THE DISGRACED DAUGHTER

LYNNE FRANCIS

PIATKUS

PIATKUS

First published in Great Britain in 2025 by Piatkus

1 3 5 7 9 10 8 6 4 2

Copyright © 2025 by Lynne Francis

The moral right of the author has been asserted.

*All characters and events in this publication, other than those
clearly in the public domain, are fictitious and any resemblance
to real persons, living or dead, is purely coincidental.*

A CIP catalogue record for this book
is available from the British Library.

ISBN 978-0-349-43368-4

Typeset in Caslon by M Rules

Printed and bound in Great Britain by
Clays Ltd, Elcograf S.p.A.

Papers used by Piatkus are from well-managed forests
and other responsible sources.

MIX
Paper | Supporting
responsible forestry
FSC® C104740

Piatkus
An imprint of
Little, Brown Book Group
Carmelite House
50 Victoria Embankment
London EC4Y 0DZ

The authorised representative
in the EEA is
Hachette Ireland
8 Castlecourt Centre
Dublin 15, D15 XTP3, Ireland
(email: info@hbgi.ie)

An Hachette UK Company
www.hachette.co.uk

www.littlebrown.co.uk

PART ONE

MARCH 1828 — JUNE 1829

Chapter One

As Lizzie Carey stepped out of the house, the sun that lit the street gave even the meanest dwelling along Lower Street a more prepossessing appearance, despite peeling paint and grimy windows. Mrs Carey, Lizzie's mother, had harsh words for the neighbours who paid so little attention to their homes.

'Look at us,' she would declare, sweeping the front step with vigour. 'Eight of us living here, and from the outside you'd think it was the grandest house hereabouts, rather than the smallest cottage in the road.'

Lizzie closed the gate behind her and set off at a brisk pace, the March wind bringing an instant flush to her cheeks. Despite the sunshine, the air was still chilly. She was glad to be outside, even though her errand wouldn't keep her away from home for long. Since her eldest sister, Nell, had left to be married, Lizzie, aged sixteen, had taken up all of her duties. With five children under the age of twelve at the fireside, every day was a non-stop routine of cooking, washing, cleaning, nose-wiping and quarrel management. It felt to Lizzie that the only time she had to herself was when she fell into bed at night – a bed shared with sleeping younger family members – or when she could escape into Castle Bay to fetch provisions from old Widow Booth's shop in Middle Street.

She was on her way there now, and she was so delighted by the fresh air that she didn't notice the glances she attracted from a woman walking towards her along Middle Street. Even had she done so, she wouldn't have been aware that the woman stopped the instant she passed her, turned and watched Lizzie's journey up the street, before following her at a slower pace.

Lizzie made a striking sight, her auburn hair glinting in the sunlight, her pale skin enhancing the rosiness the wind had brought to her cheeks. She had no time to spend before the looking-glass, though, and was unaware that her petite, trim figure had blossomed into womanhood, attracting admiring glances. What she was aware of, however, was a sense of dissatisfaction. It had been accepted without question in the family that Lizzie would step into Nell's shoes and become her mother's helpmeet. Lizzie hadn't considered anything different at the time. But now, in the long hours spent taking care of the household, she found herself wondering whether this was all there was to life: hard work in her mother's house, then, if she followed the path expected of her, marriage to someone in the town and a similar life in another small cottage close by. Nell, of course, had done rather better than that and was now living in Hawksdown in a brewery cottage much the same size as the Careys' house, but occupied just by Nell and her husband Thomas.

What alternative was there? Lizzie had discovered it was better not to dwell on it, for there seemed to be no answer. So, today, she was determined to enjoy the brief moments of freedom she had been granted.

'You look to be enjoying the lovely weather.'

Focused on adjusting the purchases from Widow Booth's shop in her basket, Lizzie glanced up at being addressed.

'I couldn't help noticing you just now.' It was her follower who spoke: a woman in her late forties wearing a costume somewhat smarter than one might expect to see in Middle Street. She had blonde hair swept back under a stylish hat, and she was regarding Lizzie with a friendly expression on her handsome face.

'Yes, the sunshine is very welcome after the weather we've had all week.' Lizzie hoped she was managing to be both polite and discouraging. Why would a stranger wish to strike up conversation with her?

'Would you mind if I walk along with you a little way?' the woman continued. 'I have a question I hesitate to ask, but I will never forgive myself if I don't.'

'Oh?' Lizzie was instantly intrigued.

'Yes, I wondered whether you had ever considered a life away from here.' The woman gestured at the street they were walking along. It held a mixture of taverns and houses, most of them for the sole purpose of entertaining the sailors at anchor in Castle Bay, whether with ale or women.

'I'm assuming you've lived here all your life. It's rather a mean little place, I must say. I come every now and then to visit family and I always hope for some improvement, to no avail,' she continued. 'But you must excuse me – I haven't introduced myself. I'm Mrs Simmonds and I'm the owner of an establishment in Canterbury. I'm looking for a young woman such as yourself who might come and work with me there.'

Lizzie experienced a range of emotions. She was curious to know more, but feared what she would hear. And even though she had been feeling trapped by her life, she bridled to hear Mrs Simmonds refer to Castle Bay in disparaging tones.

'Well,' she replied, with some spirit, 'if you are referring to the kind of establishments that we are walking past,' and she gestured to a house where a woman leaned against the frame of the open door, while another sat in an upstairs window combing her hair, 'why would I travel all the way to Canterbury for such work when it's available on my doorstep? Not that I'm interested in it,' she added hastily.

Mrs Simmonds wasn't affronted, but laughed and laid her hand on Lizzie's arm. 'My dear, you are exactly as I hoped when I first spotted you in the street. A girl who is not only striking in appearance, but with something to say for herself. My establishment is far removed from such as these. I have a respectable dress shop, and I require a model to show off my designs. You have the face and the figure I have been looking for. I hope you will let me tell you more, so I can tempt you to join me.'

Lizzie, flattered but also flustered, wasn't sure how to respond.

'I can see you will need time to consider,' Mrs Simmonds continued. 'I'm sure you weren't expecting such a proposal on your outing this morning. Now, I've told you my name but you haven't introduced yourself.'

Lizzie was strangely reluctant to share such information with a stranger, but she said, 'Elizabeth. Elizabeth Carey.' She bit her lip. Perhaps she should have made something up, she thought.

'And where can I find you, Miss Carey?'

Lizzie had a sudden vision of Mrs Simmonds turning up on the doorstep of number seven Lower Street. It appeared smart enough from the outside but the minute the door opened she would be engulfed by the noisy chaos of the Carey family. They never had visitors who weren't relatives. Would there even be space to sit down? Lizzie glanced at Mrs Simmonds's smart costume and reached a decision. 'It would be better if I could visit you,' she said. 'Tomorrow, or the day after?'

'I'm staying at Throckings Hotel. Meet me there at ten o'clock tomorrow morning. I do hope you'll make the right decision.' Mrs Simmonds was brisk in her farewell and walked away without looking back.

Lizzie watched her confident progress along Middle Street and marvelled at the strange course the morning had taken. Then she turned her face towards home. Her mother would wonder where she was. She should have said, 'No,' there and then to Mrs Simmonds. Of course she couldn't take up her offer of employment. How would the family manage without her? But she wanted to savour the sudden hope it had given her, the idea that there was a world beyond Castle Bay, a world in which she could find her place. She could at least hold on to that dream for a few more hours.

CHAPTER TWO

A dark cloud, blown in from the sea, had obscured the sun as Lizzie hurried up Lower Street. The first drops of rain began to fall as she opened the gate to number seven and her thoughts went involuntarily to Mrs Simmonds. Would she have reached Throckings Hotel by now, or would her smart costume be spoiled by the rain? If so, it would do nothing to improve her opinion of Castle Bay, Lizzie thought.

She stepped through the front door to be greeted by the sight and sound of her two youngest siblings, Alice and Susan, wailing, a broken doll on the floor in front of them. Mary, the next oldest, cast a glance at Lizzie, then looked at the floor, her bottom lip stuck out. There was no sign of Ruth and Jane, or of their mother, so Lizzie knelt and picked up the doll, a simple one carved from wood by their grandfather, Walter. He had used metal pins to attach the limbs, one of which now lay on the floorboards. The sleeve of the blouse, which Lizzie had stitched from a remnant of one of her own worn-out garments, hung empty.

'Were you fighting over Arabella?' Lizzie asked. It was a regular occurrence. Walter had repaired the doll many times, before being struck by the idea of making another so they could have one each. Alas, it had made no difference. Whichever doll was being played with by Alice or Susan became the target of desire by the other. Although, in this case, Mary's expression suggested she might have been the culprit.

'Come on, don't cry. I'll try to mend her later, and if I can't do it, we'll ask Grandpa Walter.'

7

Lizzie hoped her repair would be successful, for now that Walter had moved away to the countryside and was happily ensconced in a cottage with Eliza Marsh, they saw him far less frequently.

'Where's Ma?' she asked, but receiving no answer she took her basket to the kitchen and began to unpack the few items, adding them to the meagrely stocked shelves. Mark Carey was a fisherman and his income fell far short of that required by a family of eight. Lizzie knew that, along with a great many other men in the town, he took part in smuggling runs, ferrying goods from French ships anchored a distance from the coast of Castle Bay in the safety of the waters known as The Downs. On dark, moonless nights, tubs of brandy and flagons of other spirits, wine, tobacco, tea and coffee were transferred from the vessels to the galleys rowed by the men of Castle Bay. As soon as the boats crunched ashore on the shingle beach, the goods melted away into the myriad cellars of the town.

At its height, the trade had been lucrative and the town had felt almost prosperous. But two events had combined to make smuggling less appealing, and more risky. With the end of the French wars, the soldiers garrisoned in the town had departed, removing a ready market for many of the goods. And the raising of a new force, the coast guard, to tackle the smuggling had proved far more effective than the past efforts of the revenue men. The latter could be paid off; the coast guard were not local and much harder to corrupt.

Tonight's dinner would be soup and bread, Lizzie thought, the same tomorrow and the next night, unless fortunes changed and the sea provided a bounty of fish. Her thoughts turned to Mrs Carey, Ruth and Jane. Now that the three youngest girls had stopped fighting, the house was very quiet. Surely her mother wouldn't have gone out and left the younger ones alone at home.

The front door banged and a chatter of excited voices was added to the sniffs she could still hear from Alice and Susan.

'Ma?' Lizzie stuck her head around the kitchen door. 'Where have you been?'

'Just along the road to Mrs Watson,' Mrs Carey said. 'You were such a time and I'd promised to take Ruth and Jane to try on their new dresses.'

Lizzie experienced a surge of irritation. Where was money to be found for new dresses? And why did her mother think it appropriate to leave a five-year-old in charge of a two- and a three-year-old? She felt a niggle of guilt all the same. Had her conversation with Mrs Simmonds delayed her? Surely by no more than a few minutes.

'Where were you?' Mrs Carey persisted. 'Not wasting time with that boy who works for Widow Booth, I hope.'

'Whatever are you talking about, Ma?' Lizzie was genuinely confused. Her mother often suspected her of dallying with one or other of the local boys, but Lizzie had no time for them. If she dared contemplate her future, it didn't consist of following in the footsteps of her parents and filling a house with small children they couldn't afford. She looked to her older sister, Nell: her husband, Thomas Marsh, at least had prospects. He was well thought of at Coopers Brewery and would undoubtedly be promoted soon. All at once Mrs Simmonds's unusual proposal, which she had imagined politely rejecting, began to look more enticing.

'I could have made dresses for Ruth and Jane,' Lizzie said. 'Where are we to find the money to pay Mrs Watson? And Mary is too young to be left in charge of Alice and Susan. They had been fighting when I got home and Arabella is broken again.' She held up the doll.

Her name was far too grand for her appearance – head roughly carved from wood with eyes, lips and hair painted on, the cloth body dressed in a drab brown skirt and once-cream blouse, a plain apron tied around her waist. She ought to be wearing something rather more elegant, like Mrs Simmonds's outfit, Lizzie thought, and smiled wryly.

She and Nell had been given more elaborate names – Elizabeth and Eleanor – shortened as the other girls began to arrive, to match their simpler names. She had no memory of playing with dolls when she was small. Twelve-year-old Ruth had owned the doll first, naming her and cherishing her. As Arabella had been passed down to the younger siblings, she had become progressively more worn, so that little of her facial expression remained. Lizzie had a feeling that if she attempted to re-draw her features, Alice or Susan would be outraged. They loved their Arabella just as she was, even if their baby lisping had caused them to struggle with her name.

'Well, Mary will have to get used to taking charge more often,' Mrs Carey said, with a look of defiance.

Lizzie frowned, uncomprehending.

'Mrs Watson thinks she can get Ruth and Jane places at the charity school,' her mother continued proudly. 'And with another on the way it won't be a moment too soon.'

Lizzie stared at her mother, struggling to take in her words. Her sisters were going to school, to be educated, when she had never had that luxury, always being called upon to help around the house. And now there was to be another baby to bring up.

Lizzie turned on her heel and went back into the kitchen, slamming the door behind her. She stared out of the window into the yard, filled with a jumble of nets and other equipment that her father didn't want to leave on the beach by the fishing boat.

She had dismissed Mrs Simmonds's proposal almost as soon as it was uttered, thinking she couldn't leave her mother alone to look after so many small children. Yet Mrs Carey seemed quite unworried by her expanding family, no doubt expecting that Lizzie would simply step in to help. Her rising fury made her want to leave the house that very minute and seek out Mrs Simmonds at Throckings Hotel. She would bide her time, though, and make a plan. Any guilt she felt on behalf of her sisters was outweighed by the anger she felt towards her mother and father.

CHAPTER THREE

Lizzie's determination was further fuelled by passing a restless night. All the children slept crammed into one bedroom, which contained a double bed and a single, with barely space to walk between them. The two older ones, Ruth and Jane, had taken possession of the smaller bed, leaving Lizzie to share with Mary, Alice and Susan. The latter had developed a cough, which didn't trouble her a great deal as she slept through the bouts that struck her every hour or so. Lizzie, however, jerked awake each time, turning over so that Susan wouldn't cough in her face. Alice and Mary were bound to catch it, she thought. There would be many disturbed nights and tired, crabby days ahead.

She got up with the dawn and went downstairs to rekindle the fire in the range, shivering as she wrapped her shawl around her. March might have brought some bright days but the mornings were still chilly. She stood as close as she could to the range, willing it to heat quickly, and thought about the night just ended and the day ahead. Soon there would be another child to squeeze into the already crowded bedroom Lizzie shared with her siblings. Granted, not for another year or so, for he or she would sleep with Mrs Carey at first. Even so, Lizzie experienced a wave of despair. Her life stretched ahead, days spent in drudgery in Lower Street, or an escape into marriage and a repeat of the same pattern in another house in Castle Bay. A memory of Mrs Simmonds, in her elegant blue-grey costume, came unbidden, along with an image of Lizzie dressed in such an outfit. She almost laughed.

But why not? Why should she have to stay here and endure, when she had been offered the chance to start afresh somewhere new? She felt a little thrill of excitement, then jumped, startled, as her father came into the kitchen through the back door.

'Daydreaming, Lizzie?' he asked. He yawned and rubbed his eyes. 'Make a pot of this, will you?' He threw a packet of tea onto the table. 'I've a thirst on me, even though I'm in need of my bed.'

'Have you been out with the boat?' Lizzie asked, as she took the earthenware teapot down from the shelf and set water to boil.

'Aye, I have.' Her father didn't elaborate, leaving Lizzie unsure as to whether he'd been fishing or on a smuggling run. She was inclined to think the latter, given the packet of tea. It wasn't something they could often afford to have in the house.

'You're a good girl, Lizzie,' her father said, seating himself at the kitchen table. 'I don't know what we'd do without you.'

Lizzie didn't reply, struck with guilt for the thoughts she'd been having when he'd walked in.

'I suppose your ma told you about the new one on the way.'

Lizzie nodded, keeping her back to him as she busied herself making the tea.

'Let's hope it's a boy at last, eh? Then we can stop trying.' Her father chuckled. 'I need someone to take over the boat when it gets too much for me.'

Lizzie cut a slice from the last remaining stub of the loaf she had bought yesterday and set it before her father. The rest of the family would have to make do. She looked in the housekeeping jar, knowing that, unless a miracle had occurred overnight, there would be nothing in it other than a few coppers.

Her father noticed. 'I'm hoping to have something for you later,' he said. 'There's money owed to me. I'll go to the Ship this afternoon.'

Lizzie set her mouth in a grim line to prevent a disbelieving snort escaping her lips. If her father received any payment for whatever he had been up to, she had no doubt that the vast majority would disappear behind the bar of the Ship, or some other tavern, rather than find its way back to Lower Street. She thought to offer to collect what he was owed but knew he would be affronted.

'No daughter of mine will set foot in the Ship,' he would declare, 'or any other tavern at this end of town. They're full of unsavoury types.'

The irony would be lost on him, Lizzie knew. She saw he was casting around for something to put on his bread. She plonked a jar on the table in front of him: the last of the blackberry jam she had made at the end of the summer, from fruit collected along the path leading to Sandown Castle. She had hidden farthings from the housekeeping jar until she had had enough to buy the sugar she needed to make it. Sugar was a luxury in the Carey household, at least since Nell had left. They had had more money when she was there. Somehow, she had found the time to work behind the bar in the Fountain Inn, and for the Marsh family. She supposed there had been fewer small children at home to be cared for at that time.

Her father had drunk his second cup of tea and picked every crumb of bread from his plate. He pushed back his chair, yawning. 'I'll be away to bed, then, Lizzie. Keep those little 'uns quiet.'

Lizzie had just poured tea for herself from the rapidly cooling pot and was looking forward to a few minutes for herself when she heard feet thundering down the wooden stairs.

Alice and Susan burst into the kitchen. 'Mary's been sick,' they announced.

Lizzie made a face. That would mean stripping the bed, and Mary, to wash and dry everything before nightfall: there was no spare linen in the house.

She gulped the tea and set down the cup with a sigh. Then she divided the remaining crust of bread between the two little ones, spreading each piece thinly with a scraping of jam from the jar, before setting off upstairs. Half an hour later, Mary was tucked into Ruth and Jane's bed, the sheets and her nightgown soaking in a pail. Lizzie kept her fingers crossed that Mary wouldn't be sick again, as she stirred a pot of watery porridge on the range. If Mrs Carey didn't come downstairs soon, Lizzie would have to wake her. She was determined to meet Mrs Simmonds at Throckings Hotel at ten o'clock, as arranged. Although what had seemed quite possible yesterday no longer felt so achievable.

CHAPTER FOUR

The church clock was striking the hour as Lizzie hurried up to the door of Throckings Hotel, then hesitated. She had had to wash and dress in great haste, choosing her second-best dress – wearing her Sunday outfit would have made her mother suspicious if she'd been spotted. Now, faced with entering what passed for the grandest hotel in Castle Bay, her courage almost failed her. But, taking a deep breath, she pushed open the door and marched up to the reception desk as if she was quite used to being in such an establishment.

'I'm here to see Mrs Simmonds,' she said. 'She's expecting me.'

The desk clerk looked her up and down. Lizzie's colour rose. She sensed he was getting ready to turn her away. Then, to her relief, she heard Mrs Simmonds's voice behind her.

'Miss Carey. You are very punctual. Shall we go through?' She turned to the clerk. 'I take it there is a fire in the parlour?'

He nodded, looking a little put out by her manner.

'We'll take coffee there,' Mrs Simmonds continued, and she swept ahead of Lizzie into a room overlooking the sea. Lizzie noticed she was wearing another elegant gown, this time in a deep shade of mulberry. She seated herself at a table in the window and waited for Lizzie to join her.

'Well, have you considered my proposal?'

Lizzie was prevented from answering by the arrival of a diminutive girl, bearing a tray that was surely too heavy for her. It was laden with a pot of coffee, cups and saucers, a milk jug, sugar bowl, tongs and teaspoons, all of which looked to be in danger of sliding onto the thick rug before she could safely deposit the tray on the table.

Lizzie considered Mrs Simmonds's question as the girl unloaded her burden and poured the coffee, then went on her way. She still had not reached a decision, having veered one way and the other all the way there. It had been difficult to make her escape – as soon as Mrs Carey had shown her face in the kitchen, Lizzie had announced they had need of bread and, taking the few farthings from the housekeeping pot, she had hurried upstairs to make herself presentable. Mary was sleeping soundly in the single bed so she felt easy about leaving her. She went downstairs on silent feet and slipped out of the front door before Mrs Carey, distracted by Alice and Susan in the kitchen, could protest.

And now here she was, with Mrs Simmonds expecting a decision, while she remained torn between concern for the younger members of her family, and a desperate wish to live a life of her own.

'I trust you have come to tell me you will be accepting my offer?' Mrs Simmonds didn't wait for Lizzie's response, but carried on. 'I think you will do very well in my establishment in Canterbury. And, if you do, then I may move you to my other, in London.' She studied Lizzie's face closely, causing her to blush. 'Indeed, I think you will do very well there.'

Lizzie was taken aback. Mrs Simmonds hadn't mentioned this possibility previously. London sounded both daunting and exciting, especially when she hadn't been anywhere except Castle Bay in her entire life. But Mrs Simmonds must think she was worthy of such a prospect.

She went on speaking, even though Lizzie still hadn't found her tongue to answer. 'I will leave a ticket for you at the Castle Bay Inn, for the Canterbury stage coach tomorrow. Do not leave it too late to travel – I will expect you by the evening. Now, I am returning to Canterbury myself today, and I have things to do first. Take your time and enjoy your coffee.'

Mrs Simmonds, who had barely touched her cup, stood up,

causing Lizzie to scramble awkwardly to her feet, too. She nodded at Lizzie and swept from the room. Lizzie sat down again and sipped her coffee, but it was still too hot to drink. So, a decision had been reached, she realised, and she wasn't the one who had made it. Perhaps it was easier that way.

She should return home. Mrs Carey would demand to know why she had taken so long to make the short journey to the bakery in Middle Street. Yet she was determined to savour the unusual experience of sitting alone, drinking coffee, in such luxurious surroundings. Lizzie gazed around at the panelled walls, the thick rug on the floor. It could have hardly have been more different from the taverns in town that her father frequented. Not that she went into them, but their doors were nearly always open and, through a haze of smoke, Lizzie had glimpsed the scuffed floorboards, the mismatched wooden chairs and tables, the customers in their worn and stained work clothes.

The young girl had reappeared in the doorway, clutching the tray. Clearly, now that Mrs Simmonds had left, it was expected that Lizzie should be on her way, too. Lizzie hastily gulped the coffee, put down the cup and stood up. She hoped Mrs Simmonds had settled the bill, for her few farthings most certainly wouldn't cover it. She drew herself upright, stuck her chin into the air and marched out, unsmiling, hoping she looked as though she was accustomed to doing such things. Perhaps she would be, she thought, once she was in Canterbury. Only as she left Throckings Hotel and hastened along Beach Street did it occur to her that Mrs Simmonds hadn't told her where to leave the coach, or the address she would need to go to in Canterbury. Or, indeed, how much she would be paid.

Lizzie, previously undecided about her decision, was now determined to go, despite the uncertainties. Perhaps Mrs Simmonds would leave the address with the ticket for the stage coach, she thought. And she appeared very keen for Lizzie to come and work for her, so presumably she would pay her enough to make it worth her while. She cast aside her misgivings in this way, remembering to stop to buy bread on the way home. She could hear the wails from inside the house before she reached the front door.

Mrs Carey turned an angry face on Lizzie as soon as she entered. 'Where have you been?' she demanded. 'Dallying on the way to the bakery, I'll be bound.' She cast a critical glance over her daughter. 'You look a deal too smart to be setting about the housework. Hoping to impress someone, were you?'

Lizzie fought down the urge to tell her that she had just been in Throckings Hotel, where she was offered a very good position in Canterbury and would soon be wearing garments far more elegant than Mrs Carey could imagine. Something told her that her mother would pour scorn on such an idea. And, in any case, she couldn't risk alerting her to her plans, or she would find a way to prevent her leaving. Instead she would submit with the best grace possible to the drudgery of another day at number seven Lower Street. She would let imaginings of what lay ahead sustain her, and smile through it all.

'Mary has been sick again,' her mother informed her. 'You'd better go and change the bed, then get those sheets washed and hung out to dry.'

CHAPTER FIVE

Lizzie settled herself as best she could on the Canterbury stage coach, squashed between a large gentleman and an even larger lady, who had also managed to bring substantial valises on board. These were placed on their knees and looked set to jab Lizzie at every turn in the road. She suspected that the two passengers were related, and had each chosen a window seat so they could get some air. It was going to be a long journey.

Lizzie attempted to sit back on the bench seat, gripping her bundle tightly on her lap. She had packed her meagre belongings in a few snatched moments during the morning, leaving it as late as possible so that no one would notice her Sunday-best dress was no longer hanging from the peg on the wall, or that her hairbrush had vanished from the top of the chest of drawers. Such an observation was unlikely, she knew, but her guilt at what she had planned made her feel as if she had announced, 'I'm running away,' to the whole household.

Her heart hammered so hard in her chest that she feared one of the other passengers would surely hear it and comment. She wished the coach would leave. The hour was growing late; she had found it hard to slip away, since although Mary had recovered from her sickness, both Alice and Susan had succumbed. The morning had been filled with washing sheets and nightgowns and settling fractious children. Mrs Carey had pleaded sickness of a different kind, preventing her from helping. Lizzie had thought grimly that her mother would have no option but to deal with it if any of the others fell ill, then chided herself. She knew the burden would fall on Ruth as the eldest daughter left at home.

In the end, half despairing of reaching Canterbury that day, she had slipped away when her mother was in the kitchen, Alice and Susan were in bed, Ruth and Jane entertaining Mary. Clutching her bundle behind her back, she had muttered words to the effect that they needed something from Widow Booth's shop, before letting herself out of the front door quietly. Ruth and Jane paid her no attention.

By now, they would be wondering where she had got to. Even though she knew no one would think to come looking for her on the stage coach, she shrank back in her seat as far as her neighbours would allow, and wished it on its way. Lizzie had been unable to leave a note for her mother to explain her departure. She could neither read nor write, having been kept from even the most basic schooling by her mother's need for her to help at home. Nell, who, as the eldest, had benefited from an education, had tried to teach her whenever they had a snatched moment to spend together, but it had proved fruitless. Lizzie had little aptitude for it. Now she fretted that the family would worry. Her mother would be furious if she knew she was running off, but would that thought enter her head? Would she think something had happened to Lizzie while she was on the way to the shops? Most likely she would believe Lizzie was with one of those boys she had suspected her of meeting every time she left the house.

Lizzie sighed. Then, from the folds of the shawl she wore, she pulled out a note she had been handed at the Castle Bay Inn when she had enquired about her stage-coach ticket. She unfolded it but, as she had feared, her limited learning meant she could only recognise the odd word. She presumed it had been left by Mrs Simmonds, and would contain details of the arrangements in Canterbury. Could she ask one of the other passengers if they could read it to her? She glanced across at the bench seat opposite. A clergyman in a shabby cloak – he might pose awkward questions and disapprove of what she was doing. A mother travelling with two young children seemed harassed and was as squashed as Lizzie, but she, too, might not look kindly on a daughter escaping her familial duties.

She cast covert glances at the neighbours on her own seat. They didn't look as though they would welcome conversation. Embarrassed by her own inadequacy, she folded the note and tucked it away. Perhaps it would be better to wait until later in the journey, when an opportunity to ask for help might present itself.

An opportunity never did arise. There had been little conversation to enliven the long hours, but a good deal of snoring, at least from Lizzie's immediate companions. The clergyman had buried his nose in a leather-bound volume and was clearly hoping to avoid conversation. The mother had studiously avoided engaging with anyone other than her children, to the extent that Lizzie began to think perhaps she was running away, too.

So Lizzie found herself in the dark and cold of Canterbury, at an hour long past the one at which Mrs Simmonds might have expected her. A light drizzle was falling and Lizzie pulled her shawl over her hair, then stood uncertainly in the yard of the coaching inn, as the other passengers disembarked. Once they had shaken out the creases from their clothes and collected any luggage from the roof, they melted away in the darkness, all sure of their destinations. Lizzie stood on, feeling anxious. Would Mrs Simmonds think to send someone to meet each arrival from Castle Bay? Or would she have been angered by Lizzie's failure to arrive earlier, and assumed she wasn't coming? Perhaps the answer lay in the note. She would have to find someone to read it to her.

Lizzie felt in the folds of her shawl, but the note wasn't there. She was struck by panic – where was it? Had she dropped it in the coach? It had been driven away out of sight, but presumably not far as the horses would need to be unhitched to rest. She was about to start out in search of it when something white on the ground caught

21

her eye in the gloom. It was the note, which must have fallen from her shawl as she covered her hair. She bent and seized it with relief, then regarded it in dismay. It was no longer a crisp piece of folded paper. It had been trodden on and pressed into the wet cobbles. The ink on the front had run and, as Lizzie tried to unfold it, the paper began to disintegrate in her hands.

Tears welled in her eyes. This was her only link to Mrs Simmonds. Presumably it contained the address Lizzie was to go to, or at least the name of the person who would meet her from the coach. And now here she was in Canterbury, alone in the dark in a strange city, with no idea of where to go. She felt a surge of longing for home, for the crush of the double bed shared with her sisters. But even if she could have faced getting back on the coach for several more hours, she knew she couldn't return. Her mother would never forgive her for leaving as she had. And, anyway, there wouldn't be a coach until the morning. She must set about finding a safe place to shelter for the night. More tears welled as Lizzie realised she had no money, other than a farthing or two in her pocket. She hadn't considered that she might need any.

CHAPTER SIX

Lizzie wiped the tears roughly from her face with the corner of her shawl. She would have to see whether she could use the little information she had to track down Mrs Simmonds. While that would not have been impossible in a town the size of Castle Bay, it was already evident to Lizzie that Canterbury was considerably larger. They had stopped at a coaching inn close to the city walls – she had no idea what lay beyond. She pushed away the nagging doubt that threatened to overwhelm her again and turned to the door of the inn. She would start by making enquiries there.

She entered with some trepidation, but the man standing behind the desk opposite the door didn't seem unduly surprised at the sight of a woman on her own. Lizzie supposed a great many travellers passed through the inn every day. She approached him, not quite sure where to begin.

'I was expecting to be met off the Castle Bay coach,' she began, 'but I am late and there is no one here. And I – I have had a mishap and lost the address of where I am to go.' The note she had received was now a soggy ball, clutched tightly in her fist. 'I am in search of a Mrs Simmonds who owns a dress shop in the town.'

The man regarded her. 'A dress shop?'

'Yes. I don't know whereabouts.' Lizzie began to feel the enormity of the task. There could be many dress shops in such a town. And what would the man on the desk know of such things?

The desk clerk frowned and bit his lip as he thought over her question. 'Well, you might start in Mercery Lane,' he said at last.

'There's a few drapers there. If you can't find her, they might be able to help you.'

Lizzie, her spirits lifting, was about to ask for directions when he added, 'But they will be closed now. You'd best wait until the morning. Do you want a bed for the night?' He began to look down the page of the ledger on his desk.

'No, no,' Lizzie said hastily. 'But thank you. Can you tell me how to get to Mercery Lane? It may be that Mrs Simmonds lives over her establishment.'

The man gave her directions, which were thankfully straightforward.

'Turn right outside, then take the broad road ahead of you, running to your left. Keep walking until you see the tower of the cathedral. Mercery Lane runs up towards the entrance, at Christ Church gate. You'll find it on your left.'

Lizzie thanked him, picked up her bundle and set out into the night. The rain was a little more persistent now. She hoped she didn't have far to go: she had wanted to look her best to meet Mrs Simmonds, not appear before her as wretched and bedraggled.

Even though the hour was late, the streets were busier than Lizzie expected, although she was not used to being out of the house at this time. She supposed Castle Bay, or at least the inns and other premises in Middle Street, would be just as lively. As she drew closer to the cathedral, its pale stone tower visible even through the gloom, she saw that it was the focus for many of the people on the street. There were stalls selling pies and hawkers selling trinkets: wooden crosses, beads, crudely carved representations of the cathedral tower. She was startled more than once by someone stepping out in front of her and thrusting merchandise into her face, in an attempt to persuade her to buy. She shook her head and hurried on, glad of the crowds, yet made uneasy by them. What would she do if she couldn't find Mrs Simmonds? Once the hour grew later and the crowds melted away, where could she go with no money for a bed? She cursed herself for her folly, then pushed away the thought.

24

Perhaps Mrs Simmonds would be close by, in rooms above her shop. She would be angry with Lizzie for arriving late, and for the mishap with her note, but surely all would be well in the end.

The road had broadened into an open space, lined with more stalls around the edge, and Lizzie realised she had reached the cathedral gate. Where had the man said to go next? 'You'll find it on your left.' She could hear his words in her head. She looked around and sure enough, directly opposite the grand entrance to the cathedral grounds, she saw a narrow street, the overhanging upper storeys of the buildings opposite each other almost meeting in some places. She pushed her way through the jostling crowd, trying to ignore the nagging hunger created by the aroma of meat frying on the stalls nearby. Lizzie glanced up at the street name, on a plaque high on the first building. She could make out the first letter 'M', and felt sure this must be the right place. There were signboards hanging outside more than one of the shops and, as she drew closer, her heart beat faster. Lengths of cloth were draped in the windows and, as she peered into the interiors, she could see ghostly outlines of garments suspended around the walls.

Could one of these shops belong to Mrs Simmonds? And, if so, which one? The names of the owners were written on the boards but the letters meant nothing to Lizzie. Why hadn't she paid more attention when Nell had tried to teach her? She stepped back to see whether she could make out a light in any of the rooms above the shops and, as she did so, she collided with a passer-by who had come up on silent feet behind her.

'Oof,' he said, temporarily winded.

Lizzie, startled, began to apologise. 'I'm so sorry, I didn't see you there.'

'No, no, my fault. I wasn't paying attention.' The man rubbed his side, where Lizzie realised she had elbowed him. She was sure she had stepped heavily on his toes as well.

Seizing her chance to enlist help, she began to explain. 'I'm looking for a dress shop belonging to a Mrs Simmonds. I was directed here but I can't ...' she hesitated '... I can't make out whether any of these shops might be hers.'

She avoided looking at the man as she spoke, gazing at the signs instead.

'Let me see ... George Claris, linen draper. And William Claris.' The man pointed at the two boards nearest to them. He took a few steps away from her. 'John Brooke, ironmonger,' he read. 'William Cobb, cheesemonger. There is another draper, but that's a man's name, too.' He returned to her side.

'Perhaps there are more drapers, further along,' Lizzie ventured, disappointment threatening to overwhelm her.

The man shook his head. 'I know the street. They are all to be found at this end.' He gave her a sharp look. 'Is all well?'

Lizzie, overwhelmed by tears, couldn't speak. What was she to do now?

'I take it you're a stranger to this place,' the man said. 'I'm on my way to the Chequers Inn.' He indicated a building on the corner of Mercery Lane and the cathedral square. He scrutinised her in the dim light. 'Why don't you come along to get out of the rain? You can sit down and tell me all about it.'

Every fibre of Lizzie's being told her it was not a good idea to enter an inn in a strange city with a man she had only just met on the street. About to shake her head and turn away, the realisation that she had little money and no idea where to go next made her reconsider. Surely she would be safe in such a public space. Her spirits at a low ebb, she nodded mutely, and followed him into the bustling interior. She was dimly aware of candlelight and a throng of people, but she kept her head down while the man guided her to a quiet table tucked away from the crowd. She glanced up at him as she murmured her thanks, and for the first time caught a glimpse of his face. The smile he offered her crinkled the skin around his dark eyes, and the raindrops caught in his curly hair sparkled in the candlelight.

'I'll be back in a moment. Sit tight,' he said, then vanished into the crowd around the bar.

Lizzie sat quietly, staring at the table, while her thoughts scattered this way and that. She could only hope that this stranger was as genuine as he seemed, but a dull sense of foreboding lurked at the edges of her mind.

CHAPTER SEVEN

Lizzie was glad to be inside, out of the rain. But she had barely ever set foot in an inn, other than to fetch her father home, and she was nervous and wary. Now she had put herself in the position of being beholden to a stranger. Yet how else was she to discover the whereabouts of Mrs Simmonds?

At that moment the man returned, bearing a tankard of ale and a smaller glass of dark liquid, which he set in front of her. 'Brandy,' he said. 'I thought you might need it.'

Lizzie wasn't sure what he meant but she lifted the glass and took a sip. Taken aback as the fiery liquid hit the back of her throat, she began to cough. She made a face – it wasn't pleasant.

The man was smiling. 'Try again,' he said. 'It will warm you up and bring some colour back to your cheeks.'

To be polite, Lizzie, better prepared this time, took another sip. She could feel the warmth spreading through her as the liquid went down her throat.

'That's better. Now, I'd best introduce myself. I'm Adam Russell.' He was looking expectantly at Lizzie.

'Lizzie – Elizabeth – Carey,' Lizzie said.

'Well, Miss Carey, tell me how and why you find yourself here, looking for a Mrs Simmonds.'

Lizzie took another sip of the brandy. 'I met Mrs Simmonds in Castle Bay and she offered me work in Canterbury, in her dress shop.'

Adam Russell seemed surprised by her words. 'And the nature of this work?'

'To model her dresses. And if I did well, she said I would move to her London establishment.'

'Ah. And can you describe this Mrs Simmonds? It may be that I know her.'

Lizzie experienced a surge of hope. 'An older lady, very elegant,' she said. 'Quite tall, with blonde hair. She is forthright ...' Lizzie remembered Mrs Simmonds's assured manner when she had met her in Throckings Hotel. Despite her wish to do her justice, she could add little else to her description. In truth, they had spent hardly more than half an hour in each other's company.

'I think I may know her. Or know of her,' Adam said. He hesitated. 'Although I'm not sure she is the owner of a dress shop. Her establishment is a rather different one.'

Lizzie, delighted by his recognition of Mrs Simmonds, barely registered the import of his words. 'Where can I find her?' she asked. 'She will be wondering what has happened to me. I must go at once and apologise for the lateness of the hour.'

'If Mrs Simmonds is who I think she is, the lateness of the hour will scarcely trouble her. Why, her business for the day will only just have begun.' Adam was grim-faced.

Lizzie, bending to pick up her bundle from beneath the table, once again missed the clues Adam was offering her. 'Thank you for the drink, Mr Russell,' she said, straightening and taking another sip, then another. She had to restrain a cough and her eyes began to water. 'Once I am settled with Mrs Simmonds I will repay you. I find myself without money at present.'

Adam was frowning. 'Miss Carey, I fear you are a little too unwary for the streets of Canterbury. I can't believe you have your family's blessing to be here. Have they met Mrs Simmonds?'

Lizzie felt unaccountably hot. How was she to answer? And what business was it of this man? A sharp retort rose to her lips, but she remembered she was reliant on him to lead her to Mrs Simmonds. He was regarding her with frank brown eyes, waiting for her reply.

'I'm well able to look after myself,' she said at last. 'And others

29

too. I've been taking care of all my sisters ever since the eldest, Nell, left home. Now it's my turn to lead my own life.'

She wasn't sure she had been able to supply him with a satisfactory answer but he nodded. 'In that case,' he said. 'Drink up and I'll show you the address you seek.' He drained his tankard and stood up as he spoke.

Lizzie swallowed what remained in her glass and followed him back through the throng of cheerful drinkers and out into the street. It was raining still but she barely noticed, filled with relief at the thought of a successful end to her long day.

She struggled to keep up with Adam's long strides and, as they progressed through the warren of interconnecting lanes, she wondered at her light-headedness. She supposed it must be from the brandy and lack of food: it was many hours since she had eaten. The need for secrecy meant she had been unable to take anything from home to sustain her on the journey to Canterbury. Lizzie tried to concentrate on her surroundings but the dark streets defeated her. They had moved away from the cathedral and the streets had broadened out from the cramped lanes surrounding it. Here the houses were more substantial and several had well-lit interiors. She could see people in the candlelight and even hear the noise of chatter and laughter as they passed. Lizzie could make little sense of it, but her weariness and hunger were making her feel most peculiar.

She was glad when, shortly afterwards, they came to a halt. A carriage had pulled up outside one of the houses and four men spilled out onto the pavement. Lizzie shrank back behind Adam; the men had clearly spent the evening at an inn and they were in high spirits. They bounded up the steps to the house and the door opened to admit them before they had even knocked.

'This is it,' Adam said. 'Mrs Simmonds's establishment.'

Lizzie was bewildered. 'Is it her home? It's not a dress shop ...' She looked up at the building, scarcely able to believe how grand it was. The broad steps to the front door had pillars on either side, and a great many candles burned within the drawing room at the

30

front. The recent arrivals were now visible there, being greeted by their hostess. As she turned towards one of the men, Lizzie caught a glimpse of the upswept blonde hair and elegant figure of Mrs Simmonds, a sparkle of jewellery at her throat. Her business must be very profitable, she thought. She looked down at herself in some alarm. How could she enter the house in such a bedraggled state?

'Oh, Miss Carey.' Adam sighed. 'You still don't understand, do you? Mrs Simmonds does employ young ladies but her establishment is not a dress shop. She finds young women such as yourself to satisfy the desires of her customers, who are the kind of men we saw entering a minute or so ago.'

Lizzie looked from the lit window to Adam and back again. The gentlemen they had seen earlier had now been joined by women. Mrs Simmonds was moving around the group, filling glasses. She could almost hear the laughter outside on the roadway as she watched the young ladies drape their arms around the men's necks and whisper in their ears. In that moment, all her dreams of the new life that lay ahead of her in Mrs Simmonds's establishment crumbled into dust. She had believed every word Mrs Simmonds had uttered, flattered by the attention. Now she could see how she had been lied to and deceived. She had run away from home without a word, intent on bettering herself, and for this?

CHAPTER EIGHT

L izzie turned on her heel and set off blindly, intent on escaping from the truth before her eyes.

'Miss Carey, wait. Where are you going?'

She barely knew what to do, other than to get away from this place as quickly as possible. Tears ran down her cheeks, tears of rage and humiliation. How could she have been so foolish and gullible?

Adam was alongside her now. He let her walk in silence for a few minutes. Then he said, 'I'm sorry, it must have come as a shock. But I can't let you wander the streets of Canterbury alone like this. I can offer you shelter for the night.'

Lizzie shook her head and walked on, staring at the ground. She had been caught out once in a naive belief and wouldn't let it happen again. This Adam Russell must have seen at once how it was. He, too, must hope to take advantage of her.

Adam, evidently sensing her reluctance, pressed on: 'I can assure you that you aren't the first to be misled by Mrs Simmonds, and enticed to what she calls her establishment. At the cathedral we have helped several unfortunate souls who fell prey to her persuasive words. I have remonstrated with her, to no avail. There is no love lost between us.' He paused, glancing at Lizzie to see the effect of his words.

'My home is not far from here. My wife, Hannah, would never forgive me if I left you out here to fend for yourself.'

Lizzie slowed her pace. The mention of a wife was reassuring, but was it true?

'She'll still be awake. At least come and meet her. We live in

New Street, just the next street along.' Adam was pointing through the darkness.

Lizzie, with no idea what to do other than to find a doorway to curl up in, nodded, defeated by her day. He seemed genuine, but her faith in her ability to judge people had just been sorely tested.

She walked in silence by his side through the rain, which had now eased to a drizzle. Even so, the hem of her dress was soaking and her shawl had barely kept her shoulders dry. They stopped at the door of a house fronting directly onto the street, where a single candle burned in the window. Once more, Lizzie was reminded of what an unsightly mess she must appear. If Adam really did have a wife, whatever would she make of her?

She didn't have time to think further, for he had opened the door and was ushering her in. A figure stood in the narrow hallway, a candle held in front of her so that Lizzie could barely make out her features.

'I've brought you a waif from the streets,' Adam said cheerfully. 'I found her in Mercery Lane, looking for a dress shop she'd been led to believe belonged to Mrs Simmonds.' He shut the door behind him. 'It took a trip to Mrs Simmonds's house to convince her she had been misled. She finds herself all alone, a stranger to the city, so I thought it best to bring her home.'

'Did you need to drag her around in the rain to show her the truth?' the lady with the candle scolded. 'She's half drowned. Come into the kitchen – it's warmer there and you can dry off.'

She addressed the last remark to Lizzie as she led the way down the dim passageway. Lizzie followed meekly, stepping into the kitchen where another candle stood in the centre of the scrubbed table, casting the rest of the room into shadow. She could feel the warmth from the range and instinctively moved closer to it.

'Now, Adam Russell, are you going to introduce us?'

Adam, who had been in charge of the evening until they reached his house, was quick to oblige. 'Miss Carey, may I introduce you to Hannah, my wife. Hannah, Miss Carey.'

33

'Have you a Christian name, Miss Carey?' Lizzie had begun to realise that Hannah wasn't as fierce as she sounded. Adam wasn't put out by her chiding and was, indeed, smiling fondly at her.

'Of course ... It's Elizabeth. But everyone calls me Lizzie.'

'Well, Lizzie, let's get some of your wet things off you before you take a chill. Adam, go and make sure the children are sound asleep. Frances was coughing earlier.'

Hannah was pulling the wet shawl from Lizzie's shoulders as she spoke. 'Have you anything dry to wear in your bundle, or is that soaked, too?' She regarded Lizzie doubtfully. 'If not, I'm sure I can find you something, although I'm rather taller than you.'

Lizzie, who was beginning to shake with cold and hunger, tugged at her bundle and was relieved to find that a skirt and blouse, rolled up in the middle, were only slightly damp. She didn't wish to inconvenience Hannah more than she had already. And it was true, Adam's wife was a good head taller than Lizzie – she would have been hard pressed to find something suitable.

'Strip off those wet things,' Hannah instructed. 'Adam will know to stay away. I expect you are hungry, too,' she continued, helping her to pull the dress over her head.

Lizzie was glad Hannah couldn't see her confusion – she had no doubt heard her stomach rumbling loudly. She emerged from the wet dress red in the face.

'I'm sorry to be such a trouble,' she said.

Hannah smiled. 'I'm used to it. Adam goes around town collecting up those who have found themselves in a predicament. Barely a week goes by without him returning home with someone in need of help.'

She didn't seem at all put out, Lizzie thought, as she quickly donned her skirt and blouse. Tears started to her eyes as relief and gratitude overwhelmed her. If she hadn't met Adam, she would have found herself in an even worse situation. She shuddered, causing Hannah to give her a sharp look.

'Pull up that chair and sit by the range,' she said. 'I'll fetch you something from the larder. There's a slice of pie left over from Adam's dinner.'

Lizzie sat down as instructed, straightening the sleeves of her blouse and trying to control her emotions. She heard footsteps in the passage and Adam called, 'Can I come in?'

'Yes, please do,' Lizzie answered for Hannah, who had her head in the larder.

'All's well upstairs,' Adam said, and Lizzie nodded, suddenly awkward.

Hannah returned to the table, bearing a slice of pie on a plate, as promised, along with a hunk of bread and a glass of cordial.

'Eat up,' Hannah encouraged, setting the plate in front of Lizzie and fetching a knife and fork from a drawer in the dresser.

'How many children do you have?' Lizzie asked, once she had taken the edge off her hunger.

'Two – a boy and a girl,' Hannah replied.

Lizzie, reminded of the family she had left behind, looked around the kitchen. It was in considerably better order than the one in Castle Bay. Mrs Carey liked to keep up appearances outside for the neighbours, but was less concerned about the interior. Although, Lizzie thought, as she ate another mouthful of pie, the Russell family seemed somewhat more prosperous than the Careys.

She was just thinking of how she could ask a question of Adam about his occupation without appearing rude, when he addressed his wife: 'How was your sewing this evening, my love?'

Hannah sighed. 'My eyes grew tired very quickly. I am a long way behind with my order.' She shook her head. 'I could barely make out where the white thread met the white fabric. I fear I will have to unpick it all tomorrow.'

Lizzie, trying not to bolt what remained of the food in front of her, asked politely, 'What are you sewing?' She imagined it would be something for one of the children.

Adam answered for his wife. 'Hannah is very skilled in white-work. Ladies who wish to impress but struggle to create the designs themselves employ her to do the work on their behalf. I wish I had half her talent.'

Lizzie, who had very little idea of what whitework might be, finished the last crumbs on her plate and asked him, 'And what is it that you do?'

'He's a clerk of works at the cathedral.' It was Hannah's turn to speak on his behalf. 'Now, Lizzie, I'm ready for my bed so if you've finished we'll settle you on the sofa in the sitting room.' She turned to her husband. 'Adam, fetch me a pillow and a blanket. I dare say you'll find it comfortable enough there, Lizzie. The fire is still lit although it has burned well down. The children might disturb you in the morning, but if you keep the door closed they may not know you are here.'

Adam had returned with the bedding and beckoned Lizzie to follow him. He showed her into the front room, where the candle burned in the window.

'Here you are,' he said, pointing to the sofa. 'It will do for tonight. Talk to Hannah in the morning – I will have left early for the cathedral. I'm sure she will help you decide what to do next.'

CHAPTER NINE

Adam closed the wooden window shutters and wished her goodnight. Hannah came in as he left, picked up the candle and put it by Lizzie's makeshift bed. 'Goodnight, Lizzie,' she said, and was gone.

Lizzie couldn't face changing out of her clothes now that she was warm and dry. She lay down on the sofa and pulled the blanket around her, gazing across the room into the glow of the fire. She willed sleep to overtake her but, although she was weary, thoughts of the day, and particularly of that evening, came crowding in. What a mess she had got herself into. And it would have been far worse if she hadn't met Adam by chance.

She couldn't lie there with all the what-ifs plaguing her, so she got to her feet and went over to look at the shelves beside the fireplace. There were some small china ornaments: a shepherdess, and a lady dressed in all her finery. And several books, but Lizzie couldn't read the lettering embossed on the spines. A wicker basket on the topmost shelf caught her eye. Seeing fabric peeping from one side, she lifted it down and took it over to the sofa. Raising the lid exposed a square of neatly folded white fabric, a needle and thread piercing the top layer.

She lifted out the cloth and spread it on the blanket, then picked up the candle and held it closer to the work. Lizzie had never seen such intricate stitching – swirling arcs of foliage and flowers, all worked in white thread on the white linen, the stitches formed in such a way that they raised the texture of the petals and the leaves.

With her free hand, she gently traced the lines of the design. Then, fearful of dripping wax, she set the candle-holder on the floor, folded the piece, returned it to the basket, and the basket to the shelf.

Lizzie lay down again on the sofa and blew out the candle. It was late, she knew, and the household would be awake early in the morning. She must thank Adam for his kindness before he left for work. She felt a little nervous of being left alone with Hannah. She, too, had been kind but Lizzie sensed a reserve. Hardly surprising, she supposed, if Adam was in the habit of bringing home strangers who had fallen on hard times. She ought to make a plan, so that she imposed as little as possible on Hannah and her family. But with precious little money in her pocket, and her eagerly anticipated role with Mrs Simmonds now shown to be a deception, she didn't know where to begin. She fell into an uneasy sleep, which deepened with exhaustion just before dawn, so that she missed the sounds of Adam quietly moving around the kitchen, and his departure, the front door closing behind him.

Lizzie woke to the sound of giggles and the sight of two small heads peeping around the door to the sitting room. For a moment she was confused, imagining herself at home in Castle Bay with her siblings. An instant later, memories of the night before flooded back and she sat up.

'Mama says you're to come to the kitchen when you're awake,' one of the children, the owner of a mop of curls, informed her. Then both heads vanished. Lizzie blinked and tried to shake off the fuzziness of sleep. She stood up and gazed in some dismay at the creases in her outfit. She attempted to smooth them, then took a deep breath and went along the corridor to find the family. She was only too aware of what Hannah must think of her: a foolish young girl who had arrived bedraggled, had now overslept and no doubt looked even worse.

Hannah, busy at the stove, had her back to Lizzie as she entered the room. The two children were sitting at the kitchen table, steaming bowls in front of them.

'Take a seat,' Hannah said, without looking round. 'There's porridge on the stove, or bread on the table if you prefer.' She was neatly attired in a brown sprigged cotton dress, her hair pulled back from her face, and had clearly been awake for some time.

'I'm sorry if I overslept,' Lizzie said. 'I'm very grateful for the bed for the night, and the food. I'll be on my way as soon as possible. I had hoped to see Adam ...' she glanced at the children '... Mr Russell, to thank him for his help, but I must have missed him.'

Hannah smiled briefly. 'He leaves for work at an early hour. Now, don't feel you must hurry to leave. Indeed, I don't know where you would go with no money in your pocket. Adam and I discussed it before he left and I have a proposal to make to you. But let me introduce you to the children while you eat some breakfast. This is Gabriel,' she indicated the child with the curly hair, 'and this is Frances.' Frances appeared to be a couple of years younger than her brother, Lizzie thought, and whereas Gabriel resembled Adam, she had the look of her mother.

Despite the late meal she had eaten the night before, Lizzie found herself hungry again and, while she ate some bread, spreading it with a delicious home-made preserve, she concentrated on drawing out the children, who were a little shy at first. Frances was the first to overcome her reserve, reaching out to touch a lock of Lizzie's hair that had worked loose from the hastily inserted clips.

'You have curls,' she said, 'like my brother. I don't.' Her bottom lip stuck out a little and she looked as though she might cry.

Lizzie saw that Hannah was about to admonish her for her forwardness and hastened to speak first. 'I think my hair must be very unruly, after getting so wet last night.' She was aware that she hadn't looked in a glass that morning and she undoubtedly needed to retrieve her hairbrush from her bundle to restore some sort of order. 'But you have beautiful hair, Frances – you will be able to make it do exactly as you wish as you get older. I have to battle with mine every day to keep it in order.' Lizzie was reminded of how the wind off the sea in Castle Bay whipped knots into it throughout the winter, and the painful brushing she had to endure to tease them out.

Gabriel now decided that his younger sister shouldn't take up all of their visitor's attention.

'Why did you get so wet?' he demanded.

Lizzie smiled at his abruptness. 'I arrived in Canterbury last night, ill prepared for the weather, became lost and your father was kind enough to help me by bringing me here to spend the night.'

'Why were you lost?' Gabriel's curiosity wasn't yet satisfied.

'I was expecting to be met off the coach but arrived later than expected. And the note of the address I should go to was ruined by the rain.'

Lizzie glanced at Hannah, but she was still busy at the stove. Even as she recounted her tale she realised it didn't show her in a very good light. Rather, it highlighted impetuous behaviour and a lack of planning. What would Hannah think of her?

'Why couldn't you remember where you had to go?'

Lizzie blushed. Children had an unerring knack of putting you on the spot, she thought ruefully. Their questions were so direct – they hadn't yet learned to read the signs that told them they were treading on delicate ground.

'Gabriel!' Hannah, frowning, was giving them her full attention now. 'That's quite enough questioning. Miss Carey – Lizzie – is a stranger to the city and can't be expected to know her way around. Now, off you go, the pair of you, and find something to do. I need to talk to Lizzie. Then I think we might go out for a walk as the weather is fine.'

Hannah wasted no time in turning to Lizzie as soon as the children could be heard scampering up the stairs.

'As I said, I have a proposal for you. Adam tells me you are experienced in looking after children, and that you are perhaps a little unwilling to return home.' Hannah's eyebrows rose in question, but she pressed on. 'Our maid-of-all-work keeps an eye on Gabriel and Frances when I have stitching I must finish. Otherwise I must sew at night when they are asleep. If we engage you to look after them, I can do so much more. We will provide bed and board, and an allowance, in exchange. There is a small bedroom you can have. I once thought it would be my work room but I find I prefer to be in the sitting room, alongside the fire.'

Was this Hannah's idea or Adam's? The little she had seen of the house had told Lizzie the family was more prosperous than her own, yet Hannah seemed to feel it was important to take on sewing to earn more money.

Did she want to agree to the exact same work she had run away from? What else could she do? She had no money to return home and for now she was dependent on Adam and Hannah's kindness. She should be grateful for the offer, she knew.

'What would you expect of me?' she asked, adding, when Hannah seemed puzzled, 'My daily duties?'

She could tell by her hesitation that Hannah hadn't really thought about this, which confirmed at once that it must have been Adam's suggestion.

'I suppose much as I do,' Hannah said. 'Get the children up and dressed in the morning, give them breakfast, then occupy them if I am working. Take them out if the weather is fine, a little reading and writing, drawing . . .'

Hannah paused, taking in Lizzie's expression.

'I can't read or write,' she blurted, and immediately felt her cheeks burning with shame. 'I can count, though,' she added, feeling the offer of work slipping through her fingers. 'And sew. And draw.'

'Then you can listen while I teach Gabriel and Frances,' Hannah said. 'And in return perhaps you can help me with some sewing.' Her smile was encouraging.

For the first time in Hannah's company, Lizzie began to feel at ease. She smiled back. 'Then thank you,' she replied. 'I would be very happy to take up your offer.'

CHAPTER TEN

During the days that followed, Lizzie was surprised to discover that caring for someone else's children was easier than caring for her siblings. Gabriel and Frances listened to her, whereas Mary, Alice and Susan would have argued. And, it had to be said, Hannah was a better mother than Mrs Carey: her children had a healthy respect for her and knew what would happen if they didn't do as they were told. In any case, as they got to know each other, she became very fond of them and delighted in taking them for walks, one small hand clasped in each of her own as they walked on either side of her. Passers-by often smiled at them, and mothers would sometimes engage her in conversation as they walked in the little park by the River Stour, just a few streets away from the house, remarking on how charming and well behaved her charges were.

Lizzie missed her own siblings, but she didn't miss the drudgery she had experienced at number seven Lower Street. In Canterbury, she didn't have to do the laundry, cooking and cleaning, as well as look after the children: Judith, the maid-of-all-work, did most of that. She wasn't living the sort of life she had once imagined Mrs Simmonds to be offering, but she felt she had certainly moved up in the world.

Hannah had taken stock of Lizzie's few belongings, and had adapted one of her own dresses for her, shortening it and letting out the bodice seams, so that she had something else to wear, other than the dress she had travelled in and her Sunday best. A blouse and skirt were the only other things she had managed to pack. She was as proud of the altered dress as if it was a brand-new outfit, but Hannah had frowned at her own handiwork when she saw her wearing it.

'I'll make you a new dress, to the correct fit,' she promised. 'I shall start as soon as I have completed the work for the cathedral. I do believe I have a length of fabric put away somewhere that will suit you perfectly.'

Once Hannah had seen that Lizzie was competent to take care of Gabriel and Frances throughout the day, she had devoted herself to sewing, leaving the housework and the basic cooking to Judith. Adam had complained, but in a good-natured way. 'Mutton stew again,' he said, as they were served it for dinner two nights in a row.

'It's something Judith knows how to cook,' Hannah said briskly, 'so I asked her to make a large pot.' Then she relented. 'I've nearly finished the embroidery for the Dean's robes. As soon as I have delivered it, I promise I will roast a chicken.'

'On Sunday, perhaps?' Adam asked hopefully.

Lizzie had discovered, within the first day or so of being at the house in New Street, that Adam worked in the Dean's office at the cathedral. He had been a stone mason until an injury to his back had made the painstaking work, often in cramped spaces, too hard to bear. His knowledge of the cathedral and its many statues had led him to a position working on the preservation of the existing works and the commissioning of new ones – or, at least, that was what Lizzie understood from Hannah. Coming from a town where all the work revolved around the sea, whether it was related to fishing, boat-building, smuggling or the inns that serviced the sea-faring folk, she had marvelled at the strangeness of such an occupation.

Within a few days of arriving in Canterbury, she had a chance to see for herself the interior of the cathedral that lay at its heart. The family attended the Sunday service as a matter of course and Lizzie, who had believed St George's Church, in Castle Bay's Lower Street, to be the largest and finest in the area, had been astonished by the scale and grandeur of the cathedral. She felt extremely small as she

43

sat quietly in her pew, Frances and Gabriel next to her, Hannah and Adam seated beyond. St George's could have been swallowed up by the cathedral several times, she thought, trying to pay attention to the service but finding her eyes drawn to the vastness of the vaulted ceiling and the huge, worn flagstones of the floor, trodden by the feet of pilgrims for hundreds of years.

Adam engaged her in conversation as they walked home. 'An impressive building, is it not?' he asked.

Lizzie sensed the pride in his voice. 'It is. I have never seen anything quite like it,' she admitted. 'It gave me a sense of ...' She stopped, unsure of what she wished to say. 'The sense of a greater being, perhaps,' she said, a little embarrassed. 'It is a very calm place, even when filled with people.'

'I'm glad you felt it,' Adam said quietly. 'It has that effect on me, too.'

Lizzie knew from Hannah that some of his wanderings about the streets after dark, as on the evening she had been rescued, had come about as a result of a wish to help people, inspired by the days he spent in and around the cathedral.

'It seems to have permeated his blood,' she said with a sigh, then laughed. 'Although it has brought work to me, too, in the embroidery of vestments. We are quite the cathedral family. If Gabriel could sing, no doubt he would be a chorister, but he seems to have inherited my inability to hold a tune.'

Lizzie wondered when Adam would bring home the next lost soul, but he seemed to have curtailed his wanderings, an indirect result of her arrival: she looked after the children, allowing Hannah to sew for most of the day. This meant Hannah no longer worked into the evenings and Adam felt less inclination to leave home now that he had the company of his wife and Lizzie.

After a month had passed, Lizzie felt like part of the family. Hannah's initial reserve had faded and she had proved to be a warm friend and guide to Lizzie, staying true to her word with regard to teaching her to read and write. She set aside two mornings a week to work with Gabriel and Frances on their books, and Lizzie was encouraged to join in. Spurred on by competition with a six-year-old and a four-year-old, she had remembered some of what Nell had previously tried to teach her and improved quite rapidly, although not without privately shedding tears of frustration.

When Hannah had confided that Gabriel would go to school before long, Lizzie had felt some alarm. Would the Russells feel the time was right to let her go, with just Frances, a very biddable child, to be cared for at home? She had resolved to make herself useful in other ways around the house, considering offering to help with the cooking, then discounting the idea as her skills were not much greater than those of Judith, who preferred to bake. But perhaps she could help Hannah with her sewing. Now that the intricate embroidery for the cathedral vestments had been completed, Hannah had announced she would start work on some private commissions, mainly whitework. Lizzie knew from the piece she had examined on her first night in the house that such embroidery was beyond her, but perhaps she could manage something simpler. She imagined them sitting together, companionably sewing, Frances playing nearby in the room, while Gabriel was at school. She found it to be an image that appealed, and decided to set about trying to make it happen in the weeks that remained until Gabriel's school term was due to start.

CHAPTER ELEVEN

As the weeks passed, with no talk of Lizzie leaving the family in September, she ceased to worry. She had shown Hannah that she was competent with a needle by helping with the general household sewing tasks, but it was clear she had much to learn if she was to master the techniques involved in whitework.

They had settled down before the fire one unseasonably cool summer evening when Adam was away on church business. He had journeyed to York, to visit a stonemason who was fabricating a gargoyle to replace one on the South-west Porch, damaged by exposure to the elements over the years.

'Tell me about your whitework,' Lizzie said. 'When did you learn it? And where? Have you any pieces you can show me?'

The last question was disingenuous – she had seen the embroidery in the basket on the shelf near the fireplace but didn't want Hannah to know she had been snooping on her first night in New Street.

'My mother taught me,' Hannah said. 'She'd learned it when she was in service in Scotland – there's a town in Argyll where the girls are apprenticed from the age of nine. She was fascinated by it and begged one of them – the daughter of the gardener – to show her some of the skills she had learned. She began to teach me when I was about twelve, I suppose.'

She stood up and pulled a slim notebook from the shelf next to her work-basket. 'I sketched each piece made on commission before it went to its new home. I like to make sure that each one is unique.'

She looked proud as she spoke, Lizzie thought, and rightly so as Hannah began to reveal the drawings that filled the pages.

'This is drawn threadwork,' Hannah said, stopping at a rectangular sketch. 'You can create a border by removing the warp or weft threads – the ones running vertically or horizontally. First, make sure you have stitched all around the area of the design using a strong white thread, then snip and draw single strands of the muslin or linen from within to form a lattice pattern. You can leave it like that, or form additional patterns by connecting the remaining warp or weft threads with tiny stitches.'

She pointed out the details on page after page of the exquisite drawings.

'I cut eyelets into this design, outlining the circles first with running stitches, then using small binding stitches to strengthen the edges. This one has been padded with several layers of stitches to increase the raised effect.'

Lizzie longed to see the originals. She was particularly drawn to the babies' bonnets: little mob caps of fine muslin, pin-tucked into embroidered circlets at the top and adorned with fine examples of decorative eyelets and something that Hannah described as needle lace.

She shook her head in amazement as each new creation was revealed. 'It seems impossible that you could have stitched these,' she said. 'They look like pieces of fine lace,' she pointed to a particularly intricate collar, 'or something only fairy folk could make.'

Hannah laughed. 'I assure you, no fairies were involved. Although many times I've wished for an extra pair of hands to help.' She regarded Lizzie. 'I'm hoping that might be you.'

Lizzie was alarmed. 'I could never work anything as beautiful as this,' she exclaimed. 'I can turn a seam or stitch a hem, but this . . .' She trailed off, staring at the notebook.

'It just takes the finest of fabrics, a good needle and the right thread,' Hannah said robustly. 'We're lucky to have Canterbury muslin here – it's a match for anything from Bengal and it's beautiful to work with. But your hands, the thread and the work area must be spotless – it picks up the slightest mark.'

It was a marvel that the babies' bonnets remained pristine, Lizzie thought. No doubt they were bought as christening gifts by wealthy patrons. Perhaps they were never intended to be worn other than once and, in any case, she supposed there were nursemaids and laundresses in the big houses to take care of such matters. It was a far cry from her home in Lower Street, where such a fine bonnet would have been a limp rag within minutes.

She sighed as she contemplated the pages, then realised Hannah had retrieved her work-basket from the shelf.

'I have only one piece I can show you,' she said. She unfolded the fabric that Lizzie had seen on her first night. 'I work on it whenever I can, which isn't often. It's the only piece that isn't a commission.' She looked almost shy as she spoke.

'It's beautiful,' Lizzie exclaimed, as the light once more picked out the raised petals and leaves in the arching foliage. The piece was a long way from being finished. 'What is it for?' she asked. It wasn't clear to her how it might be used.

'It has no real purpose,' Hannah confessed. 'Other than to show my work.'

'Is it for your customers to see?'

'No, I suppose it's for the family, for Frances. She's too young to learn and I want her to know what I did, in case I can't pass it on.'

Lizzie was puzzled. 'But she could learn in a few years' time, if she has the aptitude.'

Hannah, her back to Lizzie, was busy packing away her basket and returning the notebook to the shelf. When she turned around, her eyes were bright, her cheeks flushed. 'I'm finding it a little warm in here,' she said. 'I'll make us both a drink and then it's time for bed. The morning will be upon us before we know it.'

She left the room, leaving Lizzie to contemplate the strangeness of Hannah's words, forgotten within minutes as the enormity of learning whitework dawned on her. She would never master it, she knew, having only half understood the techniques Hannah had described to her. She had neither the patience nor the skill in her fingers. Her thread would be knotted and grimy before she'd begun, no matter how many times she scrubbed her hands. She would have to find other ways to help Hannah — especially if she wanted to keep her position within the household.

She sighed and stood up to join Hannah in the kitchen. There were still several weeks of summer before Gabriel would begin school: she must make herself indispensable in that time.

CHAPTER TWELVE

As the weeks progressed, Lizzie's life in Castle Bay felt more and more remote. She marvelled at this – how could she have lived somewhere for sixteen years, only to cast it off so easily? She supposed it was because her life in Canterbury was so different. In Castle Bay, the sea and the weather played such an important part in day-to-day living: everyone was affected by it in some way – the fishermen, the sailors, the innkeepers, the smugglers. In the city, life ran to different rhythms; it carried on regardless of the weather.

At the beginning, Hannah had made gentle enquiries as to her circumstances and why she had left home. Lizzie had been discouraging: she didn't want Hannah to know she had abandoned her siblings to the care of their mother, who couldn't cope with them and who was expecting yet another child. She feared it reflected badly on her.

Did she miss them, Susan, Mary and Alice, who had been such a part of her everyday life? She had been glad to get away from them, and the daily grind, but now, as she watched Gabriel and Frances grow, she found herself imagining how they would have changed in the few months she had been away. Would she visit them before the year was out? She could ill afford the coach fare, or the time, she told herself.

Developments in New Street drove the thoughts from her mind. Gabriel started school and within the week Lizzie could see a change in him. From days dominated by domesticity, with activities dictated by his mother and Lizzie, he was plunged into a new world of structure and study. He was just seven years old, yet the discipline and routine appeared to suit him. He became serious and rather fussy, saying, 'But the master said . . .' at every opportunity. Lizzie rather missed the Gabriel of old and hoped he would regain some of his childish ways once he had settled.

Neither Hannah nor Adam appeared to notice: they had other things to occupy them. Hannah was expecting a baby. Adam was overjoyed and solicitous, Hannah rather pale and quiet.

'I am fearful,' she confided in Lizzie, one day, as they sewed by the fire. Autumn had set in early and leaves swirled outside in a brisk wind, rain lashing at the window panes. A planned outing to the park by the river with Frances had been abandoned, but the little girl was busy in the kitchen 'helping' Judith roll out the pastry for a pie, so the two women found themselves alone.

Lizzie raised her eyebrows at the word 'fearful' and set aside her sewing to encourage Hannah to go on.

'I've lost three babies already, all before they were ready to be born. I'm not sure I can bear to go through it again.'

Hannah's face was pinched and anguished and her hands shook. Lizzie reached over and gently took them in hers. 'I'll help in any way I can,' she soothed. 'You must rest every day, and Judith should make you beef tea to build up your strength.'

Hannah was too thin, Lizzie thought, casting a critical eye over her employer. Never one to carry weight, she appeared to have lost it over the last few weeks. Her wrists, almost concealed within the fabric of her sleeves, were bony, her face gaunt.

'I've been feeling unwell,' Hannah confessed. 'I'm finding it hard to eat, but it will pass. It's been like this every time.'

'You need your strength for the baby.' Lizzie didn't really know what this meant but she'd heard it said often enough to her mother, who could hardly have been more different from Hannah. Mrs Carey was unaffected by sickness, but took every opportunity to rest, despite appearing as strong as an ox. Perhaps all the resting was why being with child seemed to suit her so well, Lizzie reflected.

Hannah's weakness surely meant that the family would still need Lizzie, even though Gabriel was at school. She felt her position was assured, but her peace of mind was short-lived. Hannah was seized with a bout of coughing, not alarming in itself since it had begun with the onset of the damp autumnal weather. She had assured Lizzie it happened every year.

'The streets around here hold dampness in the air. We are low-lying and too close to the Stour. I dare say these were water meadows once. It will pass, once the rains ease.'

Hannah had spoken confidently, even though her narrow frame was racked by the cough. Lizzie wondered why they didn't move further from the river, but the house was tied to Adam's work, she realised, so they must stay.

'I'll fetch you a drink.' Lizzie got to her feet, alarmed as Hannah continued to cough. Her face was red, her eyes streaming and she could barely catch her breath.

She shook her head but couldn't speak, then covered her face with her handkerchief. When the coughing at last subsided, Lizzie, still standing, gazed anxiously at Hannah. Her face was white. In her lap she held the handkerchief, now stained scarlet with spots of blood.

She looked up at Lizzie. 'Don't tell Adam,' she whispered.

CHAPTER THIRTEEN

In the weeks that followed, Adam, preoccupied with his tasks at the cathedral, worked longer and longer hours, and it fell to Lizzie to adopt many roles in the house. She continued with her childcare duties, looking after Frances and collecting Gabriel after school each day. She was a companion to Hannah, and also the family seamstress. Frances had grown and her dresses needed letting down, while Gabriel treated his school clothes in a cavalier fashion and his knickerbockers required regular patching.

As Hannah's belly grew larger, her fatigue increased, as did the coughing. She was desperate to hide this from Adam but, since she was so exhausted each day, she was fast asleep in bed by the time he returned from the cathedral. Lizzie found she had become Adam's companion, too, sitting with him at the kitchen table once he had finished his meal. Sometimes he entertained her with stories from the cathedral – of the day's events, mistakes that had been made, words spoken out of place. She often had little understanding of what he was describing, but she nodded, smiled and laughed in what she hoped were appropriate moments. He seemed content just to have an audience: she supposed it helped him process the frustrations of the day. At other times, he was too tired to converse, or his dark brows were drawn together in a frown, perhaps over some work incident that had irked him. Then she would serve him a glass of ale and take up some sewing, keeping him company while he worked through his thoughts. Often, she was on the point of mentioning Hannah's cough and how worried she was. She wanted to beg him to fetch a doctor to see his wife, but she had given her word to Hannah to keep her illness a secret.

On Sundays after church, Hannah often pleaded sewing to be done, and hid herself in the sitting room. Lizzie could hear her muffled coughs but Adam appeared oblivious. He was happy to spend time with his children and would sit at the table in the kitchen, going through Gabriel's lessons with him, and helping Frances with work her mother had set.

On a rare occasion when Adam commented on Hannah's cough, his wife reminded him that it returned every year in the autumn.

'It's the damp in the air from the river,' she said. 'One day, we will move from here and then you will see how healthy I become.'

Adam looked as though there was something further he wished to say, but Hannah quickly changed the subject to distract him.

Lizzie hoped that a succession of bright, crisp days in October would restore Hannah to health, but she remained pale and prone to coughing fits. Lizzie took Frances to the little park by the River Stour, enjoying the crisp crunch of the fallen leaves underfoot. She couldn't help regarding the river with suspicion as they crossed the bridge, watching it roll on by, still swollen with the rains of September. She hoped neither she nor Frances would be afflicted as Hannah was, and encouraged her charge to gather some of the most colourful fallen leaves so that they could draw and paint them when they got home.

'We mustn't leave your mama alone too long,' she cautioned Frances, when she showed signs of becoming mutinous, having been cooped up in the house throughout the wet September. 'She will miss you.'

Frances gave her a frank look from under the brim of her hat and Lizzie was instantly reminded of just how much she resembled her mother.

'Is Mama going to die?' she asked, causing Lizzie to come to an abrupt halt.

'Whatever gave you that idea?' Her thoughts flew at once to

Judith, who had an unguarded tongue. Perhaps Frances had been spending too much time with her, while Lizzie helped Hannah with the sewing.

'Gabriel,' Frances replied. She was bending down, busy picking up leaves, and Lizzie couldn't see her expression.

'Your mama has a cough, that's all,' Lizzie said, hugging Frances to her as she straightened. Her little body was unresponsive so Lizzie continued, hoping to ease her worries: 'And you know there's a new baby on the way, so she's extra tired. That's why I've been helping her as much as I can, so don't you worry.' Lizzie didn't want to promise that everything would be all right, because she was by no means confident that that would be the case. 'Have you collected enough leaves?' she asked Frances. 'Are you ready to go back now? We can ask Judith to make us some chocolate.' She thought the little girl was cold, and it wouldn't do any harm for her to have some treats. It upset Lizzie to think she had been keeping her worries to herself.

'Where are your leaves?' Frances asked.

'I thought I could share yours,' Lizzie said.

Frances shook her head, solemn. 'Mine are all special,' she said.

'Then I will take these,' Lizzie said, barely looking as she gathered a few specimens from around her feet. It seemed Frances had no more to say on the subject of her mother, and Lizzie was glad.

'Race you to the gate,' she said, having glanced quickly around to make sure there was no one to see them behaving without decorum.

Frances needed no encouragement. She was at the gate in half a minute, leaves still clutched firmly in her gloved hand, leaving Lizzie, who had decided she perhaps shouldn't run after all, to hurry after her.

Chapter Fourteen

During the autumn afternoons, Frances preferred to stay in the kitchen with Judith rather than sit by her mother and Lizzie as they sewed. It gave the two women a chance to talk, at first about everyday matters but, as the weeks wore on into November, Hannah gradually opened up and took the chance to speak about things she wouldn't have wanted her daughter to hear.

At first, she spoke about her whitework commissions. It weighed heavily on her mind that she was struggling to work as quickly as she had in the past: she had to immediately set the work aside when she was seized by a fit of coughing for fear that the pure white fabric might be marked. Then it took her a while to recover enough to start stitching again, for her eyes streamed and made it hard for her to see. Her hopes that Lizzie might help with the delicate work had been dashed.

'It took you many years to gain the level of skill you have,' Lizzie pointed out. 'How am I to achieve that in a matter of weeks? But I can help with some of the basic stitching, and I can sew the babies' bonnets together and add the ribbons.'

It was small consolation for Hannah. Lizzie had attempted to reassure her that, once she had recovered from the birth of the new baby, she would be able to get back to her work and take up her commissions once more. But as the weeks progressed and Hannah grew weaker, despite her swelling belly, Lizzie was no longer convinced by her own words.

One afternoon, as they stitched in silence, Lizzie working on a bonnet and her employer on an elaborate cloth, Hannah spoke up. 'If anything should happen to me, will you take care of Gabriel and Frances and make sure that they are all right?' Before a startled Lizzie could speak she hurried on, two spots of bright colour burning on her cheeks. 'I fear Gabriel will become angry, and Frances – Frances is very self-possessed but she must be allowed to grieve. As for Adam ...' Hannah shook her head '... Adam will be broken.'

Lizzie struggled to find the right words. 'Hannah, I'm sure it is natural to be fearful, after you have lost your babies, but you have given birth before and all was well. I am sure all will be well this time, too.'

She reached out and put a hand over Hannah's, shocked to find her fingers chilly despite the high colour in her cheeks.

'I'm not talking about the birth.' Hannah was impatient. 'Although I suppose, in a way, I am. I don't know if I have the strength.' She cast her eyes down to the work in her lap. 'Even if I survive the birth, I don't believe I'm long for this world. This cough ...' She shrugged.

'Then let me ask Adam to send for the doctor,' Lizzie urged.

Hannah shook her head. 'It will be money ill spent. What can he do? There's no cure for what afflicts me.'

'But won't you even try?' Lizzie could hardly think how to formulate her plea. 'For the sake of Gabriel and Frances, for Adam? For the baby?'

'It's too late. I know it. It's a matter between me and God now. But you – you are young, fit and healthy. You can take on my role.' She gripped Lizzie's hand hard, her eyes burning bright.

Lizzie could scarcely comprehend what Hannah was saying. Was she asking her to step into her shoes and take care of her family? She compared herself to Hannah, so calm and well organised, managing a household with no apparent effort, and feared that she couldn't match up. She felt like a child herself in comparison.

'It's the best way,' Hannah continued, as Lizzie remained silent.

'I've thought about it a good deal. Everything will go on much as it did before.' She cast Lizzie a look of appeal. 'Can you promise me that you will do it? It would be a great comfort to me.'

Lizzie hardly knew how to respond. She could see how much it mattered to Hannah, but she couldn't promise something she might not be able to deliver.

'Hannah, you're worrying unnecessarily,' she said firmly. 'I'm sure you will be here this time next year, sitting stitching by the fire, while the baby plays on the floor. I'm going to visit the apothecary and ask his advice. We will find something to make you feel well again.'

She was relieved when Frances burst into the room, wanting to tell them about the pastry decorations that Judith had allowed her to make for that evening's pie. Lizzie was effusive in her praise but, glancing at Hannah, who remained quiet, she could see the disappointment on the older woman's face. Lizzie feared it wouldn't be the last time that the subject was raised.

CHAPTER FIFTEEN

That week, Lizzie wrapped up as best she could against the chill November wind, laced with icy flurries of rain, and ventured out into the streets of Canterbury. It felt strange to be walking on her own – she had always been accompanied by one or both of the children, or by the whole family on their Sunday trips to the cathedral. She was intent on finding some treatment to ease Hannah's coughing and breathlessness, and remembered passing an apothecary on Stour Street, not far from the park by the river.

A rich aroma of herbs, with an underlying note of bitterness, filled her nostrils as she entered the shop, dimly lit by candles on such a gloomy day. She cast her eyes over the array of wooden cabinets, their small drawers neatly labelled. Large ceramic jars, some with metal taps close to their base, stood within a glass-fronted cupboard at the back of the shop. Shelves along one wall were filled with small sacks of dried materials, and brown glass jars. Two pestles and mortars of different sizes sat on the counter, along with a set of brass scales. The apothecary was busy attending to another customer and Lizzie had a minute or two to look around, intrigued by what was on offer.

'I'm looking for something to treat a bad cough,' she began, when the customer had gone.

'For yourself?' The apothecary looked at her enquiringly.

'No, no, for my employer. The coughing is making her weak, and she is with child, too.'

The apothecary nodded slowly. 'And does she have a fever? A high colour?'

'Not always,' Lizzie said. 'She is very pale much of the time, but then her cheeks become flushed. She blames it on the weather, and the dampness that comes from living near the river.' She waved her hand vaguely in the direction of the Stour.

'Hmm.' The apothecary nodded, already turning to his glass-fronted cupboard and taking a small glass bottle from the shelf below. He held it beneath the tap on one of the ceramic jars and filled it, then sealed it with a cork. He set it on the counter, then opened one of the cabinet drawers and lifted out a small pot.

'This ointment is extracted from the leaves of foxgloves. Each morning she must rub a little on her breast, above her lungs.' He pointed to his chest by way of illustration. He picked up the glass bottle. 'This is an infusion of figwort – dilute a teaspoon in a small glass of water or weak ale and take it twice a day. When wild garlic is in season, she should eat it whenever she can.'

He wrote his prescription in an ornate script on a pad of paper, then handed it to Lizzie. The sum for the medicines was written at the bottom – it was far more than she had expected, but the money Hannah had given her would just cover it. She counted out the coins onto the counter, took up the pot and the bottle and left the shop, trying to feel hopeful that she held Hannah's cure in her hands.

Preoccupied by her thoughts, Lizzie failed to notice a woman walking directly towards her until she was brought to a halt, finding her way blocked. Puzzled, Lizzie looked up, straight into the eyes of Mrs Simmonds.

'Well,' Mrs Simmonds said pleasantly, 'I thought I had seen you in Canterbury before but believed myself mistaken.' She raised her eyebrows and looked at Lizzie.

Lizzie, aghast, was immediately filled with guilt. She had barely thought of Mrs Simmonds since her rescue by Adam on her first night in Canterbury. She had been so absorbed by her work with the Russells. Her would-be employer was undoubtedly annoyed that Lizzie had failed to appear, and had never even offered an explanation. She began to stumble out an apology. 'I'm so sorry. I did come to Canterbury on the coach, as arranged, but late in the day. When I arrived, I dropped the piece of paper you had left for me. It was ruined by the rain. I didn't know how to find you.' Lizzie was growing hot and flustered under Mrs Simmonds's cool gaze.

'How unfortunate,' Mrs Simmonds said. 'I had someone wait all afternoon at the coaching inn to meet you. I had high hopes for you at my establishment.'

'I'm sorry,' Lizzie said again. 'I didn't mean to let you down. I was delayed and couldn't get away from Castle Bay.'

'And would you care to join me now?'

Lizzie had a sudden memory of standing outside Mrs Simmonds's house in the dark and the rain, Adam at her side, as he revealed to her the nature of her business.

'Why, no!' she exclaimed, then corrected herself on seeing Mrs Simmonds's expression. 'I mean, thank you, but I managed to find other employment here and I am quite settled.'

Mrs Simmonds nodded. 'Then you owe me money.' She named a sum that made Lizzie gasp. 'For the coach fare, and recompense for the disappointment. I had clients who were looking forward to your arrival. You put me in an awkward position.'

Lizzie noted that Mrs Simmonds had given up all pretence of the dress shop. She must have presumed Lizzie had learned the true nature of her business by then. 'I don't have that sort of money,' she said, hoping she sounded firm but fearful that her voice wavered. 'I could pay you back the coach fare, but not today.' She was conscious that her pocket was all but empty after her purchases from the apothecary.

She tried to step around Mrs Simmonds, who put out an arm to detain her.

'Then where will I find you?' she asked. 'Debts must be repaid, you know.'

Lizzie began to tremble. She couldn't give her the Russells' address: Adam would be furious if Mrs Simmonds came to their house and, in any case, she didn't want her to know where she lived.

'I'll bring it to you,' she said faintly.

Mrs Simmonds frowned. Then, having considered, she said, 'A good idea. Perhaps you will change your mind once you have seen what I can offer you.' She rattled off the address – which, of course, Lizzie already knew, though she made a show of committing it to memory. 'I will expect it before Christmas Day,' continued Mrs Simmonds. 'The full sum. Of course, if you don't have the money, you could always work for me to pay off the debt.' She smiled and stepped aside, allowing Lizzie to pass.

Lizzie, anguished, hurried on, bending her head against what was now driving rain. Where could she find such an amount? She earned little money at the Russells' and most of that went on necessities. Mrs Simmonds had demanded it by Christmas, now just a few weeks away.

Chapter Sixteen

Lizzie was still agitated when she arrived back at the house in New Street, but she tried hard to shake off her worries before she saw Hannah. She wanted her to feel encouraged by the treatments her money had provided, and to believe that a cure was in sight. So, barely pausing to shake off the rain from her hair and clothing, she was quick to seek her out. Hannah was settled in her usual spot by the sitting-room fire, her eyes closed and, for a moment, Lizzie feared the worst.

Then Hannah yawned. 'I must have fallen asleep,' she said, opening her eyes. 'I think the room is too warm.'

'It's far from warm outside,' Lizzie said. She deposited her purchases on Hannah's lap, briefly grasping her hand as she did so.

Hannah gasped. 'Goodness, your hands are like ice. Thank you for going out for me in this weather. What did the apothecary say?'

Lizzie, aware that Hannah was now mainly confined to the house, described the man and his shop to her.

'Take a teaspoon of the tincture twice a day in water or ale,' she said, 'and rub on the ointment in the morning.'

'I don't want Adam to see these,' Hannah said, handing them back to Lizzie. 'He will only worry. Can you find a place to keep them?'

Lizzie thought for a moment. If she took them into the kitchen, Judith and Frances would see them and ask questions. Frances might mention something to her father. Privately, she thought it would be good if Adam was alerted to the fact that Hannah's health was failing fast, but that was a decision for her employer to make.

'Why don't you keep them on the shelf, here, behind your work-basket?' she suggested. 'No one will see them and you can take the doses without being observed.'

She tucked the two items to the back of the shelf, then went to the kitchen in search of a spoon and a glass of water, determined that Hannah should take her first dose at once. That done, she devoted herself to Frances for the rest of the afternoon, trying to banish all thoughts of Mrs Simmonds from her mind. When it was time to collect Gabriel from school, the rain was falling even more heavily and Hannah insisted that Frances stayed at home rather than take her usual daily walk.

'I don't want her catching a chill,' she said. 'She can stay here with me – we'll do some sewing together. Take my cloak – it has a hood you can throw over your hair and it will be long enough to keep the worst of the rain off you. Gabriel, at least, has his winter jacket.'

Once again, Lizzie found herself out on the streets alone. She passed very few people on her walk to the cathedral – the weather was keeping most of them indoors. She was sure Mrs Simmonds wouldn't venture out in such a downpour and, besides, Hannah's cloak, its hood thrown over her hair, provided her with protection and anonymity.

She hurried through the cathedral precincts as the great clock chimed the hour. Was the rain easing a little? Could she get Gabriel home before he was soaked?

'Hannah?'

She almost didn't register the voice calling, until it came again, louder this time.

'Hannah!'

She spun around, almost losing her footing on the wet flagstones. Adam was striding towards her. He was all but upon her before she thought to lower her hood.

'Not Hannah,' she said. 'Just Lizzie, here to collect Gabriel. I'm sorry to disappoint.' She offered him a smile. As the rain began to trickle down her face she wrinkled her nose and pulled the hood back in place.

'Oh!' Adam said. 'I thought Hannah had come, seeing the cloak. I thought she must be feeling better.'

Lizzie looked up from under the hood, which had fallen across her brow. Perhaps she should take this moment to tell Adam that Hannah was far from well, that she had been to the apothecary on her behalf that very morning and that he should, perhaps, prepare himself and his family for the worst if the medicine didn't work. But the clatter of feet as the scholars began to emerge from the cloisters reminded her she was there to collect Gabriel.

'Hannah lent me her cloak,' she said hastily, in case Adam should think she had helped herself to it, 'but she's a good deal taller than me – I'm surprised you couldn't tell it wasn't her.'

Adam was regarding her with a curious expression, then he stepped a little closer. He reached out and gently wiped raindrops from her face. 'Don't let me detain you,' he said. 'Gabriel will be waiting.' Then he turned and walked away.

Lizzie stood for a moment, unsure of what to make of him. Then she went in search of Gabriel. She didn't have far to go – he was just a few yards away, sheltering under the arches of the cloisters. Lizzie felt her colour rise – had he witnessed what had just happened? Should she say something and, if so, what? She didn't know how to interpret his father's action. So she greeted him with 'It's going to be a wet journey home, Gabriel. We must walk very fast or you will be soaked to the skin.'

'You're wearing my mother's cloak.' Gabriel spoke quite coldly.

'She lent it to me, Gabriel, so that I wouldn't get too wet. Now, hurry along. Tell me what you did at school today.'

Lizzie shepherded him out of the cathedral grounds and along Mercery Lane, where the overhang of the buildings kept the worst of the rain from them. Unbidden, a memory of the first time she had seen Adam came back to her. It had been a wet night, although not as wet as this, and distracted by being unable to find Mrs Simmonds's establishment, she had stepped back onto his foot and elbowed him as he tried to pass by. She laughed in embarrassment at the memory and Gabriel glanced up at her.

'Is something funny?' he asked. He had a pinched look about his face and she didn't think it was entirely due to the cold.

Her heart sank. He was behaving oddly – rudely, in fact. She was certain he must have witnessed Adam's strange behaviour. She couldn't think of anything she could say that wouldn't make matters worse.

'I was just remembering the first time I walked along this street,' she said. 'I couldn't read any of the shop signs. But your mother helped me and now I can barely remember why reading seemed so difficult. You are a lucky boy to have the advantage of your schooling.'

It was a partial truth, but Lizzie was determined not to let a seven-year-old boy discomfit her. 'Not too far now,' she said. 'Are you very wet? Judith can make you some chocolate when we get in.'

CHAPTER SEVENTEEN

Lizzie had decided that Christmas in the Russell household would be a joyous occasion, no matter what. Over the previous weeks she had rarely thought of her home in Castle Bay but as Christmas Day approached, she felt a sadness she found hard to shake off. Did her family wonder what had become of her? Did they hope she might reappear in time for Christmas? Every year they would attend church the night before, the younger children fractious at the lateness of the hour and the restriction of their Sunday-best clothes. They would make a late start the following morning, excitement building at the prospect of their Christmas dinner. It was always chaotic around the makeshift table her pa created for the occasion. At other times, they ate in shifts at the small kitchen table, but for Christmas, Mr Carey constructed an extension using pallets and bits of wood, from his store in the backyard or down by his boat. It was a rickety affair and, more often than not, came with an aroma of fish, which caused Ruth and Jane to wrinkle their noses and declare they couldn't sit there: they wouldn't know whether they had fish or fowl on their plates.

With the table extension in place, there was barely room to get around the kitchen, causing Mrs Carey to become hot and lose her temper, but with Lizzie's help dinner always made it to the table, even if it didn't all arrive at once. Nell had been the great cook in the family, Lizzie reflected. Since she had married, standards had fallen. Who would help this year? Ruth, she supposed, as she was now the eldest one at home. With a shock, Lizzie remembered there would be a new member of the family. Mrs Carey must have given birth in the autumn, and Lizzie hadn't once thought of it. Was it another girl or had her father's wish for a boy been granted? The baby would be passed from lap to lap as the family ate, just as each successive child had been in the past.

Once dinner was over and the kitchen put to rights, it would be time to open presents. There was rarely more than one each, money being so short. Lizzie had often been asked by her parents to make something for her siblings, which they could offer as their gift. Then they would play games, which usually led to arguments and Mrs Carey threatening to send everyone to bed. Despite that, it had always been the best day of the year in the Carey household.

Lizzie thought it would be rather different with the Russells. She broached the subject with Hannah one wintry afternoon, when the frost already lay on the roadway outside, suggesting that the journey to collect Gabriel from school would be treacherous.

'How do you spend Christmas here?' Lizzie asked. 'Do you have a big dinner? Invite family or friends? Are there presents for Frances and Gabriel?'

A shadow crossed Hannah's face and she sighed. 'After the morning service we go out visiting – the cathedral supports many of the local poorer families and Adam likes to make sure that Frances and Gabriel accompany him, so they can appreciate their own good fortune. I usually go with them but that will be out of the question this year. Then we have dinner – a goose if we can get it, if not beef.' She shook her head. 'I don't know how we will fare. Judith always has the day off so she can be with her family and I'm not sure I can manage it all on my own. But I will try.'

Lizzie was puzzled. 'I'll be here. You must just tell me what's to be done, and I will do it.'

'You won't be returning home to your family?' Hannah was surprised.

'No, they won't expect me. So you can decide what you'd like to have and then you need worry no further.'

The relief on Hannah's face was obvious. 'I'm so pleased you'll be with us, Lizzie. I feared this year would be a miserable quiet time, with just a cold meal prepared by Judith the day before. But now I know you will be here I can rest easy. Adam will have company, and the children will be delighted, I know.'

Lizzie thought it unlikely that Gabriel would delight in her presence. He had been surly with her ever since her encounter with Adam in the cloisters – she was always glad of Frances's chatter when they collected her brother from school. She felt momentary anxiety at Hannah's words about keeping Adam company, then shook it off – after all, it was no different from every evening, when Hannah retired early to bed.

She turned her mind to practical matters. 'We must plan what needs to be done. Shall I decorate the house with greenery? Shall we make gifts for the children? Will Judith deal with the butcher's order?'

It was good to have something to distract Hannah, Lizzie thought. As the baby grew in her belly, she appeared to be shrinking: her strength was failing, her face gaunt. She barely left her chair in the sitting room, other than to go upstairs to bed, and although she carried on sewing, the concentration frequently exhausted her. Despite the tincture and the ointment from the apothecary, she continued to have coughing fits, which racked her body and left her gasping for breath, her eyes running with tears. Once the tincture had been used up, she didn't ask Lizzie to buy more. Lizzie thought of volunteering to return to the apothecary, to ask whether there was anything else he might suggest, but she held her tongue. Partly this was down to a lack of belief in his treatments but also for fear of running into Mrs Simmonds again. Although she could just as easily come across her anywhere else in the city, she was filled with a superstitious dread about Stour Street. Perhaps Mrs Simmonds favoured the same apothecary with her custom. She couldn't risk an encounter: Lizzie was only too aware that her would-be employer had demanded repayment of the debt by Christmas Day, and she was in the same position as she had been when she saw her, with no money in her pocket.

By the time Lizzie needed to cajole Frances into venturing out into the cold with her to collect Gabriel, she and Hannah had come up with a plan to make the house in New Street a happy and special place on Christmas Day. Neither woman gave voice to the thought, but it loomed large in the back of Lizzie's mind: this might be the last Christmas that Hannah would spend with her family and for that reason alone she wanted to make it a very special one.

CHAPTER EIGHTEEN

The dark days of December were traditionally enlivened by small celebrations with family and friends, but this had rarely happened in the Carey household where money was in such short supply. It wasn't a tradition in the Russell family, either, Lizzie discovered. They hadn't been visited by relatives during the ten months she had lived with them, and no friends came to the door, either. Eventually curiosity got the better of Lizzie. 'Will any family join us on Christmas Day?' she asked Hannah, as the day drew closer and final plans needed to be made with Judith for the butcher's order.

'My mother and father have passed on,' Hannah said, 'and Adam's parents live a distance away. The journey is too great to undertake at this time of year, or at any time. We rarely see them. Adam is too busy with cathedral business to travel to visit them.'

It was a shame that Gabriel and Frances didn't have the benefit of grandparents, Lizzie thought. She had always loved her grandfather, Walter. He became grumpy at times at the noise of all the Carey children together, but he was happy to take them out in his cart and carve wooden toys, such as Arabella, for them. If Hannah's parents had still been alive, they could reasonably have been expected to lend a hand now that their daughter was so ill, but that was clearly out of the question. The Russell family were very much on their own.

The worry this knowledge caused faded into the background as Christmas week arrived. Lizzie worked with Frances to make decorations for the festive greenery they would collect on Christmas Eve: sticks of cinnamon bound together with red ribbon, and oranges studded with cloves. Collected together on the kitchen dresser, they filled the air with a glorious scent. On Christmas Eve afternoon, they wrapped up against the cold and went out in search of evergreens to garland the mantel over the kitchen range. The yard at the back of the house furnished them with long strands of ivy, but they had to go to the park for the conifer boughs, with their distinctive sharp, fresh scent. Frances, enchanted by the glistening red berries on the holly, was keen to take this, too, but Lizzie dissuaded her. 'We'll leave it for the birds,' she said. 'They love to eat the berries.'

They had a happy couple of hours decorating the kitchen, where they would be spending the majority of Christmas Day. Even Gabriel, who had the day off school, was persuaded out of his recent sulkiness to help. Adam surprised Lizzie by bringing home a bunch of mistletoe: she had imagined such a thing too frivolous for him. The imminent festivities seemed to have raised his spirits. She realised he had barely smiled over the last few weeks, but now he was lifting Gabriel up to the kitchen doorway and instructing him to hang the mistletoe from the nail that was already in place from previous years.

'Now go and fetch your mother,' he instructed the children.

He turned to Lizzie and smiled when they left the room. 'Thank you for this,' he said, gesturing to the decorations in the kitchen. 'I'm grateful – for everything you've done for Hannah, the children and for me.'

Frances's excited chatter as the children led their mother down the passageway prevented him from saying anything further, but he smiled at Lizzie again before turning to welcome his wife into the room. He swept her up briefly and gave her a warm kiss on her lips, causing her to blush and laugh. 'Put me down,' she protested. 'I'm too heavy for you.'

Under normal circumstances that might have been the case, Lizzie thought, but she was sure that, even with child, Hannah was hardly a burden. Now it was Frances's turn to receive a kiss from her father, then he was encouraging Gabriel to kiss his mother's cheek, which he gladly did. He was less keen to kiss Frances, but she took matters into her own hands. Lizzie was enjoying the spectacle. Had they done the same thing last year, before she had joined them and before Hannah had become ill?

Then Adam was holding out his hand to her. 'Come, Lizzie. Your turn now.'

She shook her head, only too conscious of how Gabriel might react, but Hannah was smiling and nodding encouragement. Adam strode over to her and pulled her into the doorway, planting a kiss on her cheek. She felt her cheeks flame as she saw Gabriel's expression. Then, smiling, she reached out and drew Gabriel and Frances to her, giving each a light peck on the cheek. She kissed Hannah on both cheeks with rather more feeling. Lizzie felt a brief moment of pure happiness before the anxiety that had been growing over the last few weeks returned. Was she the only one to feel it? She looked around the kitchen: the cloud had lifted from Gabriel's brow and he was sitting at the table with his father, eating Christmas sweetmeats Judith had prepared. Adam was teasing him about something – a rare moment of levity for he was normally serious. Lizzie had assumed work cares to be the cause, but now she wasn't so sure: did he bury himself in his work to avoid worrying about his wife?

'There were so many berries on the holly,' she heard Frances say. 'Perhaps we could go back and collect some?' She looked hopefully at her mother.

Hannah shook her head. 'A lot of berries mean a harsh winter ahead and the birds will need them. And our decorations look splendid just as they are.' Her gaze swept around the kitchen. 'How lovely it looks – far better than any previous year. I hope you will do this every year from now on.' She drew Frances to her and kissed the top of her head.

Lizzie glimpsed the glisten of tears as her eyes met Hannah's. She knew then that Hannah was thinking the same thing: that this would be the last Christmas she would spend with her family. It was a thought very hard to bear and she turned away after a few seconds, taking herself to the larder to check yet again that they had everything they needed for dinner the next day. She stood in the cool, dark space, barely seeing the food on the shelves before her, and took a moment to wipe away her tears. She couldn't imagine how hard it must be for Hannah to contemplate the idea that next year Adam, Frances and Gabriel would be spending the day without her.

Lizzie decided to slip away to her room: it was rare that the Russell family were all together in the kitchen. She wanted them to be able to look back on this Christmas as the best they had ever spent.

CHAPTER NINETEEN

O n Christmas morning, Lizzie excused herself from attending church, pleading that her mind would be elsewhere – planning how to get the dinner on the table – throughout the service.

Adam frowned, but when Hannah declared her intention of joining the family outing, his expression cleared and he put an affectionate arm around his wife. 'You must wrap up warm,' he said. 'You know how chilly the air can become in the cathedral. And we won't spend too long visiting afterwards – we mustn't overtire you.'

Privately, Lizzie thought that the walk to the cathedral and back would be more than enough for Hannah, without spending time on charitable visits, but she waved them off, promising a splendid dinner on their return.

Then she set to in the kitchen, scrubbing and peeling potatoes, carrots and turnips. Next, the goose went into the oven. She had been shocked at the size of it, but Judith had assured her three hours' cooking should be sufficient.

'It looks big but it's mainly ribcage,' she said. 'There'll still be plenty of meat to feed the five of you.'

There was a raised pork pie in the larder, too; Lizzie decided she would bring that out if the goose wasn't enough. She'd never cooked a goose before – in fact, she had never had responsibility for the full Christmas dinner, having previously acted as helper to her mother. She'd rather hoped Hannah would be on hand, sitting on a chair in the kitchen, to ask for advice. As it was, she would have to manage alone.

Judith had mentioned fruit of some sort would be a good accompaniment to cut through the richness of the meat. There were still some apples stored in the larder from the September harvest, so she peeled, cored, chopped and cooked them, hoping neither Adam nor Hannah would find the combination unusual.

After two hours, she checked the goose, which was browning well, and added the potatoes to the roasting dish. The rest of the vegetables could wait until the family arrived home. Judith had made a plum pudding earlier in the month, and now she set it on the range to steam, then began to lay the table. She felt as though everything was under control, and rather wished the family would return home there and then.

By the time Lizzie heard the front door open nearly an hour later, she had begun to pace the kitchen floor. She had removed the goose from the oven, set water to boil, lifted the pan off again, and considered whether she should make the gravy. Instead of feeling in control, she was now quite flustered. The family's arrival threw her careful timings into chaos, for Frances was full of excitement and wanted to tell her about the people they had been to visit.

Gabriel, on the other hand, flung himself into a chair and sighed. 'It was very tiring. I'm starving – is dinner ready?'

Adam frowned and began to admonish Gabriel. 'Did you learn nothing from our visits today?' he asked. 'Those unfortunate souls have known what it is like to be on the verge of starvation. You most certainly haven't.' Then he stopped abruptly, arrested by the sight of Hannah's wan face.

'You must sit down at once,' he exclaimed. 'What was I thinking of? I have overtired you.'

Lizzie had to turn her face away as he pulled out a chair for his wife, for she didn't wish him to see her expression. He had been wrong to keep Hannah out so long – she hoped he hadn't ruined the rest of the day for her. She went to the dresser and, without being asked, poured a small glass of brandy, setting it on the table in front of Hannah, before she turned her attention to finishing the dinner.

'It won't be long,' she said cheerfully to Gabriel, who was now sulking following his father's scolding.

'Come and tell me what you liked most about your visits,' she said to Frances, who was crestfallen at the loss of attention. As she set the vegetables to boil, Lizzie cast a glance over her shoulder at Hannah, who, she could see, was doing her best to put on a brave face for the children. Adam was encouraging her to take small sips of the brandy and telling her she would feel better very soon, but Lizzie caught his look of anxiety as he did so. She remained expressionless, still angry with him for being so thoughtless.

In the event, after Lizzie had encouraged Gabriel to help her finish laying the table and the serving dishes were set out, Hannah regained herself enough to say, 'Why, Lizzie, this is quite the most magnificent Christmas dinner we have had. You have cooked it to perfection!'

Lizzie flushed pink with pleasure and protested, 'You haven't tasted it yet.' But she was proud of herself for what she had achieved. Gabriel was already spooning roast potatoes onto his plate and had to be restrained by his father, who was carving slices of goose. Lizzie helped Frances to a small selection of vegetables, then looked enquiringly at Hannah.

'Thank you, Lizzie,' Hannah said. 'Not too much, mind.' She had at least regained her composure, Lizzie noticed, so she felt able to serve herself once she was sure everyone had what they needed.

For the first few minutes, there was very little conversation. It was beginning to grow dark outside and Lizzie realised the afternoon was wearing on; it explained why everyone was so hungry, breakfast having been eaten many interminable hours before.

'The dinner tastes every bit as good as it looks,' Adam said at last, his eyes fixed on Lizzie. 'We are very lucky to have you here with us, Lizzie. Thank you.'

Hannah was nodding at his words. 'I couldn't have managed without you over the last few weeks. And now this . . . ' She gestured at the table. Lizzie saw Gabriel's plate was empty and he was looking hungrily at the remaining potatoes; Frances was eating slowly and dreamily, as usual; Adam had also finished everything on his plate, while Hannah had at least made a good attempt.

'Well, finish up the potatoes and gravy,' Lizzie said, since there was very little goose remaining. 'But do save a bit of room for the plum pudding.'

Adam and Gabriel needed no further invitation and Lizzie bent her head to her plate, delighted at how well it had gone. She had the briefest flash of curiosity as to how the day was progressing in her family home in Castle Bay, but pushed it away. Her place was here now, and there were still things to be done before the day could be counted a total success.

CHAPTER TWENTY

With the dishes cleared from the table, Lizzie paid attention to the pudding, turning it out of its cloth onto a plate. Dark in colour and full of fruit, it had a delicious aroma and Lizzie, who had believed herself far too full to eat another mouthful, thought she might, in fact, manage a morsel or two after all. She set a jug of white sauce on the table beside it, and fetched small plates and spoons from the dresser.

'Did you make it?' Gabriel asked, gazing hungrily at the pudding's glistening surface.

'Judith did,' Lizzie said, as she cut slices to serve.

'Oh,' Gabriel said. He looked less eager. 'Then I'm not sure I'll have any.'

It looked a little dry, Lizzie thought, but the white sauce would disguise that. She poured it lavishly onto each slice, then shared them around the table.

'It smells lovely,' she said. 'I'm sure it will taste good, too.'

Privately, once she had tasted it, she felt it lacked sweetness and, as she'd suspected, was a little dry, but Gabriel and Adam ate all of theirs, although they declined seconds. Hannah and Frances picked at their portions.

'Can we open gifts now?' Gabriel asked.

'Once you have helped to clear the table,' his father said.

Gabriel stuck out his lower lip in a mutinous fashion, but did as he was asked. Lizzie got to her feet, ready to start washing the stacked dishes, but Adam wouldn't hear of it. 'Sit and rest awhile,' he said. 'We can take care of this later.'

So she sat back and watched as Gabriel and Frances opened the gifts from their parents – a cardboard fort and soldiers for him, and a jigsaw for her. Shyly, Lizzie presented a small gift to each of them too. She had worried over what to give them, but she had asked Hannah if she could use some scraps of left-over fabric from her work-basket. From them, she had created a cloth doll for Frances, dressed in an outfit made from cotton that matched the little girl's own dress. She had embroidered a face and added hair made from brown wool. Frances was delighted and set aside her jigsaw at once, which embarrassed Lizzie but made Hannah laugh.

It had been much harder to create something for Gabriel. Lizzie had racked her brains but she couldn't see how she could make something from cloth for him. Wood, perhaps, but not cloth. She'd wished she could have asked Grandpa Walter for help. Then she had a moment of inspiration – Gabriel loved his food, particularly sweet things. She would make something for him. She hoped Hannah and Adam wouldn't mind that she had, in effect, used their house-keeping to provide the gift. It would have been churlish of them to object on seeing Gabriel's delight at unwrapping his jar of biscuits, she thought.

'These are all for me,' he declared. 'I will keep them safe in a special place.'

Adam looked as though he might deliver a few choice words on the importance of sharing, then apparently thought better of it. 'My turn,' he said. He got up and left the room, then returned with two wrapped packages.

'One for you,' he said to Hannah, kissing the top of her head. 'And one for you,' he said to Lizzie.

She gazed at him, aghast. It hadn't occurred to her that she might receive gifts from her employers – she had nothing to give in return.

Adam held up his hand. 'I know what you are thinking,' he said to Lizzie, 'but I wanted to let you know how much I value your help, in the house, with the children and with Hannah. I know she will join me in this.'

It was the second time in just a few hours that Lizzie had been praised and tears came to her eyes. 'Thank you,' she said, her voice trembling. She wanted to open the package, but alone in her room, not in front of the family. She looked to Hannah to open hers, but saw at once that she was exhausted. 'Oh, Hannah!' she exclaimed. 'We have worn you out.'

'I'll take her upstairs to rest,' Adam said. 'But first, open your gifts.' He looked pleased with himself, so Lizzie obediently began to tear off the paper, while Adam helped Hannah with hers. She saw at once he had given them almost identical items, just in different colours. Hannah held a shawl in fine blue wool, while Lizzie shook one in green out of the paper.

'It's beautiful,' she said. 'Thank you so much.' She was embarrassed all over again. Not only because her gift was equal to Hannah's, but also by her lack of anything to offer in return.

She looked at Hannah, worried that she might be offended by what he'd done. But she was smiling and didn't appear at all put out, as Adam raised her to her feet and guided her to the door.

'Thank you, Lizzie. For today, and for everything,' she said, as she left.

Gabriel and Frances were absorbed by their gifts and paid no attention, so Lizzie got wearily to her feet and turned to the piles of dirty plates. She set water to heat on the range, scraped leftovers into the slop bucket and gradually began to restore order. It took well over an hour, by which time Adam had returned to the kitchen. He settled himself with a glass of ale and observed Gabriel and Frances, without attempting to join in with what they were doing. Lizzie continued to clear up, wiping the final crumbs from surfaces, then wringing out her cloth.

'Come and sit down, Lizzie,' Adam said. 'You've been hard at work all day. Will you take a glass of ale with me?'

Lizzie was longing to escape to her room and reflect on the day. It was clear, though, that Adam wished for company. She supposed it would be rude to deny him, but she would take the chance to slip away when the children went up to bed. She poured a small glass of ale for herself and sipped it, while they watched the children in companionable silence.

After twenty minutes had passed, and Frances had yawned at least once, Adam spoke up. 'Time for bed, both of you. Up you go and I'll check on you in ten minutes.'

'I'll see to them.' Lizzie pushed back her chair and prepared to rise.

Adam laid his hand over hers to detain her. 'No, no, please stay. There's something I wish to discuss with you.'

Lizzie, alarmed, glanced up but Gabriel, busy folding the pieces of his fort, didn't appear to have noticed. She suspected Adam had finally realised how ill his wife was; she could hardly refuse a much-needed discussion.

CHAPTER TWENTY-ONE

Adam barely waited until the children had left the room before he began. 'Lizzie, I've had cause to be thankful many times since our chance meeting in Mercery Lane, back in February. You've been such a help with the children and a good companion to Hannah during a very difficult time for her.'

Adam stopped and a bleak expression crossed his face. Lizzie was glad of the pause – surely enough praise had been heaped on her already that day. But he hadn't finished.

'And then, today, your presence made our celebration so special, on a day that could have been very difficult. You gave Hannah a Christmas Day to remember and I can't thank you enough. Hannah wanted me to express her gratitude again, too. And to ask you ...' he hesitated, then plunged on '... to ask you whether you will stay on after the baby is born. Hannah fears she will be too weak to care for it at first. And if the worst should happen ...' Adam tailed off.

Lizzie was shocked, although she wasn't sure why. Thoughts of what would happen in a few weeks' time had frequently consumed her but she had shaken them off. Hannah had already tried to elicit a promise of help from her, but Adam had seemed remote from his wife's illness. She had felt impatient with him on several occasions for seemingly failing to recognise how poorly she was. Now she questioned whether he had simply hidden his concern.

He stood up abruptly. 'I must go and say goodnight to Gabriel and Frances. I hope we can talk further when I come down.'

What else was there to say? Lizzie wondered, glad of a few

moments to herself. Of course she would stay and help with the baby, and with Hannah. Anything else that happened would have to be dealt with when it arose. She supposed Hannah had urged Adam to speak up, even though she and Hannah had already touched on the subject.

Lizzie turned her glass slowly between her fingers, watching the amber ale spin within it. She had barely touched it, not having much liking for it. She hoped Adam wouldn't take too long with the children: she was longing for her own bed. Yawning, she was tempted to rest for a few minutes, cradling her head on her arms on the table. Then she heard Adam's footsteps on the stairs.

'Both abed,' he said, with some satisfaction. 'And tired. Frances has your doll on the pillow. I had to take Gabriel's biscuit jar from him; otherwise I feared they would all be eaten by morning. You have quite a way with children, Lizzie.'

He smiled at her and she looked away in confusion. 'I have many sisters,' she said hastily, wondering even as she spoke whether she also had a brother, 'so I've had a good deal of experience with little ones.'

They sat in silence for a minute or two, Lizzie taking small sips of ale and debating whether it would be impolite to excuse herself to go up to bed. She was poised to rise when Adam began to speak. 'Lizzie, if the worst should happen, Hannah wants to be sure that the children will be well cared for. She wants their lives to go on much as before, even though it will be very difficult for them.'

Lizzie nodded. 'Of course. I understand. I hope that Hannah will make a good recovery after the birth, but I will be here, whatever happens. I don't intend to leave.'

She hoped that would reassure him, and Hannah, if he passed on her words in the morning. But he continued: 'Hannah wants to be sure that the house will run much as before. She saw today how skilled you are and it gave her hope.' Adam seemed to have more he wanted to say, but he was struggling to find the words. He took a swig of his ale and blurted out, 'And she wants to be sure that I will be well looked after, too.'

Lizzie was puzzled. It was understandable: should the worst happen, Hannah wanted life to go on much as it had, ever since Lizzie had been there. She felt a sudden pang – how hard must it be to imagine your family continuing without you. To think of your children growing up without your guiding hand, to visualise Christmases rolling by with an empty place at the table. It was natural that she wanted to do everything she could to ensure consistency. Lizzie felt honoured by Hannah's trust in her.

'Of course,' she said firmly. 'Hannah mustn't worry. I will tell her so myself. I will do whatever I can – for the children, the house, for you, but I hope it won't be necessary. Once the child is born, Hannah can devote herself to getting stronger again. Next Christmas Day, she will be here at the table with us all, just like today.'

Lizzie spoke with a confidence she didn't feel, but she was keen to avoid upsetting Adam. He and Hannah had a devotion she had never seen in her own parents. It was no surprise he found it hard to face up to her illness.

She smiled at Adam and stood up. 'All will be well, you'll see. Now, it's getting late and it has been a long day. I will wish you good night.' She took her glass to the scullery and tipped away the ale, then set it on the side. She would deal with it in the morning – now every bone in her body ached.

As she passed the kitchen table on the way out, Adam leaned back in his chair and grasped her wrist. 'Thank you, Lizzie, for everything.'

Startled by his touch, she looked into his dark brown eyes, trying to fathom what was hidden there, what was unsaid. She smiled again, disengaged herself and moved to the door.

'Goodnight again, Adam. Don't stay up too late – it's St Stephen's Day tomorrow and there will be work to do.'

She went up to bed, a little unsettled by their conversation. Surely Hannah understood she wouldn't just up and leave the family. She resolved she would have that conversation with her again, to put her mind at rest. Lizzie still doubted that she could run the household as efficiently as Hannah but she would do her best to reassure her. She didn't like to think of her employer lying in bed, ill and worrying. Lizzie climbed into her own bed and blew out the candle, intending to ponder the events of the day, and pick over Adam's words that evening. But barely a minute passed before her eyes closed and sleep claimed her.

CHAPTER TWENTY-TWO

After the excitement of the Christmas festivities, life went on much as before in the Russell household. Adam went back to the cathedral on St Stephen's Day, when services were performed for the poor, and Judith returned to the kitchen. She had been prepared to be irritated that her space had been usurped, but could find no fault with Lizzie: all was spotless, apart from two unwashed glasses left in the scullery from the previous evening.

Gabriel had a few free days before he must return to school, and Lizzie was glad to see him lose some of his sulkiness and difficult behaviour. Was something amiss at the cathedral school with the other boys? Or was he struggling to keep up with the work? She resolved to speak to Adam about it, not wanting to worry Hannah. Meanwhile, it was encouraging to see him playing happily enough with his sister. He had even shared his biscuits with her, which must have been hard for him.

Lizzie kept a watchful eye on Hannah, and was pleased to see that she went on much as before. At least, her health didn't appear to be worse. With the birth fast approaching she was still thinner and paler than Lizzie thought she should be, so she asked Judith whether there were any foods that would help build her up. Judith rose to the challenge with daily beef tea, and marrowbone jelly, but Hannah grew impatient of invalid food.

'There's no need to make a fuss of me and give Judith extra work. I will eat whatever the family is eating,' she said firmly.

Lizzie forbore to point out that she ate the smallest of portions,

87

citing lack of appetite, or discomfort caused by the baby pressing on her stomach. She conspired with Judith to find ways to add nourishment to Hannah's food – a spoon of cream in her chocolate, soup made with rich stock. Hannah refused again to seek advice from either a doctor or the apothecary, but allowed that the midwife be called at the end of January, to check the baby's position and hazard a guess at an arrival date.

'The baby is small,' the midwife, Mrs Lawrence, said to Lizzie, as she took a glass of ale in the kitchen after making her visit. 'And the mother is sick.' She frowned. 'I fear this will not be an easy birth. Mrs Russell is weak so if her pains are prolonged she will fade fast and have little strength to push. I will send over some tea she must drink – it will fortify her blood and help prepare her body.' She shook her head. 'You must call me out at once, as soon as the pains start. Make sure her husband knows.'

Lizzie and Judith looked at each other in silence after Mrs Lawrence had gone. Then Lizzie returned to Hannah, who had decided to stay in bed after the midwife had finished her examination.

'What did she say?' Hannah, propped against the pillows, appeared impossibly pale in the afternoon's fading light.

Lizzie decided to be economical with the truth. 'She thinks the baby is small. But she is confident about the birth and is sending over some tea to help prepare your body for what's to come. I will take Frances with me to collect Gabriel, and you can rest.' She turned to leave, then looked back to say, 'As soon as the pains start, we are to let Mrs Lawrence know. She wishes the birth to be a swift one.'

Hannah gave a weak smile. 'And I wish for the same. Gabriel and Frances were both reluctant to face the world; I hope this new baby will be more eager.'

Lizzie left the room, hoping her expression hadn't betrayed the worry in her heart. So Hannah had a history of difficult births. But the midwife had said the baby was small – perhaps that would be helpful when the time came.

The time came rather sooner than had been hoped. Barely two

weeks had passed since the midwife's visit before Lizzie was roused from a deep sleep by Adam's voice in her ear.

'Lizzie, Lizzie, wake up. I'm going to fetch Mrs Lawrence and you must sit with Hannah.'

Lizzie could only blink and stare, confused by Adam's presence at her bedside. Then she sat bolt upright and fought herself free of the covers. 'Go, go at once. I will be with her.'

Adam, who was already dressed, nodded and left. Lizzie, heart thudding, seized a shawl and hurried to Hannah. She was moaning, her face buried in the pillow, her fingers clutching at the sheet. Lizzie went to her side, easing strands of hair away from her hot forehead.

Although her mother had given birth to five children after Lizzie, she hadn't been present at any of the births. Instead, she and her sisters had huddled together in one bed and tried not to listen to Mrs Carey's cries of pain. Mercifully, each birth was swifter than the last so their torment was short-lived. But Lizzie had little idea of what she should do. She had a notion that water should be set to boil, but she didn't want to leave Hannah. She wished to make her more comfortable but should Hannah sit up or lie down? She could only stroke her forehead, pat her hand and offer words of encouragement.

'Adam has gone to fetch Mrs Lawrence. They'll be here very soon. Try to save your strength.'

Lizzie was already worried that Hannah was exhausting herself, her body racked with pain as she contorted and writhed beneath the sheet. She had managed to contain her cries to avoid disturbing Gabriel and Frances, but the effort required must have cost her dearly.

Lizzie was almost panicking by the time Adam burst into the room, Mrs Lawrence behind him.

'How is she?' he gasped, out of breath. 'I'm sorry we have taken so long. Mrs Lawrence was attending another birth and once I'd knocked up her household I had to go in search of her.'

'Well, I'm here now,' the midwife said briskly, rolling up her sleeves and washing her hands in water poured from the ewer on the washstand. She turned to Lizzie. 'Set water to boil if you haven't already. And find me clean cloths.'

Adam hovered at the end of the bed, until he was despatched by Mrs Lawrence to sit outside the children's bedroom door in case they should wake. Relieved to have the midwife in charge, Lizzie turned her attention to the tasks she had been given, hoping with some fervour that she wouldn't be called upon to assist at the birth.

CHAPTER TWENTY-THREE

Lizzie's hope that the baby being small would lead to a quick delivery was dashed as the hours passed without the welcome sound of a newborn's cries. Instead Hannah's moans, no longer contained, were weaker and Lizzie grew more anxious. She went in to Mrs Lawrence at regular intervals, to check whether she required anything, but was mostly waved away. Hannah lay against the pillows, eyes closed, face as pale as parchment except for a livid spot of colour on each cheek.

Lizzie, in need of something to occupy herself, sent Adam to the kitchen for breakfast, although she doubted he would force much past his lips. She persuaded Gabriel to get ready for school and Frances to dress so they could all walk together. They would leave early and go slowly, she thought. The children's faces were pinched with anxiety every time their mother cried out. Getting them out into the fresh air might take their mind off her suffering. They joined Adam at the breakfast table; Judith was now in the kitchen and Lizzie was relieved. If Mrs Lawrence needed anything while she was out, Judith could step in.

Both children were quiet as they set off for Gabriel's school. Lizzie tried to distract them from their thoughts along the way – pointing out potatoes rolling down the road as a bag burst during a delivery to the greengrocer, a dispute between two carters, neither prepared to give way to the other in a narrow lane – but gave up after a short while. Perhaps it was best to let them be. She could talk to Frances on the way home, but Gabriel was worryingly morose.

They were almost at the cathedral gate when he turned to her. 'Will Mama be there when I get home?'

'Of course, Gabriel.' Lizzie was brisk. 'Where else would she be? And you will have a little brother or sister, too.' She spoke with more confidence than she felt. 'You mustn't worry – all will be well, I'm sure.'

'But she sounded—' Gabriel broke off, unable to express himself.

He would have been too young to remember anything of Frances's birth, Lizzie supposed. The sounds of his mother's torment must have been very distressing.

'It's all quite normal,' Lizzie hastened to reassure him. 'I remember from when my sisters were born. Now, off you go into school and try not to think about it. Frances and I will see you later – I'm sure we will have some news.'

He joined the tide of boys flowing into school, head down as he trudged along. He didn't turn to wave as he usually did.

What if everything wasn't well when he left school in the afternoon? How would she explain it to him? Seized with the urge to get home as quickly as possible, she turned to Frances. 'No lessons for you today,' she said to the little girl, knowing that neither of them would be able to concentrate. 'What shall we do instead? Shall we draw? Or make some of Gabriel's favourite biscuits to surprise him when he gets home?'

Lizzie shivered her way back to New Street – the February weather was cold and she was weary after being woken in the night. She feared it would be a long day, trying to keep Frances occupied as far away from her mother's bedroom as possible. Perhaps, though, it was all over and the baby had been born. She opened the front door and stepped into the hallway, ears straining for sounds from upstairs. All was quiet and, heart full of hope, Lizzie thought she would leave Frances in Judith's care while she hurried upstairs. But then she heard Hannah cry out, so she hustled Frances into the kitchen, where Adam still sat at the table, much as they had left him.

'Anything?' she asked him, hoping her cryptic question would mean nothing to Frances.

He shook his head.

Lizzie longed to go upstairs to see how things progressed, but she focused her attention on settling Frances at the table with paper and a pencil. Then she quizzed Judith as to when they might make biscuits without getting in her way.

Adam roused himself enough to send word to the cathedral that he wouldn't be there that day. The adults passed a tense few hours, attempting to mask their anxiety in front of Frances. Every so often, Adam rose abruptly from the table and went upstairs, returning ten minutes or so later. Lizzie assumed he stood outside the bedroom door, anxiously listening. Each time he returned, he shook his head and sat down again.

Lizzie felt Mrs Lawrence could be left no longer without offers of assistance so, leaving Frances with Judith and the ingredients for the biscuits, she made her way upstairs with some trepidation. She listened outside the bedroom door but all was quiet. She knocked and walked in. Her eyes went first to Hannah, who lay against the pillows, drained of all colour, her hair plastered to her face by sweat. She looked at Mrs Lawrence, who was grim-faced.

'I'm glad to see you. I was beginning to think you'd all abandoned us. I'm fearful for mother and child. She's exhausted and barely has the strength she needs to deliver this baby. I think we must send for the doctor.'

Lizzie nodded. It would be expensive, but she knew Adam wouldn't hesitate to do what was best. 'I'll go and tell her husband,' she said, turning to leave.

'And I'll have something to eat and drink when you return.' Mrs Lawrence's tone was plaintive. 'I've been up all night with another mother and I'm famished.'

Lizzie was ashamed not to have thought of this. She nodded more vigorously and hurried from the room. With Adam despatched to fetch the doctor and Frances reassured that her mama was in good hands – Lizzie didn't feel she could promise all would be well – she returned to Mrs Lawrence with a bowl of soup, some bread and cheese, and a small glass of ale. She felt shame again at her reluctance to enter the room, worried at what she would find. But Hannah lay in the same position as before, eyes closed.

While Mrs Lawrence fortified herself, Lizzie drew up the wooden bedroom chair and sat at the head of the bed. She hesitated before taking Hannah's hand, stroking it gently. Her skin was hot and clammy, despite the pallor of her face.

'Hannah, can you hear me? It won't be long now – Adam has gone for the doctor.'

Hannah's eyelids flickered and she opened them. She looked at Lizzie but didn't seem to recognise her.

'It's me, Lizzie. Don't worry. The doctor is coming to help Mrs Lawrence.'

She heard a contemptuous snort from Mrs Lawrence. Lizzie supposed she had a poor opinion of doctors attending childbirth, but she had clearly exhausted all the tricks she knew to encourage a reluctant baby into the world.

'Adam?' Hannah whispered. 'Frances?'

'Adam has gone for the doctor,' Lizzie repeated. 'Frances is downstairs with Judith.'

'See them.' Hannah said. She gripped Lizzie's arm. 'Must see them.'

'Adam will bring the doctor up,' Lizzie soothed. 'You can see Frances when the baby is here.'

There was a wild look in Hannah's eyes and her grip grew stronger as a contraction seized her. 'Now,' she panted. 'It will be too late.'

Lizzie, puzzled, looked to Mrs Lawrence. She stood up, wiping crumbs from her mouth and came over to the bed. 'Now, Mrs Russell, don't you go upsetting yourself. You can see you husband and daughter all in good time. Let's get this baby born first.'

Hannah's eyes closed and Lizzie watched as a tear trickled from beneath an eyelid.

'She's tired, that's all,' Mrs Lawrence said. She meant it to sound reassuring, but her expression told a different story.

A brisk knock at the door announced the doctor, Adam hovering in the background. Lizzie took her chance to excuse herself and join him on the landing

'How is she?' he asked anxiously.

'Tired,' Lizzie replied. 'And weak. But I'm sure, now the doctor is here, it will be over very soon.'

Her words were prophetic, but not in the way she would have wished.

CHAPTER TWENTY-FOUR

Within the hour, a thin cry could be heard downstairs in the kitchen. Adam, Lizzie and Judith looked at each other, straining their ears for more. After what felt like a lifetime it was repeated, and Adam got to his feet, Lizzie too.

Once again, Lizzie was anxious as they went upstairs. They hesitated outside the bedroom door. Adam knocked.

'One moment, please.' It was Mrs Lawrence's voice. Lizzie could hear a murmur of voices within, then the midwife opened the door. She was flushed, her hair escaping from its cap, a bloodied bundle of sheets in her arms. She thrust these at Lizzie.

'More hot water,' she said, 'and linen.'

Lizzie caught a glimpse of the doctor, sleeves rolled up, bending over Hannah, before she turned and hurried down the stairs. She couldn't allow Frances to see the sheets but she was absorbed in her jigsaw and Lizzie was able to slip into the scullery unobserved. Water had been simmering on the stove throughout the morning and she filled a jug and took it upstairs, collecting sheets and the few remaining clean cloths from the linen cupboard on the way.

Adam stood close to the door in the bedroom, dazed. He was holding a bundle in his arms. Lizzie took in the scene at a glance: the doctor and Mrs Lawrence were attending to Hannah, who was even paler than before, if that was possible. Lizzie deposited the water jug on the stand and set the linen on the chair, catching a glimpse of Hannah's bloodied nightgown as she did so. Then she turned her attention to Adam. 'Can I see?' she asked.

He lowered the bundle and she glimpsed a tiny face, topped with tufts of dark blonde hair, all swaddled in a blanket. The baby was pale, too, like its mother, and its eyes were closed, the lids with a bluish tinge.

Lizzie's heart lurched. Had the baby not survived?

'Is it— can I ...' she whispered, unable to express what she wanted to ask. If she could hold the baby, she would be able to tell whether or not it breathed.

'Here.' Adam thrust the bundle at her. 'Take her.'

So they had a little girl, Lizzie thought. She took her, amazed at how light she was, and cradled her in her arms. She stroked her face and her eyelids fluttered but didn't open. Adam had eyes only for his wife.

Mrs Lawrence came over to the little group at the end of the bed. 'Mrs Russell is very weak,' she said. 'She's lost a lot of blood. But she lives. She will need nursing over the next few days. I will arrange for a wet-nurse I know to come and take care of the little one.' She gestured to the baby in Lizzie's arms. She hesitated, then continued, 'The baby is weak, too. I think you must have her baptised as soon as you can.'

Then she turned back to the bed. Lizzie looked up at Adam. He was swallowing hard, and she could see he was trying to hold back tears as he stared at his wife.

'I'll take the baby down to show Frances,' Lizzie said. Frances could not be brought up to see her mother yet, and Adam needed time to compose himself.

She slipped out of the room, her head in a whirl. A nurse for Hannah and a wet-nurse for the baby, as well as the doctor's fee – it was a lot for Adam to manage. Perhaps she could nurse Hannah – but then who would look after Frances and Gabriel?

Frances exclaimed in delight when Lizzie entered the kitchen with the swaddled baby in her arms.

'Let me see! Let me see!' She reached up, trying to tug the blanket free.

'Wait, let me sit down,' Lizzie said. 'There, now you can see her properly.'

'She's a girl!' Frances was delighted. 'What's her name?'

'Your mama and papa haven't named her yet,' Lizzie said. The baby slept on, undisturbed by Frances's chatter.

'Can I go and see Mama?' Frances was already halfway to the door.

'Not yet,' Lizzie said hastily. 'The doctor is still with her.' Her eyes met Judith's. 'In a little while.'

Frances stuck out her bottom lip and returned to the table. 'Can I hold her?'

Lizzie was torn, fearful that Frances, being so young, would be clumsy, but also wanting to distract her from her wish to see her mother.

Judith came across and peered at the baby. 'She's a wee scrap of a thing, isn't she?'

Lizzie nodded. 'Mrs Lawrence thinks she'll do well enough, with a wet-nurse.' She deemed it best not to share the rest of the midwife's words, which had not been so encouraging.

Frances was growing restless. She had settled herself into a wooden kitchen chair, her feet dangling some way from the floor, her arms held out wide. Lizzie carefully lowered the precious bundle into her arms, then knelt beside her on the floor, nervous in case the little girl dropped her sister. But Frances held her tightly – too tightly, at first, so that the baby squirmed uneasily. Then she opened her eyes and stared straight at Frances, who cooed with delight.

'She's looking at me! Hello,' she said, beaming all over her face. She was entranced for a good five minutes, until the baby started to cry – a small bleating sound that stabbed Lizzie to the heart. She sounded so very weak.

She was about to take the baby back when the door opened and Adam came in.

'Papa!' Frances thrust her sister at Lizzie, jumped off the chair and ran to her father. 'Can I go up now?'

'Not yet.' Adam ruffled her hair. 'Your mother is very tired and needs to rest.' He turned to Lizzie. 'Mrs Lawrence would like to speak to you.'

She hesitated, unsure whether to take the baby with her or leave her behind. Judith stepped in and took her; Adam looked too shocked and weary to be left in charge.

Lizzie trudged up the stairs with a heavy heart. What was she about to hear? She feared it wouldn't be good news and she tried hard to prepare herself. But when she knocked and entered the bedroom, all was restored to order. Hannah was peacefully asleep, the doctor was writing in a notebook and Mrs Lawrence was folding bed linen. She looked drained, Lizzie thought, as well she might after such a difficult birth following a sleepless night.

The doctor peered at her over his spectacles but continued to write. Lizzie went to the midwife.

'Mr Russell has been told what to expect.' The midwife's words struck Lizzie with some force – it could only mean the very worst news. 'He has agreed that you should have charge of the baby. As soon as I get home I'll arrange for the wet-nurse. She'll need to sleep in at first but once the baby is stronger and has a routine, she'll come in several times a day. Can you prepare a bed for her?'

Lizzie nodded, stifling a sigh. She would have to share her room, and no doubt the baby would be in with them, too, since Hannah needed to rest.

'Then I'll be on my way,' Mrs Lawrence said. 'The doctor will arrange for a nurse to come in to attend to Mrs Russell. I'll see myself out.'

She was understandably keen to get away, Lizzie thought, following her down the stairs a minute or so later, laundry tucked under her arm. She, too, was exhausted after the events of the last hours. And now the quiet routine of the household was to be further disrupted, by the arrival of two nurses to care for mother and child. Lizzie fought down a sense of foreboding, telling herself it was just tiredness making her feel so gloomy. She took a deep breath and entered the kitchen, a bright smile pinned to her lips.

Chapter Twenty-Five

Within a few hours, the Russell household was thrown into further disarray. Lizzie remembered just in time that Gabriel needed collecting from school. She rather hoped Adam would offer to go but he was sitting at the kitchen table, head in hands, and Lizzie judged it a good idea to get Frances away from the house.

'You should be able to see your mama when you get back,' she said, hoping fervently that that would be so.

Judith was happy to take charge of the baby, although Lizzie could see they would be lucky to have any dinner on the table that night. She and Frances returned forty-five minutes later with Gabriel in tow, the cheeks of all three bright red from the cold wind, to find the baby being fed by a small woman, who introduced herself as Eliza Hawkins. Gabriel declined to meet the baby but demanded to see his mother.

'The doctor's nurse is here.' Judith's lips were pursed. 'A Mrs Thornhill. She's asked for a fire to be lit and tea to be brought up. I'm not sure how I'll go on if I'm to be up and down the stairs all the time.'

'I'll help,' Lizzie said, worried that the extra demands might drive Judith to walk out. A thought struck her. 'She isn't staying, is she?' She had no idea where they would put her if she was.

'No. She's coming in three times a day.'

Judith turned back to the range and Lizzie ushered the children out of the room.

'We must be quiet,' she warned. 'Your mother is very tired. We'll only be able to stay a few minutes.'

In fact, they had barely a minute. The nurse, a tall woman in a plain grey gown with a white apron over the top, glared at them so fiercely when they entered that Lizzie quailed but said bravely, 'The children would like to see their mother.'

Adam was sitting by the bed, holding Hannah's hand. He hardly glanced at his family. Hannah's skin was so pale it resembled the alabaster statues in the niches at the cathedral.

'She is very ill,' the nurse said, 'and not to be disturbed by children's chatter.'

Frances, frightened, burst into tears, earning herself another glare.

'Look, she's sleeping peacefully,' Lizzie said, bending to be at the same level as Frances and Gabriel and speaking quietly. 'We'll come back and see her before bedtime.'

She heard the nurse harrumph behind her, but ignored her and shepherded the children out of the room. Then she did her best to provide as near-normal a routine as possible for them. She settled Gabriel with his schoolwork at the kitchen table along with two of the biscuits they had made. Then, seeing Frances was content to sit and chatter to the wet-nurse, she helped Judith get on with making the dinner. They would have at least one extra mouth to feed but she doubted Adam would eat a great deal and she supposed Hannah would require, at most, a little broth. She was seized with a great weariness after her early start and found herself peeling the potatoes in a very haphazard way.

Judith took the knife from her. 'Sit yourself down and I'll make you a cup of tea. Then you take Mrs Hawkins,' she indicated the wet-nurse, now holding the baby to her shoulder, patting her back and humming a tune, 'up to your room. We'll have to find a drawer to serve as a crib until we can trouble Mr Russell to go down to the cellar and find the family one.'

Adam slept the night in a chair beside his wife, although Lizzie doubted he got a great deal of rest. She found him in the kitchen, his face grey and drawn, when she came down early to make tea for the wet-nurse, who was feeding the baby. Lizzie was tired too, despite an early night, for the baby had been restless. Although her mewling cries barely disturbed the silence, Lizzie had awoken instantly each time and lay there listening to the comforting murmurs of Mrs Hawkins as she tried to settle her.

Lizzie drew her shawl around her shoulders, conscious of being attired only in a nightgown, her hair loose around her shoulders. But Adam was oblivious, lost in deep thought. She set about making the tea, and set a cup before him.

'How is Hannah?' she ventured. 'Did she pass a quiet night?'

Adam started, as though he hadn't registered her presence. 'Too quiet,' he said gloomily. 'She barely breathed. I had to check her several times to make sure she still had a pulse.'

He must have passed a desperate night, Lizzie thought, while the household slept around him and he had only his deepest fears for company.

'What time will Mrs Thornhill arrive?' Lizzie asked. She wasn't eager to see the woman but it would give Adam a break from his bedside vigil.

'Soon,' Adam said. 'I think she said seven o'clock.'

That was another hour away. Lizzie considered. 'I can sit with Hannah until then if you like. You could rest in the sitting room,' she offered.

Adam seemed unable to make a decision, so she picked up the tea she had set before him and took it into the sitting room. The room was cold but Adam, following obediently, didn't seem to register it. Lizzie fetched a blanket from the closet on the landing and, finding him already curled on the sofa, eyes closed, placed it over him. Then she took tea to Mrs Hawkins and made her way to Adam and Hannah's bedroom. She didn't care for the idea of Mrs Thornhill finding her still in her nightclothes, but she didn't want to risk leaving Hannah alone any longer while she got dressed.

It looked as though Hannah hadn't moved since Lizzie had last seen her. She lay on her back, her breathing imperceptible so that the covers, tucked tight over her breast, didn't appear to lift at all.

Lizzie sat beside her and took her hand. 'Hannah, you have a beautiful daughter.' It occurred to her that she hadn't seen the baby since the birth, something they must remedy that day. She had a feeling Mrs Thornhill would prevent it, so the visit would have to be made during the hours she was away.

'Frances is very taken with her, Gabriel less so.' Lizzie chuckled, remembering his reaction on his return from school. 'You and Adam must choose a name for her.' She was conscious of the midwife's words, *I think you must have her baptised as soon as you can.* Not accustomed to talking to someone who didn't answer, Lizzie hurried to fill the silence.

'She's being very well cared for by the wet-nurse, so you mustn't worry. And she has a good pair of lungs on her.' Lizzie chattered on, embroidering the truth, looking for a sign – a flicker of the eyelids, a sigh – that her words were reaching Hannah. But there was nothing, and eventually Lizzie couldn't think of anything else to recount and sat in silence, watching her mistress. She had no experience of serious illness. She had encountered only a succession of childhood ailments back home in Castle Bay. They were violent for a day or so – high temperatures, vomiting – then the child was right as rain, if a bit pale and lacking in appetite. Hannah's silent immobility was a great deal more worrying, but perhaps the lack of a temperature and her apparently peaceful sleep were good signs. Lizzie was surprised to find herself longing for Mrs Thornhill's arrival, so that she could ask her.

CHAPTER TWENTY-SIX

Mrs Thornhill was not disposed to be forthcoming about Hannah's health when Lizzie pressed her. On arrival, she had cast a disparaging glance over Lizzie's night attire, being herself well turned out in a navy dress and a fresh white apron.

'I can't answer any questions about Mrs Russell until I've had time to observe her properly,' she said. 'And when I have, I will answer to the doctor or Mr Russell. Now, if you would be so good as to fetch me a cup of tea.' She stood in front of the bed, hands on hips, until Lizzie felt she had no alternative but to leave the room.

Judith had arrived and Adam slept soundly in the sitting room, so Lizzie delivered the tea to Mrs Thornhill as requested, then went to wake the children.

'Time to get up,' she said, pulling back the curtains. Gabriel groaned and buried his head deep into his pillow, but Frances went from being fast asleep to sitting bolt upright.

'How is Mama?' she asked.

'Asleep,' Lizzie said. 'Now, start getting dressed both of you. I must do the same, and then I will come and we'll go down to breakfast.'

Lizzie hurried to her room, fearful that Frances might take it into her head to run along the landing and burst in on her mother. She didn't like to think about the reception she would get from Mrs Thornhill.

To Lizzie's relief, Mrs Hawkins was up and dressed, preparing to take the baby downstairs. She had felt awkward at the prospect of washing and changing in front of her. The wet-nurse had even dealt with the chamber pot and refilled the water ewer. Lizzie wished Mrs Thornhill was so easy and efficient.

'I hope you weren't too much disturbed,' Mrs Hawkins said. 'This little mite was restless last night.' The swaddled baby was fast asleep in her arms: would she be sufficient distraction to stop Frances demanding to see her mother?

As soon as the door shut behind the wet-nurse, Lizzie washed and dressed, then pulled a brush through her hair and pinned it up. There would just be time for a hasty breakfast before they left for school, provided Gabriel had roused himself from his bed.

In fact, she suspected he only tumbled out of the sheets when he heard her footsteps along the landing, so she sent Frances, who was fully dressed, down to the kitchen with a promise of seeing her baby sister, while she chivvied Gabriel along.

'Can I see Mama before I go?' His question was partly muffled by the shirt he was pulling over his head.

'We haven't time. But tonight when you get back,' she promised.

'It's not fair.' His face was flushed and she could see he was close to tears. 'Frances is here all day and she will see her. What if, by the time I get back, she has ... she is ...' He stopped, unable to continue.

'Oh, Gabriel.' Lizzie wanted to hug him but feared he would push her away. 'I'm sure all will be well. She just needs a lot of rest at the moment. Now, hurry downstairs. Judith will have made your chocolate. But you might have to take biscuits for breakfast and eat them on the way to school.'

She gave him a gentle push towards the door while she quickly tidied the room, plumping the pillows, smoothing the sheets, tucking them in and throwing the blankets over the top. Judith would normally do this, but she had extra duties with two nurses in the house and Adam at home, so Lizzie felt she must do whatever she could to help.

Down in the kitchen, Frances was gazing, rapt, at the sleeping baby. Gabriel had stationed himself at the opposite end of the table and was drinking his chocolate.

'Frances, have you had your breakfast? Gabriel, drink up quickly.' Lizzie went to the jar and removed two biscuits then, looking at Frances, took out another. Best to avoid a squabble breaking out when they were in a hurry. She hadn't yet eaten or drunk anything herself but it would have to wait until she returned: Gabriel's school was strict and they had been late more than once this term already.

Twenty minutes later she was wiping crumbs from his mouth as he did his best to turn away from her in the cathedral grounds. She wondered whether to mention seeing his mother when he got home, then thought better of it. He had seemed his normal self on the walk to school; she didn't want him to start the day with worry for Hannah filling his mind.

She and Frances waved him off although he didn't look back. Then they turned homewards, Frances chattering about the baby as she skipped along at her side.

'What will she be called?' Frances asked.

'I don't know,' Lizzie said. 'What do you think?'

'Frances?' the little girl ventured.

Lizzie laughed. 'I don't think so. That would be confusing, two girls with the same name in the house. What do you think your mama and papa might choose?'

Frances seemed stumped by the question and they went along in silence for some time. 'I don't know,' she said, as they neared their front door. 'I'm going to ask them as soon as I get in.'

She ran a few steps ahead of Lizzie, who hurried to catch up. She would have to stop her waking Adam, or running upstairs to her mother. Frances wasn't tall enough or strong enough to open the front door on her own, though, so she was forced to wait for Lizzie, who was already anticipating the tea and slices of buttered bread she would breakfast on.

But as she opened the front door it quickly became apparent that all was not well. The doctor stood in the hallway, conferring with

Adam, who looked dishevelled, as though he had not long woken up. They glanced at Lizzie and Frances but didn't acknowledge them, so Lizzie shepherded Frances past them and into the kitchen, where Judith, usually so busy, stood twisting her apron between her hands. Mrs Hawkins was nursing the baby, and when she looked up, there was no welcoming smile on her lips but, rather, a grave expression.

Lizzie's blood ran cold. They had been gone barely forty-five minutes. What had happened in that time?

Chapter Twenty-Seven

I mmediately fearful, Lizzie looked from one woman to the other. 'What is it?' she asked. 'I saw the doctor in the hall.'

She couldn't bear to ask the question to which she dreaded the answer and didn't want Frances to hear it, either. She had perched beside Mrs Hawkins and the baby and seemed oblivious to the atmosphere for now.

'The doctor called in on his rounds.' Judith spoke carefully. 'He thinks—' She broke off, struggling to find the right words. 'He thinks Mrs Russell hasn't done as well as he had hoped overnight.'

'What does that mean?' Lizzie asked, although Judith's expression told her what she needed to know. They couldn't talk freely in front of Frances, but there was nowhere to send the poor child. In the silence that had fallen in the kitchen, they heard the front door close. The doctor must have left. Lizzie slipped out of the room, hoping to speak to Adam. She found him still standing in the hallway, staring up the stairs.

'Oh, Adam,' was all Lizzie managed to say, of all the words that were crowding into her mind.

'The doctor told me I must say goodbye.' Adam's expression was bleak. He still made no move to mount the stairs.

'Then you must,' Lizzie said firmly. 'You won't forgive yourself if . . . ' She didn't finish the sentence but she was seized with a sense of urgency. What if something had happened while Adam was speaking to the doctor? And Frances – she must be told.

'I think Frances should go up with you and then I'll take her away,' Lizzie said, trying to sound as though she knew the right thing to do. She feared that if it was left to Adam he would still be standing in the hall when it was time to collect Gabriel.

Gabriel! The thought hit her like a blow. He would be devastated, and angry no doubt. She had told him he would be able to see his mother when he came home from school. Should she run and fetch him? A sense of urgency took hold: she turned on her heel and went back to the kitchen.

'Frances, come with me,' she said, holding out her hand. 'Your father is going in to see your mother and you should come too.'

Frances stood up at once. She looked a little surprised that Lizzie hadn't referred to Mama and Papa as she usually did. Adam was still standing in the hallway, but he roused himself when he saw his daughter. Frances ran to his side and they climbed the stairs, Lizzie following a few steps behind. Mrs Thornhill opened the bedroom door to them and when she stepped aside, Lizzie caught a glimpse of Hannah, still and pale, much as she had been earlier that morning.

Lizzie hung back and shook her head slightly at Mrs Thornhill, to signify that she wouldn't be coming in. Then she wandered along the landing and waited. She waited for some time, conscious of feeling hungry and thirsty, then being annoyed at the intrusion of such mundane feelings when a terrible event was being played out behind the closed door.

Eventually the door opened and Frances emerged, her face hot and tear-streaked. Lizzie held out her hand without a word and took her down to the kitchen. Judith served food and drink, the only thing she felt able to do under the circumstances. She, Mrs Hawkins, Lizzie and Frances seemed compelled to stay at the table, waiting, although for what Lizzie wasn't sure. For Adam to appear and tell them it was all over, she supposed. She longed to go up and ask to see Hannah, but felt it wasn't her place. She wished she had said her goodbyes that morning, had said something profound instead of the stream of nonsense she had come out with in an attempt to fill the silence.

The baby stirred and let out a loud wail that startled them all.

'Goodness,' Mrs Hawkins said, raising her to her shoulder and rubbing her back. 'It must be wind.'

They all watched, for lack of anything else to distract them. The baby writhed a little, red in the face, then whimpered, settled and fell asleep again. Ten minutes later, Adam came into the kitchen. His face was grey, his eyes red-rimmed and his expression wild.

'She's gone,' he said, and slumped in a chair, burying his face in his hands. Lizzie longed to put an arm around his shoulders and comfort him but felt it would be inappropriate. And, in any case, Frances had burst into loud sobs: all her attention was devoted to trying to comfort her.

Afterwards, Lizzie struggled to remember the course of the rest of that day. The doctor came back; Mrs Thornhill appeared downstairs at some point and said her goodbyes; Lizzie asked whether she might see Hannah and found herself standing in the silent bedroom, unsure what to say. All was much as it had been early that morning, but this time she had no sense of Hannah inhabiting the pale, still body on the bed. Lizzie stood for a moment or two, then went away again.

Gabriel had to be fetched from school. When Lizzie appeared without Frances, who had refused to accompany her, he took one look at her face and knew at once. He was white with fury. 'You told me I could see her when I got home. You promised,' he said.

Lizzie wasn't sure she had promised but she was too tired to argue. 'I'm so sorry, Gabriel,' was all she could say, over and over again as they walked home.

When they got in, Adam took him up to see his mother. Afterwards, Lizzie had heard a storm of sobbing. Then his bedroom door slammed. She had paused halfway up the stairs, wondering whether to go to him but Adam, descending, had shaken his head, without a word passing between them.

Food had appeared on the table at intervals that didn't match normal mealtimes; the baby had cried and been fed, and was mostly

110

ignored by everyone other than Mrs Hawkins. Frances had gone to bed far later than her normal time, and Gabriel had refused to come downstairs to eat. Lizzie lay in bed with a headache, her brain filled with foggy fatigue. She woke in the night when the baby cried and remembered at once what had happened, then tossed and turned, struggling to return to sleep. How were they all to go on, without Hannah, the backbone of the family, to guide them?

CHAPTER TWENTY-EIGHT

It seemed appropriate to Lizzie that the weather was bleak and grey on the day Hannah was buried. After all, that had been the mood in the house on the intervening days since her death. She looked around at the small group gathered at the graveside: Frances and Gabriel, Adam, his hands resting on their shoulders; Judith in black, which made her look tired. No doubt she was, Lizzie reflected; they all were. There were acquaintances from the cathedral, one or two people Adam worked with and others Lizzie suspected of simply being curious. Adam's parents weren't there. Lizzie supposed it was too far to come in the uncertain winter weather. Mrs Hawkins had stayed behind with the baby, who still had no name. As Adam and the children each threw a handful of earth onto the coffin, their faces contorted with grief, Lizzie vowed the baby would be named and baptised. She seemed to be thriving under Mrs Hawkins's care, but the midwife's words still echoed in her head.

Lizzie, Judith at her side, followed the family back along the graveyard path, her head bowed. Judith wept, but Lizzie had been unable to shed a tear. She couldn't work out why. Was she simply cold-hearted? Was it the rawness of everyone else's grief that compelled her to try to comfort them, while disregarding her own? For she was not unmoved by Hannah's death, far from it. She was deeply sorrowful and struggled to comprehend that she would never see her again. She simply couldn't weep.

The group of mourners made their way to the old infirmary building in the cathedral grounds. It had been arranged that tea would be served there, rather than at the house, perhaps in honour of Adam's position. Lizzie was glad to be inside, away from the chill wind, but dreaded the prolonging of this public grief. She longed for them to be at home, behind closed doors, gathered together as a family.

She had a purpose now, at least. Adam was obliged to talk to the mourners and Gabriel and Frances were standing alone, looking lost.

'Shall we find you something to eat?' she said, steering them towards the table. Frances shook her head, but changed her mind when she saw cake. Gabriel took a plate and piled it with oatmeal biscuits and shortbread. Lizzie accepted a cup of tea and looked for Judith, conscious she was unlikely to know anyone at the gathering. She was sitting alone at a table, so Lizzie left the children in her charge and returned to the table for more tea. She hesitated, then took a biscuit, too. She wasn't particularly hungry but who knew when they would eat that day?

After half an hour, their plates now empty, the children were growing restless.

'Can we go home?' Frances was plaintive.

Lizzie sighed. She felt much the same, but knew they must stay. 'Just a little longer,' she said. The gathering was scheduled to last for an hour, so the family could leave then, their duty done. She noticed the unfamiliar mourners had loaded their plates, eaten fast and were preparing to slip out of the door, without bidding farewell to Adam. It was customary to allow anyone to attend a funeral, and the gathering afterwards, but Lizzie felt the least they should have done was offer condolences to Adam.

At last he came towards them. Lizzie leaped to her feet.

'Let me get you a cup of tea. And something to eat,' she said. She'd noticed he'd partaken of neither.

He shook his head wearily but she ignored him and fetched tea, with one or two of the remaining savouries. 'Thank you,' he said, drinking the tea very quickly. 'I hadn't realised how thirsty I was. All that talking.'

'There's ale, too,' Lizzie offered, although she rather hoped he'd refuse. She feared it might make him maudlin.

He picked at the pastries. 'Perhaps more tea.'

He looked up at her and she saw his eyes were brimming with tears. Hastily, she picked up the cup and went back to the table, where the helpers were starting to pack things away. They would be able to go home now, without appearing disrespectful.

When she returned, Adam was on his feet again as mourners approached to say goodbye. Gabriel had his head on the table and Judith was trying to cajole him into sitting upright.

'Come on, children.' Lizzie spoke briskly. 'You must be at your father's side now. And then we can go home.'

Reluctantly, Frances and Gabriel stood either side of Adam but stared mostly at their feet as one person after another came up to offer final condolences. It was overwhelming for them, Lizzie thought, and who could blame them? She longed to get them back to the safety of their familiar house, where they could gradually start to rebuild their lives. But Gabriel would be expected at school, and she supposed she must begin lessons again with Frances. Although how they would go on without Hannah's guidance, she didn't know. To ward off rising panic, she helped Judith gather plates and cups from the table; anything to keep busy and hold her thoughts at bay.

Then, thankfully, it was all over. They could leave the old infirmary and venture back out into the cold, where the wind drove drizzling rain into their faces throughout the silent walk home. Lizzie was sure she wasn't the only one to feel a sense of relief as they removed their damp cloaks and jackets, and made their way to the warmth of the kitchen.

'There you are.' Mrs Hawkins was in her usual spot, the baby swaddled and asleep. She didn't enquire further and Lizzie was glad. She didn't think anyone would want to talk about what they had just endured. Now, with Hannah gone and a baby to find her place within the family, they must move on and try to find a new way of living. And the baby was still without a name. Lizzie stared down into her face, peaceful in sleep, and waited for a name to suggest itself. Nothing came to mind – she was yet to develop a personality, she supposed. She remembered Frances suggesting her own name as a good choice and the ghost of a smile crossed her countenance, quickly suppressed. She didn't want Adam to catch her looking cheerful. It was hardly the day for it, although she couldn't help feeling that Hannah wouldn't have minded at all.

CHAPTER TWENTY-NINE

The day after the funeral Mrs Hawkins announced her intention of returning home and taking the baby with her.

'It's more usual,' she said, when Lizzie protested. 'My family need me at home, and this little scrap is happy enough anywhere.'

Lizzie could hardly deny her right to be with her family, but every ounce of her being told her that the baby should stay. Did no one else in the family think of her as the embodiment of Hannah? Lizzie did, and she couldn't bear the thought of her being taken away. 'What did Mr Russell say?' she demanded.

Mrs Hawkins shrugged. 'He's quite happy. He'll pay less for me to be nursing her at home. And I think he finds the baby difficult. She reminds him too much of his wife's death. I've noticed he doesn't so much as glance at her.'

Lizzie had noticed that, too, but imagined he was preoccupied with his own thoughts. He'd returned to work, which in some ways was a relief: his brooding presence in the kitchen had been hard for Judith, Lizzie and Mrs Hawkins to bear.

'Let me speak to him tonight,' Lizzie begged. 'Will you at least stay until then?'

Mrs Hawkins frowned. 'My eldest is looking after the little ones. I don't want to leave her to manage for much longer. I'll have to be home tonight.'

'I could care for the baby,' Lizzie said. Judith stopped what she was doing to stare at her and Mrs Hawkins laughed.

'And how will you nurse her?'

Lizzie coloured. 'Well, I can't do that. But I can look after her in every other way.' She'd had plenty of experience with her sisters, she reasoned.

'I dare say you can.' Mrs Hawkins nodded comfortably. 'But there's a while to go before she's weaned.'

Lizzie left the subject, and turned her attention to Frances, who had been listening, wide-eyed.

'Is the baby going to be taken away?' she asked.

'Mrs Hawkins needs to get home to her family,' Lizzie said. 'We were just discussing how best to manage it.' She didn't want Frances worrying. She had become attached to her little sister – an argument she could perhaps use with Adam. Frances was waking with nightmares, always about something she had lost. It wasn't hard to work out what that might be about. Lizzie feared that not having the baby at home would only make matters worse.

Gabriel was presenting his own set of problems. Lizzie knew he was angry with her: his grief had focused on what he believed to be the broken promise that he would see his mother after school. He ignored her most of the time, so she supposed he couldn't be accused of being impolite, but she was starting to dread her dealings with him. She told herself it would pass, that he, too, was grieving in his own way.

Adam was withdrawn, but Lizzie knew she must discuss some important things with him. The wet-nurse was one, a name for the baby another. And all the decisions that Hannah had made in the running of the house – organising the purchase of food and the meals to be put on the table – he would have to make them. Otherwise it would be impossible to return to some sort of normality. She and Judith were doing the best they could but it was hardly their place to step into Hannah's shoes.

Every so often, the loss of Hannah hit Lizzie like a body blow. She missed her quiet good humour, the way she organised the household so unobtrusively. Most of all, she missed the time they had spent stitching companionably in the sitting room, Frances running in and out with tales from Judith and the kitchen.

That night, Lizzie was waiting for Adam when he returned from work. She would have preferred to have her discussion with him when the children had gone to bed, but Mrs Hawkins was determined to return home and it couldn't be put off. Lizzie knew better than to speak out before he had eaten, so she waited patiently while he ate his pie and drank his glass of ale. Judith usually returned home as soon as dinner had been served and cleared away, but tonight Lizzie was aware that she loitered. There was no point in further delay so she took a deep breath.

'Adam, I gather you've agreed that Mrs Hawkins should take the baby home with her, and nurse her there?' It was a question but Lizzie didn't give him time to answer. 'I think it would be better for the baby to stay here, in this house. We have already suffered a loss. Frances, I know, would take this further loss very hard. I can look after the baby during the day, if Mrs Hawkins is prepared to come in just for the feeds. And if she took her home with her at night, Frances and I could collect her in the mornings, after we've taken Gabriel to school.'

Lizzie stopped, pink in the face. There was still a lot she needed to say, but some of that could wait until the children were in bed. The question over the baby was the most urgent to resolve. 'And the baby needs a name,' she added.

Adam stared at her, his expression hard to read.

He shrugged. 'As you wish. If you think you can look after another child, so be it. You can name her, too, for all I care.' With that, he got up from the table and left the room, closely followed by Gabriel.

Lizzie sighed. She didn't like to see the family so divided. But she had got her way. Judith, smiling, was gathering up her gloves, bonnet and shawl. Mrs Hawkins rose to her feet.

'Then I will see you and Frances in the morning,' she said. She didn't seem unduly put out by the change of plan. Lizzie hoped fervently that she could make it work.

CHAPTER THIRTY

Lizzie was relieved to have her room to herself, without the presence of Mrs Hawkins and the disruption of the baby's cries. But Frances cried out in distress during the night and Lizzie, somewhat disoriented at being woken from a deep sleep, stumbled along the landing to comfort her.

'Ssh, ssh,' she soothed, stroking Frances's brow. The poor little girl barely seemed awake but was sobbing hard. Gabriel turned over in his bed with a noisy sigh. Lizzie, keen to avoid him waking fully, began quietly to sing a song half remembered from comforting her siblings during times of illness. Her murmured, indistinct words had the desired effect and Frances, after shifting uneasily for a few minutes, drifted back to sleep. Lizzie was glad to see her brow had smoothed, but she carried on with the song, humming rather than singing, until she judged it safe to rise and creep from the room.

Back in her own bed, she struggled to fall back to sleep. She was seized by memories of her family. They would all have grown since she last saw them – their faces would have changed, their personalities developed. Were Alice and Susan still squabbling over Arabella, the doll? Was Mary still taunting them? And was the new baby a boy? She should write: her mother wouldn't be able to read the letter, but perhaps Ruth or Jane could. Weren't they supposed to go to school? She was seized with anxiety when it occurred to her that anything could have happened – the family might have moved and she would no longer know how to reach them. Her father might have had an accident with the fishing boat. Her mother could have died in childbirth. Lizzie gasped and covered her face with her hands. She should never have left them without a word. She would write to them the very next day if she could.

She drifted into a restless sleep, only to wake with a start at a rap on the door. It was Adam's voice. 'Lizzie, wake up. You've overslept. I need to go to work and you must get Gabriel up for school.'

Flustered, Lizzie stumbled from her bed and hurried along the landing, hearing Adam talking to Judith in the kitchen below. She hadn't been able to speak to him the previous night for answers to all her other questions and now she was at a disadvantage. If she couldn't even get up in time to attend to his children, would he revoke permission for her to look after the baby by day? Anxiety made her sharper with the children than she would normally have been, and she saw Frances's lower lip start to tremble as she urged them to hurry and get dressed.

'Go down to Judith and have some breakfast while I get ready,' Lizzie said. 'And, remember, we're going to pick up the baby on the way home.'

Gabriel curled his lip in disdain but Frances brightened and positively skipped down the stairs. When Lizzie emerged from her own room, properly attired with her hair brushed and pinned up, she could hear Frances chattering to Judith about the baby. Lizzie smiled as she descended to the kitchen. A name would have to be chosen. Perhaps that was something they could do that day. Or they could make a list of names and let Adam choose, despite his apparent indifference.

Once more, Lizzie's breakfast would have to wait. 'Time to go,' she said to Gabriel and Frances. The little girl was out of her seat at once, but although Gabriel stood up, he carried on taking bites of his bread and butter and didn't move beyond the table. Lizzie tried hard to curb her irritation. She knew he wasn't fond of school and now his home life had suffered a terrible disruption. Even so, he would be punished if he was late again. She opened her mouth to speak but, as if he had read her mind, he made a sudden move to the door and they joined Frances, already waiting in the hallway.

Lizzie set a fast pace and she was out of breath by the time they reached the gate to the cathedral garden. For once, though, they were in good time. She wished Gabriel a good day, as always, and expected him to walk off without acknowledging her.

But he turned suddenly and said, 'I think you should call the baby Grace.'

Lizzie was astonished. She barely knew what to say but managed to stumble out, 'Why, Gabriel, Grace is a lovely name.'

'It was one of Mama's favourites,' Gabriel said. 'She couldn't decide between that and Frances when Frances was born.' And he walked off to join the other boys.

Then baby Grace it should be, Lizzie thought. Not least because it was the first interest Gabriel had shown in her, but if it truly was a favourite of Hannah's that should be honoured. And, after all, it was a lovely name.

'Baby Grace,' Lizzie said to Frances. 'What do you think?'

'Let's try it and see if she likes it,' she suggested.

Lizzie smiled, turning Frances in the direction of Mrs Hawkins's house, which was not far from the school.

Her first impression was of a small house, filled with children but very clean and neat. Either her eldest had done a good job while her mother was away, or Mrs Hawkins had spent the evening cleaning and tidying on her return.

'Where's the baby?' Frances demanded, as soon as they were inside.

'Frances!' Lizzie said, trying to reprimand her by her tone of voice.

'Well, that's why we're here.' Frances was puzzled.

Mrs Hawkins laughed. 'Did you miss her? My brood are quite taken with her. My eldest is looking after her – come and see.'

They followed Mrs Hawkins into the kitchen where a girl of

about twelve was sitting on a kitchen chair, holding the peacefully sleeping baby.

'We have a name for her,' Frances announced. 'We're going to call her Grace and see if she likes it.'

The baby stirred a little, opened her eyes and closed them again.

'See? She does!' Frances exclaimed.

'Best be getting home with her,' Mrs Hawkins said. 'She's been fed and changed. I'll be there before noon but if she gets restless before then, just walk around with her and let her suck your finger.'

She addressed Lizzie but Frances nodded solemnly. She was all for taking the baby from the other girl but Lizzie stepped in and scooped her up, tucking her inside Hannah's cloak, which she had worn with the walk home in mind.

'Let's get her back quickly,' she said to Frances. 'And maybe we can make a bed for her in the kitchen. Do you think she'd like that?'

Frances clapped her hands in excitement. 'She can have my Lizzie doll,' she said, referring to her favourite, the one Lizzie had made as a Christmas gift.

Lizzie made a point of thanking Mrs Hawkins's daughter, who, she discovered, was called Nell, like her own sister. She experienced a momentary pang of loss, a wish to know what her Nell was doing. Shaking it off, she elicited a promise from Mrs Hawkins that she wouldn't be late, before following an impatient Frances out of the door. Thank goodness for baby Grace, she thought, as they walked home, Frances checking constantly that she was well protected from the wind. At least she was a distraction for the little girl, if not for Adam and Gabriel.

CHAPTER THIRTY-ONE

During the days that followed, a routine became established and, luckily for everyone, Grace was perfectly amenable to all of it. Lizzie and Frances collected her from Mrs Hawkins on the way back from school. She slept soundly for a while, in the drawer repurposed as a bed, which was now in continuous use in the kitchen, while Frances did her lessons and Judith bustled around. Then, when she woke, Frances kept her entertained, chattering away to her and waving dolls in front of her, until Grace grew restless. At that point, Lizzie picked her up and walked her around until Mrs Hawkins arrived, promptly as promised.

Grace fell asleep after her feed, Lizzie and Frances ate bread and cheese or leftovers from the previous night's dinner, and the routine was repeated. This time, though, when Mrs Hawkins appeared in the late afternoon to feed Grace again, she took her home with her. Lizzie was in two minds about this. It meant that neither Adam nor Gabriel saw her, except at the weekends, but it was less restrictive: she could give her undivided attention to Frances. And Lizzie knew that, as Grace grew, the regime would change again. She looked forward to spring, and milder days, when she and Frances could take Grace to the park and not have to be so tied to the house.

She was thinking very much along those lines one morning as she and Frances left Gabriel at school and began their walk to collect Grace. The sun was shining and there was a feeling of expectation in the air; the leaf buds on the trees were beginning to unfurl and primroses were about to join the daffodils already adding bright splashes of colour to the cathedral grounds.

'Well, here you are, with your pretty charge.'

At first Lizzie couldn't place the woman who had planted herself in front of them on the pathway. The sun, still low in the sky, was behind her, casting her face into shadow. But the lack of recognition was swiftly replaced by a sinking feeling: it was Mrs Simmonds.

'I haven't seen you for some time, Lizzie,' Mrs Simmonds continued. 'Have you been in hiding? It makes no odds – I haven't forgotten that you owe me money. And I intend to collect the debt, one way or another.'

She turned to Frances. 'And what's your name, my dear?'

Frances, who hadn't understood the content of Mrs Simmonds's words, just the polite tone and easy smile with which she delivered them, saw no reason to be shy and answered at once. 'Frances,' she said. 'We've just left my brother Gabriel at school and now we're going to collect my baby sister, Grace.'

Lizzie closed her eyes briefly at Frances's openness.

'Ah. Then don't let me detain you further,' Mrs Simmonds said, stepping aside. She laid her hand on Lizzie's arm, gripping it firmly. 'I look forward to seeing you again one morning very soon.' She smiled again and ruffled Frances's hair before moving off.

Frances turned to watch her go. 'She's a nice lady. Is she your friend?' she asked Lizzie.

Lizzie chose her words carefully. 'I don't know her well enough for that. Now, we must hurry. Mrs Hawkins will be expecting us.'

She did her best to appear her normal self to Frances as they walked along, but her heart was thumping in her chest as she tried to take in what had just happened. How could she have forgotten about the debt owed to Mrs Simmonds, repayment due by Christmas? The memory of it had been submerged by the festivities, and then by the tragedy that had befallen the family not long afterwards. But Mrs Simmonds clearly wasn't going to forget, and now she was fully aware of their morning routine. Lizzie felt sure she would engineer another meeting before too many days had passed. On top of that, she knew rather too much about the family, thanks to Frances's guileless candour.

Aware that she was monosyllabic in her answers to Frances, she tried to shake off her anxiety and focus on the day ahead. But still her head whirled. How might she repay the money, which she felt sure Mrs Simmonds was inflating regularly, when she had so little to call her own? Could she ask Adam to help her? She would have to explain why she needed such a sum. She was sure he would understand, but as to whether he had it, that was another question. In addition to Judith's salary, he had had to pay the doctor's and Mrs Thornhill's fees and he was still paying Mrs Hawkins, and would be for some while. Hannah had paid Lizzie from the extra income her sewing had brought in, so she had received no money for a few weeks. It all seemed impossible.

Lizzie sighed as they arrived on Mrs Hawkins's doorstep, earning herself a questioning look from Frances. She managed to give her a weak smile as the door opened, but the sight of baby Grace drove her worries from her mind. She was still awake after her feed, and Nell was carrying her around. Both Frances and Lizzie were convinced that Grace smiled as soon as she saw them.

'She's a happy girl this morning,' Mrs Hawkins said. 'Not that she isn't always content, but I think spring is in the air and she can sense it.'

Lizzie carried Grace home, tucked into Hannah's cloak as usual, but facing out for the first time so that she could look around, her head and soft downy hair protected from the breeze by a bonnet. She could feel her little legs kicking against her every now and then, while Frances exclaimed and pointed things out on their journey – a clump of daffodils, nodding in the wind, a robin pouring its liquid song from a bough, a horse and cart rumbling down the road. Lizzie held Grace to her and delighted in the warmth of her tiny body, the regular beat of her heart, the way she turned her head every now and then to look up at Lizzie. She wished she could preserve every moment of that journey in her heart for ever. If nothing else, it successfully drove all thoughts of Mrs Simmonds from her mind.

CHAPTER THIRTY-TWO

Lizzie had managed to have her discussion with Adam about how the house should be run, without Hannah to take charge of all the day-to-day responsibilities. As she had expected, he had been impatient, and keen to have done with it.

'I think it best if you manage it as you see fit, Lizzie,' he said. He looked helpless as he spoke. 'I wouldn't know where to start. I gave Hannah a housekeeping allowance and she took care of everything.' He stood up abruptly and left the room, but Lizzie wasn't offended. His lip had begun to tremble at the mention of his wife and she knew he was struggling to hold his emotions in check.

She, too, had been ambushed by a wave of sadness the previous day, when she had gone into the sitting room, now little used, to find some threads in Hannah's work-basket for a sewing project with Frances. Hannah's whitework piece, the one she had intended to work on for her own family, was neatly folded on top of the work-basket, gathering dust. It struck Lizzie forcefully that the piece would now never be finished. She shook it out to look at it once more. Could she complete it, in Hannah's memory? One look told her it would be impossible. Hannah's work was exquisite, the result of years of practice, and of natural talent. Lizzie's eyes were brimming with tears as she folded the work and replaced it. She stood for a moment, gathering herself, before she took the spools of thread for Frances. She felt ashamed: Grace had been such a delightful distraction over the last few weeks that she had allowed Hannah to begin to fade from her mind.

Now, with Adam handing over the household responsibilities to her, she was forcefully reminded of her employer. Hannah had dealt effortlessly with the purchase of everything needed for the house, and Lizzie had little idea of what was involved. But Hannah had kept meticulous records, so that night Lizzie took the household accounts up to her room and studied them by candlelight. Every order, whether it was for the butcher, the fishmonger or the grocer, was listed along with the date and the amount paid. The price of coal and candles, fabric and threads, all were detailed.

Lizzie stared at the pages. She wasn't sure she wanted to undertake this task. She felt a rising sense of indignation. Surely she was fully occupied with the children. Then she reminded herself that she was no longer spending time sewing with Hannah. If she didn't take charge of the purchasing, who would? She sighed. She would have to visit the shops on the way home from school, with Frances and Grace, and explain that she was now in charge. No doubt there would be bills to pay – knowing the circumstances, the shopkeepers had continued to supply the household over the last few weeks, at Judith's behest. Perhaps she and Judith could share the duties, with Judith purchasing food, while she dealt with the rest. Lizzie brightened at the thought. She would have to ask Adam for the household allowance in the morning, and request the bills from the shops. Even as she felt close to resolving the issue, another crept into her mind. She would need to ask Adam about being paid. Hannah had always taken care of this and Lizzie hadn't received a penny since her death.

She had considered drawing on the housekeeping money, so she wouldn't have to bother him, but seeing how closely the allowance matched the expenditure, she could see it would be impossible. She had managed so far, but now the debt to Mrs Simmonds loomed large. Her savings had dwindled and she simply didn't have enough.

Lizzie tossed and turned in her bed, sleep proving elusive. In the early hours, half awake and half asleep, memories of Hannah came to her – she thought she could see her at the end of the bed, her brows drawn together in a frown, as she contemplated Lizzie. Then she faded from view, only to be replaced by Mrs Simmonds, who was asking for such an unfeasibly large sum that Lizzie gasped in horror and Frances, standing beside her, burst into tears. Lizzie woke with a start and realised that Frances was indeed crying, but in the bedroom along the landing. She jumped from her bed, wondering if she had been crying for long. As she hurried along the landing, she met Adam coming from the other direction.

Lizzie, embarrassed, clutched her nightgown to her throat. 'I'm sorry Frances woke you. I dreamed she was crying – it took me a while to realise she actually was.'

'Don't worry, Lizzie. Go back to bed. I'll go in to her.' Adam put his hand on her shoulder and smiled at her.

Lizzie almost flinched. She returned to her room, feeling the pressure of his fingers on her collarbone as though they had burned their imprint through the thin fabric. She lay in her bed, listening as Frances's sobs eased, then ceased. The quiet click of the door told her Adam had returned to his own bed.

Why did you leave us, Hannah? Lizzie thought. The family was struggling to deal with its grief, all of them affected in quite different ways. Gabriel and Adam had closed in on themselves; Frances appeared to be coping well by day but was tormented by night. And Lizzie was trying to hold them together. But now she had a problem of her own. What would Hannah's advice have been for dealing with Mrs Simmonds? And if she had still been alive, would Lizzie have dared to ask her?

CHAPTER THIRTY-THREE

The next morning Lizzie was weary after her restless night. It was an effort to chivvy Frances and Gabriel to eat their breakfast and leave the house for school. She had time only for half a cup of tea and she was monosyllabic as they walked along, despite the lovely weather. Gabriel and Frances didn't appear to notice, though, and they arrived in good time. Lizzie and Frances had waved Gabriel off and turned in the direction of Mrs Hawkins's house, when Mrs Simmonds stopped them again.

'Good morning to you both, and what a beautiful one it is,' she remarked, falling into step beside them. 'But I declare you look out of sorts, Miss Carey. Are you unwell?'

Lizzie was taken aback. 'No, just tired,' she muttered.

Mrs Simmonds shook her head. 'These are your best years, my dear. You have a fine face and figure and you should be capitalising on them, not wasting your time as a nursemaid.'

She smiled sweetly at Frances, who smiled uncertainly back.

Her tone changed. 'It's been more than a year now since you promised to work for me and still you haven't paid me what you owe. And, of course, the debt keeps growing, what with the interest.'

She named a sum that made Lizzie gasp. 'That's far too much,' she protested.

'Then come and work for me. The debt will be wiped clean, you'll earn enough to keep yourself in the fine clothes you deserve, and you'll be able to send money home to that family of yours in Castle Bay.'

Lizzie grimaced. Mrs Simmonds knew how to hit hard. She glanced down at herself, noticing for the first time how drab and worn her clothes had become. And it had never occurred to her to send money home. Imagine the difference it would make to the family if she could. For a moment, she was almost swayed by Mrs Simmonds's words. Then she remembered the nature of the work.

'I will have money for you soon,' she promised. 'But not the amount you want. It's too much.' She spoke defiantly although her heart was beating uncomfortably hard.

Mrs Simmonds shrugged. 'I'm patient. I can be here every week until it's all paid. Or you can decide to do what's sensible.'

With that, she walked back towards a carriage waiting at the roadside. Frances glanced up anxiously at Lizzie. 'She wasn't very nice this time, was she?' she asked.

'No, not so nice,' Lizzie agreed. 'But don't worry, it will be all right.'

But would it? How had she been so foolish as to get herself into such a situation?

Their arrival at Mrs Hawkins's house to collect Grace pushed the worry from Lizzie's mind. And for the next few weeks, even though Lizzie expected to see her every morning, there was no sign of Mrs Simmonds. Adam had given Lizzie money to pay the outstanding tradesmen's bills, which left a little for the housekeeping jar, although not as much as she had expected. She had briefly considered whether she might use it to help pay off her debt, then discounted the idea. She saw it as borrowing, but Adam might've considered it stealing. Yet as April went by and May arrived, with no further sightings of Mrs Simmonds, Lizzie once more began to forget all about the monies owed.

As they returned home one particularly fine May morning, Lizzie said, 'I think we should take Grace to the park today.'

'Oh, yes!' Frances almost danced with excitement. 'Let's ask Judith for a picnic.'

'We have to be back by noon for Mrs Hawkins to feed Grace,'

Lizzie warned her. Seeing Frances's face fall, she added, 'But we can take something to eat and drink. And a blanket to sit on the grass. It's such a beautiful day.'

For the first time in many weeks, she felt a lifting of her spirits, along with restlessness. She was tired of the daily routine: it would be good for them to do something different. And Grace would be weaned before long, so there would be fewer restrictions on their lives.

'No lessons today,' she promised.

Frances skipped at her side for the remainder of the journey home, and rushed into the kitchen as soon as they arrived. By the time Lizzie joined her, she had ordered a vast array of foods to be packed and Judith's brow was heavily creased with a frown.

'We just need some of your delicious lemonade, and a biscuit or two,' Lizzie hastened to assure her. 'We won't be gone long – we'll save the picnic for another day, when Gabriel can join us.'

Frances looked as though she was about to make a fuss so she sent her in search of a blanket and a toy or two to entertain Grace.

'It's a good idea,' Judith said, as she poured lemonade from the big jug into a glass bottle. 'You've been looking a bit pale and out of sorts. A change might do you good.' She shook her head. 'You do too much for this family – and never get any time off.'

Frances arrived back in the room, clutching a blanket and more toys than she could sensibly carry, which put a stop to the conversation. Twenty minutes later, with the blanket, two dolls, the lemonade and some biscuits stowed in a basket, Lizzie and Frances stepped outside the door again. Lizzie breathed deeply: the air was fresh, with a faint sweet scent carried on the breeze, and the birds were singing. Her spirits lifted at once.

'To the park,' she said, and they turned off the roadway, away from the wagons and carts rumbling through, onto the quieter side streets that led towards the river. They hadn't been to the park since Christmas, she realised, when they had collected greenery to decorate the house. A wave of sadness hit her. Hannah had been alive then, just five months ago. It felt much longer – time had weighed heavily on them all since her death. And now here they were, without Hannah but with baby Grace, who was alert in Lizzie's arms. She was looking around at everything they passed, wriggling and kicking in excitement. She was heavier now – Lizzie was finding it hard to carry both baby and basket and thought she might have to ask Frances to stop so she could catch her breath, but the sight of the gates to the park spurred her on.

As soon as they were through them she told Frances to take the blanket and find a good spot to spread it out. 'Somewhere with a bit of shade for Grace,' she said. 'Beneath a tree.'

The park was quiet: there was just a lady walking with two small children. Lizzie kept Frances in view as she ran across the grass and laid the blanket beneath a horse chestnut in bloom. 'You've chosen well,' she said, arriving beside her and setting down the basket, then sitting with Grace on her lap.

'Can we have the biscuits now?' Frances asked.

Lizzie laughed. 'It's a bit early.' Then, foreseeing trouble if she didn't agree, she said, 'One now and another before we leave.'

She poured them a glass of lemonade each, too. The less she had to carry back, the better.

CHAPTER THIRTY-FOUR

Lizzie laid Grace on her back and watched her gurgling contentedly as she looked up at the leaves moving above her, the sunlight filtering through the branches. When Frances bent over her with a doll she began to kick enthusiastically, her arms stretched out and little fists clenched. All at once, Lizzie became aware of two children silently watching them.

She smiled at them. 'Hello,' she said, wondering who they were with. Worryingly, she couldn't see anyone nearby, so she patted the blanket encouragingly. 'Would you like to sit down?'

She thought she recognised them as the children seen at a distance with their mother when they had first entered the park. They didn't respond, continuing to stand silently and watch. Lizzie cast another glance around but couldn't see their mother anywhere.

'Would you like a drink?' she offered. They shook their heads.

'A biscuit?' She saw Frances glaring at her, but ignored her. Judith had packed more than enough for the two of them.

The boy shook his head again but the girl, younger than Frances, hesitated. Lizzie held one out to her. Then, seeing the boy's expression, she offered one to him as well.

'It's quite all right,' she said. 'I'm sure your mother won't mind.'

'She told us not to move.' The boy had found his tongue. 'And not to talk to anyone. But *she* wouldn't listen to me.' He pointed to his sister.

Lizzie smiled at him. 'I'm sure your mother won't be cross – she'll see you are quite safe here. Do sit down. I'm Lizzie, this is Frances and the baby is Grace.' She wanted them both to feel at ease so she could find out just where their mother had gone.

They did as she suggested but remained quiet, although they watched every move that Frances and Grace made. Lizzie chatted to them, despite their silence, hoping to discover their names and where they lived. Eventually, after twenty minutes, she had discovered the boy was called Christopher and his blonde-haired sister was Agnes, and they lived in one of the houses overlooking the park. That was a relief: Lizzie was beginning to fear the time would come for her to leave with Frances and Grace and then what to do? She could hardly leave the siblings on their own, and she couldn't take them home with her for fear of being accused of abduction. At least she would be able to knock at the door of the house Christopher had pointed out; hopefully someone would be about. But it was odd that the children were alone – Lizzie kept glancing at the house's blank frontage, as though it might reveal the answer, to no avail.

Shortly afterwards, to Lizzie's relief, a lady approached them across the grass. Agnes scrambled to her feet and ran to her, calling, 'Mama,' and clung to her skirts. Christopher stayed on the blanket, a mutinous expression on his face. Frances looked on in some puzzlement.

Lizzie supposed she should get to her feet to greet their mother.

'No, please, don't get up for me,' the lady exclaimed. 'Such an idyllic scene. I didn't want to disturb it.' She smiled at Lizzie, who awaited further explanation.

Christopher spoke up: 'I told Agnes not to move but she wouldn't listen. She wanted to come and look at the baby.'

His mother turned her charming smile on him. 'Well, there's no harm done. I can see you have been well looked after by Miss—' she turned back to Lizzie.

'Carey,' Lizzie said. 'Elizabeth Carey.' She was still waiting for an explanation.

'You must be puzzled as to how two young children came to be alone in the park?'

Lizzie raised an eyebrow but didn't speak.

'We live just across the road. Well, we are staying just across the road – in fact, we live in the countryside. I felt a little unwell – the warmth of the day – but the children didn't want to return to the house with me, so I could have a cold drink. They said they had only just got here. So I made them promise they would stay where they were and not speak to anyone. Then the housekeeper stopped me and asked me a multitude of questions, and I glanced out of the window and saw they were in good hands so here I am at last.'

The lady turned her smile on Lizzie again, who had the impression she was well practised in using it to get out of difficult situations.

'Well, children, we must leave Miss Carey and her charges in peace.'

'Can't we stay longer?' Agnes protested. Lizzie rather thought she had her eyes on the remaining biscuits wrapped in the cloth.

Their mother hesitated but didn't immediately demur.

'They are welcome to stay for another twenty minutes,' Lizzie said. 'Then we will have to leave so baby Grace can be fed. I can bring them both to your door, if that suits.'

Their mother looked delighted. 'Would you like that, children?' She barely waited for an answer before she said to Lizzie, 'Thank you. We're at number forty-two. And I'm Mrs Bullivant.' Then she hurried from the park. Lizzie wondered briefly why she didn't have a nursemaid, then turned her attention to the children. Frances and Agnes ran off to play on the grass, but Christopher stayed at her side. He seemed more at ease now they had permission to be there, and he took over the duty of entertaining Grace, who was thankfully still happy, although Lizzie knew it wouldn't be long before she became tired and fretful.

She was tempted to quiz Christopher about his lack of a nursemaid but thought better of it, and confined herself to asking his age and that of Agnes – eight and four – and telling him a little about Frances and Gabriel. He was far more interested in Grace than Gabriel was, she thought, as the two little girls came back and flopped onto the blanket, quite red in the face from running around.

'Lemonade time,' she declared, giving Frances and Agnes a glass to share and donating her own to Christopher.

'But what will you drink from?' he asked, and her heart went out to him for his thoughtfulness.

'I will have something when we get home,' she said, sharing out what remained of the biscuits. Then it was time to pick up Grace, who was thankfully now sleepy rather than grumpy, pack away the blanket, and shepherd the children across the park to number forty-two.

As they stood on the doorstep, Lizzie saw a familiar figure at the corner of the square. Mrs Simmonds was watching them. Lizzie turned her back on the woman and prayed for the door to open quickly. The maid ushered them into the hall, shutting the door behind them, to Lizzie's relief. Mrs Bullivant appeared shortly after.

'Say thank you to Miss Carey,' she said to her children.

'Thank you,' they chorused, Agnes adding, 'Can we play again tomorrow?'

Lizzie hesitated. She had no objection – they had been easy play-mates – but she didn't know what the weather might bring.

'Now, we can't impose on Miss Carey,' Mrs Bullivant said. 'And we will be returning to the country very soon.'

'If you see us in the park, you are most welcome to join us,' Lizzie said, smiling at Agnes and Christopher.

'Now run along and wash your hands, then see whether Cook can find you something,' their mother said. She turned to Lizzie. 'I'm without a nursemaid at present – and I find it's a role I'm not well suited to. I don't suppose you are looking for a position?'

Lizzie, astonished by the question, looked down at Grace, sleeping in the crook of her arm, and Frances, thankfully too distracted by the grandeur of their surroundings to pay any heed to the conversation.

Mrs Bullivant gave her disarming smile and shrugged. 'I can

see you are well suited. But if things should change ... Let me give you my address in the country, just in case. It's quite remote – I've found it hard to get girls to stay. There, now I've given you a good reason not to come.' She left the hall, returning shortly with a sheet of paper, an address written in beautiful copperplate script. Lizzie barely glanced at it before folding it and putting it into the basket.

'It was very nice to meet you, Mrs Bullivant,' she said, being polite rather than truthful. 'And Christopher and Agnes. They are lovely children.'

Mrs Bullivant looked surprised. 'Do you think so? I've been finding them tiresome and disobedient.' She sighed. 'But, as I say, I'm not good with children.'

'I'm sure you have other demands on your time,' Lizzie said, finding it hard to imagine the life of a lady in a house as grand as the one in which they stood. She hurried Frances out of the door, knowing that she must get Grace home before she woke and realised her belly was empty.

Back on the doorstep, she was relieved to see Mrs Simmonds had gone. This was neither the time nor the place to discuss a debt with the woman she now feared was one of the more notorious residents of Canterbury, despite her elegant appearance.

CHAPTER THIRTY-FIVE

Frances was eager to return to the park the next day so she could play with Agnes, her new friend, but the weather was against them. It was too windy for a picnic, and although the sun was shining on their walk home from collecting Grace, showers soon set in. Frances was forced to submit to lessons, which she did with ill humour. Grace was unsettled and cried a good deal, forcing Lizzie to pace around the kitchen while she tried to supervise Frances's work.

'Here, let me take her,' Judith said, just as Lizzie was wondering how long it would be before Mrs Hawkins arrived. Grace was not only heavier, but stronger, too – she kept pushing herself away from Lizzie and arching her back. Lizzie wished she could tell them what ailed her.

'By the way, when I emptied the basket yesterday there was a piece of paper in it. I tucked it behind the flour jar in case you needed it.' Judith nodded in the direction of the dresser.

Lizzie had forgotten about the address Mrs Bullivant had given her. 'Thank you,' she said. She took it and put it into her pocket, although she couldn't imagine that she would ever need it.

The day proved trying. Grace fought against being fed, turning her head away and wailing so that even the placid Mrs Hawkins became exasperated. 'She's either sick or decided she's ready to be weaned,' she declared. Lizzie, Mrs Hawkins and Judith all regarded Grace. She was red in the face from crying but not overly hot.

'I'll try her with some milksop tonight – if she takes to it, my job is done,' Mrs Hawkins told Lizzie. Grace had now fallen asleep, worn out by crying, so she deposited her in her makeshift drawer bed. The family crib sat, unused, in the children's bedroom. If Grace was ready to be weaned, she would remain at home at night, sleeping in the crib.

Lizzie had mixed feelings. Although it would be welcome not to have the additional job of collecting Grace each morning, she wasn't sure about having charge of three children full-time. Gabriel, at school, was little trouble but, much as she loved Grace, she was always glad when Mrs Hawkins took her in the late afternoon. Without that respite, she feared she would become exhausted. Adam left the house early and arrived home late, and Lizzie supposed that what she did was no different from mothers throughout the land – but she wasn't the children's mother.

Grace slept for a long time, which was a relief, but when she woke she was very irritable. Lizzie was sure she was hungry and considered trying to get her to take bread soaked in milk from a spoon, but thought she ought to wait and let Mrs Hawkins do it her own way. She and Judith were very glad when Mrs Hawkins reappeared on the doorstep; this time Grace fed eagerly and the wet-nurse declared that maybe she'd had a touch of colic but she'd try her with milksop in the morning, just to see.

Lizzie hoped that getting out into the fresh air to collect Gabriel would ease the headache she had developed, but the wind whipping at her hair just made it worse. She'd left Frances at home for once – Judith said she would watch her until they returned – and she hurried along, head down, thoughts elsewhere, until she almost collided with a passer-by in Mercery Lane.

'I beg your pardon,' she said, then realised whom she was addressing. Despite the blustery weather, Mrs Simmonds looked immaculate, in a dove-grey silk outfit, not a hair out of place under her stylish bonnet.

'I was hoping to see you, Miss Carey,' she said, laying a gloved hand on Lizzie's arm. 'It's been quite a while now, and your debt is still growing. Although,' she glanced around and her voice dropped so that Lizzie had to strain to hear against the wind, 'I have a proposition for you. You can pay it all off in one night, if you so wish. I have a gentleman who is most interested in meeting a young woman who is ... how can I put it? ... fresh and untouched. I'm assuming you are? No dalliances with the handsome widower you share the house with? Or trysts with young fishermen on the beach in Castle Bay?'

Lizzie drew back, her face red with anger.

Mrs Simmonds laughed. 'You'd better think about it, my dear. I've tried to be accommodating but my patience is fast running out. I'll give you a week – find the money you owe me or agree to my terms.'

Lizzie hurried on, her mind in a whirl. She was never going to be rid of Mrs Simmonds and her demands, she could see that. She would have to speak to Adam that night about her wages. If he could pay her what she was owed, she might have just enough to cover the wretched debt. Lizzie couldn't bear to reveal why she had such an urgent need of the money, though. She feared it reflected badly on her.

She collected Gabriel and made a special effort to give him her full attention. It was rare for them to spend time alone, without Frances and Grace there, too. But Gabriel hadn't enjoyed his day at school and wasn't disposed to talk a great deal, so they lapsed mostly into silence on the way home. He cheered up when he saw that Judith had made a meat pie for dinner, and it seemed to suit Adam, too: he came in shortly afterwards. Lizzie noticed that he was in a better mood than he had been for some weeks, so she resolved that she must speak to him that evening, despite the headache that refused to leave her.

She came down from putting Gabriel and Frances to bed to find Adam nursing a glass of ale at the kitchen table, deep in thought. They hadn't used the sitting room since Hannah had died – it felt too much like her room, with all her sewing things still there, her presence still strong, as if she was about to come in and take a seat by the fire.

Lizzie sat down opposite him, declined a glass of ale and took a deep breath, ready to launch into her plea for help.

'I've been meaning to speak to you, Lizzie,' Adam said, before she could begin.

Lizzie was startled, then worried. Had she done something to earn his displeasure? Had he somehow learned about Mrs Simmonds and her threats?

'And I to you,' she said, hoping to explain her troubles before he could judge her.

'Then I very much hope we will find ourselves on common ground,' Adam said, puzzling Lizzie. He looked at her over the top of his glass, smiling.

Mrs Simmonds had spoken the truth – he was a handsome man, she thought, in a dispassionate way. He would make someone a good husband in the fullness of time. But how would he react to what she had to ask him?

'You are very good with the children, Lizzie,' Adam said. 'As good as a mother to them.' He gave her a meaningful look. 'So, I was thinking, why don't we make you their actual mother?'

Her head full of Mrs Simmonds and her demands, and her need to ask Adam for money if she was to look after Grace full time, Lizzie was confused.

'I think we should marry,' Adam said. 'It's the obvious thing to do. The children like you, you run the house well and you will have a home, a respectable position. People are beginning to talk.' He elaborated; 'About you still living in the house, with me, now that Hannah has gone.' He took a mouthful of ale. 'You are young. We could have another child or two, together.'

Lizzie stared at him. For a moment, she thought he was going to reach for her hand, and she stood up abruptly and went in search of a glass. She poured a small amount of ale into it, then feared it looked as though she was joining him in celebration.

The evening's conversation was not going the way she had imagined.

CHAPTER THIRTY-SIX

Lizzie sat down again, her thoughts whirling. Would marrying Adam solve her problems? Would he deal with Mrs Simmonds for her, and rid her of the debt? She discounted the idea almost immediately. It would mean starting married life beholden to him – she needed to find her own way to deal with that predicament.

Even as the thought clarified, she began to see something else. It had never been her intention to leave her family responsibilities in Castle Bay, only to take up a similar role in someone else's family. She had fallen into that through circumstance: perhaps the time had come to make another change. But what could she do?

Adam was looking at her, waiting. She took a nervous gulp of ale. Her thoughts skittered in yet another direction. She was fond of Gabriel, Frances and Grace, and the status that married life would offer was briefly attractive. But she was only seventeen – did she want to be a wife and full-time mother so young? She gazed back at Adam. There were none of the feelings she associated with falling in love, but had never experienced. There was no thrill, no catching of breath, no excitement. He was a kind man, and good-looking – the sort of man she supposed she ought to be proud to call her husband. He was at least ten years older than her – was that the source of her doubts? Or perhaps this was normal. Wouldn't it be better to marry someone calm and steady? She certainly didn't want to follow the example set by her own parents: their arguments, followed by passionate making up – and another child in the family. As she struggled to marshal her thoughts, Adam spoke again.

'Are you worried that it is too soon after Hannah's passing? It's quite usual, you know. Hannah and I spoke about it before she died.'

Lizzie was shocked. 'You did?'

Adam nodded. 'Yes. She felt there was no one better suited to her role.'

Lizzie knew that a widower often took a new bride soon after his wife's death, to help with the children and the house. She had just never envisaged herself in that position. She tried to imagine herself attending Sunday services on Adam's arm, rather than in the background with the children. Would she still be looking over her shoulder for Mrs Simmonds? Or would she give up her demands if the marriage took place? Perhaps Adam would give her an allowance that she could use to pay off the debt once and for all. Then she remembered Hannah's meticulous accounts – no personal allowance was mentioned.

'I can see I have startled you,' Adam said gently. 'I thought perhaps you had an inkling of my intentions.'

He reached out and took her hand before Lizzie could snatch it away. 'I've expressed myself clumsily. I do have feelings for you, Lizzie. I'm not suggesting this just to make life easier for myself. I'll give you a week or two to get used to the idea, and then we can have the banns read in church.'

He spoke confidently. Lizzie's heart sank – he hadn't considered that this might not be something she wanted. In an instant, she saw that her life must change. She must marry Adam or, if she refused him, she must leave the house. She would not be able to stay on and care for the children if she turned down his proposal.

'Yes, a little time, please give me a little time,' she said. 'Grace isn't well, and I can't think properly about anything else at the moment.'

Adam frowned and withdrew his hand. 'Grace is unwell? Why didn't you tell me?'

'I was going to,' Lizzie said. He hadn't given her chance to speak about her concerns and now there was little point. She could hardly ask to be paid when he had asked her to be his wife. And perhaps Grace wasn't unwell, just ready to be weaned. She would know more tomorrow. 'She was fractious today,' she said, 'but she wasn't hot. Mrs Hawkins thought she might have a touch of colic. I'll know more tomorrow when I collect her.'

Her headache threatened to overwhelm her. The few sips of ale she had taken hadn't helped, and she was overcome with a great weariness and the need to be on her own. She stood up abruptly. 'I'll bid you goodnight,' she said. 'It's been a long day.'

She took her glass to the scullery and tipped away the remaining ale. Adam reached out and caught her hand as she passed on her way out of the kitchen. 'Think on it, Lizzie,' he said. 'This house, the children, children of your own. It could all be yours.'

Was there a hint of desperation in his plea? What would he do if – when – she turned him down? Who would look after the children? But she couldn't add that to her worries. She had hoped that this evening would provide a solution to them and instead they had grown.

She gave him a small smile. 'I will think – I promise.' Then she disengaged her hand and went up to her room. She longed for deep, dreamless sleep but instead she feared she would toss and turn all night, haunted by indecision. She must remain steadfast in whatever she decided, but she couldn't make a decision to suit someone else, a decision that might leave her with a lifetime of regret.

CHAPTER THIRTY-SEVEN

Lizzie hoped to find Grace restored to her usual placid self when she and Frances went to collect her the following morning. But Mrs Hawkins appeared troubled when she opened the door to them. 'She refused the bread soaked in milk,' she said. 'And she's had a difficult night. I hope she settles for you. I'll come a bit earlier, just in case.'

Her face was grey with fatigue and Lizzie's heart went out to her. She was tired, too, but for a different reason. As she had expected, she'd had a troubled night, filled with anxious dreams when she eventually drifted off. She was almost sure she didn't want to marry Adam, but was that foolish of her? She looked down at Frances and felt a surge of affection. It would be hard to leave the children. Should that alone persuade her to rethink?

As it turned out, looking after Grace gave her little time to dwell on the matter. The baby became more difficult as the morning wore on, refusing to sleep and grizzling when she wasn't outright crying. By the time Mrs Hawkins appeared, Lizzie was exhausted from walking her, and from the worry of not knowing what to do for the best.

Grace fed a little, then turned her head away. Mrs Hawkins pursed her lips. 'She's hot,' she declared. 'I think she's running a fever.'

Lizzie put her hand on the baby's forehead – she was burning. 'I thought she was just hot from all the crying,' she said, mortified. She tried to remember whether her sisters had run a fever like this, but couldn't – at least not when they were babies. It was so much easier when they were grown and could tell you what was wrong.

Mrs Hawkins was unbuttoning Grace's gown and pulled it over her head, causing vigorous protest. 'We must make sure she doesn't overheat,' she said. 'I used to wipe down my little ones with water – warm, not cold, mind – to cool them.'

Judith presented her with a clean linen cloth from the drawer and Mrs Hawkins soaked it in a bowl of warm water. Lizzie was dubious – the weather was unsettled and it wasn't particularly warm. Surely this treatment would just make Grace worse. But, to her surprise, she quietened and her eyelids drooped, snapped open, then drooped again. Within a minute, she was fast asleep.

Mrs Hawkins laid her in the makeshift bed and covered her lightly with a single blanket. 'I'll be going then,' she said.

'But won't she be hungry when she wakes?' Lizzie said, panicking at the thought of an afternoon spent pacing the floor with a wailing baby.

Mrs Hawkins shrugged. 'She might sleep awhile. She must be exhausted after last night. If she's hot again when she wakes, repeat what I just did.'

'Should we send for a doctor?' Lizzie asked.

Mrs Hawkins shook her head. 'Not unless you want to kill her. She'll do better without their tender care. A doctor will only recommend bleeding her and, in my view, she's too young for that.' She left, refusing offers of sustenance, and Lizzie sat down at the table, consumed by anxiety.

'Here, eat this soup,' Judith said. 'You look as though you barely slept last night.'

Lizzie was filled with an urge to tell her about the conversation she'd had with Adam the previous evening. Then she looked at Frances, now quietly drawing beside her, and knew she couldn't. So she bent her head over the bowl and focused instead on spooning up the hot broth, telling herself that each mouthful would be restorative.

Grace slept for a long time, Lizzie frequently getting up to check on her: she was so quiet that Lizzie worried she had stopped breathing. She feared she was neglecting Frances's lessons, so used the time to work on her reading and writing, much to the little girl's disgust.

'I don't need to do this.' She pouted, after struggling to make sense of one particular sentence in a book of Gabriel's that he had outgrown.

'Why not?' Lizzie asked.

'Because I'm going to marry a rich man and have a lot of servants and they can do everything,' came the reply.

Lizzie tried not to catch Judith's eye, for she knew she would be unable to keep a straight face.

'Well, even so, you will still need to be able to read and write,' she pointed out. 'You will receive invitations to suppers and gatherings. How will you know who they are from or when they are to be held if you can't read? And you will need to keep household accounts, or you won't know whether the tradesmen are cheating you, will you?'

She heard Judith snort behind her.

'I will have a secretary,' Frances announced.

Lizzie was silenced. Where had she come across such an idea?

She had no chance to pursue it further, for a splutter, then a wail, from Grace's bed told her that their peaceful time had passed. Judith got there first and lifted her out. 'She's hot again,' she said, and sighed.

Lizzie hurried to prepare another bowl of water to the correct temperature, and repeated the cooling-down procedure. But this time Grace wasn't placated and fought against it, arching her back and screaming. She had calmed a little by the time Mrs Hawkins arrived, to find Lizzie pacing, Grace nestled into her shoulder and a blanket lightly covering her little body.

'No better?' she asked.

Lizzie shook her head. 'Although she did sleep for a few hours.'

'I'll see if she'll feed,' Mrs Hawkins said. 'Then I'll take her, but I don't think it's good for her to be outside – the change in temperature might make her worse. It would be better for her to stay here, really.'

Lizzie, worried, regarded her. 'And would you stay, too?'

'There seems little point if she won't feed.'

Lizzie couldn't bear the thought of having to pace the floor all night, too. And if Grace wouldn't feed she would surely die. 'Please take her tonight,' she begged. 'Perhaps she will be better.'

Mrs Hawkins agreed, with some reluctance. 'But if I have another night like last night, we'll have to put an end to the arrangement. Mr Russell doesn't pay me enough to be up half the night.'

Judith, no doubt sensing Lizzie's despair, pressed a parcel of biscuits, wrapped in a striped cloth, on the wet-nurse. 'For the family,' she said. 'I dare say, with the extra work of Grace, you haven't had time to make any yourself.'

Mrs Hawkins chuckled. 'The only time they get biscuits is when my eldest, Nell, stirs herself to make them. But I thank you.' She seemed a little mollified, and Lizzie was encouraged to see that Grace was feeding, although not very enthusiastically, stopping to gaze around the room every minute or so.

Once Mrs Hawkins had left, it was time for Lizzie and Frances to fetch Gabriel. For the first time, Lizzie felt like screaming at the predictability of it all. Was this to be her life for the next few years? If she married Adam, would he agree to employ someone to take up her current role? She thought not – despite his professed fondness for her, she feared his proposal was a way to kill two birds with one stone: he would gain a wife and also have the security of his children being cared for by someone who knew them well.

CHAPTER THIRTY-EIGHT

Lizzie dreaded Adam's return from work. She didn't relish spending the evening in his company. What if he pressed her on her decision, even though he had said he was prepared to wait? So she took the initiative and the minute he stepped into the kitchen, she warned him that Grace was still unwell, and Mrs Hawkins appeared reluctant to continue caring for her if she didn't improve, at least without an increase in pay. She left out Mrs Hawkins's suggestion that Lizzie might take over – she didn't want Adam to seize on it as a way to save money and an encouragement to advance the marriage.

As she had expected, Adam frowned and objected, but then appeared to think better of it. 'Poor mite. How can I refuse her a chance at life? Hannah would never forgive me.'

Lizzie slept better that night, but when she knocked at Mrs Hawkins's door the next morning, she could tell as soon as the wet-nurse appeared, that she had had another disturbed night. She thrust Grace at Lizzie and shook her head when asked if she had fed. 'She's barely taken anything at all. If this carries on for much longer I won't have anything left to give her. Not that I'm prepared to get up through the night again.'

'I spoke to Mr Russell,' Lizzie said hastily. 'He's willing to pay a little extra to help.'

'Hmm.' Mrs Hawkins was unimpressed. 'To be honest, I'm not sure she's long for this world.'

Horrified, Lizzie glanced down at Frances. Had she understood the woman's blunt words? She settled Grace into the crook of her arm, stroking her downy hair, and felt a fierce protectiveness. No doubt Mrs Hawkins had seen a great many babies fail to thrive, hence her apparent callousness, but Lizzie was determined to do her absolute best for Grace.

'We'll see you later?' Lizzie said. It was framed as a question, but she was determined to give her no choice.

Mrs Hawkins nodded and shut the door. Lizzie began the walk home with Frances, glancing down frequently at Grace, who was quiet in her arms.

Grace remained wakeful, but peaceful, all morning. Lizzie tried to see this as a good sign, but there was something about her list-lessness that was more worrying than all the wailing of the previous day. Frances attempted to engage her interest with a rag doll, but she barely bothered to follow it with her eyes and after a while she drifted off to sleep. She was still asleep when Mrs Hawkins arrived. 'It seems a shame to wake her,' she said, 'especially after the night she had.' She accepted a bowl of soup from Judith, dipping her bread roll into it and slurping noisily. 'We all enjoyed your biscuits,' she said, taking a look around the kitchen as if to check whether more were cooling on a rack.

Judith was pleased, and cut her a slice of the pie she had just baked. Once it was eaten, Mrs Hawkins using her fingers to chase every last crumb, Lizzie suggested they wake Grace and see whether she would feed.

To everyone's surprise, she didn't object to being woken, but nei-ther would she feed, turning her head away. Lizzie began to think there must be something in the wet-nurse's milk she objected to, until Mrs Hawkins pointed out the rash forming around Grace's neck and ears. She raised the baby's gown and it was spreading across her chest too. Lizzie was filled with terror. Surely this was a bad sign.

Mrs Hawkins, however, was more sanguine. 'Probably just a result of the fever,' she said. 'She's cooler now. I think she might be on the mend. After another good sleep she ought to regain her appetite. I can give her some soothing syrup tonight if you like.'

Lizzie didn't know how to respond. If she said no, how could she be sure whether or not Mrs Hawkins had administered it? She suspected the suggestion was to ensure the wet-nurse had a good night's sleep, rather than Grace. She bit her lip and said, 'Whatever you think best.'

Mrs Hawkins left, looking satisfied, and Lizzie put Grace back to bed, where she dozed the afternoon away. Lizzie checked her anxiously at frequent intervals to see whether the rash had spread, but it appeared unchanged.

'You'll wear yourself out, fretting about that baby,' Judith scolded, although Lizzie knew she was just as worried.

'She's so helpless,' Lizzie murmured.

'You're as good as a mother to those children, particularly Grace,' Judith said, in a low voice. 'In fact, Grace won't ever know any other mother.'

Judith had her back to Lizzie as she spoke and didn't notice her stricken expression. It was true: Grace would think of Lizzie as her mother, especially if she married Adam. And although he had been distracted by Grace's illness and hadn't mentioned marriage again, she knew that couldn't last. She must make her decision, for the sake of Grace as much as for Adam. She couldn't bear the thought of Grace becoming too closely attached to her, only to lose her. At least she currently saw as much of Mrs Hawkins as she did of Lizzie: now was the time to decide.

'Is everything all right?' Judith, turning, was stilled by the sight of Lizzie's troubled face.

Once again, Lizzie longed to confide in her, but Frances was at her side, so she smiled weakly.

'I dare say by this time next week she'll have regained her strength and you'll be wondering what all the fuss was about,' Judith said.

Lizzie could only hope she was right. At that moment, it felt unlikely.

CHAPTER THIRTY-NINE

That night, Lizzie reached a decision. She would write to Mrs Bullivant at the address she had given her, to see whether she still needed a nursemaid. The thought of earning a wage, having a uniform to wear and not being on duty all day, every day, suddenly seemed very enticing. Once she had plucked up the courage to tell Adam of her decision not to marry him, she would need to move on swiftly. And hadn't Mrs Bullivant said her house was buried deep in the countryside? That would solve another pressing problem: Mrs Simmonds would never find her there.

At midday, Grace fed enthusiastically for the first time in a very long while. They were all delighted, apart from Frances who was too young to appreciate the significance. After Mrs Hawkins had left, her mood significantly improved now that her role was important once more, Lizzie announced Frances could have a free afternoon. 'No lessons,' she said. 'You can do what you like – within reason.'

It was hardly necessary to add the last bit – Frances was generally well-behaved, unlike Gabriel, who would immediately have planned something naughty. She announced she wanted to play with her dolls in her room, alone. Lizzie agreed, but told her she would be in her bedroom along the landing, if she needed her.

'You go and have a rest,' Judith said. 'I can keep an eye on Grace, although I doubt she'll wake until it's time for Mrs Hawkins to return.'

'I have a letter to write,' Lizzie said. She hesitated, unsure whether or not to tell Judith what she planned to do. Then she thought better of it: she might try to convince her to stay and Lizzie wanted to act while her determination was still strong. Also, she would need to ask Judith to get the letter to the post office for her: if she went herself she would have to take Frances, which might lead to awkward lies.

An hour later, after several attempts, which she had discarded due to unsightly blots or ill-thought-out phrasing, she had a letter she was content with. It read:

> *Dear Mrs Bullivant,*
>
> *We met when I came across your children, Christopher and Agnes, in the park near your house in Canterbury. You mentioned that you were looking for a nursemaid for them and, although I was well suited in my employment at the time, circumstances have changed and I am now thinking of moving on. I wondered whether the position was still available.*
> *Yours,*
> *Elizabeth Carey*

As she folded the paper, she had a moment of doubt. Would Mrs Bullivant suspect something was amiss, with her sudden decision to leave? Should she have explained it a little more? But how to do so? 'My employer wants to marry me now that his wife has died but I don't want that'? It raised too many questions and was better left unsaid. She could only hope that Mrs Bullivant was still in need.

Now that she had made the decision, it became desperately important to Lizzie that her request should succeed. What if Mrs Bullivant didn't reply or, worse, turned her down? Lizzie didn't think she could bear the disappointment. She kissed the letter lightly, wishing it well, then took it downstairs to ask Judith whether she could take it to the post office in the morning on the way to work.

Judith looked curiously at the address as Lizzie pressed a few coins into her hand. 'Betsanger Court,' she spelled out hesitantly. 'It sounds rather grand.'

Judith was curious to know more, Lizzie could tell, but she just said, 'I don't know, I've never seen the place.' Then, having checked that Grace was still peacefully asleep, she went back upstairs to Frances, leaving Judith to continue preparing the dinner.

That evening, Lizzie was happy to share the news with Adam that Grace finally appeared to be on the mend. 'She fed well twice today,' she said. 'Mrs Hawkins is convinced that she has recovered from whatever ailed her.'

'That is happy news indeed,' Adam said. He glanced at Frances and Gabriel, finishing up their roast fowl and potatoes. 'And soon we will have more happy news to share.'

Lizzie's blood ran cold. She should have been more careful, but her spirits had been so lifted that afternoon by Grace's recovery that she couldn't wait to reassure Adam. And now he would be pressing her for a date for their marriage. He clearly couldn't conceive of the idea that she might turn him down.

Thankfully, Gabriel and Frances appeared oblivious. They were both intent on finishing their roast dinner, which Judith had made as a special mid-week treat to celebrate Grace's improvement. Lizzie knew that, as soon as they were in bed, the topic would be raised once more.

As she had suspected, when she came downstairs after saying goodnight to the children, Adam was waiting, his usual glass of ale in hand. 'So, Lizzie, have you an answer for me? I've been a patient man but I need to know.'

Lizzie took a deep breath. She needed to play for a little more time. She had reached a decision, but she wasn't ready to share it just yet.

'Adam, I've been so worried about Grace that nothing else has filled my thoughts these past days.'

She saw by the lowering of his brow that her words hadn't been well received, so hastened to add, 'But I promise now I will think on it. Will you give me the week you first promised me for an answer?'

'I can't see what there is to think about, Lizzie.' Adam was impatient. 'It makes perfect sense. The children know and respect you – as I do. You will have far more status as a married woman than as a nursemaid. Far more than you might ever have expected, I might add.'

His last words took Lizzie's breath away. So he was prepared to marry beneath him to secure a nursemaid, for that was what she would remain, and a companion for his bed.

Before she could respond, he continued, 'I'll give you until Saturday. I want to talk to the minister on Sunday about the banns being read.'

She bit back the words she longed to let fly. Tomorrow was Wednesday. If Judith had sent the letter, would she have a reply by Saturday? If not, she would have to leave, with nowhere to go, or reluctantly submit to marrying Adam.

He saw the expression on her face, and adopted a softer tone. 'Perhaps you feel unsure now about being my wife, but it's the right thing to do. I think we will rub along well enough. And I have seen how you are with Grace. Imagine how you will feel when you have a baby of your own – our baby – to love.'

Lizzie managed a small nod. She knew marriage as a business transaction was the lot for many women, but she had no intention of being one of them. She could only hope that Mrs Bullivant was at home to receive her letter, and that she would respond favourably to Lizzie's request. Otherwise, she didn't know what she would do.

CHAPTER FORTY

O nce Lizzie had ascertained that Judith had indeed sent the
letter, she could barely contain her anxiety. Long before Mrs
Bullivant could possibly have received her missive, Lizzie began listening out for the knock on the door that might signify the delivery
of a reply. She passed Thursday and Friday in a fever of impatience,
and was hard pressed to give her full attention to Frances and Grace.

What would happen if she didn't hear from Mrs Bullivant, or
the answer was no? The sensible thing would be to do as Adam
wished and marry him. That would relieve her anxieties over the
children, but she couldn't see Adam as anything other than her
employer. Might that change with time? Lizzie was doubtful. And
he wouldn't give her time in any case. He would expect her in his
bed – the bed that had once belonged to Hannah – on the night of
the wedding.

Each day when she asked Judith whether a letter had arrived,
Judith shook her head. 'What is it that is so important?' she asked.

Lizzie's disappointment was so great she could barely reply.
'Nothing,' she mumbled.

By the time Friday came, Lizzie was in a quandary. If the letter
didn't come that afternoon, just a few hours would remain until
Adam demanded her answer. Her head throbbed. How could she
tell him she wasn't going to accept his proposal? He would be so
angry – not because she was hurting his feelings, but because she
would be thwarting his plans. Marrying Lizzie would be a neat
solution for him and any worries he might have over the care of

his children and the running of his house. Would he throw her out in a rage? She must prepare herself that night, gathering her few belongings together.

When Lizzie came down to the kitchen the following morning, fully dressed but yawning after a bad night, the house was quiet. Adam had already left but would return shortly after midday. Gabriel, unusually, had no school that Saturday so Lizzie had left him and Frances to sleep in. She was looking forward to a quiet half-hour or so to drink some tea and eat some bread and butter, before she needed to think about collecting Grace.

Judith was already in the kitchen, boiling water and slicing bread in preparation for breakfast. 'I have something for you,' she said, taking a folded letter from her apron pocket and holding it out to Lizzie. 'I met the post boy on the doorstep. Luckily I had some coins on me to give him.'

Lizzie all but snatched it from her, broke the seal and unfolded it. There was no need to wonder who could have sent it – it was the only letter she had received so far in her life. And she recognised the flowing copperplate script from the address Mrs Bullivant had written down. Her hands shook as she read and she almost dropped the letter on the floor after the first sentence but she forced herself to carry on.

Dear Miss Carey,

I regret to say the position of nursemaid has now been filled. However, Betsanger Court is always in need of competent servants so if you would be prepared to take up another post, then do come. You will need to speak to my housekeeper, Mrs Bailey, on arrival and she can allocate your duties.
Hermione Bullivant

Lizzie burst into tears. It was a mixture of elation at receiving the letter, disappointment that the position she had imagined herself in was filled, and nerves at the thought of what she must do next.

'Why, whatever is the matter?' Judith was at her side, full of concern. 'Is it bad news? Family?'

Lizzie was unable to speak. She held out the letter to Judith by way of explanation. Judith took it. Then, reddening, she passed it back. 'I can't read the hand,' she said.

Lizzie suspected that, in fact, she didn't read very well, no matter how clear the handwriting.

'You'll have to tell me what's amiss,' Judith continued. 'Sit down and I'll get you a cup of tea.'

Lizzie, realising her legs were trembling, did as she was told. Judith set a steaming cup in front of her, and joined her at the table. 'Now, what's all this about?' she asked.

Lizzie poured out her story: how she had become beholden to Mrs Simmonds over an unpaid debt; how Adam had asked her to marry him but she had no wish to; how she had sought a new position at Betsanger Court following her chance meeting with Mrs Bullivant.

'And now I have been offered something, but not what I hoped for, and I must give an answer to Adam by the end of the day so the banns can be read in church tomorrow, and I feel so bad at the thought of leaving the children with no one to care for them.' Lizzie burst into tears afresh.

Judith had been shaking her head throughout most of Lizzie's outpouring of woe. 'You are quite certain you don't want to marry him?' she asked. 'He's a decent man, and I can tell you love the children.'

Lizzie considered for a few moments. 'You are right – he is a decent man, which makes it all the harder, and I do love the children. But I don't love him and I don't want to marry him. He will be angry, I know it.'

Judith nodded slowly. 'His pride will be hurt. But it's nothing he won't recover from. And there's plenty who will be happy to step into your shoes, Lizzie, for security and the status of being a wife.'

Lizzie felt a stab of jealousy at the thought of someone new in the children's lives, particularly Grace's. Still she shook her head. 'I don't understand how or why anyone would do that.'

Judith sighed. 'You are young. In a few years you may look back on this and regret it. But if you are set on leaving you must go before Adam returns today. Write him a note and explain why. Otherwise, he will make you stay until he engages someone else to do your work.'

'Or finds someone to marry,' Lizzie said darkly.

'Either way, it could be awkward,' Judith said. She stood up and went around the table to Lizzie, crouching to give her a hug. 'I don't want to lose you. I don't like change, what with Hannah leaving us so suddenly and now you. You have been such a blessing for this house. But if it isn't the life you want for yourself, I won't try to change your mind. Go and write your note and send the children down to have breakfast. Then you will need to collect Grace. You can slip away later when Mrs Hawkins comes to feed her.'

'But what will I tell the children?' Lizzie could feel tears starting to her eyes again.

Judith considered. 'It's best to say nothing. Grace is too young to understand, of course, but Frances will be upset and cling to you, and Gabriel, well,' she shrugged, 'Gabriel has reached an age where he finds it hard to show his feelings.'

Lizzie took a deep, shuddering breath. Could she really leave them without a word? Then the thought of Frances's tears made her shut her eyes briefly. Whatever she did, it would be hard.

'Go!' Judith said. 'Write your note, but send the children down first.'

And so the routine of the morning began, but one that felt so different from any other. With everything she did, Lizzie was conscious that this was the last time she would perform this particular duty. She got the children up and dressed, with many a grumble from Gabriel, and sent them down to Judith. Then she sat at the desk in her room and wrote her letter to Adam, trying her best to express her regret in turning him down and her hopes for a happy future for him and the children. She hoped he would excuse her departure in such an abrupt manner, and explain to the children that she loved them, but she had to leave. Then she sat back and read what she had written. Would he offer an explanation to the children, finding an excuse to cover her leaving, or would his bitterness cause him to speak ill of her? She sighed. It was out of her hands. Once she had gone he could do what he liked.

She cast a swift glance around the room. She had already packed her few belongings in a bundle; she had little more than when she had arrived. Folding the fine green woollen shawl that Adam had given her for Christmas to add to it, she remembered Judith's words. Would she have cause to regret this decision in the years to come?

She wished she had a small gift she could leave for the children but there had been no time to think of it. She would send them something, she thought. She would like them to remember her fondly. Then she went downstairs, ready to chivvy them out into the sunshine to go and collect Grace. The thought of this being her last morning with them caused her bottom lip to tremble. They should do something special together, but what? She supposed a trip to the park would have to suffice. Gabriel, being at school, always missed their outings. Perhaps he was still young enough to take pleasure in them. She would soon find out, but whatever happened, she wanted them to remember this particular morning for the right reasons.

Before she joined them in the kitchen, she slipped into the sitting room, took down Hannah's work-basket and extracted a pair of fine pointed scissors, a spool of pink thread and a short length of narrow cream ribbon, tucking them into her pocket. The neglected white-work still lay, neatly folded, on top of the basket. On impulse, she ran back upstairs with the piece and added it to her bundle. Perhaps there was a gift she could offer the family after all.

Chapter Forty-One

The outing to the park was more successful than Lizzie had hoped, although her morning with the children had an unpromising start. Gabriel had complained about accompanying Lizzie and Frances to collect Grace.

'I have the day free of school and you want me to walk the same route as I do every day, when I have no need to?' he asked. 'Well, I'm not coming. I'm old enough to stay here. Judith is in the house.'

Lizzie argued with him, to no avail, until Judith stepped in.

'You can stay here until Lizzie gets back, Gabriel, but I'm too busy to be giving you attention. After that, you do as she tells you.'

Gabriel glowered. He'd won a victory, but not a straightforward one. He recovered his mood, though, when Lizzie and Frances returned with Grace. Gabriel was a stranger to her during the week, since he was at school during the hours she was at New Street. She usually saw him only on Sundays, when he was a great novelty to her. Today she kicked and squealed in delight at the sight of him and Gabriel couldn't help but smile.

'We're all going to the park,' Lizzie declared, taking advantage of his good humour. 'Just for an hour or two. It's lovely weather.'

Surprisingly, Gabriel didn't demur. He walked at her side, tickling Grace's toes every now and then so that she squirmed and shrieked with laughter. When they reached the park and laid Grace on the grass in the usual shady spot, he sat with her, brushing her nose with a blade of grass that she tried to snatch from him, going cross-eyed with the effort.

'Why don't you run around a bit with Frances?' Lizzie suggested, after a quarter of an hour. Frances, disconsolate, was a little distance away, kicking the grass and glancing over at them every now and then. To her surprise once more, Gabriel got to his feet and went over to his sister. They had a brief conversation, then Lizzie saw Gabriel cover his eyes while Frances ran swiftly to a clump of shrubbery to hide. Lizzie was tempted to call to her to be careful of her dress, then thought better of it. Let them enjoy themselves.

She slipped the scissors and thread from her pocket. Then, glancing across the grass to make sure the children weren't watching, she snipped a fine, curling lock of Grace's soft baby hair. She bound the cut end quickly with a length of pink thread, tied the cream ribbon around it, then slipped the scissors, thread and lock of hair into her pocket just as Frances arrived, panting, at her side. She would write Grace's name, and the date, on the ribbon when they went home, so that she would always have a memory of this day.

'I can't find him,' Frances wailed. 'I've looked everywhere.'

Lizzie stood up and gazed around the park. A tiny movement caught her eye: Gabriel was peeping at them from behind the trunk of the largest tree in the park, set back against the railings.

'Try once more,' she suggested. 'Look around the edge of the park, near where Agnes and Christopher live.'

It gave her a little thrill to mention their names. Was it possible that she might be in the same house as them later that day? The thrill gave way to panic. She had given no thought as to how she was to get there. Mrs Bullivant had said they lived in the middle of the countryside, but had given no directions. Lizzie had the address – Betsanger Court, Northbourne – and nothing else, not even a street name.

Suddenly, overcome with nerves, she wanted to get back to New Street. She would have to be on her way before Adam returned. But she forced herself to watch the children play for another half an hour before suggesting it was time to return.

'Perhaps Judith has been baking while we were out,' she said. 'Or making lemonade.'

The children, who had been grumbling, brightened at the prospect. Lizzie took a last look around the park. Would she ever see it again? Then she hoisted Grace up to her shoulder, so she could take a good look around as they walked back. She listened to Frances and Gabriel's chatter. He was so much happier when he wasn't in school, she thought, with a pang. What happened there to make him so surly? She supposed she would never know.

As they walked through the door of the house on New Street, the delicious aroma of baking filled their noses.

'Biscuits!' Gabriel declared, and hurried for the kitchen.

'Wash your hands – both of you,' Lizzie called after them, following at a more leisurely pace. She felt a rush of gratitude towards Judith, who was doing everything she could to make this last morning, and her departure, easier.

In the kitchen, Judith had just taken the biscuits from the oven and was batting Gabriel's hand away.

'They're too hot to eat,' she scolded. 'Do as Lizzie said and wash your hands. I'll pour you a drink. You look hot, the pair of you.'

'They've been running around the park,' Lizzie said, as she deposited Grace in her makeshift bed. It really was too small, she decided – it was beginning to restrict her movements. It was time for her to move to the crib.

While the children were in the scullery, washing their hands, Judith spoke to Lizzie in a low voice. 'Take money from the house-keeping pot for your journey,' she said. Seeing Lizzie's hesitation, she went over and seized the pot, removing the lid. 'Quickly,' she urged. 'I know Mr Russell hasn't seen fit to pay you since Hannah died. It's not stealing – it's hardly even what you are due.'

She was right. Lizzie dipped her hand into the pot and extracted several coins, slipping them into her pocket. Judith replaced the jar just as the children came back into the room. Frances seemed to have spilled a quantity of water down the front of her dress.

'Gabriel splashed me,' she said, giggling, on seeing Lizzie's expression.

Lizzie decided to overlook this, for the sake of harmony.

Judith flapped a linen cloth over the biscuits, then tested one with her finger. 'There, much cooler,' she said, sliding several onto a plate and setting it in the middle of the table. 'Now, don't eat them all. Save one for Lizzie – and I'm expecting Mrs Hawkins any minute now.'

On cue, there was a knock at the front door. Heart beating fast, Lizzie went to open it. Mrs Hawkins's arrival meant that it was almost time for her to depart. Her smile, as she stood back to let Mrs Hawkins enter, was tremulous. Had she made the right decision? She shook off the doubt: it was too late to change her mind now.

Chapter Forty-Two

Fearful of meeting Adam on his way home, Lizzie hurried down New Street, her shoulders shaking with sobs she was trying to suppress. Once Mrs Hawkins was settled and feeding Grace in the kitchen, she had slipped upstairs to collect her bundle, leaving the note for Adam to find on the desk in her room. Then she had gone downstairs and listened outside the kitchen door. Mrs Hawkins was telling Judith about something that had happened in their street the previous night. Frances and Gabriel were obviously listening because she heard them laughing.

She had longed to go in and say her goodbyes – it seemed so wrong to leave them all without a word – but she knew she mustn't. She couldn't change the happy mood in the kitchen just to satisfy a selfish wish and, in any case, Adam could return at any moment.

She was quietly opening the front door when she heard footsteps behind her and turned to find Judith, a small cloth-wrapped parcel in her hands.

'Some food for you,' she said, then flung her arms around her and gave her a hug. 'Now, on you go. And may luck go with you.' Then she gave her a gentle push out of the door and shut it behind her.

So Lizzie had found herself out on the street, with no clear plan as to how she was to reach Betsanger Court. It seemed unlikely that it would be on a stage-coach route, but she supposed she should ask at the coaching inn first. She hadn't been near it since her arrival in Canterbury, over a year ago now, and when she found herself standing in the yard, the memory of how helpless she had felt flooded back to her. She didn't know then where she was going, and it was little different today.

At least it is daytime, and not raining, she told herself, as she looked around for someone she could ask. The young ostlers were all busy, leading away the horses from a recently arrived coach, and did not look as though they would welcome being disturbed. In any case, Lizzie was nervous of going near the horses, which were flecked with sweat, tossing their heads and whinnying as they were coaxed from the traces. An elderly man was sitting on a wooden bench in the yard, smoking a pipe and watching the proceedings. Lizzie went over to him.

'Excuse me,' she said. 'I need to get to Northbourne today. Do you know whether I might do that from here?'

'Northbourne.' The man scratched his chin, then turned to look at her. 'Where be that, then?'

Lizzie was taken aback. 'I don't know,' she admitted.

The man puffed on his pipe. 'See, if it's out Whitstable way, you leave through West Gate. If it be out on the London road you want the Postern Gate. From here, you go out towards Castle Bay and Dover.'

'It's in the countryside, that's all I know,' Lizzie said. She was on the verge of tears once more. Would she have to walk all around Canterbury, trying to find how to reach this place?

'Ah.' The man seized on this bit of information. 'Then the stage coach is no use to you – it only stops in the towns. Try asking at the inn along the road – that's where the wagons and carts stop. They come and go from all over. I'll be bound someone there will know the place.' Pleased with himself, he returned to sucking his pipe.

Lizzie thanked him and hurried away. The inn, the King's Arms, was situated at the corner of the cattle market, which was all but closed now after a busy morning. The yard was crammed with wagons and carts belonging to visitors to the market. She couldn't see anyone there and she didn't want to walk among the horses, looking for someone to ask, so she would have to go inside.

Taking a deep breath, she opened the door and stepped straight into the bar. It was crowded and, once her eyes had become accustomed to the gloom after the bright daylight outside, she could see she was the only woman in there, apart from the barmaid. Lizzie pushed her way through the crowd, avoiding the men's eyes and trying to ignore the coarse comments she heard. Her cheeks were hot and pink by the time she reached the counter.

The barmaid looked at her curiously. 'What can I get you?'

Lizzie didn't really want anything but felt obliged to order a cordial. As the barmaid handed it over she said, 'I need to get to a place called Northbourne. Have you heard of it? Would any of the carts or wagons leave here to go there?'

The barmaid shrugged. Lizzie, crushed, took a sip of her drink.

'Anyone here bound for Northbourne? Or know where it is?' The barmaid's voice was so loud that the room fell silent. Lizzie, startled, slopped drink from her glass.

There was a hush for what seemed like a very long time before a voice piped up, 'Aye, I know. Who's asking?'

'Lady here needs to get there.' The barmaid jerked her head in Lizzie's direction. The man who had spoken started to push his way through to the bar, accompanied by ribald laughter from some of the others.

'Now then,' he said, when he reached Lizzie's side. 'Northbourne, is it?'

'Betsanger Court,' Lizzie said. 'Do you know it?'

The man's eyebrows rose. 'Aye, I've been past it.'

'Are you going that way today?' Lizzie asked eagerly.

The man shook his head. 'No.'

Lizzie's heart sank. Then she gathered herself. 'But this is the right place for the Northbourne road?'

The man nodded. 'But there's not many carts go out that way. 'Tis a small place, just a few houses.'

Lizzie tried hard to get herself under control. Since she had left the house in New Street, and the children, without a word, she hadn't been far from tears.

'Don't upset yourself.' The man spoke kindly. 'I'm only bound halfway there, but if we leave now I'll take you where you need to go.'

Lizzie could hardly believe her ears. 'You will?' Her face was wreathed in smiles. 'I have money. I can make it worth your while.'

She made to put down her bundle and retrieve the coins from her pocket. The man put out his hand to stop her.

'Don't go showing money in this place. Thieves and ruffians, the lot of them.' He laughed as he said it, but added, 'Not a fit place for a young woman. I'd not want a daughter of mine to step over this threshold. Now, finish your drink and we'll be on our way.'

Lizzie drained her glass and handed it back to the barmaid. 'Thank you for your help,' she said.

The barmaid nodded, then turned back to serving customers.

'John,' Lizzie's saviour introduced himself.

'I'm Lizzie,' she replied, and followed him as he pushed his way through the crowd, whose remarks had become even coarser.

Outside, she took a deep breath.

'All right?' John asked.

Lizzie nodded, although she was shaking.

John's cart was quite close to the inn's entrance and required only a small amount of manoeuvring before it was out on the road. Lizzie climbed up and sat beside him. Then, with a shake of the reins, they were on their way, leaving behind the broad stretch of the cattle market.

Lizzie turned back to watch the town recede into the distance, the great tower of the cathedral visible long after the rest had faded from view. What had Adam said to the children about her absence? Were they upset? Had Frances cried? She wished now she had left a letter for the children, too, for him to read to them. But would he have done so, or would he have torn it up and thrust the fragments into the fire of the kitchen range?

PART TWO

JUNE — OCTOBER 1829

CHAPTER ONE

As the cart moved further from the town and deeper into the countryside, Lizzie's anxiety eased. She opened the cloth parcel and discovered Judith had packed bread, cheese and ham, as well as a couple of biscuits. Lizzie had little appetite, but John was more than happy to help out and soon the cloth contained nothing apart from a few crumbs.

John was a man of few words and, once the food was finished, most of their journey was conducted in silence. Lizzie didn't mind: it was a companionable silence rather than an awkward one. The cart passed along narrow country lanes lined with cow parsley and campion, with just the occasional cottage beside the road. Every now and then Lizzie glimpsed a church in the distance, signifying a village nearby, but John clearly preferred the solitude of his route. The air was filled with the fresh scent of greenery, and it struck Lizzie that she had become used to the odours of the city – horse manure and worse on the streets; wood smoke, winter and summer, especially in the evenings; roasting meat; the dank smells that rose from the river. Occasionally, she glimpsed distant figures at work in the fields and now and then a dog came from nowhere and began to chase the cart in a half-hearted way.

Lizzie tried to rouse herself from the stupor she had sunk into to ask John where he was originally bound and to apologise for taking him out of his way. But he seemed content to drive the cart through the late-afternoon sunshine, occasionally whistling a refrain she half recognised from the streets of Canterbury. She was just summoning the strength to ask him what he knew of Betsanger Court and its inhabitants when he drew the cart to a halt alongside a bank of trees.

'Here we are,' he said.

Lizzie looked around. There was no sign of a house.

'Just up there,' John said, pointing. Lizzie followed his finger and saw a narrow drive, just wide enough for a carriage, cut through the trees. The exposed earth looked bright and raw against the grass. 'I can't take you any further,' he said, without explanation, 'but it's not far.'

Lizzie gathered up her belongings and began to climb down, feeling unaccountably tearful once more. She could have wished the cart journey to go on for ever: the rolling of the wheels through the tranquil countryside had had a calming effect on her. Now, she must face up to what lay ahead, and the consequences of her decision.

'You look after yourself now, Miss Lizzie,' John said.

Lizzie remembered her manners. 'I can't thank you enough for bringing me here. I don't know how I would have found it otherwise.' She gazed around helplessly. Mrs Bullivant had spoken the truth: the house was definitely remote.

She took her bundle in one hand and tried to extract a few coins from her pocket with the other.

'Nay,' John protested. 'I don't want your money – I ate nearly all your food and that's enough payment for me. Now on you go, and don't worry. And may luck go with you.'

Lizzie gave him a tremulous smile of thanks, and walked ahead of the cart to turn into the driveway he had pointed out. As she followed it through the trees, she heard the rumble of wheels behind and her heart lifted. Had he decided to accompany her after all? She turned to see, but he was just manoeuvring to turn and go back the way they had come. She raised her hand in farewell and John tipped his hat to her. Then she squared her shoulders and set off in search of the house.

John was right: it wasn't far. The driveway curved round, giving a fine view of parkland surrounded by trees, and all at once the house

172

was visible. Lizzie stopped, taken aback. The name had led her to expect a grand old property. Instead, she found herself looking at a square villa, built in pale brick so new it shone in the landscape. It appeared perfectly symmetrical, with windows at either side of the stately porch and equal sized windows in a row on the first floor.

Conscious that she might be observed, Lizzie set off once more. There must be a door at the back for the servants, she decided. She couldn't believe she was expected to approach the front. It was only as she came abreast of the house that she saw a slightly lower building attached at the right, set back from the main frontage. Instinct told her this was where she must go. She found an ordinary door, without pillars or a portico, but with a bell pull. As Lizzie hauled on it and heard the jangling within, her heart began to beat faster. A minute passed and she was just contemplating pulling it again, when the door swung open. A harassed-looking girl of a similar age stood there.

'Yes?' she said.

'I'm Lizzie – Elizabeth Carey. I've come about a position. I'm to speak with Mrs Bailey.'

The girl frowned. 'What position?'

'I don't know,' Lizzie admitted. 'I was originally asked to be nursemaid but that position is filled. Mrs Bullivant asked me to speak to Mrs Bailey when I arrived.'

The girl was glaring at her and Lizzie began to feel uncomfortable. 'I'm the nursemaid,' the girl said.

'Is Mrs Bailey here?' Lizzie pressed. The girl seemed disinclined to allow her to enter. 'I have a letter from Mrs Bullivant.'

'You'd better come in, then.' The girl stood aside and Lizzie stepped into the narrow hall, blinking to adjust her vision to the gloom after the brightness outside.

'This way.' The girl led her down a passage to the left and knocked on a door halfway along.

'Yes?' came a voice from within.

The girl opened the door, stuck her head around it and said,

'Someone to see you, Mrs Bailey.' Then she hurried off, leaving Lizzie to enter the room.

Mrs Bailey was younger than Lizzie had expected. She judged her to be in her late twenties, neatly dressed in a dark skirt and blouse, a brooch at her throat, her glossy brown hair swept up on her head. She was sitting behind a desk, a ledger open in front of her.

'I'm Elizabeth Carey,' Lizzie said. 'I have a letter from Mrs Bullivant about employment.' She held it out and Mrs Bailey took it and studied it.

'Mrs Bullivant didn't mention this to me.' She handed the letter back to Lizzie, who stood there, at a loss. Was she about to be sent away?

Mrs Bailey looked her up and down. 'What is your experience, Miss Carey?'

'I've mainly looked after children,' Lizzie said, adding, 'and a baby. But I can mend and sew, and cook.'

'And do housework?' Mrs Bailey asked.

Lizzie hesitated. Did it count that she had cleaned up after her siblings, and the Russell children? She felt it was unlikely to amount to the same thing as dusting and polishing the fine furniture and porcelain that undoubtedly filled the rooms of Betsanger Court.

'No matter.' Mrs Bailey waved an impatient hand. 'I expect you can be trained. Mrs Bullivant is correct to say we need competent servants.'

Lizzie felt it pained her to agree with her employer.

'I will add your details to the servants' ledger and then I will call Susannah to take you to the room you will share. I hope you have a dress, or a blouse and skirt you can wear. Something a little smarter, perhaps.' Mrs Bailey cast a critical eye over Lizzie, who blushed, knowing herself to be shabby. 'If not, we can find you something.

'Now, Elizabeth Carey, you said?' The housekeeper was poised to write in a ledger she had taken from the shelf. 'And your address?' She stared at Lizzie in an unsettling way.

Lizzie didn't know how to answer. She had now run away from two homes – was she prepared to give either address to Mrs Bailey?

'Fifteen Mercery Lane, Canterbury.' She stumbled over the lie. From the sharp look the housekeeper gave her, she sensed disbelief, but Mrs Bailey didn't challenge her and wrote it down.

'Wait here and I will fetch Susannah.' Mrs Bailey rose from her chair and Lizzie was struck at once by her elegance and fine figure. While she was out of the room, Lizzie gazed around, not really taking in her surroundings.

Mrs Bailey returned, a slender blonde girl in tow. 'This is Miss Susannah Griffiths,' she said. 'I will leave you to her care now. I will see you both in an hour, at supper. And we will discuss your duties, Miss Carey.'

Lizzie followed Susannah along the passage, catching a brief glimpse of the kitchen as they passed. Then they climbed two sets of stairs to the attic bedrooms, Lizzie's apprehension growing with every step. Her experience so far hadn't prepared her for anything like this. There would be a lot to learn.

CHAPTER TWO

Two beds were set side by side in Susannah's room, with a narrow gap between them, just large enough to squeeze in a chest of drawers.

'I've taken the top two,' Susannah said, pointing at the drawers. 'The bottom one is deeper, but it doesn't look as though you have much, anyway.' She cast her eyes over Lizzie's bundle as she spoke. 'Just a warning: I once caught Mrs Bailey in here, having a good look through everything. If you have something you want to keep from prying eyes, I can show you a hiding place.'

Lizzie shook her head.

'Suit yourself. Use the pegs on the wall to hang dresses.'

She stood by expectantly. Lizzie was reluctant to unpack her few belongings in front of her, but undid her bundle, shook out the rolled-up skirts and blouses and placed them in the drawer, then hung her one dress from the peg. Susannah made space on the drawer top for Lizzie's hairbrush, and the small prayer book she had brought with her from New Street.

'Are you going to change?' Susannah looked doubtfully at the clothes in the still-open drawer.

Lizzie coloured. 'I think I'll keep on what I have. Mrs Bailey said something might be found for me to wear.'

Susannah laughed. 'It might. But I think you'll have to alter something to fit. You're on the small side. Now, quickly back down-stairs. We might just catch the end of tea.'

Lizzie followed her out of the room, conscious all at once of

Susannah's height. Her blonde hair was tucked neatly under her cap, a crisp white apron tied tightly around her slender waist. Lizzie could see she would have to work hard on her own appearance to measure up.

Tea was already under way when Susannah and Lizzie arrived at the big table set in a side room off the kitchen. They slid into two empty chairs and Susannah reached for the nearest teapot, filling Lizzie's cup and her own, then offering the bread-and-butter plate.

'Go on, take another,' she urged Lizzie, who had taken a slice. 'It will be at least three hours before you'll eat again.'

Lizzie looked around the table, which had places for far more people than were seated. Four women and three men were deep in conversation at one end and, once they had glanced up at Susannah and Lizzie's arrival, they paid no further heed to them.

'Will you tell me who everyone is?' Lizzie whispered to Susannah. They might not be interested in her but she was curious to know about them.

'Well, that's Cook at the head of the table,' Susannah said. Lizzie had guessed as much from her rolled-up sleeves and the traces of flour on her dark dress, despite her apron. 'Amy is sitting beside her, and next to her is Ann. They do the light housework upstairs. The kitchen maid, Alice, helps Cook.'

'I don't see Mrs Bailey,' Lizzie said. 'Or the girl who let me in.'

'Mrs Bailey takes tea in her room,' Susannah said. 'And I expect it was Hester who let you in.' She made a face. 'She likes to take tea in the nursery, even when the children aren't here. Fancies herself a cut above the rest of us.'

'Where is Mrs Bullivant, and the children?'

'She's in London with Mr Bullivant,' Susannah said. 'I don't know why she hasn't left the children here, or taken Hester with her. Hester has only just become nursemaid. Mrs Bailey suggested her when she couldn't find anyone else to come and work here. I don't think Mrs Bullivant was very happy. She would have preferred to have a choice.'

Lizzie thought back to her chance meeting with Mrs Bullivant and the children in the park. If only she had seized the opportunity when it was offered to her, she could have filled that post. 'Does the family spend much time here?' she ventured.

'I expect Mrs Bullivant will be back in a day or two,' Susannah said. 'She won't stay long. There will be shopping to do, or a play to see, in Canterbury or back in London.'

'And Mr Bullivant?' Lizzie asked.

Susannah laughed. 'We might see him twice a year. When he last came, he brought half the servants from the London house. Caused a commotion – there wasn't really room for them all, and Cook resented the London woman interfering in her kitchen. But there was a lot more work, what with the guests and parties. I suppose that's why he built this place – for entertaining.'

The servants at the top of the table were setting down their cups and standing up.

'Quickly, finish up,' Susannah urged.

She turned as one of the men called down to them, 'Susan, aren't you going to introduce us?'

'This is Lizzie,' Susannah said. 'She's going to be a housemaid alongside me.'

Lizzie, while wondering at Susannah being addressed as Susan, couldn't help staring at the man who had spoken. He was a few years older than she was, his brown hair curling around his collar and framing his lightly tanned face. The sleeves of his white shirt were rolled up and he wore a leather waistcoat. Lizzie guessed that he worked outside and his next words confirmed it.

'Well, since Susan doesn't see fit to introduce us, I'll do it myself. I'm Joe,' he said. 'I look after the horses and drive the carriage when the usual coachman is away. And this is Samuel, the head gardener, and Abraham, his assistant.' He indicated the men to his left and right, but Lizzie barely registered them. She was so drawn to Joe she could barely take her eyes off him.

He gave her a broad smile, which made her blush, and said,

'Welcome to Betsanger Court, Lizzie. I hope you'll be happy here. And stay a bit longer than most of the staff.' With that, he took his cup and plate to the scullery, following Samuel and Abraham.

Lizzie noticed that none of the women paid her any attention. She turned to Susannah. 'Susan?' she enquired.

Her fellow housemaid sighed. 'Yes. Only Mrs Bailey calls me Susannah. We like plainer names down here.' She picked up her cup and plate. 'I'd better make a start on showing you what to do. Mrs Bailey joins us at dinner and she'll want a full report.'

Chapter Three

It didn't take Lizzie long to discover that the life of a general housemaid was much harder than anything she had yet done. Once tea was over, Susan took her to the scullery to show her where to find the things she would need for her cleaning duties the next day.

'While the family are away, we get up at six and make a start on cleaning out the grates and laying the fires, even in the rooms that aren't being used. Mrs Bailey likes them to be kept ready at all times. When the family are here, you'll need to set water to heat on the range so Ann and Amy can take it up to their rooms. Then there's time for a cup of tea before bringing up the cold food for breakfast.' Susan had led the way to the dining room as she spoke, and pointed at the large polished table in the centre of the room.

'The breads, preserves and butter go in the centre here. When the family come down, hot food goes on the sideboard. It's usually just Mrs Bullivant, though, and she doesn't eat a great deal in the morning. The children take their breakfast in the nursery and one of us will have to carry it up to them.' Susan looked Lizzie up and down. 'Mrs Bullivant won't like to see you serving dressed like this. We'll have to hope Mrs Bailey has found you something to wear.'

Standing in the dining room, Lizzie felt even shabbier than she had in the housekeeper's room. It was a light-filled space, painted in pale shades. Even the furniture was pale wood. Lizzie supposed it must all have come from London, and Susan's next words confirmed it.

'Mrs Bullivant has had the place decorated to suit herself. I'm not sure it is to Mr Bullivant's taste. He's a big, bluff man, the sort you might imagine sitting with his dogs by the fire after a day's shooting. There hasn't been a shoot yet, but I suppose there might be.'

'What does he do?' Lizzie looked around the walls, hoping for a portrait of the sort of man Susan described, but they displayed only small flower paintings.

'He's in the tea trade, I think. Or, at least, he has ships bringing goods here from around the world.' Susan was vague. Lizzie got the impression she wasn't much interested.

She ushered Lizzie upstairs to show her the bedrooms – just four, but large. Two overlooked the lawn at the front, the others the back where Lizzie could see that a garden was being constructed. They were fresh and bright, too, with painted furniture and pale flower-patterned curtains at the windows. Susan was right: Mrs Bullivant had decorated the house to her own taste.

'You won't have much to do with these rooms, other than sweeping the floors and cleaning the grates. Oh, and emptying chamber pots when guests are here.' Susan wrinkled her nose. 'Now I'll show you the nursery.'

She led the way to a door at the side of the main staircase, which opened into a corridor. Susan knocked at the door at the end, then opened it.

'The nursery,' she said, nodding at Hester, who was sitting by the fire with some needlework.

Hester frowned. 'What do you want?' she asked.

'I'm showing Lizzie around,' Susan said. 'She's going to be working alongside me as a housemaid.' She turned to Lizzie. 'One of us will make up the fire here each morning, and bring up the water for washing. The children have their meals served here.'

Lizzie took in the two small beds, coverlets neatly folded back, the table in the window, the shelves holding a few books, a teddy bear and a doll, and a small collection of lead soldiers. She could imagine Christopher and Agnes here, playing on the rug by the fire. She saw the bed behind the door, a narrow single.

'You sleep in here with the children?' she asked.

Hester nodded, lips pursed. 'Yes, Mrs Bullivant insists. There's a perfectly good bedroom next door and I would hear them call out. But she won't have it, so I have to go to bed at the same time as they do. I've asked Mrs Bailey to persuade her to change her mind.'

Susan ushered Lizzie out and shut the door. 'Never happy, that one,' she said, not bothering to lower her voice. 'Gets one of the best jobs in the house and wants to alter things to suit herself. Well, good luck to her. If Mrs Bullivant suspects she isn't looking after those children properly, she'll be out of here.'

Lizzie listened with interest. Could a position as nursemaid open up for her after all? She had no time to dwell on it for Susan listed all the jobs that must be done before dinner.

'We need to check all the fires – I noticed one or two were burning low. I'll show you where to get the wood.'

Lizzie followed Susan out of a back door in the servants' area, and along a short passage, with walls on either side but open to the sky. It led into a cobbled yard, lined by low buildings with divided doors along one edge, which Lizzie took to be stables. On the opposite side, pitchforks and spades were propped against a wheelbarrow, and whistling could be heard from the open door of a wooden lean-to.

Susan pointed to the row of stables. 'The firewood is stored in the archway at the end, the one with no door. You'll find a basket there – take as much as you can carry, then come back for more. I'll see you in the kitchen.'

Susan turned on her heel and was gone, leaving Lizzie standing. She looked around to see whether anyone else was about, then went to the wood store and began to load the wicker basket she found there. She was just testing its weight, considering whether she could manage to carry it the short distance back to the house, when the light coming in from the doorway was blocked by a figure.

Lizzie couldn't see who it was, their face cast into shadow.

Nervous, heart pounding, she turned to face them, holding up the basket in front of her, like a shield.

'Here, why don't you let me carry that?' The man stepped forward and Lizzie saw at once it was Joe.

'I can manage,' she protested.

'I'm sure you can,' Joe said comfortably, 'but I'm about done with my jobs for the day and it will give me an excuse to talk to you.'

Lizzie blushed furiously, rueing her pale skin, which betrayed her so easily. She hoped the gloom of the wood store hid her reaction. She let Joe take the basket, following him back out into the sunlight. She didn't know what to make of it – he had barely spoken more than three sentences to her since he had introduced himself, but his very presence cast her into confusion. Even her legs felt weak as she followed him across the yard.

CHAPTER FOUR

When Lizzie climbed into bed that night, she was exhausted. She would surely sleep as soon as her head touched the pillow. But thoughts whirled around her brain. Was it really just that morning she had been in the kitchen with the family in Canterbury, the offer – or threat – of marriage hanging over her? And now here she was, tucked away in the attic bedroom of a house in the middle of nowhere, faced with starting out all over again.

She ran over everything that had happened after Susan had given her the tour of the house and explained her duties. Joe had helped her bring three loads of firewood back to the scullery, chatting easily all the way, while she had remained all but dumb. She had found herself staring as his strong arms lifted the logs as though they weighed nothing, then blushing again as she realised his hazel eyes were fixed on her as he talked.

After that, they had been called to dinner. Lizzie had sat beside Susan lower down the table, Joe in his place near the top.

Mrs Bailey had appeared, looking troubled. She had seated herself at the head of the table, displacing Cook to the side, and without preamble had announced, 'Mrs Bullivant has sent word that she will be returning from London tomorrow, bringing friends with her to stay for a few days. She would like them to see the house at its very best.' She paused to look around the table, then addressed Samuel. 'Mr Briggs, tomorrow morning you will cut flowers from the kitchen garden so they can be placed in all the rooms. Mrs Hammond, we will consult on the menus this evening so that Mr

Powell can be despatched to place our order with the butcher.' Here Joe nodded.

'Miss Griffiths and Miss Carey, I expect to see the house sparkling by the time the party arrives.' Next, she had turned to Ann and Amy, the upstairs maids, 'Miss Brooke and Miss West, you will have extra duties unless the visitors arrive with their own maids. You must arrange the flowers in the bedrooms and, indeed, in all the rooms.'

She had stood up abruptly, saying, 'I will take dinner in my room,' causing Alice to leap to her feet and go in search of a tray to carry her food through to her. Mrs Bailey had stopped at the door and turned back. 'Miss Carey, come to my room after you have eaten.'

Everyone looked at Lizzie, causing her to blush yet again. Fear gripped her that Mrs Bailey had seen her talking with Joe and was going to dismiss her.

'It will be about your uniform, I expect,' Susan had said, helping herself to potatoes from the tureen then passing it to Lizzie.

Relieved, Lizzie had turned her attention to the food on her plate, a delicious and aromatic stew rich with gravy. Despite her hunger, she struggled to finish it, her stomach cramping with anxiety at the thought of what was to come the following day. Would she be able to fulfil the duties expected of her?

She had tried to talk about that further with Susan as they had climbed into bed. 'Mrs Bailey seemed worried about the visitors,' she began.

'She's always like that,' Susan interrupted her with a yawn. 'The house already looks perfect. Don't worry – Cook will have the worst of it. I expect they'll have to send out to the village for extra help.'

Lizzie was curious about Susan's background. She was no older than Lizzie but clearly very competent in her duties. 'Have you always worked in service?' she ventured.

'Yes.' Susan seemed surprised at the question. 'Since I was nine or ten. I started in the kitchen as scullery maid, doing all the jobs nobody else would do, then worked my way up to kitchen maid. When a position came free above stairs I talked my way into it. I've got my sights set on a job like Ann's or Amy's.' She yawned again. 'I think everyone here has always worked in service, except maybe Joe. And Mrs Bailey.'

Lizzie wanted to ask her more about Joe but couldn't think how to do so without laying herself open to teasing. Before she had formulated a plan, Susan's regular breathing told her she was asleep. With a sigh, Lizzie turned to face the wall. The dark shape of her dress for the next day hung from the peg on the wall. Mrs Bailey, spurred on by the arrival of important guests, had found her something to wear.

'I remembered we had set this aside,' she had said, indicating a black dress, folded on her desk. 'One of the maids left it behind when she departed in a hurry. It no longer fitted her . . .' She trailed off, then gathered herself. 'Her figure wasn't dissimilar to yours, when she arrived, so it should fit you without alteration.'

'Did she gain weight while she was here?' Lizzie was puzzled.

'In a manner of speaking.' Mrs Bailey was brisk. 'Now, I have much to do. I will be watching you and expecting the best from you over the next few days, Miss Carey.'

Lizzie had left her and taken the dress back to her room to try on. It fitted her perfectly. What had happened to the girl it had belonged to? Mrs Bailey had been quite reticent on the subject.

Susan had come in then, and offered to lend her an apron and cap for the morning.

'Do you know anything about the girl this dress once belonged to?' Lizzie asked.

Susan shrugged. 'I don't know. What was her name?'

'Mrs Bailey didn't say. Just that it didn't fit her any more. She'd put on weight.'

Susan laughed. 'Indeed she had, if it's who I think it is. Only she wasn't getting fat.'

Lizzie frowned. 'Then what was the matter?'

'She was having a baby, you silly goose. Don't you know anything?' Susan was laughing at her expression. 'She was dismissed as soon as Mrs Bullivant realised.'

'But who – how?' Lizzie looked doubtfully at the dress, as if the same fate might befall her if she wore it.

Susan shrugged again. 'Someone in the house.'

Lizzie thought rapidly. Samuel and Abraham were surely too old. That just left Joe. The thought put a shard of ice in her heart. His easy manner was far too appealing – she must be on her guard against him. She couldn't allow such a fate to befall her.

This resolution now joined the thoughts chasing each other around Lizzie's head and keeping her from sleep. Betsanger Court was a strange, cloistered world, with its own rules, which she must learn. How would she ever grasp what was expected of her, when it all seemed so strange? She was relieved to have left her problems with Mrs Simmonds and Adam far behind her but it seemed she must tread carefully here, if she was to keep her place. Would she ever have a life in which she felt at ease, content – and safe? Lizzie thought of her sister, Nell, and her marriage to Thomas. Why couldn't she have followed such a straightforward path herself?

CHAPTER FIVE

Lizzie felt a hand on her shoulder and a voice broke into her dreams. 'Wake up!'

'It's too early, Frances,' Lizzie mumbled. 'Go back to bed.' Then, as sleep receded, she thought she must get up and return her charge to her room. She opened her eyes and was confused to see someone staring down at her who most definitely wasn't Frances. Gradually, it came to her. She wasn't in New Street with the Russell family, she was in Betsanger Court and she was a maid-of-all-work now.

'Who's Frances?' Susan enquired. Then, without waiting for an answer, she said, 'Get up or you'll be late. Mrs Bailey is going to be watching us like a hawk today.'

Lizzie, still groggy from her restless night, saw that Susan, already dressed, was pinning her blonde hair under her cap. It took all Lizzie's resolve to throw back the covers, swing her legs from the bed and go over to the washstand to splash her face with cold water. Gasping, she patted it dry with the linen towel, then took her new dress down from its peg. Shy, she turned her back on Susan, pulled her nightgown over her head and quickly replaced it with her shift and stays, then the dress. She fumbled with the buttons in her haste to be ready; she needed to follow Susan closely or she knew she would forget everything she had been told the previous day.

As she pinned her cap in place, Susan cast a critical eye over her. 'You'll do,' she said. 'Now, follow me.'

Lizzie discovered there was no time for tea in the kitchen, where Cook and Alice were already hard at work.

'Tea and bread and butter at eight,' Susan said firmly. 'We have to clean all the grates, lay the fires and light them before then.' She led Lizzie into the scullery and pointed out the ash bucket, then showed her where to collect everything she would need for the job: a lidded pail to bring the ashes and cinders downstairs, a small brush and dustpan, the kindling to start the fires.

'The logs are already upstairs in the baskets,' Susan said, 'and you'll find the tinder boxes on each mantelpiece. Watch out for cinders that are still hot. And don't get smuts on your apron, or your face, or you'll hear what Mrs Bailey has to say about it.'

She saw the uncertainty on Lizzie's face and relented. 'Come and watch what I do in the dining room, then I'll watch you clean and light one on your own. But we'll have to work fast.'

And work fast they did. Between them, they cleaned the grates in the four bedrooms, the drawing room, the library, the nursery and the housekeeper's room, as well as the two in the dining room. Lizzie was thankful that Susan undertook to do the nursery and Mrs Bailey's room – she was keen to avoid both Hester and the housekeeper.

With all the fires laid and lit, they arrived back in the kitchen just as Alice was setting two large earthenware teapots on the table. Lizzie's stomach rumbled at the sight of the bread and butter; she had begun to feel quite faint as she lit the last fire. But before she could eat, there were ashes to dispose of, the brush, pan and cinder pail made ready for the next morning, and then she had to scrub her hands at the sink in the scullery. Lizzie began to fear there would be nothing left on the table by the time she took her place, until she saw Alice in the kitchen, cutting more bread.

She slid into her seat next to Susan, then had to restrain herself from bolting a slice of bread, such was her hunger.

Susan poured her a cup of tea and passed it to her. 'After this, go up to the nursery and collect the laundry. A girl is here from the village today to take care of it. Then re-stock the firewood and once that's done I'll show you where to find what you need to whiten the front step. Mrs Bailey wants that done, and the hall floor polished, in good time before Mrs Bullivant arrives.'

The morning flew by for Lizzie. Despite her resolution of the previous evening, she couldn't help but look around for Joe when she went out to collect the firewood. He'd been at breakfast, but deep in conversation with Samuel and Abraham, and Lizzie had avoided glancing more than once in his direction. Out in the stable yard, on her own, she looked and listened, but all was quiet. She supposed he had been sent on the errands Mrs Bailey had spoken of. Disappointed, she filled the firewood basket and struggled with it back to the scullery, repeating the journey twice more until she was hot and out of breath. It was going to be a glorious day, the sun already beating down out of a clear blue sky. But there was no time to stop and take it in – she must move on to whiten the front step so that it would be fully dry before the visitors arrived.

She was on her knees on the front porch, conscious of the heat of the sun on her back as she applied all her strength to the job, when she heard a voice.

'Miss Carey.'

Looking up, she found Mrs Bailey watching her. Lizzie scrambled to her feet.

'Miss Carey, your cap is awry, your hair is coming loose, your face is flushed in an unseemly way and your apron is marked. As soon as you have finished, you must change it. I cannot have Mrs Bullivant or the guests seeing one of our household in such a state. When they are here, you will stay out of their sight at all times.'

She turned on her heel and walked away, leaving Lizzie with her indignant protestations still on her lips. How was she supposed to do such a job in the warmth of a summer's day without becoming flushed? She attempted to push her hair under her cap with the back of her hand, but sensed she had only made matters worse. She knelt down and set to work again. Five minutes later, the sound of hoofs on the drive made her look over her shoulder in horror. Surely the visitors weren't arriving already. She began to gather up her equipment, ready to scramble to her feet again, when Joe came into view, driving the horse and cart. He gave her a cheery wave as he went around the back of the house to the stable yard. Lizzie felt her cheeks grow even redder.

CHAPTER SIX

The afternoon went by just as quickly for Lizzie. She had washed, but failed to polish, the hall floor before being called for a midday meal, where bread, ham and pickles were laid out on the table, and Alice set down two of the large brown teapots for everyone to help themselves. Nor had Lizzie changed her apron, reasoning that it would be soiled again after she had knelt to apply the beeswax, linseed and turpentine polish that Susan said must be used. She was anxious, though, that Mrs Bailey would notice, or that she would be chastised for falling behind in her duties.

Susan reassured her. 'Mrs Bailey will be upstairs most of the afternoon, supervising the preparation of the bedrooms. And if she comes downstairs, just keep your head down and avoid catching her eye. I'll give you a hand with the floor once I've finished folding the linen for the press.'

Lizzie's agitation eased a little but she had found herself wishing everyone else would hurry up and finish eating. They couldn't leave the table, Susan warned her, until Cook pushed back her chair and stood up, signifying the end of the meal. She noticed Joe drumming his fingers on the table and glancing at the kitchen clock. He, too, must have an urgent task to finish.

At last Cook, who surely was the most under pressure of them all, stood up with a sigh. 'I suppose we must get on,' she said. 'I'm told they will arrive about five o'clock, no doubt ready for their dinner and demanding hot water to wash away the dust of the journey. If I can find the time to make us something to eat, we'll have it around eight o'clock.'

She looked severe as she spoke, but gave herself away with a chuckle. It was a long time to wait until eight o'clock that evening, Lizzie thought, looking longingly at the few slices of bread and butter still on the table. She remembered the kitchen in the Russell household, and the biscuits Judith baked nearly every day. She feared hunger would be a part of the daily routine at Betsanger Court. Then she forced herself back to reality – such a different reality – and went in search of the cloths and polish Susan had pointed out earlier. She was thankful to find a kneeling mat, too. The hall was a good size and she would be spending at least an hour on her knees.

With the help of Susan, the job was indeed done within an hour, just in time for Ann to place an arrangement of flowers on the circular central table. Lizzie and Susan hastily gathered everything together and retreated to the scullery.

'Now you'll have to wash out all the cloths that have been used today,' Susan said, pointing to a pile on the floor. 'You can't hang them in the yard to dry, as we usually do, in case they are seen from the bedroom windows. So squeeze them out as best you can and hang them over there.' She pointed to a fine rope strung between the shelves in the scullery.

It made no sense to Lizzie. The sun was hot – they could surely be put to dry outside for an hour before the visitors arrived. She resolved to do just that, once Susan had gone.

Just before five o'clock Lizzie was sitting down with more bread and butter and a cup of tea made by Alice, while Cook, now very red in the face, sweated over a variety of pans set on the range. Mrs Bailey hurried into the kitchen.

'The guests will be here soon. Miss Brooke and Miss West, you are to come and wait in the hall while I welcome them. Mr Powell, wait in the yard until you hear the carriages, then come around to help with the luggage.' She cast a critical eye over Joe. 'Find a clean shirt. And a comb.

'Miss Griffiths and Miss Carey, go up to the attic bedrooms at once and make up all the spare beds. I have no idea how many servants the ladies will be bringing with them but we must be prepared. And open the windows to air the rooms.'

Everyone scrambled to their feet to do as they were bade. As soon as Mrs Bailey's back was turned, Lizzie took the chance to cram the last piece of bread and butter into her mouth and finish her tea. Then she followed Susan up the back stairs, collecting armfuls of linen from the press as they passed.

It was only as Lizzie opened the last window, leaned out to breathe deeply and take in the scent wafting up from the flowers in the cutting garden that she remembered the cloths she had left outside on the line. Bits of rag, stained by regular use despite their wash, swayed in the gentle breeze. At the same moment, she heard carriage wheels on the drive and the jangle of harnesses. She froze in horror. She had to get downstairs at once and retrieve the cloths before the visitors or, far worse, Mrs Bailey, spotted them from the bedroom windows.

She hurried from the room, clattering down the stairs and back through the kitchen, past a startled Cook, Alice and the girl from the village who was peeling potatoes.

'They're here,' she called over her shoulder, hoping to deflect any curiosity over what she was doing. She had gathered the washing from the line and was back in the scullery in two minutes flat. At least they were fully dry, she thought, quickly folding the cloths and putting them back on the shelf. Then she took a deep breath and went back up towards the attic, meeting Susan on her way down.

'Where did you go?' Susan asked, suspicious.

'To warn Cook that the visitors were here,' Lizzie said. 'I heard the carriages arrive.'

She didn't think Susan believed her, judging by the look she gave her, but they returned to the kitchen to stay out of sight and await further orders. Cook declared that since they were there they might as well be useful. Lizzie actually enjoyed it – she felt on safe ground helping to chop vegetables and gathering up the plates needed for the various courses. As she stood stirring the soup that was to be the servants' dinner, with cold meats and slices of pie from the larder, she was hard pressed not to sneak morsels of food into her mouth, such was her hunger. With an effort, she managed to control herself. She couldn't risk getting into trouble on only her second day at Betsanger Court.

CHAPTER SEVEN

By eight o'clock, Lizzie could barely keep her eyes open while she ate her soup and the rest of her supper. The talk around the table was subdued, despite the arrival of Mrs Bullivant and her guests. There were four extra servants at the table, brought from London by the ladies: two lady's maids, and two coachmen who had had to be accommodated alongside Joe over the stables. Lizzie guessed no one wished to gossip in front of strangers. Also, it was clear that Cook and Alice were exhausted, too.

She fell into bed shortly after nine o'clock and was asleep within moments. Once again, when Susan shook her awake, she struggled to place where she was. One thing was clear to her, though – it was very early.

'It can't be time to get up,' she protested.

'Afraid so.' Susan gave her a grim smile. 'We have to start work an hour earlier when guests are here, so that we can get as much done as possible before they're about.'

By the time she and Lizzie were leaving the scullery, laden with the ash and cinder pails, brushes and kindling, Cook, yawning, was standing in the kitchen, contemplating an array of ingredients laid out on the work table.

'I don't imagine they'll take breakfast early,' she said, 'so I'll make a start on tonight's desserts.' She was talking to herself rather than to them, Lizzie thought, as she struggled past. They could only clean out and light the fires in the downstairs rooms – the bedrooms would have to wait until Mrs Bullivant and her guests were at breakfast. But Susan had warned her there would be no time for slacking. 'You'll have to whiten the front step again, after they traipsed all over it yesterday, and sweep the hall floor, then start laying out plates and dishes in the dining room.'

Lizzie looked longingly out of the window as she started work on the dining-room fires. The early sunshine was already beginning to disperse the mist that had crept across the grass during the night. A rabbit sat at the edge of the lawn, ears twitching, then bounded off into the hedge that ran around the property. It was going to be a glorious day. The only fresh air she would get was while she whitened the front step, or went out to bring firewood in from the stable yard. It was a far cry from what she had been used to. Was this form of imprisonment a better alternative to the marriage she would have been forced to endure if she had stayed in Canterbury? Lizzie pursed her lips and sighed. She would not allow herself to think in this way. She knelt down in front of the first fireplace and began work. It was hard to imagine why anyone would need the fires lit on what was likely to be a very warm day. But it was not her place to question Mrs Bailey's rules.

Breakfast was a hasty affair – she was seated for barely ten minutes before the housekeeper entered and said, 'Miss Brooke and Miss West, hot water is needed upstairs. Miss Griffiths, I need you on standby to start laying the fires in the upstairs bedrooms the minute the guests come down for breakfast. Miss Carey, that leaves you to make sure the dining room is properly prepared. You must not be seen, so do it now.' She turned to the two maids who had arrived the day before. 'Your mistresses will be ready for you now, I believe. Miss Sutton,' she turned to Alice, 'make some fresh tea for them to take upstairs.'

It took Alice, unused to hearing herself addressed by Mrs Bailey, a moment or two to realise she was being spoken to. Flustered, she sprang to her feet while Lizzie, too, stood up, although rather more reluctantly. The table had been laid the night before, so she took plates for the hot dishes through to the sideboard in the dining

197

room, and set up the little spirit stoves used to keep the food warm. Her back to the door, she was laying out platters of prepared fruit, when she heard someone enter the room. She was about to turn, thinking it must be Susan come to check on her, when she heard a chair being pulled out from the table.

Lizzie froze. Mrs Bailey's words came back to her: *You must not be seen.* She could hardly sidle from the room, face to the wall, so she would have to hope whoever it was would pay her no attention. She kept her eyes cast down and prepared to make as hasty an exit as possible.

'Bring me my chocolate, please. And I will take an egg, lightly boiled.'

Lizzie recognised Mrs Bullivant's voice at once, although she daren't look up. She bobbed an acknowledgement and mumbled what she hoped sounded like 'Yes, madam,' before attempting to make her escape.

'Wait, Miss Carey, isn't it?'

Lizzie was forced to look up. Mrs Bullivant was seated at the head of the table in a loose, brightly patterned silk robe, her hair flowing around her shoulders. Lizzie was startled to see her other than formally dressed, but supposed she was at liberty to behave as she liked in her own house. Her surprise must have been too clearly written across her countenance for Mrs Bullivant laughed.

'I like to breakfast early, before my guests appear, then take time over my morning bath. But tell me, Miss Carey, are you settling in?' She looked Lizzie up and down, then frowned. 'You are wasted here, doing such work. I will speak to Mrs Bailey about moving you.' A gleam of satisfaction appeared on her face. 'In fact, she has foisted a nursemaid upon me, a young woman who is totally unsuited to the job. I can't imagine what she was thinking – the girl has no aptitude for working with children. Mrs Bailey will have to tell her today that she must take your place and you will take hers.'

With a contented smile, Mrs Bullivant shook out her napkin, spread it over her lap and turned her attention to the bread rolls.

Lizzie managed an awkward curtsy, having no idea whether or not that was appropriate, and stumbled from the room, legs like jelly and cheeks aflame.

Mrs Bailey would be furious that Lizzie had been seen, despite her express instructions, and angered by Mrs Bullivant's interference in her household. As for Hester, Lizzie could hardly bear to think how she would react. She gave Mrs Bullivant's order to Cook and Alice, then begged Susan, now back in the kitchen, to deliver it to the dining room. 'Remember, I'm not supposed to be seen,' she said.

Then, as she went to gather a scrubbing brush, pail and soap for the front step, a little flicker of joy took hold. She would be spared the drudgery of the housework and instead she would be spending nearly all of her time with the children. She would no longer be confined to the house: instead she would be at liberty to take them outside into the grounds and perhaps even as far as the village. Betsanger Court suddenly felt like a far more enticing place than it had just a few hours earlier.

Chapter Eight

Christopher and Agnes had been delighted when, the afternoon of Lizzie's encounter in the dining room, Mrs Bullivant had taken her up to the nursery and introduced her as their new nursemaid.

Agnes ran up and took Lizzie's hand, while Christopher hung back with a shy smile. 'Have you brought Frances with you?' Agnes asked. 'And the baby?'

Lizzie felt a tug on her heartstrings as she thought of the family so recently left behind in Canterbury. 'No, they have stayed at home with their father,' she said.

'You aren't their mother?' Agnes seemed puzzled.

Lizzie smiled. 'No, I was their nursemaid.' She had been more than that but it seemed best to keep it simple.

'I thought you were their mother. You loved them very much.'

Agnes was tugging her towards the shelves in the room, bent on showing Lizzie her favourite toys. Lizzie glanced back towards Mrs Bullivant, who was watching, an inscrutable expression on her face. Did Mrs Bullivant love Christopher and Agnes very much? she wondered.

'Is there a routine you would like me to follow with the children?' she asked her employer, as she bent down to look at the doll Agnes was holding out to her. 'Are there particular lessons you would like them to take? Are you happy for them to be out in the gardens?' Now that she was no longer confined below stairs she was eager to get outside in the fresh air as much as possible.

Mrs Bullivant shrugged. 'As long as they have their meals at a regular time, you are at liberty to occupy them as you think fit. Christopher has started work with a tutor on Saturdays, so it would be useful to make sure he keeps abreast of his reading and writing.'

Although she was still in the room, Lizzie sensed that Mrs Bullivant was withdrawing, eager to spend time with her guests. That suited Lizzie well enough – it looked as though she would have minimal interference.

'Then let's find your hats, children,' she said. 'We'll go out into the garden and see what we can collect to draw on our return.'

She turned to speak to Mrs Bullivant again, but she had already slipped away. Neither child seemed put out by her disappearance, so Lizzie found a basket they could take with them to the garden, then led them out of the nursery. She hesitated at the door, inclined to follow the back stairs as she would usually. But the children were already at the top of the main staircase, so she followed them down, unable to hide her smile. How quickly her life had changed!

They spent a very happy hour in the garden. Christopher found a snail with a shell patterned in a whorl of black and yellow, which he was determined to draw. He and Lizzie made it a bed of leaves in the bottom of the basket, while Agnes collected petals fallen from the roses. They added some colourful pebbles and Agnes picked some daisies from the lawn.

'Another day, we will go to the kitchen garden and ask for some flowers to take back to the nursery,' Lizzie said, emboldened by her new role. She was feeling the heat of the sun on her head. All her belongings were still in the room she shared with Susan, including her bonnet, so, reluctantly, she declared it was time to return to the nursery. Should she go to the kitchen and ask for some lemonade to be brought up? Surely the children must be hot, too. But they were already running back to the main door and she hurried after them. It wouldn't do for them to collide with any of the guests, or for Mrs Bullivant to think they were out of control on Lizzie's first day in charge. The house was quiet, though, as Lizzie went quickly up the grand staircase. The children were already at the table in the window, getting out paper and pencils. To Lizzie's amazement, a jug of lemonade and three glasses stood on the table, along with a plate of biscuits.

'You must wait for me, Christopher and Agnes,' Lizzie admonished them, but gently. 'I need to keep you in view at all times. Now, what a surprise – I was just thinking how lovely it would be to have a glass of lemonade on such a warm day.'

'We always have a drink in the afternoon,' Agnes said.

'And biscuits. Or cake,' Christopher added.

Lizzie poured the lemonade and reflected again on how lucky she was. No more slices of bread and butter to fill her. She might even have a chance to sample some of Cook's legendary cake, which was usually reserved for guests.

Lizzie soon discovered that all her meals were of a superior quality to those below stairs. Mrs Bullivant had given orders that the children were to eat well, and the food cooked for them was served to Lizzie, too. Porridge and eggs in the morning, a light lunch of bread and ham, or a slice of pie and, at the end of the afternoon, a simpler version of what would be served to Mrs Bullivant in the evening, when she was at home. The only drawback for Lizzie was that the evening meal followed hard on the heels of the lemonade and biscuits. She found it hard to do it justice at the time, but the long evening that followed left her feeling hungry by bedtime. She daren't leave the sleeping children to slip down to the kitchen, so she took to saving her afternoon biscuit for later. Considering the overall improvement in her circumstances, it was no great hardship.

Lizzie had few qualms about replacing Hester, but she could see that Susan, who had so much more experience than Lizzie or Hester, was unhappy at remaining in her below-stairs position. She now brought up the meals to the nursery and delivered them without a word, greatly upsetting Lizzie. She was eager for some news of what was going on downstairs, but Susan's frostiness discouraged her. After two days, though, Susan broke her silence.

'I'll not be the one serving you soon. Mrs Bullivant is taking Ann as her lady's maid when she returns to London, and I'll be taking over her duties upstairs.'

She was trying hard to maintain what had become her habitual look of annoyance, but couldn't help a smile spreading across her face.

Lizzie leaped up and gave her a hug. 'Oh, Susan, I'm so pleased for you. You deserve it. You know so much about running this house, you ought to have Mrs Bailey's job.'

Susan gave her a wry look.

'You'd be better at it than she is.' Lizzie thought back to the way in which Mrs Bailey had summoned her to deliver news of her promotion to nursery maid.

'Mrs Bullivant is insistent that you are to take Hester's role in the nursery, and refuses to follow my advice. I can't help but think you have twisted her thinking. From what I have seen so far, you are basically incompetent and ill-suited to a life of service. I'm warning you that I'll be watching your every move and if I suspect anything amiss in your dealings with the children, you and your belongings will be out on the road in an instant.'

The housekeeper's face had been quite pink by the time she had finished her speech. Lizzie had experienced a tremor of apprehension. What if she wasn't as good as she believed herself to be with the children? Then she had reassured herself: she had years of experience. And Mrs Bailey didn't have time to follow her around all day.

'You know what needs to be done,' Lizzie continued, 'and how to ask people to do it without annoying or upsetting them.'

Susan gave a short laugh. 'Don't underestimate Mrs Bailey. She's not going anywhere. And she has favourites: Hester has been one for a while. You've made two enemies by being given this post. So you'd best watch your step.' She saw Lizzie's expression and added, 'Don't worry. I'll keep an eye open for you. And I'll ask Alice if she can bring the meals up to the nursery. Otherwise it'll be Hester. She'll probably spit in your food.'

Lizzie looked around in horror to make sure the children weren't listening, but they were busy eating at the table in the window.

Susan gave a wry smile. 'Don't worry. I suspect Hester is too lazy to carry trays up here. And they are taking on the girl from the village through the summer to help Alice, so I think she'll manage.'

Susan was halfway along the corridor when she turned back. 'By the way, Joe was asking after you. Wanted to know why you weren't at the table any more. I told him you'd left and he looked disappointed.'

Lizzie's heart gave a lurch. 'Why did you do that?' she protested.

Susan grinned. 'I let him sulk his way through Cook's roast fowl, then told him where you were. He cheered up no end. Think you've made quite an impression.'

CHAPTER NINE

Lizzie soon established a daily routine for the children. After breakfast, she set Christopher to work on his books, reading passages aloud to her, or practising his handwriting, which left much to be desired. He was an unwilling student, so she broke up his desk work with spells of painting his lead soldiers, reasoning that there was still much to be learned with this activity. She had him read about the battles they might have fought, and learn the significance of their coat colours, braiding and epaulettes.

Agnes was too young to have had any formal education so far, but Lizzie saw no reason why she shouldn't learn to read and write. The little girl would not have a tutor; no doubt she was intended to become a pretty adornment for some wealthy man in the future, but Lizzie was only too conscious of the consequences of her own lack of education.

What the children saw as the hard work of the day ceased with the arrival of lunch, after which Lizzie insisted on a rest of half an hour. It gave her a chance to look over Christopher's work, or to take up some mending. Then came the favourite part of her day, provided the weather was good: they would go out to walk around the grounds and visit the stables, where the two horses, Captain and Lady, had become firm favourites of both children. Or they would take their sketchbooks and go to the kitchen garden, where Lizzie set them simple tasks: drawing a selection of leaves, or capturing the different shapes of flowers, from simple flat-faces to more complex tubular petals. Samuel or Abraham always cut them a few stems to take back to the nursery, where their sweet perfume served as a reminder of the warm afternoon while Lizzie sat stitching by the window after the children were in bed. It was also a reminder of Joe, whom they invariably saw on their outings: he was always in evidence at the stables, ready with a carrot or an apple for Agnes and Christopher to feed to the horses. And with a special smile for Lizzie that carried her through the rest of the afternoon on a cloud of happiness, no matter how much she scolded herself.

Sunday at Betsanger Court revolved around going to church, whether or not Mrs Bullivant was in residence. She was still there with her guests on Lizzie's first Sunday, and they set off in good time in three coaches, the ladies smartly dressed in costumes rather more reserved than Lizzie had observed them wearing previously. She had the children ready early, in case Mrs Bullivant requested they travel in the coach with her, but she didn't so Lizzie walked with them. She took delight in discovering what lay beyond the trees surrounding Betsanger Court, which kept them completely private from the outside area.

She remembered the fields from her drive to the village with John, the carter, and the glimpse of a church tower in the distance. Mrs Bailey led the party. She had taken one look at Lizzie and said, 'Your outfit will not do, Miss Carey.'

Lizzie, wearing what she considered to be her Sunday best, feared she would be turned back and humiliated in front of the other servants but Mrs Bailey continued, 'I will find something more suitable for you when I go up to Canterbury next week. There are shops where you can purchase clothes that are ... no longer new.' She wrinkled her nose in distaste at her own description. 'I will take an amount from your wages each week until it is paid for.'

'Thank you,' Lizzie said, surprised by her thoughtfulness, but already worried about how much such an outfit might cost her, even at the presumably lower price of one that was 'no longer new'.

'I am merely thinking of the reputation of the household, Miss Carey.' Mrs Bailey swept past her and set a brisk pace along the drive and through the gates, while Lizzie busied herself with Agnes's gloves and hat to hide her discomfort. She heard Hester snigger behind her but didn't look round.

Up ahead, Susan, Amy and Ann walked behind Mrs Bailey. Joe, Samuel and Abraham followed; Joe wasn't required to drive the family carriage since the head coachman, Isaac Turner, had returned from London with Mrs Bullivant. Lizzie allowed a discreet gap to develop between her and the men so that she wouldn't have to walk so close to Joe. Christopher, however, had other ideas. He broke free of her hand and ran up beside Joe. Lizzie heard him say something about Captain and Lady. Joe nodded, and Christopher ran back.

'You must walk beside me,' Lizzie chided him. 'We're supposed to make our way to church in an orderly fashion.'

Christopher ignored her, leaning across her to address Agnes. 'Joe said we can go and visit the horses in the stables when we get back.'

Lizzie sighed. It seemed as though she was destined to be in Joe's company, even if she tried to avoid him. Then she shook off the thought and concentrated on their route, which had brought them to the outskirts of a village. Houses straggled along the road leading towards the centre: a mixture of small terraced cottages and larger buildings, one half-timbered and another with Dutch gables, although nothing on the scale of Betsanger Court. As they passed, she saw families gathering on cottage doorsteps, men and women dressed in their Sunday best, the mothers trying to smooth the wayward curls of their young sons, and tie the ribbons on the bonnets of their daughters. She realised they must have been waiting for their party to pass before falling in behind them, and experienced an unusual sense of self-importance. It was the same in the church, a grey stone building with a sturdy tower. Mrs Bullivant and her party were already seated at the front and Mrs Bailey led the way to the pews behind them, waiting for the servants to file in before she seated herself beside the aisle. Lizzie took a quick look around: the interior was light and airy, with high archways lining each side of the nave, and memorial tablets forming the main decoration on the austere walls. Above the altar, though, a panel of painted gold-rimmed medallions caught her eye. They were clearly old: the paint in each had flaked and the colours had faded over time, but she thought she could make out a lion and a dove, images that were repeated across the panel. Her eyes returned to it many times during the course of the sermon, which she found very dull. She maintained a rigid-backed appearance of attentiveness, though, to set an example to the children and to satisfy Mrs Bailey, who glanced along the pew at regular intervals to check on the household members.

Lizzie was glad to be back outside in the fresh air and, judging by the laughter and chatter that erupted as soon as the congregation were outside the church door, the relief was shared. She was hard pressed to keep Christopher and Agnes in order while they waited for Mrs Bullivant and her party to exchange a few words with the vicar. The children wanted to run around the churchyard and play hide and seek among the gravestones. She sympathised, but it would have earned her more than the glare that Mrs Bailey was already bestowing on her. At last, Mrs Bullivant made her way to the churchyard gate and the household party fell in behind, followed by the rest of the congregation.

Lizzie's stomach rumbled in anticipation of food. Cook and Alice had stayed behind to prepare the meal for Mrs Bullivant's party; she hoped there had been time to make something for the rest of them, too. The walk back to Betsanger Court seemed to take longer than the journey there, and Lizzie tired of trying to keep the children in order. She let Agnes pick flowers from the grass verge, so that she had quite a posy, albeit wilted, by the time they reached the entrance to the drive. Christopher had forsaken her to skip alongside Joe and she left him to it. Mrs Bailey might not approve but Mrs Bullivant was her employer, and unless she said something, Lizzie was content to let him be.

She had both children back at her side by the time they reached the front of the house. Mrs Bullivant's party was already safely inside, so she ushered the children up the stairs to the nursery to wash their hands. She put the flagging posy into a jug of water and set it on the table, by which time there was a knock on the door and Susan entered, with lunch for them all. Lizzie looked with some dismay at the array of cold meats and bread on the tray. She thought longingly of the hot meal Judith had prepared for the family's return from church: a full roast dinner with a pudding to follow.

Susan laughed at her expression. 'Don't worry. We'll have a proper dinner tonight. And I gather Mrs Bullivant is moving on to Canterbury tomorrow, so we'll be back to our usual quiet selves when she goes.'

Would their mother ask to see the children before she left? Mrs Bullivant had spent little time with them, but she supposed her other guests must be keeping her busy. It was such a different way of life from any Lizzie had known before. She thought back to her own childhood in Castle Bay, the life that Gabriel and Frances led in Canterbury, and now this one. Which was best?

CHAPTER TEN

Christopher was all set to bolt his food and scramble off his chair so that he could visit the horses, until Lizzie told him Joe would be eating his midday meal so he must wait. He sat, swinging his legs and sighing until Lizzie and Agnes had finished. Agnes wanted Lizzie to tell her the names of all the different flowers she had collected, which Lizzie was hard pressed to do.

'This one is red clover.' She pointed to a cluster of pink-tipped tubular petals that formed a rounded flower head. 'It has sweet nectar, which the bees love. And this one is a vetch of some kind.' She picked up a deep-throated purple flower on a stem of leaflets, each one ending in tendrils to allow them to cling to the surrounding plants. 'The yellow one is a buttercup, of course, and that's red dead nettle. This purple one is bugle, or maybe ground ivy. Perhaps we can find a book to help us identify them. Now, if you have finished, Agnes, I think Christopher will burst with impatience if we don't go down to the stables now.'

She made sure the children still looked presentable before they left via the main staircase, in case they came across their mother. Laughter and the tinkling of cutlery and glassware told her that Mrs Bullivant's guests were still at the table, so she allowed Agnes and Christopher to scamper along the side of the house, then take the narrow passage to the stable yard. Joe was seated on an upturned barrel, eyes closed and face to the sun. He stood up, stretched and smiled as the children ran to him.

'Are we disturbing you?' Lizzie was apologetic – it was a free afternoon for him, after all.

210

'Not at all. I was just enjoying the sunshine while I waited for you.' Joe gave her the smile that turned her insides upside down, so that she had to switch her gaze to the children, now running over to the stables, to hide her blushes.

'Wait,' Joe called. 'Don't startle them. I've got carrots here for you to give to them.' He fished in his pocket and produced two, which he presented to Agnes and Christopher. 'Now, remember what I told you before. Hold them flat on your palm – we don't want them mistaking your fingers for a carrot, too.' He squatted beside Agnes and, seeing she was nervous, he supported her hand by placing his palm beneath it. 'There, he's a big fella, isn't he?' He stroked the nose of the big grey horse affectionately, then looked to see how Christopher was getting on. He was fearless around the horses and had already fed Lady, whose head was bent low over the stable door as she tried to nuzzle her way into Christopher's pockets, to his delight.

'Nothing there for you, madam,' Joe said to Lady.

'Do you have more?' Christopher asked hopefully.

Joe shook his head. 'No. I'll have Cook after me if I take any more carrots from her store. Now, who wants to sit on Captain's back?'

Lizzie smiled as she watched him. The routine was always the same but the children never seemed to tire of it. And Joe had such patience with them.

'Do you have brothers and sisters?' she asked, once he was back by her side, the children now playing with the stable-yard cat.

'Two of each,' Joe said. 'I'm the eldest. I haven't seen them in a while, though.'

'Why?' Lizzie asked.

Joe shrugged. 'They live a distance away. It's too far for me to get there and back when I have an afternoon off. I plan to ask for a bit longer in the autumn, when the family aren't here, so that I can make the journey.' He turned to Lizzie. 'And you? Do you have family nearby?'

'Not nearby,' Lizzie replied, without knowing whether or not this was true. 'I have six sisters. Although I might have a brother too, I suppose.' She spoke the last sentence aloud, without intending to.

She became aware of Joe's gaze.

'It sounds as though you aren't close to your family?' he asked.

'Not really,' Lizzie admitted, unwilling to say more.

He nodded and looked back at the children. 'The cat has had kittens,' he called. 'Who wants to see them?'

They spent a delightful half an hour watching the kittens stumble around in the corner of the stable where their mother had made their home, before Lizzie reluctantly said it was time to go. Agnes in particular protested bitterly.

'Why can't I take a kitten with me?' she wailed, after Lizzie had refused point blank to allow it.

Joe stepped in. 'Because they are much too young to leave their mother. They wouldn't survive without her.'

'And your mother, and Mrs Bailey, wouldn't be happy. Cats are for the kitchen and the stables, not for the nursery,' Lizzie said sternly. 'Now, it's time for a rest, Agnes. And Christopher must read – he's falling behind with his book.'

Agnes complained all the way back and Christopher dragged his feet, scuffing the ground with his boots. Lizzie was glad that all was quiet in the house and their mother was nowhere in sight.

'We can see the horses, and the kittens, again during the week,' she promised, as she shut the nursery door behind them. The jug of lemonade on the table, and the plate of biscuits, placated the children for a while, long enough at least for them to forget about their disappointment. Lizzie promised Agnes they could paint the flowers she had picked that morning, once she had had a rest, and she allowed Christopher to sit with his book in the window seat, even though she knew he would spend more time gazing outside than at the pages.

She took up her sewing but she, too, was barely concentrating on what was in front of her. Instead, she pondered the time they had spent with Joe. Why was she drawn to him? It was the first time ever she had experienced this. Was it the mysterious 'love' she had heard others refer to? She had certainly never felt this way about Adam Russell. But then Joe was undoubtedly given to flirting with any new maid who crossed the threshold of Betsanger Court. She thought about the girl who had had to leave in disgrace, whose outfits she now wore.

Lizzie smoothed the fabric of her skirt, a frown creasing her brow. Was it unlucky to be wearing it? She gave a little sigh at her folly, and looked up to catch Christopher watching her.

Embarrassed, as though he could read her mind, she spoke crisply: 'Eyes on the page, please, young man. I'll be asking you questions on this later.'

He looked back down at his book, his lips set in a stubborn line. She hadn't been fair, Lizzie reflected. Why did he have to study on such a glorious sunny Sunday? To be like his father, perhaps. She hadn't met him yet, but she imagined him a force to be reckoned with, if he was anything like his wife.

CHAPTER ELEVEN

The following morning, the children were summoned to bid farewell to their mother and her party. Lizzie made sure they looked presentable, and stood on the steps with them, beside Mrs Bailey and in front of the rest of the household, as Joe and Isaac loaded her luggage. The carriages for the other ladies were ready and waiting, as Mrs Bullivant beckoned the children forward.

'My darlings, I'm sorry not to have spent more time with you. These ladies have kept me far too busy.' She gestured to the visitors, who laughed obligingly. 'But I promise we will do something together very soon. In the meantime, I will leave you in the very good hands of Miss Carey. Be sure to do as she tells you.'

She bestowed a kiss on the head of each child, then turned to Mrs Bailey, as the ladies climbed into their carriages. 'Thank you, Mrs Bailey. We have all had a delightful time, due in no small part to your excellent management of the household.'

Mrs Bailey, who rarely showed emotion, turned quite pink with pleasure. Lizzie considered how little she knew of the housekeeper. She didn't even know her Christian name, let alone how old she was or, indeed, where her husband was. She resolved to ask Susan at the first opportunity. But now it was time to bend down beside Agnes and Christopher and encourage them to wave farewell to their mother. Would they be upset by her departure?

Far from it – they were playing on the front steps before the carriages were even out of sight, Christopher encouraging Agnes

214

to jump down one, then two steps beside him. He was embarking on three by the time Lizzie saw what he was doing.

'That's quite enough, Christopher,' she said, speaking loudly enough for Mrs Bailey to hear. 'We don't want any broken legs, or necks.'

Then she ushered the children inside to the nursery and settled them at the table, Christopher to his studies and Agnes to complete her flower painting from the day before. Lizzie had embarked on one, too, and she was rather pleased with the result.

When Susan brought up the midday meal, she was disposed to loiter, so Lizzie drew her away to the passage, where they could take a few moments undisturbed.

'I'm glad they've all gone,' Susan said. 'Mrs Bailey has been watching our every move ever since they arrived. It made all the extra work we had to do seem even more painful.'

'I'm curious about Mrs Bailey,' Lizzie began. 'Where is her husband?'

'She's a widow,' Susan replied.

Lizzie was surprised. 'She seems young to be a widow. Was her husband much older?'

'I don't think so.' Susan smiled. 'The rumour downstairs is that she drove him away with her constant carping. Either that or she poisoned him.' She giggled at Lizzie's shocked expression. 'I expect the truth is a lot simpler. But she's a prickly character. It doesn't do to get on the wrong side of her. Which is where I'll be if I don't get back down the stairs. Now that Ann's gone to be Mrs Bullivant's lady's maid, we're a pair of hands less. And there's a lot to do to set the rooms to rights now the visitors have left. The mess they make ...' She wrinkled her nose in distaste. 'Never a thought for those who have to clear up after them.'

She took up the tray and departed, leaving Lizzie to return to the nursery table and join her charges. Today's meal was chilled soup, most welcome when the day looked set to be a hot one, with freshly baked bread on the side. The servants' meals would no longer be such scratch affairs, Lizzie thought, now they had Betsanger Court back to themselves.

On Thursday morning she received word that she must prepare the children for a trip to Canterbury.

'Mrs Bullivant would like them to spend a few days with her, and for you to accompany them.' Mrs Bailey had arrived in the nursery unannounced, thankfully finding the children quietly occupied with their morning work. 'Mr Powell will drive you there in the carriage we keep here, as Mr Bullivant has need of his carriage in London again. You will depart straight after breakfast tomorrow. Take a small bag for each of you.'

Lizzie nodded, hoping she looked composed. Her heart and mind were racing: her heart at the prospect of Joe conducting them to Canterbury, her mind at the idea of returning so close to where she had lived with the Russells. She would like to see Judith and the children, but had no wish to encounter Adam. Or Mrs Simmonds.

She told herself it was unlikely in both cases. Adam would be at work, and there was no particular reason for Mrs Simmonds to be loitering in the vicinity of Mrs Bullivant's house. She resolved to turn her attention to making sure the children's clothes were clean and pressed, ready to be packed along with her own few things. Their mother would expect Agnes and Christopher to be in a different outfit each day, perhaps even more than one, and it wasn't clear how long they would be staying. She must be well prepared.

Lizzie and the children were waiting on the steps, bags beside them, at nine o'clock the next morning. There was no farewell party to see them on their way, just a stern-looking Mrs Bailey. Lizzie's heart picked up its pace as Joe brought the spare carriage round. He looked unusually smart in a uniform of tailcoat and breeches, a high white collar framing his face. She noticed him tug surreptitiously at his neck tie and smiled to herself. He wasn't used to such finery.

'Remember, the children must be well behaved at all times,' Mrs Bailey warned her. 'Mrs Bullivant will judge you by them. I hope you know how to acquit yourself in company.'

Lizzie smiled, although she had to grit her teeth to do so. Would it hurt the housekeeper to wish the children a happy time? she thought, ushering them into the carriage while Joe loaded the bags. She didn't bother to check whether or not Mrs Bailey waved them off.

Chapter Twelve

Lizzie had little time to pay heed to the scenery on their journey to Canterbury for Agnes and Christopher kept her busy with their questions, most of which she couldn't answer.

What were they to do in the city? Why did their mama want them there? Were they visiting for a treat? How long would they stay? Would they have to do lessons?

The last one at least, which came from Christopher, Lizzie could answer.

'If we stay longer than two or three days, I will have work for you to do,' she said firmly. It was Friday already, and Christopher would be having a Saturday morning free of his tutor. They could begin again on Monday, although she suspected Mrs Bullivant would be more likely to disregard such demands on his time than his father would.

They were within the walls of the city by the time the children became restless. Lizzie began to recognise many of the streets they passed. She knew they were close to the house where she had lived for seventeen months and she longed for, and dreaded, a glimpse of Frances or Judith. But Joe's route took them a different way, bringing them to a halt outside the front door of Mrs Bullivant's house opposite the park.

Lizzie waited for him to open the carriage door for them, then stepped down and helped the children jump out. The front door opened before they had reached it and the maid she recognised from their previous visits stood there.

She addressed the children: 'Welcome! Are you thirsty after your journey? Your mother will be down shortly but come to the kitchen with me and we will see what we can find.' She turned to Lizzie, standing awkwardly on the step. 'You must come too. I'm Ellen.'

Lizzie cast a glance over her shoulder. Joe had unloaded the bags and was preparing to move the carriage. She could hardly leave the luggage standing on the step, so she quickly moved it into the hallway before hurrying after Ellen.

'Leave it there,' Ellen said. 'One of the footmen will carry it up for you.'

They didn't have footmen at Betsanger Court, Lizzie thought, casting a glance around as they moved to the back of the house. From the little she glimpsed through open doors, the rooms were decorated quite differently, too, with dark furniture, walls covered with richly patterned paper and heavy curtains blocking out a good deal of the light. Then they were through the door leading into the servants' area, where silence gave way to bustle and noise. Lizzie relaxed: this already felt like familiar territory. Ellen made quick introductions but Lizzie struggled to retain the names of the cook, the two footmen, an upstairs maid and a kitchen maid. She comforted herself that she probably wouldn't have much to do with them, if her experience of Betsanger Court was anything to go by.

Indeed, she had no sooner drunk a cup of tea and watched the children eat rather too many biscuits, washed down with raspberry cordial, than they were summoned to see Mrs Bullivant. She was sitting in her parlour, dressed for going out in a smart navy costume and a hat trimmed with feathers, a sun parasol at her side.

'Well, children, I thought it was time to purchase some new clothes for you, since you are both growing so fast.' She studied them and nodded. 'You will do for now. We will go to my dressmaker and take some measurements, then have cake in town. How does that sound?'

Christopher's face had fallen at the prospect of spending time being measured for clothes, but his face brightened at the mention of cake. 'And can we go to the shop in the arcade? I need some more soldiers,' he said.

'Of course.' Mrs Bullivant nodded, so that the feather on her hat trembled. 'And Agnes shall choose something, too.'

Lizzie was careful not to let her feelings show, but she could already see that their visit to Canterbury would consist of unsuitable meals taken at the wrong hours, and rather too much spoiling of the children. But she must not judge how Mrs Bullivant chose to live. Her life was so far removed from anything Lizzie could have imagined: three houses, in two different cities as well as the countryside, all staffed and managed while she and her husband were elsewhere. Once again, Lizzie wondered what Mr Bullivant did to earn enough money to support such a lifestyle.

She was to be amazed even more as the days passed. Mrs Bullivant indulged the children with presents and outings in the carriage to visit her friends for tea, where they were cooed over and petted while Lizzie remained discreetly in the background. On their first evening, Mrs Bullivant went to the theatre and on their second she held an elaborate dinner for friends. The children were expected to make an appearance as the guests had their pre-dinner drinks. When Mrs Bullivant proudly explained that Christopher was already showing a mastery of Latin, while Agnes displayed signs of having great skill in watercolour, Lizzie had to bite her lip hard to keep her composure. She inclined her head and smiled when Mrs Bullivant turned to her for confirmation, all the time thinking of what Christopher's tutor might have to say on the subject.

When Sunday morning came, Lizzie was disturbed to discover that they would be attending the service in the cathedral. It would be impossible not to see the Russell family, she thought, but they would not be expecting her. Perhaps they might not notice her in the congregation.

Luck was on Lizzie's side that morning. The cathedral was busy with worshippers, and they were a little late in arriving. Mrs Bullivant took a pew on the other side of the nave to the Russells', and several rows back. Lizzie could see Frances and Gabriel's heads, and Adam's. But who was that between him and the children? A young woman, that much was apparent, wearing a costume in light blue, with a neat hat perched on top of upswept blonde curls. She turned to speak to Gabriel as Lizzie watched, then to Adam. She thought she recognised her as the daughter of one of the families who always stopped to converse when the service was over and Hannah was still alive. There was something in the way she spoke to Adam and Gabriel that suggested intimacy more than a nursemaid. Lizzie was taken aback, then reflected that three months had passed since she had left. Adam had been eager for a wife, and it looked as though he had found one.

Chapter Thirteen

Since they had arrived in Canterbury, Lizzie had seen little of Joe other than when he brought the carriage round for them, and held the door while they got in. He always gave her a quick smile when Mrs Bullivant wasn't looking, and she wished she could have spent time in the kitchen, lingering over a cup of tea while he was off duty. But Lizzie had no free time: she was either out with Mrs Bullivant and the children or sleeping beside them in the nursery. Ellen brought up all the meals they took at home and, as she had suspected, she had no reason to be in the kitchen with the other servants.

After a few days of social engagements, Lizzie was relieved when Mrs Bullivant announced she would be going out alone that morning so Lizzie should entertain the children as she saw fit.

'Don't go too far from the house,' Mrs Bullivant said. 'If I return in time we may do something this afternoon.'

'I'll take Agnes and Christopher to the park across the road,' Lizzie said. 'It will be good for them to spend some time outdoors.'

'Stay out of the sun,' Mrs Bullivant warned. 'Agnes, be sure to wear your bonnet.'

Christopher should really have been doing lessons, Lizzie knew, but after he had spent several days fidgeting in drawing rooms while his mother paid social calls, she felt it unfair to confine him to the table in the nursery. In any case, she was longing for some air: she found the Canterbury house stuffy and she was impatient to return to Betsanger Court. With the children suitably attired for the warm sunshine, she took them downstairs, stopping at the kitchen first.

'We're planning a picnic in the park,' she said. 'Could we have something to take with us – lemonade and biscuits, perhaps?'

The cook was looking a little harried: Mrs Bullivant had another dinner planned for that evening. She didn't respond immediately and Lizzie's heart sank. Ellen wasn't there and the other servants seemed otherwise occupied. Joe was sitting at the table, polishing his long leather boots. He smiled at her.

'I'll bring something over to you in a little while,' he said. 'Cook here has a lot to do but I'm sure she'll find time to put something together.'

Lizzie, feeling awkward, nodded her thanks, then hurried the children out of the room. She longed even more for their return to the familiar routine of Betsanger Court.

Once across the road in the little park she relaxed. It was good to be outside, away from the restrictions of the last few days. She settled herself in the shade and encouraged Agnes and Christopher to run around while the park was empty of other visitors. When they came back to her, she set them a task as she had once done with Frances. 'See whether you can find me a feather, a pink flower, a smooth stone and a special treasure.' She repeated her instructions and watched them run off, keeping them in view.

She was observing Agnes scouring her surroundings, stooping every so often in her quest, and didn't realise she had been approached until she was addressed.

'So, Miss Carey, you are back in town. I thought I caught sight of you at the cathedral on Sunday. And here you are, with your new charges.'

Lizzie scrambled to her feet. Mrs Simmonds, cool and elegant despite the heat of the day, fixed her with a steely look.

'I haven't forgotten about your debt, you know. But if you come to work for me, it will be gone in an instant. I have many a gentleman who would pay well for your charms. They have become discontented with the familiar and seek out the new. My task is to prevent them seeking it elsewhere.'

Lizzie, shocked, began to tremble. Would she never be free of this woman? She feared Mrs Simmonds might persecute her for the rest of her life.

'I do not have money with me to pay this debt you speak of,' she said, in what she hoped was a firm voice, even though she could hear how shaky it was. 'Now I will thank you to leave me alone before the children return. Or Mrs Bullivant sees us.'

'Mrs Bullivant has gone out,' Mrs Simmonds said pleasantly. 'I watched her go. And the children will have no understanding of our conversation. Now, how are we to solve this conundrum? Am I to understand I will need to drive out into the country, to Betsanger Court, to wait while you count out the pennies into my hand? You should understand that no one ever gets the better of me in business.'

Lizzie was horrified. Mrs Simmonds had not only been watching the house, but she knew where the Bullivants had their country home.

'Is there a problem?' It was Joe, standing close by, holding a basket containing a stoppered bottle, glasses and a linen-wrapped bundle. How much had he heard? Or was it obvious, from the way she and Mrs Simmonds were standing, that they were arguing?

Lizzie opened her mouth to speak, and shut it again. What could she say? She was too ashamed to reveal her predicament to Joe.

He set the basket down, then addressed Mrs Simmonds. 'Miss Carey seems a little upset. Can you tell me why?'

'Just a little discussion about a long-standing debt,' Mrs Simmonds said smoothly. 'I think we understand each other. She hasn't the means to pay me, so I have agreed to visit Betsanger Court to collect it.'

'I see,' Joe said. He looked at Lizzie. 'Is this correct?'

Lizzie, on the verge of tears, could only stare at her feet.

'Well,' Joe said, 'I have the impression that Miss Carey doesn't see things in the same way as you.' His voice had become so hard that Lizzie glanced up in surprise. 'I suggest you take yourself on your way. I know who you are, and the type of establishment you have. I've had reason to take so-called gentlemen to your door in the past. And I don't know how or why Miss Carey would have had any involvement with you, but she is clearly disturbed by you and your threats.'

He held up a hand as Mrs Simmonds began to protest. 'Be on your way, or I will be forced to tell Mrs Bullivant you have been watching the house, and the comings and goings of the children. Don't try to deny it – I've seen you sitting nearby in your carriage. She won't take kindly to the news, especially once she knows of your character. If you don't want the constable paying you a visit, I would leave now.'

Mrs Simmonds glared at them, then turned on her heel to leave.

'And don't bother to take a trip to the country,' Joe added. 'You'll get the same reception there – but the dogs will make you even less welcome.'

Mrs Simmonds summoned all her dignity and stalked off, just as Agnes and Christopher ran up, clutching their finds.

Christopher caught Joe's last words. 'Dogs? Are we getting puppies?' he asked.

Joe smiled. 'Not puppies, no. But dogs might be a good idea, out in the countryside. I will speak to the master about it. Now, who wants lemonade? Take a look in the basket and see what else you can find.'

Lizzie was overwhelmed with gratitude. He distracted the children with the picnic while she took a minute or two to compose herself as best she could. Her thoughts were a whirl. Had he really seen off Mrs Simmonds for good? But what must he think of her? He said he knew the nature of Mrs Simmonds's business. For Lizzie to have incurred a debt, he must believe she had worked there. She was hard pressed not to break down in tears at the thought, but she tried to rally herself. She gave Joe a sideways glance, fearing he would ignore her, but he gave her a smile and offered her a glass of lemonade. She gulped it down gratefully. Her cheeks were burning, with shame rather than the heat of the sun. She must find a way to explain it to Joe, but for now she must compose herself.

'So did you find everything?' she asked, turning to the children. 'And what treasures did you choose?'

The children laid out their finds, hot and sticky from being clutched in their hands, and Lizzie congratulated them as best she could, even though her heart wasn't in it. She longed to be away from that place, and all memory of what had occurred.

'Can we go home now?' Agnes asked.

'Of course,' Lizzie said. 'Are you hot? Shall we go back to the nursery?'

'No. Not across the road.' Agnes pouted. 'Home. Back to the countryside.'

'I'm sure we will go soon,' Lizzie said, wishing she could tell Agnes how much she longed for the same thing.

She stood quietly beside Joe while the children sat on the grass and ate their biscuits.

He turned to her and, to her surprise, gently brushed her fingers with his own. 'Don't worry,' he said quietly. 'I won't let you come to any harm.' Then he gathered the glasses, putting them back into the basket with the empty bottle, and strode back across the road.

Lizzie watched him, his broad shoulders in his white shirt, his strong arms revealed by rolled sleeves. She felt a tiny spark of hope. She hoped Mrs Simmonds would think twice about another confrontation with Joe.

CHAPTER FOURTEEN

Lizzie and the children had just stepped into the relative cool of the hallway when Ellen appeared. 'There you are,' she said. 'Shall I bring your midday meal up to the nursery?'

'Could you give us a little while?' Lizzie said. 'The children have only just eaten their biscuits. I fear they'll have no appetite.'

'But we're hungry,' Agnes and Christopher chorused.

Lizzie laughed. 'Then you must ignore me. Thank you, Ellen.'

Ellen was clearly relieved. 'It's a busy day and Cook will want to concentrate on tonight's dinner.' She bent towards Lizzie and, in a confidential whisper, said, 'Mr Trent is in town. Mrs Bullivant will want everything just so this evening.'

Lizzie was confused. 'Mr Trent?' She meant Mr Bullivant, surely.

'Her special friend,' Ellen said, with a wink.

Lizzie was shocked and glanced hurriedly at the children, but they were already out of earshot, climbing the stairs to the nursery.

'I expect you'll be on your way back to the country now,' Ellen said. 'She won't have time for the children while he's around.'

'She said she might spend some time with them this afternoon,' Lizzie protested, feeling she should show some loyalty to her employer.

'I wouldn't count on it,' Ellen said, and departed towards the kitchen.

Lizzie followed the children slowly up the stairs and supervised hand- and face-washing before they settled at the table. The tray that came showed every sign of having been put together in haste:

roughly hewn slices of bread, a slab of cheese and a bowl of apples. Lizzie had no appetite but the children happily filled their stomachs.

'What will we do this afternoon?' Christopher asked.

'Well, your mother might be at home to do something with you,' Lizzie said. Christopher sighed at the prospect of more visiting but Lizzie quelled him with a look, then declared it was time for a rest. She insisted Christopher took up a book, and allowed Agnes to lie on the window seat, gazing out at the sky while she cuddled her favourite doll.

After an hour had passed, Lizzie decided Mrs Bullivant wasn't going to appear or, if she did, it would be too late to do anything with the children, given that she was expecting dinner guests that night. So she suggested Christopher might paint some of his new lead soldiers, which made him very happy, while she read to Agnes.

A little later, Ellen knocked and came in with raspberry cordial for them all.

'The mistress is back,' she said to Lizzie. 'She wants to see you in the parlour and I'm to sit with the children.'

Lizzie jumped to her feet and cast a quick glance in the looking-glass to check her appearance. She smoothed her hair, noting her high colour as she did so. Was she in trouble? Had Mrs Bullivant somehow learned of the argument in the park that morning? She hurried from the room, her anxiety increasing as she approached the parlour.

Mrs Bullivant looked as though she had only recently returned. She was standing by the window, gazing out over the park, still in her costume of that morning.

'There you are, Lizzie. I won't keep you long. I'm sorry I didn't get home in time to join you and the children. I must prepare for tonight's dinner now, but I will see the children in the drawing room before we eat. I find myself caught up with engagements in the days ahead, so you will return to Betsanger Court in the morning. Mr Powell will take you in the carriage. Please be ready for an early departure.'

Relieved that there was no mention of Mrs Simmonds and the incident in the park, Lizzie stammered, 'Yes, of course, thank you, madam.'

Mrs Bullivant turned from regarding the park and caught her smiling. 'Ah, I see you will be glad to return to the countryside. I take it the city isn't to your taste?'

Lizzie stuttered, 'Yes, no, I mean ...' She breathed deeply and tried again. 'The children have enjoyed spending time with you, but I think they are finding it hot in the city and will be glad to be back at Betsanger Court.'

Mrs Bullivant smiled. 'And you, Miss Carey? Will you be glad?'

Lizzie thought of how she looked forward to a return to the routine, the familiar faces of the household there – even Mrs Bailey – and the freedom the children had. These things made life easier for her but she could hardly say that to her employer.

'Perhaps I'm a country girl at heart,' she said. 'But I have enjoyed our time in Canterbury, and seeing quite a different side of life.'

'Well said, Miss Carey.' Mrs Bullivant moved purposefully towards the door. 'And now I must dress for dinner. Please make sure the children look their best for my guests.'

Lizzie returned to the nursery and told the children they must gather together any important belongings, for they would be returning to Betsanger Court the following morning. Ellen, collecting the cordial glasses, shot her a look, eyebrows raised. Lizzie ignored her and set about removing clothes from the chest of drawers and folding them into neat piles. She kept one set apart for Agnes and Christopher. There would be a battle later to persuade them to change for the dinner guests, but it would be for the last time. After that, they would be back to their quiet life in the countryside and a proper routine once more. But first there was a chance to see the mysterious Mr Trent. Was Ellen correct in her insinuations? Were they being sent back to the country because Mrs Bullivant wanted to devote her time to him while he was in town? It certainly looked that way and, despite herself, Lizzie was eager to see him.

At seven o'clock that evening she presented herself and the children, attired in their best clothes, hair brushed and faces washed, to the party in the drawing room. It was a small gathering and Lizzie searched their faces, to see whether she could spot Mrs Bullivant's special friend. In fact, it was hardly necessary for a man was at her side and, from the solicitous way in which he treated her, and the way in which she looked at him in return, it was clear this must be Mr Trent. He was not as Lizzie had expected. Sandy-haired, no taller than Mrs Bullivant, smartly but not fashionably dressed, he wasn't a figure to stand out in a crowd. Lizzie reflected that she had never met Mr Bullivant. Perhaps the two men were similar, or possibly entirely different. She was conscious she might be caught staring so did her best to retain her usual neutral expression as Mrs Bullivant introduced the children around the room.

'And this is dear Mr Trent,' she said, turning to him last, 'but, of course, you have met him many times before. Now, to bed with you both. I will see you again before too long. Miss Carey, I wish you all a safe journey tomorrow morning. I expect to hear great things of Christopher's studies once he is back at his desk.'

The assembled company laughed politely and Lizzie took her cue to shepherd the children from the room. Christopher had to endure some ruffling of his hair on the way.

'Now, as your mother said, it's time for bed. We have to make an early start in the morning.'

The children protested but Lizzie was firm. It was hard to settle them when it was still so light outside, and the laughter and chatter from the dining room drifted up the stairs, but after half an hour of tossing and turning, both children were fast asleep. Lizzie waited until dusk fell across the park outside, then climbed into her bed. She thought she would struggle to fall asleep, too, but she was surprised to find herself being shaken awake by Ellen in the thin light of dawn.

'Time to get up,' she whispered, depositing a fresh jug of water on the washstand. Then she was gone, leaving Lizzie to lie in bed for a few moments more, savouring the thought of what lay ahead.

CHAPTER FIFTEEN

As soon as she dismounted from the carriage at Betsanger Court, Lizzie felt she could breathe again. Agnes and Christopher were equally happy to be back, Christopher leaping down the carriage step in his haste to be home and Agnes preparing to do the same until Joe caught her. He set her gently on the ground.

'We don't want any broken heads now we're back,' he said, with a smile. She shook him off and ran after Christopher, who was already racing round the house towards the stable yard.

'Children! Come back!' Lizzie called after them, but it was too late. They had vanished around the corner of the house.

'Don't worry,' Joe said. 'I'm going to the yard now. I'll keep an eye on them. I expect they want to see the kittens. You sort yourself out, then come and find us.'

He deposited the bags at the front entrance and Lizzie prepared to take them upstairs. There was more luggage than there had been when they had departed: new outfits for the children as well as gifts Mrs Bullivant had bestowed on them. Lizzie was very hot by the time the last bag was in the nursery, and delighted to see Susan bearing a tray of lemonade. Although she was now an upstairs maid, she had carried on delivering the meals to the nursery, as Hester had refused. Although sorry for her extra work, Lizzie was glad. Cloistered in her nursery world, she looked forward to their brief interactions, and to gleaning any news from the house.

'I thought I heard the carriage but it was so early I didn't think you could be here already. Then I saw Joe in the yard. You could probably do with some refreshment after the journey.' Susan set the tray on the table.

'Thank you,' Lizzie said, pouring herself a glass and gulping it down. 'I'll go and fetch the children. We had an early start and they're probably thirsty, hungry too.' She paused and said, 'I'm glad to be back.'

It was odd to think that at one time this place had seemed so strange and unwelcoming to her. Now it felt like home. She took a lemon biscuit from the plate and nibbled it thoughtfully as she hurried down to the stables. As Joe had predicted, the children had been keen to see the kittens, which had become more adventurous since their departure.

Lizzie and Joe watched as Christopher teased them with a leafy twig, drawing it along the ground for them to pounce, then pulling it away, while Agnes tried her best to capture one for a cuddle. They were too wriggly to submit and she was thwarted every time.

'Lemonade upstairs,' Lizzie said, 'and biscuits.'

There was no response. Lizzie sighed. 'I'll give them five minutes,' she said.

She turned to Joe. 'Don't you have to return to Canterbury with the carriage?'

'Are you keen to be rid of me so soon?' Joe laughed. 'Mrs Bullivant has no need of it. Mr Trent has made his carriage available to her for the rest of her stay in Canterbury, and then she will be going to join Mr Bullivant in London. I believe they will return here after that.'

'Mr Trent ...' Lizzie said slowly, not sure how to phrase any of the questions that had been troubling her. 'Has Mrs Bullivant known him long?'

'As long as I've been employed by the family, that's for sure.' He gave her a quizzical look. 'Is there more you'd like to know?'

'Well ...' Lizzie floundered '... Ellen called him her special friend. What does that mean exactly?'

Joe chuckled. 'Just that, I suppose.' Seeing that Lizzie was becoming frustrated he relented. 'She finds it useful to have a male companion in Canterbury, as Mr Bullivant rarely joins her there. Mr Trent's wife suffers from ill-health and doesn't appear in public, so the arrangement suits them both.'

Lizzie was still confused. 'Mr Bullivant doesn't object?'

Joe shrugged. 'Object to what? His wife is happy so he is too.'

'But ...' Lizzie thought back to their early departure. She was sure that Mr Trent was still in the house. She could see no evidence within but it was as though his presence hung on the air, like the cigar smoke from the previous evening. Was that why Mrs Bullivant had wanted the children out of the house so early that morning?

Joe smiled at her. 'Best not to think about it. Grand folk live their lives in a way they would never tolerate in us. They're welcome to it as far as I'm concerned. I'm happy with this.' He gestured at the stable yard, the children playing on the cobbles. 'And I'm glad to be back to it. Now, I'd better get on with sorting out those horses. Isaac Turner would have my guts for garters if he saw me dilly-dallying with you when the horses need attending to.' He winked at her and went off to give Captain and Lady a proper rub-down.

'Up to the nursery now,' Lizzie called to Agnes and Christopher. 'We can come back down to the gardens later.'

They grumbled, but the promise of lemon biscuits drew them away. Then they became absorbed in their new toys while Lizzie unpacked, so the rest of the morning passed peacefully. Lizzie thought guiltily of Christopher's studies. His tutor would return on Saturday and it would be obvious he had done little. It was too late to do anything about that now, she thought, with a sigh. He would have to make it up with extra work over the coming days.

Susan reappeared after a while with their midday meal. 'Did you enjoy Canterbury?' she asked Lizzie.

'At first,' Lizzie said, glancing at the children to make sure they weren't being overheard. 'But then it all became too much – the visiting and the children always having to look smart and be on their best behaviour. I couldn't wait to get back here.'

Susan looked surprised. 'But the shops and the theatre – I would love to go there.'

'You've never been?' It wasn't far, Lizzie thought, but what need did Susan have of going there, let alone the means to make the journey?

Susan shook her head. 'Never. Maybe I'll go and work there one day. That's where most of the girls go from Betsanger. It's too quiet here, stuck out in the country.'

Lizzie smiled to herself. That was exactly how she liked it. Mrs Bullivant's life in the city was so very different from the life she had led there with the Russells. The situation with Mr Trent had jangled her nerves – she didn't fully understand it, despite Joe's attempt at an explanation. She looked at Christopher and Agnes, their heads bent over their plates. Did they have any idea of the lives their parents led? Was this to be their destiny too? They were so innocent – she wished she could keep them that way, so that they need never learn of the web of deceit that was the backdrop to their upbringing.

CHAPTER SIXTEEN

There followed an idyllic couple of weeks at Betsanger Court. Every day was blessed with soft late-summer sunshine and Lizzie returned to the previous routine in the nursery. Each morning Christopher studied at the table in the window, while Agnes played, drew or sewed alongside Lizzie, or simply gazed out of the window. She was quite self-sufficient, Lizzie noted, and easily able to entertain herself, unlike Christopher. After their midday meal, Christopher could sit still no longer and they went outside, for a walk around the grounds or into the village nearby. There was little to see other than a few houses, a church and a shop that sold almost everything. Bread and vegetables were piled on a long wooden table that served as a counter, while rat traps and metal pails hung from hooks on the walls. Some of the pails were empty, others filled with goods for sale: nails in assorted sizes, scrubbing brushes, blocks of soap. The woman who ran the shop had a soft spot for Agnes and Christopher and always had something to offer them – sugar mice, liquorice or barley-sugar twists from big glass jars on the counter. Lizzie had to limit the visits to once a week, partly because the shop-keeper would never take payment and partly because Christopher began to expect the gifts as his right.

On other days, she would take a blanket down to the gardens and they would sit and draw, or she would read to them and Susan would bring their afternoon drink and biscuits out to them. The children's favourite way to spend time, though, was in the stable yard, playing with the kittens and petting the horses. Lizzie looked forward to these afternoons, even though she knew, despite her determination to be wary, it was Joe she was eager to see. She tried to limit their visits to two or three a week, to avoid being a nuisance, but he always appeared happy to spend time with them, and to show the children anything new in the gardens.

'There's a badger sett in the wood,' he said one day. 'Come and see it.' He set off through the kitchen garden, the children skipping at his side, leaving Lizzie to follow. She nodded at Samuel and Abraham, hard at work among the vegetables, and paused to sniff the bed of lavender, humming with bees, before slipping through the gate in the wall and into the copse that Joe called the wood. It bordered farmland and the badgers had set up home close to the fence, digging out the soil so that it formed mounds all around the tunnel entrances.

Agnes was disappointed. 'Where are the badgers?'

'They sleep in the day,' Joe said, 'but they come out at dusk. There are cubs in the den – I came down to watch them play last night.'

'Can we come with you tonight?' Agnes asked.

Lizzie shook her head. 'It will be past your bedtime.'

Joe gave her a look. 'Maybe they could stay up late, just this once. It's not often you get a chance like this. The cubs will be grown before too long.'

'Can we go? Please say we can!'

Christopher added his pleas to Agnes's so that Lizzie was forced to clap her hands over her ears, laughing. 'All right,' she said. 'It will be good for you both to learn about them. But we must leave the house very quietly and hope no one sees us. I'm not sure what your mother would think of you being kept up late.'

It wasn't Mrs Bullivant Lizzie was worried about so much as Mrs Bailey, but she kept that to herself. She also tried to ignore her own mounting anticipation: the thought of being out with Joe in the evening was an exciting novelty. But, she told herself, there would be a perfectly good reason for her to be there: furthering the children's education.

'Good,' Joe said briskly. 'We'll need to set off at eight o'clock. I'll take a couple of lanterns from the stable. Make sure you wrap up. The evenings may feel warm, but it's cooler under the trees and we might have to wait a while before the badgers show themselves. It's better we get down here before dusk falls and settle ourselves. Then we have to sit very still and stay quiet. Can you do that?'

He addressed Agnes, who nodded solemnly, but Lizzie thought it was Christopher who was more likely to find that hard. She would have to warn him not to wriggle, and to save his questions until they were on their way back to the nursery.

They all trooped back to the stable yard, and the children devoted themselves to teasing the kittens while Lizzie and Joe watched.

'The master and mistress will be here next week,' Joe said.

Lizzie was surprised. 'I didn't know that,' she said. She supposed Joe had heard kitchen gossip. No doubt Mrs Bailey would tell her soon enough. It was a shame: it would curtail the children's freedom again. She was curious to see Mr Bullivant, though, and to discover how he would behave with his children.

'I'd best get back to work,' Joe said. 'I'll wait for you tonight by the gate in the kitchen garden.' The smile he gave her made Lizzie think for a moment that it would be just the two of them, until reality forced its way back in. She'd have a hard job quelling the children's excitement over the next few hours. And, if she was honest, her own. She hadn't been out of the house after the children's bedtime all the time she had been at Betsanger Court. It felt like a very big adventure – an illicit one, too.

Chapter Seventeen

By the time eight o'clock came, the children were overexcited and overtired. Agnes had been yawning since her usual bedtime of seven, and even Christopher was flagging. They perked up when Lizzie began to gather blankets and jackets into a basket, and were waiting at the nursery door by the time she was ready, impatient to depart.

'We have to be very quiet on the stairs,' Lizzie said. 'Tiptoe down them like little mice.' It was lucky that this side of the house was empty, she reflected, for although they did as she asked, the strangeness of the situation made them giggle. She had to make them pause in the hall to gather themselves before she opened the door and they slipped outside onto the steps.

Joe was right: the air was cool and Lizzie shivered, although more from anticipation than chill. She glanced at the children and decided to wait until they reached the wood to get them to put on their jackets. She feared they would only protest if she did it now.

'Now, we must creep past the house and hope no one sees us,' Lizzie warned. 'Stay in the shadows, don't speak until we reach the stable yard, and then only in a whisper.'

She set off behind the children, conscious that Agnes's pale dress shone in the low light as shadows fell across the garden. She was small, though, and could pass beneath the windows unseen. Mrs Bailey's parlour on the ground floor had one overlooking the gardens; Lizzie could only hope she wasn't sitting there reading to catch the last of the daylight. She bent lower and hoped for the best, risking a quick glance as she passed – the housekeeper was at her desk, back to the window, and didn't appear to have heard them.

Lizzie felt she could breathe more freely once they reached the stable yard. Joe was already there, waiting by the kitchen garden, two lit lanterns set on the wall beside him. Agnes and Christopher ran to him and Lizzie feared they would call out, but they had remembered her words, although she could hear their whispers quite clearly.

'All set?' Joe asked, handing a lantern to Lizzie.

She nodded, her hand trembling a little as she took it and her fingers brushed his.

'Right then,' he addressed the children, 'follow me in single file and when we reach the wood, watch where you put your feet. The ground's uneven and there are tree roots across the path – easy to see by day, a trap for the unwary at night.'

'Wait,' Lizzie said, as he was about to lead the way. 'Agnes, Christopher, put your jackets on now, before you start to feel cold.'

Christopher grumbled that he was hot and didn't need anything and Agnes copied him, until Joe said, 'No jackets, no badgers,' at which they obeyed at once. Then they were on their way, crossing the kitchen garden where moths fluttered around the lanterns, one brushing Lizzie's face so that she uttered a strangled squeak and nearly dropped the light.

The wood by night was quite different from earlier that day. It was immediately much darker and Lizzie could hear quiet rustlings in the undergrowth as they followed Joe along the path he picked out. A little way into the wood he stopped, turned and held his fingers to his lips. 'We have to be extra quiet from here. The badgers will sense the vibration of our footsteps underground so we need to settle ourselves quickly, downwind from the entrance to the sett so they don't catch our scent. We might need to sit a while before they come out, so make sure you're warm and comfortable. And I'll have to turn the lanterns right down so the light doesn't disturb them.'

He set off again, stopping a couple of minutes later at a

moss-covered fallen log. Lizzie quickly laid a blanket along it and lifted Agnes to perch there, Christopher scrambling up beside her. She put a woolly shawl over their legs, made sure they were supported by a branch behind them and couldn't fall backwards, then hesitated. Where should she sit?

Joe solved that by taking another blanket from the basket and spreading it along the log next to the children. He indicated she should sit, then sat next to her, handing her the remaining shawl. He was so close to her, she could feel the warmth of his body. She made a show of checking that the children were safe and secure, to hide the effect he was having on her. Then he laid a warning hand on her arm and she had to sit quietly, facing forward, eyes straining to get used to the dark. She could dimly make out the entrance to the badger sett and tried to concentrate on it but her thoughts were elsewhere. There had been no opportunity to speak to Joe about the incident with Mrs Simmonds in Canterbury, other than to thank him. Now, seated so close to him, she felt an urgent need to explain herself. What must he think of her? Yet his attitude towards her didn't appear to have changed since that horrid encounter in the park. She blushed in the dark to think of it, and turned towards him. But he held a finger to his lips and pointed forward. On her other side, Lizzie sensed the children sit up and she glanced at them to make sure they didn't slide off the log. They were transfixed, peering into the gloom, so Lizzie turned her head to see what they had all spotted.

A striped black-and-white snout was just visible at the entrance to the sett. Its owner was motionless – he was testing the air, Lizzie thought. Then he must have decided it was safe, because the rest of his bulky body emerged, quickly followed by three other badgers of a similar size. One rushed another, impatient to be on the move, and they tumbled over and over. Lizzie held her breath, thinking they were fighting, until she realised they were playing, no doubt glad to be out of the confines of the sett.

Another badger followed, moving more slowly. This one was larger – one of the parents, Lizzie assumed. He or she ignored the little ones and set off in the direction of the fence, bent on a night's foraging. What did badgers eat? She would have to ask Joe, once they were allowed to speak. She glanced at him again and he turned towards her. She could see his smile in the darkness. He reached for her hand and squeezed it briefly, holding on to it. Her heart beat faster. His hand was warm and dry, his grip firm, completely enclosing her fingers. He was still smiling at her, and she couldn't look away. She had the strangest feeling that they were speaking to each other, but without a word being uttered. Had the children noticed? Lizzie didn't care: she wanted the moment to go on for ever.

Conscious at last of the children's restlessness, she wrenched her gaze away from Joe and glanced at them, then at the badgers. The cubs had vanished, either back into the sett or they had followed their parent out into the field.

'That's it,' Joe said, in a normal voice, breaking the spell. 'They've gone for now. Time to get you to bed.'

Lizzie was surprised that they didn't protest, until she lifted Agnes down from the log and she sagged against her skirts. Then she realised how weary she was. For once, Christopher didn't seem to want to jump down so Joe lifted him, then fished in his pocket and produced a paper-wrapped package.

'I begged this from Cook.' He tore away the paper to reveal four slabs of fruit loaf. 'I told her it was for the badgers, so I hope it isn't stale.'

Lizzie, suddenly hungry, bit into her slice. It was deliciously moist. 'What do badgers eat?' she asked, through a mouthful of crumbs.

'Not fruit loaf.' Joe laughed. 'Earthworms, fallen apples, eggs, the odd rat if they can catch it.' He busied himself gathering up the blankets and putting them into Lizzie's basket, then he turned up the flame on the lanterns.

'Now, don't stumble on the way back.' He glanced at Agnes, then put both lanterns on the log and bent to scoop her up. He settled her so that her arms were round his neck and her head resting on his shoulder.

'Off we go,' he said, picking up a lantern. Lizzie followed suit, wrapping a shawl around her shoulders. They reached the kitchen garden without incident, then crossed the stable yard. She thought Joe would set Agnes down there but he strode off around the house and she hurried after him, her heart in her mouth. What if they were spotted?

Thankfully, the curtains were closed in Mrs Bailey's parlour, although a light shone dimly behind them. Lizzie tiptoed past, hardly daring to breathe. Again, she thought Joe would deposit Agnes on the steps, but he opened the front door and continued up the stairs, Lizzie hurrying after. At the door to the nursery he stopped, while Lizzie opened it and ushered Christopher through. Then Joe transferred Agnes to Lizzie's arms, lightly kissing the little girl's hair as he did so. His lips brushed Lizzie's cheek and his eyes held hers for a long moment, before he took her lantern and set off silently down the stairs.

CHAPTER EIGHTEEN

The children slept late the following morning, for which Lizzie was glad. With Susan's help, she had quietly instigated the moving of the beds to the room beside the nursery, feeling that the children would sleep better if they weren't in the room where they spent the majority of each day. She hadn't sought Mrs Bullivant's permission and she supposed it would be something she should address when the parents arrived in the next few days.

Susan was surprised to find the nursery empty when she arrived with the breakfast tray. 'Are they sick? Shall I take it all away again?' she asked, looking doubtfully at the cooling porridge and boiled eggs.

'No, it's time they were up. I'll wake them,' Lizzie said. 'They were overexcited yesterday and had trouble getting to sleep.'

It was only partly untrue, she reflected, as Susan unloaded the tray; Agnes and Christopher had been excited before they set out but had had no difficulty in sleeping when they returned. Agnes hadn't even opened her eyes while Lizzie pulled off her clothes and put her into her nightgown.

She called the children to the table, telling them they could change out of their nightclothes after they had eaten. They were ravenous, Christopher spooning down his porridge as though he hadn't seen food for days.

'Slowly, now,' Lizzie warned. 'You'll give yourself tummy-ache.'

'Can we go and see the badgers again tonight?' Agnes asked. She saw the surprise on Lizzie's face and changed to a wheedling tone. 'Please,' she begged. 'We'll be good all day, won't we, Christopher?'

Lizzie laughed. 'You're always good,' she said. 'But I don't think we can go again tonight.' She saw the threat of tears in Agnes's eyes and added hastily, 'We'll have to ask Joe. Maybe he'll take us again in a few days' time. Now, if you've both finished eating, it's time to get washed and dressed.'

Susan came to remove the tray while they were so engaged, for which Lizzie was grateful. She was sure Agnes wouldn't be able to contain her excitement over the previous evening's adventure and would be desperate to share it.

'Now, both of you,' she said, once they were settled again at the table, books open in front of them for the day's work, 'the badgers must be our secret. If anyone finds out where we went, they might tell Mrs Bailey and she will tell your mother. We might be forbidden to go again, and Joe will get into trouble.'

Agnes had been about to protest, but the thought of Joe being reprimanded stopped her.

'Do you promise to keep quiet?' Lizzie asked. She didn't like asking the children to be devious but she couldn't see an alternative. They nodded solemnly.

'We can spend the morning with the badgers in a different way,' Lizzie said. 'Christopher, you get some of the books down from the shelf and see what you can find out about them. Their size, how long they live, what they weigh. Start a new page in your book and write it all down. And then see if you can draw one. Agnes, why don't you draw me a picture of the badger sett?'

The children liked the idea and settled to the task. They were still absorbed, heads down, when Susan reappeared with their mid-morning drink.

'Goodness, you look busy,' she said.

Lizzie held her breath, but they didn't utter a word about what they were doing.

'They're good at drawing, aren't they?' Susan said, watching them for a moment or two. 'Their parents will be pleased. I hear they're coming soon.'

'I haven't heard anything,' Lizzie said, even though Joe had already mentioned it.

'I dare say we'll be told in the next day or so,' Susan said. 'Expect to be kept busy. And watch yourself.'

She had gone before Lizzie gathered her wits to ask her what she meant. She tried to put Susan's words out of her head and concentrated instead on the children's work. Agnes had drawn a picture of their outing, with the four of them sitting on the log, and some oversized black-and-white creatures apparently floating in the sky. Luckily it would be very hard for anyone to make sense of the scene, Lizzie thought, as she congratulated her on her hard work.

Christopher had done a very good job with his research. He had added a line about what badgers ate, based on what Joe had told them, including 'not fruit loaf'. Would that raise awkward questions from his tutor? She praised him. She'd worry about that if and when it happened.

'Have your drinks,' she said, 'and then we can decide what to do next.'

'Go and see Joe in the stables,' they chorused.

Lizzie laughed. 'He'll be busy,' she said. She saw the disappointment on their faces. 'Perhaps this afternoon.' If only they knew how much she wanted to see Joe, too. She would love to be able to go with him, and the children, into the woods again, seemingly watching the badgers at play, while all her senses were tuned into him sitting beside her, strong and warm, his hand holding hers.

The nursery door swung open. Startled, Lizzie broke free from her reverie and looked up.

'Daydreaming, Miss Carey?' Mrs Bailey was frowning at her. 'There isn't time for any of that. Mr and Mrs Bullivant are on their way here. They will arrive by dinner time and will no doubt want to see the children. Make sure they are presentable. And tidy the nursery.' Her gaze swept the room, but she could find no fault. 'Mr Bullivant will want to see Christopher's books to check his progress.'

'And my drawings,' Agnes said, picking up her paper and waving it at Mrs Bailey, who ignored her.

Lizzie stood up. 'Of course,' she said to Mrs Bailey. 'Children, we must make everything ready.' She went over to the bookshelves and made a show of straightening the spines, hoping that would be enough to make the housekeeper leave. Mrs Bailey stood for a moment or two longer, then Lizzie heard the door click shut behind her.

A wave of disappointment washed over her. How long would the Bullivants stay? The children would have to be on their best behaviour, ready to be summoned to their parents at any moment. There would be no chance to visit the badger sett again; she wasn't sure they would even be able to go to the stable yard to see the kittens and horses. She feared Mr Bullivant would disapprove of such activities. She had to be honest with herself, though. This was not all about the children. She was disconsolate on her own account. When would she be able to spend time with Joe again? He would no doubt be kept busy, as would everyone in the household. There would be no opportunity for secret smiles and the brushing of fingers. Everyone must be on their very best behaviour.

Chapter Nineteen

When Susan came upstairs with their midday meal, she told them of the uproar the arrival of the Bullivants had caused. Lizzie was instantly grateful to be in the peaceful surroundings of the nursery.

'Cook is in a proper flap,' Susan confided. 'There wasn't time to order in the meat and vegetables for tonight's dinner, so Joe has been sent to check the traps. Hopefully there's a rabbit or two, and the garden vegetables haven't come to an end yet. There's plums for dessert – she's got Alice working on a pudding recipe – but it has put her in a very bad mood. So I'm afraid I had to get something together for you today.'

Lizzie surveyed the hunks of bread, slices of cold meat and dollops of chutney on each plate, and hastened to reassure Susan that it would suit them perfectly. She felt guilty that Susan was still waiting on them, when no doubt there was plenty to be done, preparing all the rooms to Mrs Bailey's exacting standards. Susan hurried away and Lizzie looked at the children's glum faces.

'It's not what you're used to, but it doesn't happen every day,' she said. 'Now eat up, and then we'll walk into the village.'

Christopher brightened at the thought of the sweets to be found there, but Agnes protested. 'Why can't we go and see the kittens?' she asked, picking at her food.

'Because everyone will be busy, making sure the place is spick and span for your parents,' Lizzie said, trying not to sound resentful. After all, it was Mr Bullivant's money that provided for them all. They would have to embrace whatever whims and fancies he brought with him from London, and do so with willingness and a smile.

The walk to the village proved a good distraction, but Lizzie was surprised and alarmed to find the Bullivant coach already at the front of the house when they returned, and a footman busy unloading trunks and bags. They stepped around the pile and went into the house. Lizzie heard the gruff tones of a male voice in the drawing room and hesitated. Should the children go and see their father? Then she looked at Christopher's face, grubby and sticky from the sweets he had consumed, and Agnes's hands, stained green from the stems of the flowers she had picked.

'Up to the nursery,' she said. 'We'd better get you cleaned up in case your parents want to see you.'

In fact, it was after six o'clock before the summons came. Lizzie had kept the children quiet and tidy by reading to them for as long as she could, but her energy was flagging by the time Susan knocked and poked her head around the door.

'They're having drinks in the drawing room,' she said. 'You're to take the children down.' She smiled at Agnes and Christopher, then withdrew.

Lizzie ushered the children down the stairs, nervous that Mr Bullivant would quiz them, and somehow their secret outing of the night before would be revealed. But he barely looked up from the paper he was reading by the fire, and it was Mrs Bullivant who greeted her offspring.

'I think you have both grown since I last saw you. In such a short time, too! It must be the country air you were longing for, Miss Carey.' She smiled at Lizzie, then turned back to Agnes and Christopher. 'And you're wearing the clothes I had made in Canterbury – how well they suit you!'

She called to her husband: 'My dear, won't you say hello to your children? You haven't seen them in some weeks now.' Was that a hint of reproof in her voice?

248

Mr Bullivant grunted, sighed and folded his newspaper with an air of irritation. 'Well, come over here and let me see you,' he said.

Lizzie gave Christopher and Agnes a gentle push towards their father. It was her first chance to look at him. He was red-faced, perhaps from the warmth of the fire, and portly, his waistcoat buttons straining with the effort of holding his belly. His grey hair was thinning and his face lined; Lizzie had the impression he was somewhat older than his wife. He surveyed his children as they stood in front of him.

'Working hard, I hope?' he asked Christopher. 'Don't lie, now. I'll be speaking to your tutor in the morning.'

'Yes, sir,' Christopher said.

At least he didn't mumble and fix his eyes on the floor, Lizzie thought, but looked directly at his father.

'Good, good.' Mr Bullivant turned his gaze on Agnes. 'And I suppose I must ask your nursemaid if you have been behaving your-self?' For the first time, he appeared to notice Lizzie and beckoned her over.

'So, Miss ...?' he said, and paused, waiting for her to supply her name.

'Carey,' she said, aware of his eyes raking over her. 'Elizabeth Carey.'

'Miss Carey. I hope you are strict with these children?'

Lizzie smiled politely. 'They are always well behaved, sir. They are a pleasure to be with.'

Mr Bullivant regarded her. 'I will visit the nursery tomorrow morning. I want to see Christopher's books.'

'Of course, sir.' Lizzie felt strangely uncomfortable although she couldn't say why. She glanced at Mrs Bullivant. She was at the window, her back to them, gazing out over the lawns, apparently oblivious. Mr Bullivant had lost interest in his children, so Lizzie drew them away.

'Say goodnight to your mother and father,' she said. The children chorused their goodbyes from the doorway, then broke away and scampered up the stairs. They felt as relieved as she was to be away from Mr Bullivant, Lizzie thought. She didn't relish the idea of his presence in the nursery the following morning, but it would no doubt be brief. He appeared to have little other than the most basic interest in his family. No wonder Mrs Bullivant was rumoured to prefer the company of Mr Trent, although Lizzie struggled to see the attraction of either man. Her thoughts turned fleetingly to Joe: tall, handsome, and strong from all his outdoor work, with the most unusual hazel eyes that held her gaze and awakened something within her that she fought against with increasing weakness. She supposed it was money that drove Mrs Bullivant, and was glad it would never be a factor in her own life.

CHAPTER TWENTY

Lizzie felt unaccountably nervous the following morning. She told herself not to be ridiculous: Mr Bullivant was just her employer, taking an interest in what his children were doing while in her care. She had taken the precaution of laying out Christopher's books as soon as Susan had removed the breakfast things from the table, and had added some of Agnes's stitching and her drawings. She had left out the one of the visit to the badger sett, in case it raised awkward questions.

Her uncertain mood seemed to transfer itself to the children. Christopher became sulky and refused to go and brush his hair, and Agnes burst into tears when Lizzie asked her to pick up the paintbrushes she had knocked to the floor while arguing with Christopher over names for the kittens. Lizzie was puzzled: the children didn't usually act like this. Was the imminent visit from their father the cause?

She had just got them settled at the table, Christopher with a page of algebra set by his tutor, Agnes with a handwritten alphabet to copy, when the nursery door swung open after the briefest of knocks. Mr Bullivant's bulk seemed to fill the space. Lizzie had hoped that Mrs Bullivant would be with him, but he was alone. She jumped up and said, 'Please come in, sir.'

'Hard at work, I see,' Mr Bullivant said. 'Don't let me interrupt.'

Christopher and Agnes studiously avoided looking at him and bent to their tasks.

'I hear good things about you from my wife, Miss Carey.'

Mr Bullivant had moved over to the table, picking up one of Christopher's books. He flicked through it and frowned. 'Your handwriting is in need of improvement,' he said.

'Yes, sir,' Christopher mumbled.

Lizzie hastened to deflect what she feared might be a scolding from Mr Bullivant. 'We will make a point of practising it, sir. Agnes is good with her letters.' She hoped his focus might be drawn away from Christopher, but he hardly glanced at his daughter's book.

'It will be of little use to her. She will no doubt make a good marriage and you need only concern yourself with such skills as she might need for that. Christopher will have to make his way in the world of business. He can't ride on my coat tails. If you and his tutor can't persuade him to greater efforts, he will have to take his chances when he gets to school. They won't be so easy on him there.'

Lizzie could see Christopher was close to tears, and she felt quite fired up on his behalf. 'He does his best, sir. He has shown great aptitude for the study of his natural surroundings and he has an affinity with animals.'

Mr Bullivant snorted. 'That will be of little use to him in the future, I can assure you, Miss Carey.'

Pink in the face with indignation, Lizzie drew herself upright and prepared to continue with her argument, but Mr Bullivant forestalled her. He laid his hand on her arm and said, 'Come now, I have no quarrel with you, Miss Carey. I know my son. He is inclined to laziness and will take the easy way whenever he can. Don't let him fool you.'

Lizzie doubted his claim to know his son: his visits were clearly so infrequent that she couldn't see how he could pretend to such knowledge. But further protests died on her lips for Mr Bullivant drew her away from the table to the doorway.

'As I said, Miss Carey, I find no fault with you. Quite the opposite in fact.' His gaze raked across her once more. She felt an immediate revulsion and the urge to distance herself from him, but he still had hold of her arm, so she kept her face expressionless and remained silent. This served only to encourage him.

'I would like to be better acquainted. I think you would find it advantageous, too. My wife is planning to spend a few days in Canterbury, while I remain here. I would welcome your company of an evening. I feel sure you will be able to spare me some time.'

It wasn't a question as much as a command, Lizzie thought, as panic seized her. How could she avoid his unwanted attentions? She glanced back at the table but the children still had their heads bent over their books. A knock at the door made her start. It swung open to reveal Susan with their morning drinks on a tray.

'Beg pardon, sir, I didn't realise you were here. I'll come back.'

She began to back out of the room but Lizzie said hastily, 'It's quite all right. Mr Bullivant was just leaving.' She avoided looking at him, staring instead at Susan, hoping to convey her urgent wish to be saved from this awkward situation.

Mr Bullivant nodded. 'Don't forget my words, Miss Carey. I will expect you to act upon them.'

Susan contrived to hold the door open for him, while balancing the tray. 'What was that about?' she asked in a low voice, raising her eyebrows.

Lizzie shook her head, indicating the children. 'I must speak with you,' she said, only too aware of the desperation in her voice.

Susan thought for a moment. Finally she said, 'I could come up to you once the children are in bed and we've had our dinner downstairs. I'll say I need an early night. Heaven knows I really do, after all the extra work.' She gave a heartfelt sigh. 'I'd better get back downstairs. Mr Bullivant will be wanting his coffee.'

Lizzie gave an involuntary shudder at the mention of his name. Then she squared her shoulders and turned her attention to the children. She had a feeling they would need some soothing after their father's visit.

She hardly knew how she got through the rest of the day, such was her agitation. At times she pondered whether she had misinterpreted the master's intentions. His parting words were chosen carefully and could have referred to his earlier comments about the children's studies, Christopher's in particular. But then she remembered what he had said about becoming 'better acquainted'. She doubted he wished her to sit by the fire and read to him while his wife was away ...

CHAPTER TWENTY-ONE

Lizzie had never been so grateful to see the children safely tucked up in bed as she was that evening. There had been no more talk about visiting the badger sett, or even seeing Joe in the stable yard. They seemed cowed by their father's presence in the house.

She shut the bedroom door softly behind her and took up her sewing, moving to sit in the window seat. They hadn't stepped outside that day – she would have to remedy that the next. A dress of Agnes's, awaiting repair, remained untouched on her lap and, although she gazed out at the gathering dusk, she saw nothing. Her thoughts were turned inwards.

It was dark outside by the time there was a soft tap at the door. Lizzie got up, stretched and went to open it. Susan came in, bearing two glasses.

'Goodness, why are you sitting in the dark?' she asked.

'I don't know,' Lizzie confessed, hunting around for the tinder box. 'Well, I do but ...' She stopped, struck the flint and lit the oil lamp.

Susan thrust one of the glasses towards her. 'Here, take this,' she said. 'It's brandy – Cook had left it out so I managed to sneak a couple of glasses. You looked as though you could do with it this morning, and I thought you might still feel the same.' She settled herself at the nursery table. 'And after the day I've had, I need a little reward.' She took a sip and regarded Lizzie. 'Well, what's bothering you? Or should that be who?'

255

Lizzie had just taken a gulp of the fiery liquid and choked a little in surprise. She coughed and wiped her streaming eyes.

'It's Mr Bullivant.' She paused, then blurted it all out. 'He made – I think he made – a proposition. He said he wanted to get to know me better, and that I should spend some time with him in the evenings when Mrs Bullivant goes to Canterbury.'

Susan was grim-faced. 'Up to his old tricks, I see.'

'What do you mean?' Lizzie asked.

'He prefers servant girls to his wife. He doesn't even bother to take a mistress from his own kind. He knows a servant can't protest or she will lose her job. I thought he might have changed his ways after the scandal, but it seems not.' She stopped to take a sip of the brandy, a large one this time.

'What scandal?' Lizzie demanded.

'There was a maid – the one whose dress Mrs Bailey gave you when you first arrived. You remember you said the girl had got too fat for it, and I told you she was having a baby and was let go?'

'Yes. You said the father was somebody in the house.'

'Well, that somebody was Mr Bullivant. She'd caught his eye on one of his visits and he wasted no time. Surprised her when she was out in the gardens, looking for one of his dogs that he said had gone missing. A few months later it became obvious what had gone on, and she was told to leave. Mrs Bullivant got in a fury with Mrs Bailey. She'd been staying in London and Canterbury and arrived here to find her maid gone. She questioned Mrs Bailey's judgement, saying she was the best maid she'd ever had. Mrs Bailey let slip, accidentally on purpose I imagine, the part the master had had to play in it, and Mrs Bullivant went very quiet. The master wasn't with her on that visit but we all noticed that the next time he came he kept himself to himself. We all breathed a bit more easily, I can tell you.'

Lizzie's mind was racing. 'And you – has he ever tried ...?'

Susan laughed. 'I've always been below stairs until now. Mrs Bailey doesn't like us to be seen so that worked in my favour. She warned me this time, though, not to be cleaning his bedchamber if he was upstairs, and to keep out of his way at all times. She didn't say why, but I knew.'

'She didn't warn me,' Lizzie muttered. Then another thought struck her. 'So it wasn't Joe?'

Susan was puzzled. 'What wasn't Joe?'

'Joe wasn't the father of the baby.' Lizzie's heart leaped.

Susan was frowning. 'No. Whatever made you think that?'

'You said it was someone in the house,' Lizzie said. 'And there aren't any men of the right age in the house other than Joe. Samuel and Abraham are a bit old ...' She stopped, as Susan started to laugh.

'Oh, you silly goose. Where do you get such ideas? No, it wasn't Joe. At the time he had a sweetheart back home. I doubt he had eyes for anyone else.'

Lizzie's heart plummeted. 'A sweetheart?'

Susan shrugged. 'Yes, but that's all over now. She married someone else – couldn't cope with not seeing him for so long. He wrote letters to her every week but she never wrote back. I'm not sure she could write, to be honest.'

Lizzie couldn't believe that someone had let Joe down in that way. He was such a lovely, kind man.

Susan was looking at her with dawning recognition. 'You're sweet on Joe, aren't you? How come I didn't notice?' Then she answered her own question. 'I suppose I hardly see you, these days – just to deliver your meals. Well, you and Joe ...' She smiled.

Lizzie blushed furiously. 'There's nothing going on. Please don't say anything downstairs.' She could imagine Susan teasing Joe mercilessly. 'What am I going to do about Mr Bullivant? How can I refuse, if he demands I see him while Mrs Bullivant is away? If I don't go, he might tell her I wouldn't discuss Christopher's education with him. And if I go ...' Lizzie shuddered at the thought.

'He can't say anything to his wife if you don't go,' Susan said robustly. 'She'll know exactly what he's up to.'

'You don't think she turns a blind eye to it,' Lizzie asked, 'given that she has her friend, Mr Trent, in Canterbury?'

'Maybe.' Susan was thoughtful. 'I suppose that girl was just unlucky – she might still be working here if it hadn't been for the baby.'

Lizzie found herself wishing for a moment that that was the case. Then she chided herself. She doubted the poor girl had welcomed the master's advances any more than she did. She rested her elbows on the table and put her head in her hands. 'What am I to do?' she said aloud.

Susan let out a gusty sigh. 'Maybe the master will be called back to town on business.'

'Or maybe Mrs Bullivant will insist he joins her in Canterbury,' Lizzie said hopefully.

Susan shook her head. 'That will never happen. We all know about Mr Trent although hardly any of us have seen him.'

They sat in silent contemplation until Susan stood up, yawned and collected the glasses. 'I'm done in. I must sleep, but I'll think about it. Don't worry. I'm sure we can come up with a plan.'

Lizzie gave her a weak smile. What plan could they possibly make? Could she pretend to be ill for the duration of the master's visit? She clung to that idea as a little ray of hope while she silently prepared for bed in the room she shared with Christopher and Agnes. They slept deeply and sweetly and, once again, she was struck by their innocence in contrast to the tangled lives their parents led. She longed for better things for them – and for herself.

CHAPTER TWENTY-TWO

The next day, Lizzie awoke resolute. She had decided that feigning illness was her best hope of escaping Mr Bullivant's clutches, but when to start? She couldn't maintain such a pretence for a week, say, while she waited for Mrs Bullivant to leave. She would need to start the day she left.

When Susan came with the breakfast, she quickly whispered her idea to her. 'It's the only thing I can think of,' she said, in more normal tones. 'As soon as you hear that the mistress is leaving, let me know.'

Susan nodded. 'I will. I hope it works. I haven't managed to think of anything else.'

Lizzie joined the children at the table, determined to give them as normal a day as possible.

'There's Father,' Christopher said.

Lizzie's heart lurched. 'Where?' she asked, glancing nervously at the door.

'There.' Christopher pointed. 'Outside with his dogs.'

Lizzie half stood, and saw Mr Bullivant striding along the edge of the lawn, two large hounds at his side. She was uncomfortably reminded of the part a dog had played in his seduction of the maid. 'I didn't know he had dogs,' she said. She hadn't seen them in the house.

'He keeps them in the stable yard when he's here,' Christopher said. 'I expect Joe looks after them.'

'Can we go and see them? And Joe?' Agnes piped up.

259

'I don't think they're pets,' Lizzie said. 'They look like hunting dogs to me.'

Agnes was not to be put off. 'Please can we go? To see the kittens?'

Lizzie sighed. 'Perhaps this afternoon. I can't promise anything.' Then she busied herself starting the children on some morning activities, conscious all the time that Mr or Mrs Bullivant might decide to drop into the nursery. But the morning passed undisturbed, and when Susan came to deliver the midday meal, she had news that pleased Lizzie.

'The master and mistress are going visiting this afternoon,' she remarked. 'And they will be dining out this evening. The mistress will come up before they go to say goodnight to the children.'

Lizzie smiled. Thank goodness they wouldn't have to endure Mr Bullivant's presence. And Agnes could have her longed-for visit to the stable yard to see the kittens. She waited until they had eaten to share the good news. 'I had planned to walk to the village this afternoon,' she said, 'but I think we will go to the stable yard instead.'

Agnes squealed with excitement and ran to get her sun bonnet without being asked. Christopher maintained an air of disinterest but Lizzie knew he was pleased. As for herself, she was almost as excited as Agnes but determined not to show it.

It was a pleasure to be out in the fresh air, Lizzie reflected. There was already a hint of autumn, even so early in September. The leaves would start to fall from the trees before too long, but for now they were holding on to the last remnants of summer. With a start, she realised that soon Christopher would be sent away to school. Was this why both of his parents were here? No one had mentioned anything as yet. She glanced at him, walking at her side. He was a sensitive child. How on earth would he cope?

She was pulled back to the present by their arrival in the stable yard. Agnes had run on ahead and now she was returning to them, her face wet with tears.

'Whatever is the matter?' Lizzie was alarmed.

'The kittens,' Agnes wailed.

Had they been sent to new homes already? Lizzie was about to tell her how happy they would be with a farm or stable yard of their own to rule over, when Agnes hiccupped: 'Father's dogs.'

Lizzie frowned, puzzled. Joe was walking towards them, an inscrutable expression on his face.

'Agnes said something about the kittens.' Lizzie was troubled. 'Have they gone to new homes?'

'No,' Joe said. 'They would have stayed here with their mother.'

'Then?' Lizzie asked.

Joe hesitated. 'The master had the dogs off the lead in the grounds, unmuzzled. The kittens must have been out, exploring. The dogs are hunters . . .' He shrugged and spread his hands.

Lizzie was horrified. 'You mean, they caught them?'

'Well, two of them. Maybe all. We don't know.'

'Where are the dogs?' Lizzie asked. She fought down a wish to go and shout at them, but she was also fearful that the children might need protecting from them.

Joe gestured towards one of the empty stables. 'In there. I keep them tied up, but on long leads.'

'Can I go and look?' Christopher asked.

'Only from the stable door,' Lizzie said. 'Don't open it.'

She watched him go, with some anxiety. Agnes, clearly still upset, wandered off to follow one of the fat russet hens pecking on the cobblestones. For a few moments, Lizzie had Joe to herself. And she could look at him with fresh eyes. He was no longer tainted with her belief that he had fathered a child with one of the maids, and callously let her be dismissed.

She longed to reach out and take his hand, but it was hardly the time or place. And she still hadn't been able to explain her relationship with Mrs Simmonds. She felt an urgent need to clarify the situation and had just opened her mouth, uncertain where to start, when a shriek from Agnes startled her.

'What is it?' Lizzie spun around, imagining some new horror related to the dogs.

'Look! Look!' Agnes was pointing.

Joe and Lizzie hurried over. A tiny pink nose on the end of a muzzle spiked with whiskers was visible under the tool shed, then quickly withdrawn.

'It's the missing kitten.' Joe was delighted. 'See if you can tempt her out, Agnes. I'll go and find her some food.'

He went off and returned with a bowl of kitchen scraps, the mother cat struggling and spitting in his arms.

'She doesn't like being picked up,' Joe said cheerfully, seemingly oblivious to the scratches she had inflicted on his hands, 'but she's missing her kittens. She might help persuade this one out.'

The space beneath the tool shed was too small for the mother cat to enter, so she sat outside and mewed encouragement. Agnes spread a few scraps on the ground, Joe advising her to pick the strongest-smelling ones. Then they stood back and waited. Christopher came to join them. Lizzie was surprised at how long Agnes's patience lasted. She was becoming restless, though, keen to go closer and see whether she could grab one of the paws that appeared at intervals, patting around to locate the food. Then, at last, flat to the ground on its belly, the kitten wriggled out of its hiding place.

'Is it hurt?' Agnes was anxious.

'I don't think so,' Joe said. 'Best left to its mother to sort out.' She was now busy washing her offspring. 'I'll wait until they're more settled, then find a safer place for them. They can't be left free while those dogs are here.'

He was grim-faced as he said it. Lizzie had the idea that he, too, would be glad to see the back of Mr Bullivant. She was almost tempted to tell him of her predicament, but thought better of it. This was a problem only she could solve. The anxiety over what might lie ahead flooded back. She had forgotten all about it, down here in the stable yard. Now it was time to return to the house before the master and mistress came back from visiting.

Joe must have sensed her mood for he looked at her curiously as she chivvied the children to return to the nursery.

'We'll come back as soon as we can to see how the kitten is doing,' Lizzie promised. 'Keep it safe for us until then, Joe.'

He nodded, bending to listen to Agnes, who was pulling on his arm. 'And can we go and see the badgers again?' she begged.

'Perhaps,' Joe said, 'Not while your parents are here, though.'

Agnes sighed. 'That's what Lizzie said, too.'

Lizzie caught Joe's eye and smiled, then ushered the children in front of her, back to the house. As they climbed the stairs to the nursery, she heard the rumble of the carriage wheels. Mr and Mrs Bullivant were returning. Lizzie was glad she and the children had escaped an encounter that would surely have come with awkward questions about where they had been.

CHAPTER TWENTY-THREE

As it turned out, it was Mrs Bullivant who brought news of her departure for Canterbury. She appeared in the nursery that evening, wearing a dress that Lizzie could hardly take her eyes off, so beautiful was the fabric. It shimmered as she moved, and the colours were indecipherable. Lizzie couldn't decide if it was blue or grey.

The children were already in their nightclothes, causing their mother to exclaim: 'How angelic you look! I won't keep you long – I can see you are ready for bed. I wanted to tell you that I will be leaving for Canterbury tomorrow. I particularly wanted to speak to you, Christopher, before I do.'

He looked startled as she turned towards him, a marked change in her tone. 'Your father is very disappointed in you. I persuaded him to let me talk to you first, as I know he will not spare you. He has spoken to your tutor and been advised that you are not ready to attend school. Your Latin and mathematics are not up to scratch. Your father has arranged for the tutor to attend more than once a week in the future and he has written to the school to defer your entry. What do you have to say for yourself?'

Christopher attempted to look contrite, but before he hung his head, Lizzie caught joy on his face. Poor child, she thought. At least that explained why no mention had been made of preparing him to leave for school. His father would be demanding regular updates on his progress. From his tutor, thankfully. Lizzie had no desire to be involved.

'Well, I have no doubt he will wish to speak to you himself. He will be here for a few more days before he returns to London. I will bid you a good night, and trust you will reflect on this, Christopher, and make every effort to apply yourself.'

Mrs Bullivant left, after bestowing a kiss on the head of each child. Lizzie saw them into bed, but said nothing further to Christopher. He would have to face his father at some point and she saw no reason to upset him. He tried his best, but his heart wasn't in his studies.

Once they were settled, she returned to the nursery to contemplate the days ahead. There would, perhaps, be another encounter with Mr Bullivant, who would wish to talk to Christopher. After that, the evenings loomed large in her mind. She could, of course, make the excuse that the children could not be left alone upstairs while they were sleeping, that Mrs Bullivant would be angry at such dereliction of duty. She feared, though, that he would brush away such concerns. She would have to start her pretence of illness the next day. It would need to be something infectious, or he would no doubt pursue his intention.

She went to bed early, still uncertain of a plan, and was dimly aware of the carriage returning at a late hour, carrying the Bullivants home from their evening out. She awoke in some confusion as dawn was breaking, again to the sound of horses' hoofs and carriage wheels. Had she imagined the sounds the previous evening? But surely the Bullivants wouldn't have stayed out the whole night? Perhaps Mrs Bullivant was leaving very early for Canterbury, although it seemed unlikely after their late return. Lizzie lay in the warmth of her bed and listened. She was reluctant to get up and look out of the window to satisfy her curiosity, and eventually she drifted back to sleep. She awoke with a start at the sound of the nursery door opening, and leaped from her bed, throwing a shawl around her shoulders. In her confusion, she imagined Mr Bullivant had come to talk to Christopher, so she was relieved to see Susan standing there, bearing the breakfast tray.

Susan regarded her with some astonishment. 'It's not like you to oversleep, Lizzie,' she said.

'What time is it?' Lizzie replied. 'I was woken in the night by the carriage, then again this morning. I must have fallen back into a deep sleep.'

'It's eight o'clock,' Susan said, a hint of reproof in her voice. 'Some of us had to get up very early to deal with the unexpected guests.'

Lizzie helped her transfer the contents of the tray to the table. 'Guests?' she asked.

'Yes, friends of the family, on their way to London from who knows where? They decided to make a detour to see Betsanger Court. It seems Mr Bullivant has been boasting of it at his club, but hadn't invited anyone to visit. I barely had time to dress before I had to take coffee to them in the dining room, while Cook had to provide eggs and kidneys, which is what they had a fancy for apparently. She's not in a good mood.'

'And the Bullivants?'

'They aren't too happy, either. Mrs Bailey had to wake them, although they must surely have heard the carriage arrive. Mrs Bullivant can't go to Canterbury now as she will need to entertain the wife of the couple, while Mr Bullivant shows the husband the estate.'

The children wandered through, woken by the sound of voices, so Susan took the tray and got ready to depart. Lizzie followed her to the door. 'At least I won't have to pretend I'm sickening with a fever,' she said.

Susan looked puzzled. Then her brow cleared. 'Ah, I see. I think you might be quite safe. When I took in more coffee, I heard the master say that he and the mistress might as well follow their guests back to London. Mrs Bullivant had a face like thunder, so I suspect she'll get her way and go to Canterbury. But he'll be keen to return. He never stays here long. He might once have dreamed of being a country squire, but he soon tired of that.' Susan gave a wry laugh and departed.

Lizzie went to join the children at the breakfast table with lightness of heart. Soon they would have the house and gardens to themselves, and she would be safe from their odious father. She supposed they must endure another day or two of the master and mistress's presence, but after that they could breathe more easily. Once Christopher had had his interview with Mr Bullivant, which would hopefully be curtailed by the presence of guests, they could return to their normal routine: lessons in the morning, the grounds, stable yard or village in the afternoon. And Joe – Lizzie would be able to spend some time with Joe, even though she would be sharing him with the children. She couldn't help smiling as she spooned honey into her rapidly cooling porridge. Life seemed much brighter than it had the night before.

CHAPTER TWENTY-FOUR

Christopher was lucky: the visitors and change of plan meant that his father could spare the time for just a brief interview with him. Lizzie was present: she remained standing behind Christopher, who in turn stood in front of Mr Bullivant at his desk in the library.

'I know your mother has told you how very disappointed I am in your lack of application to your work. I have informed your tutor that this must change and he must be hard on you from now on. No son of mine is going to be a failure. You will prepare yourself to follow in my footsteps. Business is the future in this country. It is where the power and money lie. You will understand when you are older, and will want to be a part of it. To do that, you need an education. Next time I am here, I will look for a great improvement in your studies. If not, you can expect to be punished.'

Lizzie winced at the thought but Christopher stood tall and said, 'Yes, Father,' in a surprisingly strong voice.

'I am sorry we did not have the time to get better acquainted, Miss Carey. Next time, I hope, and I look forward to hearing that my son has shown great diligence in his studies.'

Lizzie nodded, 'Yes, sir,' and conducted Christopher from the room. She hoped her horror at the thought of seeing Mr Bullivant again hadn't shown on her face. As she closed the door behind them, Christopher said, 'I hate him,' in furious tones.

'He only wants what's best for you,' Lizzie admonished, while silently agreeing with him.

'I'm not like him. I don't want to sit behind a desk all day, or go to my club and pretend to be important.'

Lizzie blinked. What could he possibly know of such things?

'I want to be outside,' Christopher continued, 'like here. I could farm, or manage an estate . . ,' He tailed off, having run out of ideas.

'Well, that's a long way off,' Lizzie soothed, and hurried him back to the nursery to distract him with the morning drink and biscuits.

Susan was proved right in what she had overheard. The unexpected visitors stayed for one night and departed early the following morning. Mr Bullivant followed shortly after in his carriage. When Lizzie realised that Mrs Bullivant had had her way and would be going to Canterbury, she was cast down: Joe would have to take her there and no doubt stay so that she had use of a carriage. So she was surprised and delighted to see him in the stable yard later that afternoon, when she had given in to Agnes's pleas to see how the kitten was faring.

'I expected you to be needed in Canterbury,' she said to him, as he came forward to greet them.

'Mrs Bullivant has another carriage at her disposal,' Joe said. 'Mr Trent's,' he added, in a low voice.

Lizzie nodded. 'How is the kitten?' she asked. 'Has it recovered from being chased by those horrible dogs?'

'Let's go and see,' Joe said. He led them to the stable where he'd created a makeshift pen. 'We can let her out now.'

'It's a girl?' Lizzie asked.

Joe nodded. 'Aye, she's old enough now for me to tell.' He turned to Agnes. 'So you can name her if you like.'

'Petal,' Agnes said at once.

Christopher snorted. 'That's a stupid name for a cat.'

Agnes set her jaw. 'No, it isn't.'

Joe intervened. 'Why don't you pick her up? Sit down, take it in turns and don't drop her.'

He settled them on a bale of hay and deposited Petal on Agnes's lap, to her great delight. He and Lizzie took a few paces back and watched the scene from the stable doorway.

269

'So, peace at last,' Joe said. 'Cook and the maids are glad to see the back of the family. How did you find Mr Bullivant?'

Lizzie stiffened. She didn't want to give too much away. She settled on 'Difficult. And he was angry with Christopher for not working hard enough at his studies. He won't be sent away to school just yet. Not until he's improved his Latin and mathematics.'

'A blessing for him,' Joe said. 'He'll find it hard at school. I suppose his father plans to turn him into a copy of himself, to follow him into the business.'

They both contemplated that thought until Agnes ran up, having relinquished Petal to Christopher. 'Can we go and see the badgers again tonight?' she asked.

Joe shook his head. 'I'm sorry, Agnes. I haven't seen them since we all went together, even though I've been down there. They must have moved on. They can have more than one sett in their territory, you see. Maybe we disturbed them that night.'

Agnes looked so downcast Lizzie feared she might burst into tears.

'But the weather is set fair for the next two weeks,' Joe added hastily. 'We could go out to watch the owls hunting over the hay meadow. It was cut late this year and they're still finding prey out there.'

'Can we go now?' Agnes asked.

'We'd have to go at dusk, like before.'

Agnes was so excited she ran back to tell Christopher.

'You didn't ask me,' Lizzie protested. 'I'll have to smuggle them out of the house again. I'm not sure that's wise.'

Joe grinned. 'They'll love it. It's an adventure for them. And I know you'll love it, too.' He reached for her hand and squeezed it firmly as before. And as before, Lizzie was overwhelmed by the feelings that such a simple touch aroused in her.

'All right,' she said. 'When?'

'Tonight. In the kitchen garden at seven, with warm clothes,' Joe said. He looked at Agnes and Christopher, heads bent over the kitten. 'I doubt you'll be able to make them wait longer than that, anyway. Now I must get on. Have to clear up after those dogs. Their master didn't take them out often enough and they've fouled the place.'

Lizzie wrinkled her nose. 'Time to go, children,' she called, clapping her hands. But she let herself be persuaded to stroke Petal before they left, then led the children away with a promise that they would go out that very night to see the owls.

'Not a word to anyone,' Lizzie warned. 'And you'll have to be quiet little mice when we leave, just like last time.'

They practised walking like little mice all the way back to the nursery, which made them giggle. Lizzie was glad – they had been quick to shake off the subdued mood that had afflicted them when their parents, in particular their father, had been in the house.

CHAPTER TWENTY-FIVE

Lizzie came to consider the two weeks that followed the Bullivants' departure as two of the best in her life. That evening, she and the children had managed to sneak out of the house without being spotted, and they followed Joe to the edge of the estate, where the sweet-chestnut fence overlooked a hay meadow belonging to the nearby farm. The hay was propped in stooks, waiting to be collected, and the stubble shone golden in the gathering gloom. Agnes and Christopher were quiet and obedient, Joe lifting Agnes to sit on his shoulders so she had a good view. Christopher stood on the lowest bar of the fence, arms resting against the top, and appeared quite comfortable. They had been there barely ten minutes before Joe pointed. A bird swept across the field on silent wings, a flash of white as it turned and followed the same route back. Then it came to rest on a fence post at the edge of the field, not too far from where they stood. Lizzie held her breath for fear of disturbing it as it turned its flat face from one side to the other. Then it swooped down, and rose up from the field grasping something small and furry in its talons. Lizzie thought she heard the faintest squeak and glanced anxiously at Agnes, but she was rapt, gazing out over the field where another owl was now quartering for prey.

They watched for another half an hour, until the field had been quiet for a while. Then Joe lifted Agnes down. 'That's it for tonight,' he said. 'Time for bed.'

She was about to protest, but he fished in his pocket and produced a package.

'Badger food?' Lizzie teased.

'Better, I think,' Joe said. He unwrapped the paper, revealing four fruit scones, halved and spread with butter and jam, then sandwiched together.

'Won't Cook be angry?' Lizzie asked, biting into hers.

Joe shrugged. 'I'll tell her I got hungry in the night.'

They were in the kitchen garden now and the children wanted to run on ahead, to see whether they could spot the mother cat. Joe said she had started to teach Petal to hunt. Lizzie, aware that he was loitering, warned them to stay quiet, and watched them vanish through the gate into the stable yard.

Joe took her hand and turned her to face him. 'Is this our first time alone?' he asked. 'I think it might be.' He tipped her face towards his. Then his lips were on hers, a gentle pressure that increased until he broke away. 'Oh, Lizzie, you don't know how much I've longed to do that.'

Lizzie was filled with confusion. Her first kiss, and she felt quite overcome with emotion, but also with anxiety. What must Joe think of her? Surely it wasn't right to submit to him so easily.

She struggled to find the right words. 'I hope you don't think me—' She halted, then tried again. 'We never had chance to speak of Mrs Simmonds, and why she demanded repayment of a debt. I know it must have seemed very strange, and I want to explain how it came to be. I don't want you to think I'm the sort of person who would work for her.'

Lizzie had become hot and bothered, trying to explain herself. Joe listened, then put his finger to her lips. 'You don't need to explain. I think I'm a good judge of character, Lizzie. I like you, and I know you to be a good person. That's all that matters.'

Agnes ran through the gate into the kitchen garden. 'The cat has caught a mouse,' she said, in great excitement. 'It's playing with it. Come and see.'

Lizzie tried hard not to sigh. She wished she could have spent longer with Joe, just the two of them, talking. But it wasn't to be.

They followed Agnes, and Lizzie saw she was right. The cat indeed appeared to be playing with the mouse, holding it down with her paw, then letting it go, only to catch it again.

'She's teaching her kitten how to hunt,' Joe said.

They watched for a moment or two longer, until Lizzie judged it wise to leave, before blood was spilled. It was one thing to watch the owls hunting from a distance, quite another to see the likely death of a mouse at close quarters.

'Bedtime,' she said firmly. The children's protests were weak, and she could tell they were tired.

Back in the nursery they fell into bed without a murmur, leaving Lizzie to sit by the window, attempting to recapture the sensation of Joe's kiss. She longed to repeat the experience, but it felt impossible. She could hardly take the children away from their beds to roam the grounds every evening. They had been lucky to escape detection so far ...

The children were still fast asleep the next morning when Susan appeared with breakfast. Lizzie was up, dressed and filled with a kind of nervous energy. Somehow, she must find a way to see Joe alone again.

'I was thinking,' Susan said, as she set the breakfast on the table, 'why don't I sit up here with the children one evening, so you can have some time off?'

When she registered Lizzie's startled expression she added, 'You never get any free time, do you? I think you should. Mind you, it would be best to keep our arrangement from Mrs Bailey.'

'Has someone asked you to do this?' Lizzie immediately thought Joe had said something.

'No. Who?' Susan looked innocent.

Lizzie was prevented from probing further by the arrival of Agnes and Christopher at the table, rubbing their eyes.

'I'm so hungry,' Agnes said, pouring cream onto her porridge. 'I'm so glad I'm not an owl or a cat. Imagine eating mice.'

Lizzie looked at Susan, to see what she made of Agnes's odd comment, but she just laughed.

'How funny you are, Agnes,' she said, as she turned to leave the nursery. In a quieter voice she said to Lizzie, 'Tomorrow night, once they're asleep?' Then she departed, leaving Lizzie hardly able to believe her luck. She had another chance to spend time with Joe, and so soon. Her hopes and wishes were coming truc.

Chapter Twenty-Six

L izzie felt as though months of courtship were squeezed into the first evening she and Joe managed to spend alone. She still crept out into the gardens like a guilty thief in the night, worried that she would be spotted. But once she had found Joe in the stable yard, all worry melted away. They returned to the edge of what Lizzie thought of as the owl field, where moonlight spilled over the stubble, lighting it so that prey had nowhere to hide. But they didn't watch the owls. Instead they perched on the fence with their backs to the field and talked. Joe told Lizzie all about the village in Essex where he had been brought up, and in turn she told him about Castle Bay, and how she had run away from her family, believing Mrs Simmonds was offering her a better life. She was glad to be open about the circumstances of their acquaintance. Despite Joe's assurances, she had still felt under a cloud.

Joe told her he didn't intend to remain in service much longer. 'I want to be my own man,' he said. 'Carve a way for myself. It's very comfortable here but I don't want to fall into the trap of staying too long. It's not a job for an old man.'

Lizzie felt she should offer something in return, but she had no plan for the future. She knew she was guilty of just falling into and out of situations as they presented themselves. 'I don't know where I'll be in a year's time,' she confessed. 'I can't see myself still working for the Bullivants, unless something changes.' She suppressed a shudder at the thought of Mr Bullivant paying another visit to Betsanger Court.

'Why is that?' Joe was puzzled. 'You seem happy here. The children love you, and they're far better behaved with you than they were with any of their previous nursemaids.'

'It's a lonely job,' Lizzie said, surprising herself. It was the first time she had openly acknowledged it. 'I miss joining everyone in the kitchen for meals. I never know what's going on in the house unless Susan tells me. She's the only person I see, apart from you.'

Once more, she considered telling Joe about Mr Bullivant's advances, then thought better of it. What if it reflected badly on her or made him so angry that he felt he ought to act on it?

Joe put his arm around her shoulders. 'Oh, Lizzie. I wish I could help. I find it hard not to see you as much as I would like.'

'And then there's Mrs Bailey.' Lizzie was warming to her theme. 'I don't know why she's so sour.'

Joe squeezed her shoulder. 'It's a hard job being a housekeeper. You have to keep the maids in order, make sure the cook is up to her job, be ready to welcome the master and mistress at what feels like a moment's notice. It must be lonely, too. You can't be close to the servants or you'll be accused of having favourites, and you may appear to have a special relationship with your employers, but they aren't your friends.'

Lizzie felt ashamed: she had never looked at the situation like that. She resolved to be more understanding of Mrs Bailey, even though, thankfully, they had little to do with one another.

She and Joe sat on in companionable silence for a while. Lizzie couldn't prevent herself from smiling. This wasn't how she had imagined their evening, but she was happy. They had got to know each other, and that felt important – more important than an evening filled with kisses and unspoken longing. Although she hoped he would kiss her again before they had to return to the house.

As if he had read her mind, Joe jumped off the fence and lifted her down, holding on to her. 'I hope we can do this again soon, Lizzie,' he said, murmuring into her neck, before gently kissing all the way up to her eyelids. He deposited a brief kiss on her nose, then took her hand. 'I'd better get you back. You'll find Susan fast asleep in your bed, and then where will you be?'

Moonlight lit their path back to the kitchen garden, where Joe paused, took her into his arms once more and kissed her properly, so that she was quite breathless when he eventually let her go.

'Bring the children to the yard tomorrow, if you can,' he said. 'And every day. At least while we still have lovely weather.' He walked with her around the house, and watched her safely to the front door. Neither of them was aware that someone watched them, too, concealed by the curtains in her parlour.

Susan was indeed fast asleep when Lizzie reached the nursery, although in the chair and not in a bed. Lizzie hated having to wake her, but Susan, after a moment or two of confusion, was good-natured. 'I hope you had a nice evening,' she said, yawning. She didn't mention Joe, but Lizzie knew she could hardly believe her to have been wandering the grounds on her own.

She didn't like to ask whether she would be prepared to do the same thing again, but Susan volunteered to do just that, between yawns that threatened to crack her jaw. 'I can come again, later in the week,' she said. 'No need to ask, I'll tell you when.' Then she was gone, leaving Lizzie to take up her seat while she ran over everything she and Joe had said to each other. Even as she did, questions occurred to her that she wished she had asked. Were his brothers and sisters still at home, or did they work away, as he did? Was he close to his parents?

She thought about the shouting matches in her own home and, with guilt, remembered that she had had no contact with anyone there since she'd left. Her mother must be very angry with her, that much she knew. Yet again, she resolved to write, but her thoughts turned back to that evening, and she tried to conjure up the warmth of Joe's body when he kissed her, the grip of his hand holding hers, the way he tilted her face to be kissed. She sighed. If only he could be here by her side. If only they didn't have to be so careful to keep their relationship a secret.

CHAPTER TWENTY-SEVEN

Lizzie did as Joe asked and took Agnes and Christopher to the stable yard every afternoon. They needed no persuading and indeed always arrived there before she did, having run on ahead. She and Joe managed to snatch a few moments of private conversation, but that just left Lizzie wanting more. She was grateful to Susan for suggesting another evening when she could sit in the nursery, while Lizzie crept out.

Summer was leaving, though, and autumn was making its presence felt. The evenings had become cooler, and mist spread across the hay meadow, while she and Joe leaned on the fence and talked, making Lizzie shiver. Joe pulled her close to him, his arm around her shoulders.

'What if we married?' he asked abruptly. They were in the middle of a conversation about Mr Bullivant's plans to breed pheasants on the estate, so he could bring guests to shoot.

Lizzie stared at him, her heart beating so hard it drummed in her ears. Had she heard him correctly? 'Married?' she echoed.

'Yes,' Joe said. 'We soon won't be able to meet outside like this, and I don't like the idea of sneaking around in the house. We'll be found out in no time. Why don't we marry and have done?'

It wasn't the sort of proposal Lizzie had imagined but it thrilled her just the same. Then reality struck. 'But, Joe, one of us would have to give up our job. I doubt we'd be allowed to work here as a married couple. And I don't think either of us can afford to do that. We'd have to rent somewhere to live outside and . . .' Lizzie stopped, the enormity of the problem overwhelming her.

Joe hugged her. 'I spoke without thinking. I just wanted to spend more time with you. But would you say yes? You can have time to think about it,' he added hastily.

Lizzie didn't need time to think. 'Yes,' she said simply. 'Yes, I would.'

Joe lifted her off her feet and whirled her around, then set her down, both of them giddy and laughing.

'Then you must have a ring,' he said.

Lizzie was half expecting him to pull one from his pocket so she was intrigued when he bent down and hunted among the damp foliage at their feet. He stood up, several long stems of grass in his hand, which he deftly wove together to form a plaited ring. He took Lizzie's left hand in his own and slid it onto her finger. It was a bit large and Lizzie curled her fingers to stop it slipping off.

'It will shrink as it dries,' Joe said, with confidence.

She wanted to ask him how he'd learned to do such a thing, but she didn't want to hear that he had made one for someone else. She would treasure it, she knew. That night, after they had returned to the house, she turned it round and round her finger, admiring the intricacy of the plaiting. She wore it while she slept, and kissed it when she awoke, reluctantly removing it and slipping it inside her pillowcase before she got up.

After two weeks of glorious September sunshine, the weather broke and October blew in with storms and driving rain. There were no more snatched moments in the stable yard with Joe, or blissful evenings out in the gardens. Each day, Lizzie looked hopefully out of the window for a break in the clouds; each day she was disappointed. One week stretched into two, and beyond, and Lizzie and the children were thoroughly disenchanted by the confines of the nursery.

'Can't we go and see Petal?' Agnes wailed, one afternoon late in the first week.

Lizzie shook her head. 'We'll be soaked before we even get to the stable yard.'

By the second week, desperate to see Joe, she was willing to risk it. On a day when the rain appeared a little lighter, she persuaded the children to don their sturdiest boots and hunted around for something to keep the rain off them. She had to settle for their winter coats, for Agnes and Christopher wouldn't normally be expected to go out in the rain – they had a carriage available to them for such an occasion. There would be an umbrella they could borrow from the stand downstairs in the hallway, Lizzie thought, as she shepherded them out of the nursery. They would use it until they could take shelter in one of the empty stables.

Mrs Bailey was passing through the hallway. 'Surely you aren't thinking of taking the children outside in this weather, Miss Carey?' she asked in frosty tones.

'They need fresh air, Mrs Bailey,' Lizzie replied. 'They have been shut inside for far too long.'

'I suggest you think again. Their boots will be mired in mud before you've reached the end of the drive and your skirt will be soaked and filthy. Who is going to clean your boots and wash your clothes? And we cannot have the villagers commenting on the children at Betsanger Court looking like bedraggled street urchins.'

'We were only going to the stables,' Lizzie said, defiant. 'Agnes has a wish to see the kitten there, and Christopher to see the horses.'

'From what I have seen, Miss Carey, you have spent far too much time in the stable yard. It's hardly a suitable place for children and I suggest you don't drag them there under the pretext that it's for their benefit when it is quite clearly for yours. Mr Bullivant would expect Christopher to use his time more wisely. Why don't you return to the nursery and he can do just that?'

Mrs Bailey was standing in front of the door and Lizzie would have had to push her aside to leave the house. Cheeks aflame with indignation, she said to the children, 'We must save our outing for another day. The rain can't last for ever. Back upstairs and we will find something to entertain ourselves.'

Mrs Bailey might have her way in preventing them from leaving, but Lizzie wouldn't let her win on all fronts.

Once back in the nursery, though, toys scattered across the floor in an effort to while away the hours until bedtime, Lizzie had cause to reflect on Mrs Bailey's words. Had she been keeping watch on Lizzie's movements? She had said 'from what I have seen' not 'from what I have been told'. A chill ran through Lizzie. She wished fervently she could talk to Joe. Was he in trouble for letting them visit the stables? She would have to question Susan to find out whether anything had been said in the kitchen. In the meantime, she needed to be very careful around Mrs Bailey.

CHAPTER TWENTY-EIGHT

When the rain finally stopped, Lizzie could barely wait to leave the nursery. But she followed the usual morning routine, keeping an anxious eye on the clouds. Worried by Mrs Bailey's pointed comments, she had asked Susan if she knew anything about Joe being in trouble.

Susan shook her head. 'He's been a bit quieter than usual at the table, maybe. I just thought he was fed up of getting drenched every day.'

Lizzie had tried hard to find her words reassuring, but a niggle of doubt remained. She was both excited and apprehensive that afternoon as they picked their way through the puddles that surrounded the house to reach the stable yard. Conscious that Mrs Bailey could be watching them from her parlour, she marched past, nose in the air. The housekeeper had no right to tell her how to manage her charges.

Joe had Lady, the big black horse, out in the yard, grooming her. Lizzie wondered whether he had been riding, or planned to take the carriage out, but she focused on keeping the children at her side. She didn't want them to run up and scare the animal.

They all stood at a safe distance from Joe and watched him at work. Lizzie expected him to greet them; he must have noticed them. But he remained silent, concentrating on his work.

'Hello, Joe,' she said at last. 'It's been a long time since we've been able to come and see you – nearly three weeks.'

Joe nodded by way of acknowledgement and carried on with his task.

Agnes and Christopher glanced up at her, confused by his unfriendliness.

'Can we go and see the kitten?' Lizzie asked, in an effort to engage him in conversation.

'Gone,' Joe said. 'The farmer up the road came looking for a good mouser.'

Agnes began to cry. 'But I want to see Petal. I never said goodbye to her. Why did you let her go?'

Lizzie felt like asking much the same thing. Joe was behaving very oddly, almost cruelly. It wasn't like him at all. She had a sinking feeling that something very bad had happened.

The children shifted from foot to foot, disconsolate.

'May I feed Captain in the stable?' Christopher asked. He was tentative. Even he had sensed something wasn't right, Lizzie thought.

Joe shook his head. 'I've nothing with me to give him.' He carried on working.

'Joe's busy,' Lizzie said. 'Let's not disturb him any further. We'll go for a walk instead.'

'Lane's flooded,' Joe said. 'You'll not get to the village.'

Lizzie began to feel desperate. She needed to speak to Joe alone to find out what was wrong. Had Mrs Bailey warned him not to encourage the children's visits? It seemed likely. But, then, why was he being so taciturn? She would have expected him at least to look at her, to try to signal what was wrong. Instead, coldness seemed to emanate from him, from his stance and his refusal to meet her eyes. It created an answering chill in her heart.

'Come on, children,' Lizzie said. 'We'll have to wait until it's not so wet underfoot.'

She glanced back as they left the stable yard, hoping to catch Joe watching them. Instead, she saw him take a carrot from his pocket and feed it to Lady.

They walked as far as the entrance to the driveway, so they could see for themselves that muddy brown water blocked their route to the village. Then they walked slowly back, all of them in subdued moods.

'Is Joe cross with us?' Agnes asked, in a quiet voice.

'I don't know,' Lizzie said, trying not to let her emotion show. 'But I'm going to find out,' she added. She would ask Susan when she brought up their dinner. She would surely know something.

It was another long afternoon in the nursery. Lizzie invented a story about fish making a home in the flood in the lane, then persuaded the children to draw pictures to illustrate it. Christopher's fish looked more like a sea monster; Agnes's had a friendly smile. Lizzie did her best to stay engaged with them, but she was impatient for Susan's arrival.

When at last she appeared, Lizzie waited until dinner was on the table and the children tucking in, before she drew Susan to one side and rapidly recounted a short version of what had happened in the stable yard. 'It must be Mrs Bailey's doing,' Lizzie said. 'But I don't understand why Joe behaved towards me as he did. Do you have any idea?'

Susan shook her head but wouldn't meet Lizzie's eye.

Lizzie caught her arm. 'Please, Susan, if you know something, tell me.'

'I'll try to find out,' Susan promised, and hurried from the room, leaving Lizzie even more perturbed. There was something Susan wasn't telling her, something that had a bearing on Joe's behaviour. She resolved to push her further when she returned.

To Lizzie's surprise, it wasn't Susan who returned to collect the plates, but Hester.

'Where's Susan?' she asked.

'She couldn't come,' Hester said, her face sour. Clearly she hadn't got over Lizzie being given the position she considered rightfully hers. 'Probably doesn't want to be around you, now she knows what you're really like. Going around pretending to be something you're not.'

She slammed the dirty dishes and cutlery onto the tray and

stalked out with it before Lizzie, shocked, could formulate a question. What on earth was Hester talking about? Her thoughts flew at once to Mrs Simmonds. Had she been to the house in search of payment for her wretched debt, and managed to blacken Lizzie's name? But surely Joe would have stood up for her. He knew the truth of it – she had explained it to him. She was shaking as she returned to the table, where she found Agnes and Christopher staring at her. Hester hadn't bothered to be discreet with her words.

For a moment, Lizzie was tempted to tell them it was rude to stare. Then she recovered herself. 'Take no notice,' she said. 'A silly quarrel – nothing more.'

Agnes and Christopher seemed to accept her explanation. Once they had eaten, Christopher asked to paint his toy soldiers, and Agnes wanted to play with her dolls. Lizzie couldn't find it in herself to tell Christopher he must read, Agnes too. She needed some quiet time to herself to think. Whatever had been said, and wherever it had come from, her reputation had been tarnished. Everyone in the house thought badly of her, including Joe, yet she didn't understand why. It could only be a matter of time before gossip reached Mrs Bullivant's ears. And then what?

Chapter Twenty-Nine

Hester continued to deliver their meals, but she had very little to say when she did. Lizzie felt trapped – she longed for Susan to return so she could quiz her further. Since the children were her responsibility every minute of the day, she couldn't even slip away and go in search of her.

She was reluctant to return to the stable yard and see Joe, but was desperate to do so. Would he have unbent towards them? Or would he still be brusque, verging on rude? There was only one way to find out.

After a day of crisp sunshine and a strong breeze had helped to dry some of the puddles and standing water, Lizzie and the children wrapped up and ventured out in the afternoon to the stables. Now that Petal had gone, Agnes was less enthusiastic. The horses held far less interest for her than the kitten, but even so, once they were outside, she trotted along quite happily.

The weather was markedly colder, despite the sunshine, and the wind whistled across the stable yard. There was no sign of Joe and the stable doors were closed. Lizzie's nervous anticipation gave way to bitter disappointment. She had hoped to find an answer as to what had happened to blacken her name during the rainy weeks she had been trapped in the nursery.

'Shall we look in the kitchen garden? Maybe Joe is there and we can ask about feeding the horses.'

She hoped she sounded brighter than she felt, but her sense of isolation from everyone in the household deepened. They peeped into the walled garden: Samuel and Abraham were busy clearing beds in the far corner. Lizzie waved at them and they waved back, but quickly bent their heads to their work again.

They walked back towards the house, stopping to watch the chickens scratching in the yard. Lizzie came to a decision. 'Let's collect our drinks and biscuits from the kitchen,' she said. She led the way along the passage and in through the scullery, Agnes and Christopher glancing around curiously. Taking a deep breath, she opened the door to the kitchen. Cook was there, busy at her table with preparations for dinner, Alice slicing potatoes at her side.

Lizzie cleared her throat. 'We thought we could take up our afternoon drink, to save Hester's legs.'

Cook looked up, startled, and immediately shifted her gaze from Lizzie to the children. She wiped her hands on her apron and said, 'Let's see what we can find for you. I think there might be a piece or two of cake left. It will make a nice change from biscuits.'

She went over to one of the big tins on the dresser, Agnes and Christopher following eagerly. Alice was staring at Lizzie.

She looked through the open door into the other room. 'It's very quiet here today. Where is everyone?'

'We've had word the mistress is coming back. They're getting the house ready.'

'And Joe?' Lizzie ventured. Once more, no one had told her to prepare for Mrs Bullivant.

'Gone to Canterbury to fetch the mistress.' Alice poured three glasses of cordial, as Cook returned with two plates of cake. She set everything on a tray then looked pointedly at Lizzie. So that was the way it was going to be: she was being snubbed. If she wanted biscuits or cake, she must ask. Lizzie picked up the tray and led the children out of the kitchen. Her burden was heavy and awkward on the narrow staircase to the nursery. Susan and Hester must be fitter than she was, Lizzie thought ruefully.

They had barely removed their outer clothes and washed their hands before Mrs Bailey knocked and walked into the room.

'I won't interrupt for long,' she said, looking at the drinks and cake. 'Mrs Bullivant will be arriving late this evening. She would like to see you first thing in the morning, Miss Carey.' She made to leave the room, then stopped. 'And I'd thank you for not bringing the children into the house through the scullery. That's for the servants, not the young master.'

Then she was gone, leaving Lizzie with two spots of high colour in her cheeks. The reprimand felt unnecessary, but she told herself that Mrs Bailey was notorious for finding fault. She was rather more worried by the summons to see Mrs Bullivant.

When Hester arrived with the dinner tray that evening, Lizzie saw at once that all three portions were child-sized. Was this a genuine mistake? Or done on purpose? She looked at Hester, who had a sneer on her face. Lizzie knew she should say something, or matters would only get worse. No cake or biscuits earlier, the tray hadn't been collected, and now this. But the uncertainty of tomorrow's interview was sapping her energy. Once that had happened, she would deal with this behaviour. For now, she would let it be.

The next morning couldn't come soon enough for Lizzie, although she dreaded what she was to hear. She hoped there would be some clue as to the mysterious behaviour of Joe and everyone in the household towards her, so she was up and dressed long before the summons came. Breakfast had arrived with three small bowls of porridge, delivered by Hester with a triumphant look on her face. Lizzie ignored her, although she was already hungry after her meagre fare the night before.

Hester returned later, bearing the summons that Mrs Bullivant would see her in the library. 'I'm to sit with the children,' she announced.

Lizzie made her way downstairs, heart thudding. Why had she been summoned? Perhaps it was just to say the mistress wished the children to accompany her somewhere. Or that new clothes should be made for them in time for winter.

Mrs Bullivant greeted Lizzie without the glimmer of a smile.

289

She was sitting behind the library desk, and didn't invite Lizzie to take a seat.

'Miss Carey, it has been decided that Christopher will start school in the January term. His tutor feels he can make sufficient progress by then.'

Lizzie was surprised to hear this, but tried not to let it show.

'With that in mind,' Mrs Bullivant continued, 'we will no longer require your services from the end of December.'

Now Lizzie couldn't hide her feelings. The mistress's words came as a complete shock. Her heart felt as though it had been pierced with a dagger of ice. She was to be cast out, away from Joe, away from the children, away from security. What was she to do?

'But Agnes,' she managed to stutter. 'Who will look after Agnes?'

'I have a mind to take Agnes with me wherever I go,' Mrs Bullivant replied. 'Hester can look after her here, and in Canterbury.' Her tone was cold.

'Have I displeased you in some way?' Lizzie asked. She risked angering the mistress, but she needed to know.

Mrs Bullivant hesitated. 'There have been reports from Mrs Bailey that have made me question my own judgement. I had thought you eminently suited to your work, but issues have been raised about your moral character.'

Lizzie gasped. Was this about Mrs Simmonds? She couldn't think what else it could be. She made ready to protest but Mrs Bullivant held up her hand.

'The decision is made. You will leave after Christmas.'

Lizzie thought about how she was being treated in the house, all the little indignities being foisted upon her. Must she endure such behaviour until January? Sudden anger flashed through her.

'I would prefer to leave by the end of the week. I cannot work here if you have lost faith in me.'

Mrs Bullivant was taken aback. 'That will be most inconvenient.'

Lizzie shrugged but kept silent.

'This is unacceptable, Miss Carey. I will speak to Mrs Bailey to see what can be done.'

Lizzie felt a small sense of triumph. She would go, no matter what Mrs Bailey thought.

As she turned the door handle to leave the room, Mrs Bullivant said, 'You need not expect a character, Miss Carey. No one will employ you now.'

Lizzie left, shutting the door behind her. As she climbed the stairs, some of her confidence ebbed away. What would she do now? Where would she go? Could she get word to Joe? How would she tell the children? And who would look after them?

A look at Hester's smug face was enough to bring the anger surging back. Hester knew, she was sure. Mrs Bailey must already have offered her old position back to her. How had it come to this? What had she done to deserve the treatment being meted out to her by the household? Joe's coldness, Cook's rudeness, Hester's contempt – even Susan was keeping her distance. What had been said, and who had said it, to cause such a turn of events?

It seemed to Lizzie that everyone wanted her gone, apart from Agnes and Christopher, who had no knowledge of what was going on. How could she tell the children what was about to befall them? They would be bewildered and upset; they would think Lizzie had let them down. Or would they imagine that something they had done had caused her to leave?

Lizzie's heart felt as though it had been ripped from her breast. Mrs Bullivant's last words echoed in her head: *No one will employ you now.* Lizzie knew that leaving was the right decision, but what could the future possibly hold for her?

PART THREE

OCTOBER 1829 — JUNE 1831

CHAPTER ONE

Lizzie swept the last of the dust out of the house, then leaned on her broom in the doorway, looking up and down Middle Street. Other doors stood open to allow air into the houses on what promised to be another hot day.

She watched a group of children crouched in the road, intent on their game of knucklebones. They didn't look up at the sound of a horse and cart approaching, and Lizzie half stepped out of her door, ready to dart over and pull them out of danger. But the horse and cart stopped before it reached them. A delivery for Widow Booth's shop, Lizzie guessed, from the sacks and boxes stacked on the back.

A couple of women had come out of the houses almost opposite, one with a basket over her arm. She stopped to converse with her neighbour and Lizzie saw them glance over. They turned slightly away from her and she knew they were talking about her. She could imagine their words. What was Lizzie Carey doing back in Castle Bay, after she had swept out of town well over two years earlier, off to make her fortune, or so it was said? And now look at her. Working in one of those houses that maintained a respectable front, but they all knew what went on there at night, when the sailors were in town. Lizzie pulled a wry face. Would she ever stop being the focus of gossip?

She heard one of the sash windows on the first floor being drawn up and looked up to see Nancy stick out her head and breathe deeply. Her hair was uncombed and her nightgown half off her shoulders. An edge of indignation was added to the conversation across the road.

'Lizzie!' Nancy called down. 'Bring me up some tea – and my water jug. I've a mind to go out soon.' She withdrew her head and pulled down the sash.

Lizzie looked across to the gossips on the other side of the street. She set her chin with a defiant jut and mustered all the contempt she could into a hard stare. Let them say what they wanted about her. It was none of their business where she had been over the past two years. And they could think what they wanted about her occupation now.

If Nancy was awake, some of the others wouldn't be far behind. The house had been quiet last night, with not many sailors ashore. The girls would be expecting breakfast, beds made and rooms swept. No doubt there'd be laundry, too, and Mrs Franklin would have dreamed up some tasks to add to Lizzie's workload.

Lizzie owed Mrs Franklin, the proprietor of the house, a debt of gratitude for taking her in just a few months earlier when she thought she would have to work for her keep in one of the rooms in Middle Street, or beg for her living. She shuddered. Both were unthinkable in the town where her family still dwelled.

Down in the kitchen, as Lizzie waited for water to heat, she allowed her mind to open a door that she usually kept firmly closed, to see whether the pain had eased. She had stuck to her resolution after her interview with Mrs Bullivant and made her departure from Betsanger Court at the end of that October week. She'd written a letter to Joe and left it with a reluctant Susan, but she had no idea whether he had seen it. She could still remember her words, as if she held it before her eyes:

Dearest Joe,

I wish I knew what has happened to make you so cold towards me. Whatever it is, it has tainted everything and everyone here at Betsanger Court, making it impossible for me to stay. As I write, I do not know where I will go but I can only hope that our paths may cross again and I will have the chance to set things

right. Joe, I had never loved before. Finding you was the best
thing to happen in my life and now, somehow, I have lost you.

I will take your ring with me and wear it close to my heart in
the hope that one day we will be together again. In the meantime,
I long to know what I am meant to have done so I can make it
right again.
Your loving Lizzie

She had hesitated over how she should sign the letter, and almost scratched it out. But then she had shrugged. It was a true reflection of her feelings. If Joe didn't want to hear them, she supposed he would tear up the letter, or throw it on the fire. It gave her a stab of pain even to think it.

Giving the children the news of her departure had been heartbreaking, too. Once Agnes had understood that Lizzie was leaving for good and not just going visiting, she had let out a huge wail and thrown herself at Lizzie's legs, clutching them as if to prevent her walking away. Christopher had said nothing at first, but his face had paled and his bottom lip shook. Then, after a few minutes, as Agnes's sobs began to die away, he said, in a quiet voice, 'So who will teach me now? Will I have to see the tutor every day?'

Lizzie had hesitated, unsure whether or not to speak the truth. Then she decided it might be better coming from her than from his parents. 'You're to go to school after Christmas, Christopher, so you must work hard with your tutor between now and then to make sure you can keep up with the other boys. Can you do that for me?'

She had given him an encouraging smile and held out her arms to see whether he would come to her for a hug, but he had turned away and gone to look out of the nursery window. Lizzie almost regretted her hasty words to Mrs Bullivant. For the sake of the children, should she have stayed until Christmas? Then she remembered all the slights, and how she would have had to endure Joe's unfriendliness. She knew a little of her would have died inside every day. Early on the Saturday morning of that week, before the children had woken, she stood on the front steps of Betsanger Court, her belongings packed into a bundle just as when she had arrived.

Mrs Bailey had appeared. She held out her hand to Lizzie, who thought for a moment she meant to shake it, until she saw the gleam of the coins she was holding. 'Your wages,' she said. A small smile had crossed her face. 'I suppose you'll be returning to Castle Bay,' she said, 'if your family will have you back. Give my regards to your sister's husband.'

Then she had turned on her heel and gone into the house, leaving Lizzie lost for words. How did she know about Castle Bay? She thought back to when she had first arrived: she had given the housekeeper an address in Canterbury. Had Joe told her? But why had she mentioned her sister's husband? She must have been referring to Nell, the eldest, for it seemed unlikely that anyone else in the family would be of an age to marry. How did she know about Nell and Thomas?

Puzzling over Mrs Bailey's words, Lizzie had walked to the end of the drive and through the village, without any idea of where she was going. The woman at the village shop had been opening her shutters and smiled at Lizzie as she passed, but she hadn't responded. Numb with misery, she had allowed her feet to carry her where they would so she was astonished, not an hour later, to catch a distant glimpse of the sea. Two hours later, after walking country lanes that wove through fields and orchards, stripped brown and bare by the onset of winter, she was even more surprised to find herself somewhere she recognised: the outskirts of Castle Bay.

Chapter Two

Lizzie shook herself out of her reverie. That was as much as she could allow herself to think about her departure from Betsanger Court. She must close the door on that chapter of her life, and set about preparations for the late-rising ladies of the house. If she didn't hurry, Nancy would be storming down the stairs, berating her for not bringing her tea and warm water when asked. And she wouldn't hesitate to complain to Mrs Franklin. Lizzie couldn't afford to put a foot wrong with the formidable proprietor of Bay House in Middle Street. Martha Franklin had taken her in when she had nowhere else to turn and although it was hardly the life she could have wished for, she was extremely grateful to her.

As the water boiled on the hob, Lizzie thought about her first few weeks in Castle Bay. She had been taken aback to find herself there – she had had no idea that for all those months she had been living just five or six miles from her family. She shrank from going home, unsure of her reception. And what if the family didn't live there any more? She had decided to look for temporary lodgings as far as possible from the family house in Lower Street, using some of her precious wages, and then she would decide what to do.

As she poured warm water into a ewer for Nancy, then set the pot back on the heat to make the tea, she thought back to the room she had taken. In the end, it hadn't been as far as she would have liked from number seven Lower Street, being in the same street but much further along and tucked away in a tiny alley. Two rows of houses lined the alley, so close together that you could have shaken hands with your opposite neighbour from the upstairs windows. Lizzie would have liked that, but she was hidden in the basement, with a view of nothing but a backyard through the small and grimy pane of glass that gave onto it. She had scrubbed and cleaned to make the place fit to live in. For a few days, that had taken her mind off what had befallen her. Then the November wind and rains came and her damp and draughty basement became somewhere she was eager to escape, despite the weather outside. She tramped the streets in search of work, trying the taverns she had always avoided when she lived there, but they had all asked the same thing: 'What experience do you have? Where's your character?' When she confessed she had neither, they sent her on her way.

Lizzie loaded Nancy's water jug and teacup onto a tray and made her way carefully up the narrow wooden staircase, which turned and twisted from the kitchen up through the house. There were ten rooms and ten girls: Lizzie slept in a tiny space just off the kitchen, with barely enough room for a pallet on the floor. Mrs Franklin didn't inhabit Bay House: she owned a very nice property in Hawksdown, or so the girls said.

'There you are,' Nancy grumbled, as Lizzie pushed open the door. 'I thought you'd forgotten me.'

'It's a lovely day,' Lizzie said, ignoring her. 'Which dress will you wear?' She went over to the press and pulled open a drawer. 'The yellow? Or the blue?'

Nancy was easily diverted. She loved clothes, almost as much as she loved the gin that got her through each day. Lizzie was astonished by how much she could drink and sought to keep her away from it as long as she could. But she knew that once Nancy was up, dressed and breakfasted, she would sally forth, parasol in hand to protect her complexion from the August sunshine during the short walk to the sea front, where she would deliberate between the Pelican or the Anchor for her first drink of the day. She would make her way back to Middle Street via the taverns along the way, ready to begin her afternoon or evening's work. Then it would be

Lizzie's job to fetch whatever she and the other girls required by way of sustenance – more gin, or pies from the shop on Lower Street.

With Nancy's choice of the blue dress laid out on the bed, Lizzie turned her attention to the other girls, knocking on doors to see who wanted water, tea or breakfast. The first two needs attended to, she set to work in the kitchen, slicing bread and laying out butter and jam, while she cooked eggs to serve alongside slices of ham. Mrs Franklin charged the girls for their breakfast, as well as their laundry, cleaning and Lizzie's services, so they generally liked to make sure they got their money's worth. Lizzie received little by way of payment. She had her bed provided, such as it was, and her food, but she was expected to earn tips from the girls for running errands for them. Since Mrs Franklin wanted them kept away from gin or other spirits as much as possible, preferring them to drink ale, Lizzie spent a lot of her time finding new places to conceal the bottles she was forced to bring in. It was no great hardship, though – all the houses in Middle Street had secret panelling and hidden cupboards, remnants of the days not long past when the town had thrived as a smugglers' haunt.

Lizzie could hear movement upstairs – doors opening, the girls calling to each other. They would be down in a few minutes. She piled plates on the table and laid out knives and forks, then began making the chocolate for those who preferred it to tea. As she heated the rich mixture, her fingers strayed to the neck of her work blouse. A tiny ridge beneath the top button betrayed the outline of something, but only if you looked hard. Joe's grass ring, suspended on a piece of string, hung there, her only reminder of what might have been.

'Stop daydreaming, Lizzie! Where's my chocolate?' It was Annie, who tried to sound cross as she came up to give Lizzie's shoulders an affectionate squeeze. Lizzie swung round, a ready smile on her lips, then began pouring the chocolate into cups. The other girls followed close behind, pulling out chairs, the wooden legs scraping the tiled floor, and their chatter soon filled the room. The day had begun – there would be no rest now for Lizzie until at least midnight.

Chapter Three

Once they had breakfasted, the girls sat around, in no hurry to get on with their day. It gave Lizzie a chance to go up to the rooms, sweep the floors, straighten the covers, hide any bottles incautiously left on bedside tables and collect glasses and teacups. She opened the windows as she worked, to let in some air to clear the fug of gin fumes, cheap perfume and smoke. Usually a brisk breeze off the sea, funnelling down Middle Street, made short work of it, but today was still and sultry. By the time Lizzie had cleaned the last room, her hair was plastered to her brow and her blouse sticking to her back.

She carried the cups, glasses and water ewers down to the kitchen then chivvied the girls to get out from under her feet. 'I've the breakfast things to clear and the washing-up to do before Mrs Franklin arrives and catches sight of all your gin glasses.'

Lizzie made a start on clearing the table but still the girls sat on. And why not? Lizzie thought. Their working day was hours away – this was their time to while away as they wished. She got on with the washing-up and gradually they drifted off, making vague plans to take a walk or go to the milliner in Lower Street to see whether the new delivery of ribbons had arrived. Finally, she had the kitchen to herself, but there was no time to sit down. Annie had brought her a dress, which she had ripped at the hem, to see whether Lizzie could repair it. And there was ironing to be done – all the sheets she had washed the previous day and dried in the small backyard. Mrs Franklin insisted they should be washed and pressed at least once a week when the house was busy. Privately, Lizzie thought they should be washed more frequently and not pressed, since she doubted any of the clients noticed such things, but she wasn't going to volunteer for more work.

With the table scrubbed and dried, and the heavy iron heated on the range, she set to work. It was a mindless task and her thoughts wandered once more. She smiled to herself as she thought how shocked she had been when she first arrived at Bay House. The girls were so matter-of-fact about their occupation, laughing and joking over the breakfast table as they discussed their visitors from the night before. Lizzie's cheeks had flamed at the bawdiness of their conversation; when they noticed, they had teased her and made her blush even more. It hadn't taken them long to wheedle out of her that she had no experience of what they were discussing. To her surprise, they had been intrigued and, after that, fiercely protective of her.

'Don't let Mrs Franklin get any ideas,' Nancy had warned her. 'I'll wager after one look at your face and figure she took you on with a mind to having you working on your back before too long.'

'And watch out for the men,' Annie chimed in. 'They'll get you in a dark corner and try to sweet-talk you into all sorts of shenanigans if you don't keep your wits about you.'

Lizzie had been frightened by both prospects, but forewarned was forearmed. She'd made sure to keep out of the customers' way, learning how to manoeuvre swiftly past them in the narrow hallway. And, so far, Mrs Franklin hadn't suggested a change in her work. The girls didn't know that Lizzie had family in town, although Mrs Franklin did. Lizzie hoped it would keep her safe: the proprietor wouldn't want to compromise her position as a respectable woman in Hawksdown when she knew Lizzie's married sister lived there, too. Not that the family connection was worth anything, Lizzie thought, although Mrs Franklin wasn't to know that.

She smoothed and folded a freshly pressed sheet while the iron reheated, then set to work on another. Her thoughts took her back to the end of the previous year. By December, Lizzie had all but run out of money. One bitterly cold afternoon, it drove her to make the difficult decision to pay a visit to her family home. She had half expected to come across her mother or one of her siblings somewhere in town, but it had never happened. She supposed her father was either out on his boat or in the Ship, somewhere that Lizzie never visited. And her mother would always send a daughter out on errands – no doubt the role had fallen to Ruth or Jane since Lizzie had left. Living in Hawksdown, Nell probably made her purchases in the shops there. Or perhaps she had servants to do these things for her now. So Lizzie, half fearful of starving in her basement, had put on the best dress she owned, which had seen better days, swathed herself in every shawl she possessed and set out for number seven Lower Street.

It looked much as she had when she left it – clean and neat from the outside, although the gate creaked as she opened it. A light glowed dimly inside as the afternoon gloom deepened. As Lizzie ventured up the path, she thought she glimpsed a shadow at the window, gone in a flash. She rapped at the door and waited, heart thudding. No one came so, after a minute during which she shivered in the chill wind, she knocked again.

Lizzie hesitated, half inclined simply to open the door and step inside. But what if her family no longer lived there? She couldn't take the risk, so she turned away, glancing back once more as she closed the gate. Again, that brief glimpse of a shadowy figure at the window. A stranger, or one of her family? Lizzie began the walk back to her basement, head down against the wind. It buffeted her and took her breath away, unwinding her shawls so that she was forced to stop and adjust them, staggering as she did so. She was weak, she realised. She'd been surviving on tea and bread to eke out her last few pennies. Now she was in a desperate situation. She didn't have enough money to take her anywhere else, or even enough to stay. Tears began to trickle down her cheeks and she stopped to lean against a wall and catch her breath.

Few people were out in such weather but a woman was hurrying along the street towards Lizzie, the wind at her back and a basket in her hand. 'There's snow in that wind,' she remarked, as she passed. She glanced at Lizzie as she spoke, then stopped. 'Are you unwell?' she asked, concerned.

Lizzie shook her head and made to move off but her legs buckled beneath her.

The woman dropped her basket and seized Lizzie's arm. 'Let's get you out of this cold,' she said. She ignored Lizzie's feeble protests and, picking up her basket, steered her down a side road and into Middle Street. 'Here we are,' she said, opening a door just a few yards from the corner. She helped Lizzie down a narrow flight of stairs, where she sank into a chair close to the kitchen range, barely sensible of where she was or what she was doing.

Chapter Four

The woman didn't try to engage Lizzie in conversation, but heated some soup, already in a pot on the range, and served it to her without comment, with a chunk of the fresh bread she unpacked from the basket. The soup was hot but Lizzie had to prevent herself from bolting it. It tasted like the best thing she had ever eaten.

'Thank you,' she said, leaning back once the bowl was empty.

The woman had been unpacking the basket and moving around the kitchen while Lizzie ate. Now she came and sat at the table, with a cup of tea for each of them. 'Do you want to tell me how you've come to be in this state?' she asked. 'I can tell by looking at you that you're half starved. Where's your family?'

The last question startled Lizzie. Had she been seen trying to visit them? Then she realised the woman was just probing for details. 'I live alone,' she said. 'I've been trying to get work for the last few weeks but there's nothing to be had – at least, not anything I have experience of.'

'And what would that be?' the woman asked.

'Looking after children. And housework, I suppose,' Lizzie answered.

'Can you cook?' the woman asked.

Again, Lizzie was surprised. 'Yes – but not well enough to take it up as my line of work.'

The woman nodded. 'I know of a position that might suit,' she said.

'Really?' Lizzie was cautious, although her heart leaped at the thought of finding a way out of her predicament. 'Where? And to do what?'

'Here,' the woman said. 'My sister, Mrs Franklin, is looking for someone to watch over her girls, keep the place clean, make their breakfast, do a bit of shopping. I've taken on the job for now, but I've got my own business, a milliner's, to run and I'll be glad to get back to it. I'm sure it would suit you, after you've got your strength back. My sister will be here shortly – we'll tell her.'

She seemed to assume that Lizzie would do it, or perhaps she just saw a way to be released from her obligation to her sister. Lizzie didn't have the strength to demur, even though she had a pretty good idea of what was meant by 'the girls'. It wasn't a position she'd choose, but if she was to look after them rather than become one, she must overcome her scruples.

By the time Mrs Franklin arrived later that evening, her sister, who had introduced herself as Lydia Hayward, had discovered where Lizzie was living, and had confirmed her suspicions that she hadn't eaten properly in some time. Lydia presented Lizzie to Mrs Franklin as her new maid-of-all-work, leaving her sister little option but to agree. She further added that Lizzie would need to live in, starting that very evening.

'She can work alongside me for a day or two,' Lydia added, 'and then I must return to the shop.'

Mrs Franklin, who regarded Lizzie with some suspicion, offered grudging thanks. 'I'll be sorry to see you go,' she said. 'The house has never been so well run. But if you're sure Miss Carey is up to it . . . ?'

'She will be,' Lydia said.

Lizzie folded the last sheet, and looked at the pile with some satisfaction. She was doing a good job, she felt. Mrs Franklin, a short, stout woman who did her best to present a respectable front in the way she dressed, had little to complain of, even though she was always looking for faults. The house kept Lizzie so busy that she was rarely out and about in Castle Bay, and still hadn't encountered any of her family. She had even avoided going to church during the first few months, sure she would meet them at St George's in Lower Street. Now she had found a smaller church in the opposite direction to the family home. She didn't recognise anyone in the congregation and hoped no one recognised her. The first time she had attended, in February, she had opened her prayer book to discover the curl of baby Grace's blonde hair pressed between the pages. She had forgotten placing it there. Tears had started to her eyes and she closed the book with trembling hands. It felt as though half a lifetime had passed since she had cared for the Russell children, yet it was just a year earlier. Lizzie could scarcely believe it: so much had happened in the intervening months.

The door in her mind had tried once more to creak open on her time in Betsanger Court but she pushed it firmly closed and imagined turning the key in the lock. She couldn't afford those memories if she was to keep her hard-won peace of mind. And now, on this hot August day, she felt as though she was finally in control. She wasn't yet ready to revisit her relationship with Joe, but she could contemplate Mrs Bailey and the rest of the staff, and even wonder how Agnes and Christopher fared. Other than that, she didn't allow herself to think beyond the following day: her work and the girls kept her fully occupied from morning until night, and beyond, and for that she was thankful.

The girls had returned from town, all a-flutter with excitement. They had had word that several new ships were at anchor in the Downs, the sheltered stretch of water between the shore and the great sandbar out at sea, a hazard for the unwary mariner. They were expecting Bay House to be busy that night, which was important to them, and to Lizzie, if they were to earn their keep. All of them, except Nancy, were in their rooms, either resting or preparing themselves. Lizzie hoped Nancy would return soon, preferably before Mrs Franklin paid her daily visit, so that she could usher her upstairs and persuade her to sleep, before the proprietor caught sight of her flushed face and heard her stumbling, tipsy words.

Lizzie found no shame in her work – the girls were, for the most part, delightful, even if spats broke out occasionally when one considered another had stolen a favourite customer. She knew, though, that her family wouldn't view things in the same light. They would consider she was as good as working as a prostitute herself; in the past, Lizzie had heard her mother's opinion often enough on the girls of Middle Street.

'Their mothers must be turning in their graves,' she had declared, 'for in the graveyard they must be, or why haven't they come and dragged home their daughters? To bring such disgrace on a family – can you imagine?'

Mrs Carey had then surveyed her brood of girls. 'Don't let me catch any one of you in such a place. You'll never step across my threshold again. I'd not be able to hold up my head in the town.' Which contradicted her previous declaration that mothers should rescue their daughters from a life of vice.

Lizzie was saved from further musings on Mrs Carey's opinion by the arrival of Nancy, who was, as she had expected, much the worse for wear after her afternoon of drinking. She hustled her upstairs, despite Nancy's protestations that she just wanted to sit in the kitchen and talk to Lizzie, her 'best friend in the world'. As she closed the bedroom door on Nancy, now prostrate and snoring on her bed, she heard the front door open. Mrs Franklin's fortunate timing had averted disaster. Lizzie knew that if she had found Nancy drunk so early in the evening, she would have let her go without a qualm. And Lizzie, mindful of the girls' words when she had first started, didn't want there to be a vacancy in the house. It was why she always wore only the plainest of blouses and skirts, purchased second-hand from Mrs Voss on Lower Street. There were times when it pained her to be so poorly turned out, but if that was the price she must pay to fade into the background, then so be it.

CHAPTER FIVE

September brought an abrupt end to the warm sunshine that had favoured the long days of August. The girls had started to complain about the heat in their bedrooms, and the lack of a breeze to stir the air, even with the windows flung wide. They had reason to regret their words when the storms rolled in, bringing gale-force winds that rattled the panes, whistled through every gap in the woodwork and rippled their way beneath the roof tiles. Stepping out into Middle Street to buy essential supplies from Widow Booth's shop, Lizzie found the front door all but wrenched from her hand, as she tried to hold down her skirts with the other.

When she returned with what was needed for the breakfast table, she found some of the girls already gathered in the kitchen, shawls around their shoulders. 'We need the fires lit in our rooms, Lizzie,' they complained. 'We're so cold!'

Lizzie knew Mrs Franklin's views: no fires before mid-September at the earliest. 'They can put extra blankets on their beds. And wear more clothes,' she'd told Lizzie, at the start of the year, when she was outlining what she expected of her. Would she compromise and agree to fires being lit in the evenings? There would be more sailors in town, delayed at anchor in the Downs until the storms had died away. It would be in all their interests to make Bay House as comfortable as possible for them. She would tackle her about it when she made her daily visit.

'I'll talk to Mrs Franklin today,' she promised, placing plates of sliced bread on the table, then turning her attention to the eggs cooking on the range.

The girls groaned. 'She'll say no,' Annie predicted.

'Not if I tell her it's good for business,' Lizzie said. 'But maybe the storm will blow through and we'll be back to the hot weather you've been complaining of.'

The storm did blow through, but rain set in, accompanied by a distinctly chilly wind. Mrs Franklin grudgingly agreed to fires being lit, at first only in the evening, then all day as the house became colder. With more sailors than usual at a loose end in the town, Lizzie found she was busier than ever. Not only did she have ten grates to clean each day, with fires then to be lit while the girls were at breakfast, but the additional clients meant she was despatched more often to fetch rum, gin and ale. And she had to run up and down the stairs every hour or so to make sure the fires were kept in. The girls seemed incapable of doing this, despite the baskets in each room being well stocked with fuel.

Within a few days, their supply of wood and coal, depleted after a chilly spring the previous year, needed topping up. Further deliveries were required so Lizzie had to make time to visit the coal merchant in Hawksdown. Mrs Franklin had fallen out with the one in Castle Bay over his insistence on payment before delivery. The walk to Hawksdown was pleasant on a sunny day, less attractive on a wet and windy one, with household duties building up for every minute she was away. Lizzie was frowning while she walked as she contemplated the tasks waiting for her in Middle Street, and at first didn't realise she had been addressed by a passer-by.

'Lizzie!' Then again, louder this time, 'Lizzie!'

She stopped and spun round, knowing even as she did so that the voice was her sister Nell's.

Pink-cheeked from the wind, the damp air causing her auburn hair to curl in tendrils around her face, Nell stood there open-mouthed. 'Lizzie, is it really you? What are you doing here? Where have you been?' Emotions flitted across her face: shock, puzzlement, anger. 'Do you have any idea how worried we've all been? We thought you must be dead. Gone, without a word to anyone. Ma was convinced you had drowned. We kept expecting to hear your body had been found, washed up on the shore. And now here you are. What happened? Where did you go?'

Lizzie was speechless. They thought she had drowned! Why on earth did they think that? It had never occurred to her. Surely her mother had seen she had taken a few things – her hairbrush, some clothes. She wouldn't have done that if she was going to throw herself into the sea.

'Lizzie?' Nell was growing impatient.

'It's a long story.' Lizzie barely knew where to start, but the urgent need to return to Middle Street was nagging at the back of her mind. She began to turn away. 'I can't stop now. I must get on.'

'Oh no you don't.' Nell reached out and grabbed Lizzie's arm. 'I need an explanation – the whole family does. And you owe us one.'

'I can't stop now,' Lizzie repeated. 'I'm late. I have to go.'

They stood and faced each other, two petite women, not dissimilar in looks but very obviously differing in their station in life. Nell was smartly dressed in a velvet costume, a warm pelisse over her outfit. Lizzie was wearing her usual drab work clothes, a woollen shawl, already heavy with moisture, thrown over them. She knew herself to be at a disadvantage and, infuriated, she could feel her bottom lip start to tremble. Defiant, but close to tears, she took a long, shuddering breath and tried to disengage herself.

Recognising the effect she was having, Nell adopted a more conciliatory tone. 'I'm sorry, Lizzie. It was such a shock seeing you. I don't want to lose you again. Can I walk with you? Where are you going?'

'To the coal merchant,' Lizzie mumbled.

'Then I will come with you and you can tell me something of yourself,' Nell said. 'And then I'll let you go on your way, but not without knowing where I can find you again.'

So Lizzie let her walk at her side and, in the half-mile left of her

312

journey, she gave her a brief outline of where she had been and what she had done: working for a family in Canterbury, and another at Betsanger Court, looking after their children. She was careful to leave out Mrs Simmonds's role in her story, as well as Adam Russell's offer of marriage, and her entanglement with Joe. Mrs Bailey's words, *Give my regards to your sister's husband*, flitted through her mind, but she didn't utter them.

Even as she was speaking, Nell listening intently at her side, Lizzie was trying to work out a way of disguising where she was living now. When they arrived at the entrance to the coal merchant, she tried to persuade Nell to wait outside.

'I'll only be a minute,' she promised.

Nell was having none of it. It was as if she imagined Lizzie would make her escape through the back door, sitting astride the coal sacks on the back of one of the carts. 'It's too damp and windy out here,' she said firmly, following Lizzie inside. Then she stood beside her at the makeshift wooden counter in the sparse room, coal dust heavy on the air, while Lizzie dealt with the clerk. She concentrated hard on his grimy hands as she was forced to give out the name of the person who would pay for the order, and he wrote down the address where it was to be delivered. She was aware of Nell's sharp intake of breath as she uttered the words 'Middle Street'.

As soon as they were outside again, Nell turned to her. 'What are you doing in Middle Street, Lizzie?'

The question came out like an accusation and Lizzie bridled. 'It's not what you think,' she said. 'It's where I work, but I'm not doing what you imagine. I work for a respectable lady called Mrs Franklin, who lives somewhere around here, in Hawksdown.' Lizzie glanced about, as if half expecting to see her walking along the road.

Nell kept silent, her gaze fixed on Lizzie.

Lizzie stumbled on with her explanation. 'I clean the house, shop, cook.'

'And what sort of house is it?' Nell asked. 'Who lives there?'

'I do,' Lizzie said. Then, realising there was little point in dissembling further, she gave in. 'I look after the girls who work there. They are lovely, kind and caring. They do their work, I do mine.'

Nell sighed. 'You make it all sound so normal, Lizzie. Do you have any idea how Ma will react? She's already very upset, and now this. And Thomas – how am I to tell him?'

'I know how Ma will react,' Lizzie retorted, adding, 'and I'm sorry if you think Thomas will be upset.' Once more, she remembered Mrs Bailey's words. Why had the housekeeper mentioned Thomas? How did she even know of him?

'And now I must go.' She hesitated. 'It was good to see you, Nell.' On impulse, she reached out and pulled her sister to her in an awkward embrace. Then she hurried on her way. She noticed that Nell didn't try to stop her.

CHAPTER SIX

A week passed and Nell didn't call at the house in Middle Street. Lizzie felt her anxiety begin to ease, to be replaced by anger. Clearly, her sister thought Lizzie had fallen so far beneath the rest of the family that she was no longer worth bothering with. Her emotions were mixed – seeing Nell had been a shock but, in a way, she had been glad. It had had to happen eventually, she supposed, and she longed to find out more about the family: how her sisters fared, whether Nell had children now, how her grandfather had taken to his new life in the country with Thomas's mother. Now it seemed she was to be left in ignorance, as the price she must pay for her own neglect of them all, and what they no doubt saw as her disgraceful behaviour. She had been circumspect in the details she had revealed to Nell but she feared her sister would have been busy filling in some of the blanks.

Lizzie's days continued to be full, however, and she had little time to dwell on such thoughts other than when she first awoke. She would spend a few moments savouring the warmth under the covers, shifting her weight to find a comfortable position on the lumpy pallet, before she must get up and dress quickly, ready to start the day. The cupboard of a room in which she slept was becoming increasingly damp as the wet weather continued – the moisture seeped through the brickwork where the prevailing wind drove the rain against the back of the house.

Lizzie's previous satisfaction at the position in which she had found herself had been fading since she had seen her sister. She no longer felt as though she was managing well: she now saw herself through her sister's eyes. Not quite a fallen woman, but one who was certainly experiencing hard times, her position in life much diminished.

As soon as such gloomy thoughts took over, Lizzie would take a breath, throw back the covers and pull on her clothes before all warmth left her body. The range would need attention, water must be fetched and heated, fuel brought in ready to start laying the fires once the girls awoke. The larder would need stocking and, if the weather allowed, linen must be washed. Sunday was the only day in which the routine varied. Lizzie went to her church, and some of the girls went to St George's, which no doubt caused a flutter of disapproval among the devout worshippers there. Mrs Franklin frowned on the girls working on the Sabbath so the atmosphere in Bay House was very different, although Lizzie was no less busy. The girls washed their hair, or brought down piles of laundry or mending, sitting around in the kitchen and chatting while Lizzie prepared the roast dinner they all expected during the afternoon. Since none of them bothered to get dressed, it fell to Lizzie, as usual, to fetch the drink they fancied to ease them through the long hours ahead.

Lizzie was undertaking just such an errand, mulling over the likelihood of Mrs Franklin agreeing to take on a young girl to provide some additional help, when she came face-to-face with Nell. Her heart gave such a leap in her chest that, feeling weak, she had to stop walking. Ten days had passed since their encounter and now here was her sister again, dressed as though she had visited church that morning. Where was Thomas? What excuse had Nell given for her absence? Or had she just come from their mother's house in Lower Street?

'Hello, Lizzie.' Nell was the first to speak. 'I'm happy to see you again. Is there somewhere we might talk?'

They were standing outside the Ship, sounds of laughter emanating from it every time the door swung open to admit another customer. Lizzie was sharply reminded of her father and his strictures about the place. 'No daughter of mine will set foot in the Ship,' he had declared, 'or any other inn at this end of town. They're full of unsavoury types.' Did Nell remember, too? Lizzie had observed his ruling to some extent, taking the girls' custom to the taverns around the corner in Alfred Square, but more out of concern that she might come across him propping up the bar inside. She glanced involuntarily at the windows giving onto the street.

'We can't talk here,' she said, and walked onwards to Alfred Square. 'I can't stop,' she said. 'I'm in the middle of cooking dinner.'

'I'll come back with you,' Nell offered. 'I can help.'

Lizzie was horrified. Her sister was a very good cook, but she couldn't imagine her sitting at the kitchen table, peeling potatoes, surrounded by the girls in their *déshabillé*. Yet, not twenty minutes later, that was exactly where she was. Nell declined to go into the tavern with Lizzie to buy gin and ale, but she would not be dissuaded from joining her in the basement of Bay House. The girls were startled when Lizzie returned, bringing their drinks and accompanied by someone who, after just a moment's examination, was clearly her sister. There was an awkward pause, while Lizzie, flushed with embarrassment, managed to stutter, 'This is Nell, everyone,' and turned to the range to examine the roasting fowl.

Nell sat down next to Annie. 'Give me a job to do, Lizzie,' she said.

And Lizzie, half amazed, saw Nell set to, peeling potatoes and scrubbing carrots, while joining in the chat around the table as if she was sitting with their family and not in a bawdyhouse, surrounded by no-good strumpets, as their mother would have termed them. She stayed with them to eat too. As soon as the plates were cleared, she stood up and said she must be getting home. There was some good-natured teasing about escaping the washing-up from the girls, who never considered doing such a thing themselves, then Lizzie bustled her up to the front door. She was keen to avoid any questions about where Nell lived, and who with, although she would no doubt be quizzed when she went back downstairs.

'I'm glad you allowed me to join you,' Nell said. 'I enjoyed meeting everyone.'

Lizzie looked at her doubtfully, but it was clear from the flush on her cheeks and the sparkle in her eyes that she spoke the truth – although perhaps this had something to do with the gin Annie had poured for her.

'When can we meet again?' Nell asked.

Lizzie, her hand on the door latch, could only shrug. 'The work keeps me busy all day,' she said. Then, not wishing to sound dismissive, she added, 'But there's a great deal I want to ask you. About Ma and Pa, and our sisters.' A thought struck her. 'Did Pa get his wish? Have I –' she corrected herself '– have we got a brother?'

Nell smiled. 'We have,' she said. 'Walter, after his grandpa. But everyone calls him by his second name, Peter. He just doesn't look like a Walter.'

A mixture of emotions crowded in on Lizzie. 'I hope I get to see him one day,' she said, as she opened the door.

Nell loitered in the hallway. 'Lizzie, will you come to us one Sunday? After church? Could you manage that? Here – I've written down our address. Write to me and let me know when you can come. And don't think to avoid me. I'll come back if I don't hear from you.'

As she walked away up the street, Lizzie saw Mrs Franklin turn the corner of Exchange Street and walk towards Bay House. She withdrew hurriedly and ran down the stairs to the basement, keen to get the washing-up under way so she couldn't be chided for lax housekeeping. There was just time to warn the girls to hide some of their bottles beneath the table before they heard the front door open and Mrs Franklin's footsteps on the stairs.

Would she allow Lizzie a rare afternoon off? Lizzie was doubtful, but she would wait until she knew her employer to be in a good mood, then pose the question. She had had a tantalising glimpse of how life had gone on with her family in Castle Bay during her absence and now she yearned to know more.

CHAPTER SEVEN

Nell's unexpected visit to the Middle Street house left Lizzie unsettled. The girls' curiosity about her sister only added to her disquiet – in the week following their Sunday dinner, she found herself fielding questions several times a day and revealing far more than she cared to about her family situation.

'You're a dark horse, Lizzie,' Nancy declared. 'A whole family living in the town, but you never see them. What other secrets do you have? Why are you in such disgrace?'

Lizzie blushed to the roots of her hair and busied herself stacking the breakfast dishes in the dresser. She did her best to ignore the teasing, but amazed herself by tackling Mrs Franklin about having some time off. She'd started by suggesting they took on a girl to help with some of the daily work. When Mrs Franklin refused to countenance that, Lizzie moved to her next line of attack.

'Then it's only fair I should be allowed some regular free time. I work seven days a week, long hours, and other than going to church I haven't had a moment to myself since I've been here. I'd like to take a Sunday afternoon off as soon as possible.'

Mrs Franklin was taken aback. 'And who will cook the girls their dinner?' she demanded.

Lizzie shrugged. 'Maybe they can do it themselves. Or perhaps your sister, Mrs Hayward, could help out.' She turned her attention to the vegetables she was peeling, leaving Mrs Franklin to think about it. The proprietor made no response that day, but later in the week she told Lizzie she had arranged for Lydia to step in.

'But don't think you can make a habit of it,' she warned her. 'There's plenty of others who'd be happy to take your place.'

Lizzie doubted it – Lydia had told her how hard it had been to find someone after the previous girl had flounced out, following a row with Mrs Franklin. But she thanked Mrs Franklin and could barely restrain herself from rushing out of the room to write to Nell. She managed to despatch a note later that day, hoping it would be convenient to visit that Sunday, with apologies for the short notice.

Sunday found Lizzie nervously seeking out the address Nell had sent her. She was expecting to find a cottage and was taken aback to find herself standing outside a double-fronted house, newly built judging by the colour of the brick, with an iron gate and a flagged front path leading to a substantial front door. She checked the address from the note in her hand, then went to the door and rapped on the knocker.

A few moments later it was opened, and Nell stood there, smiling, two small girls peeping out from behind her skirts.

'Oh!' Lizzie gasped. 'You didn't say!'

'Clara and Phoebe,' Nell introduced the little girls, who continued to cling shyly to her. 'Now come through and see Thomas.'

Lizzie's nervousness, temporarily lulled at the sight of the little girls, so very like her own small sisters in appearance, returned at the thought of seeing Thomas again. Nell had worked for him and his mother at their house in Prospect Street, then continued to deliver food to Thomas when he had moved out to Hawksdown, working long hours at the brewery. Since their marriage five years previously, Lizzie doubted she had seen them more than three or four times. She hadn't even been at the wedding: instead of being pleased at her eldest daughter's good fortune, Mrs Carey had been enraged. She saw Nell as neglecting her family duty in marrying and moving away, and had declined the wedding invitation. From that day, Lizzie had had to take on the care of her sisters, as well as Nell's household tasks.

320

She barely knew Thomas and so she was fearful of her reception. She needn't have worried, though. He was as welcoming as Nell and there was no hint that he might consider her damned as a fallen woman by the nature of her work. True, her position in Middle Street wasn't touched on during the course of a delicious dinner, but Lizzie learned a good deal about the day-to-day running of the brewery, where Thomas had risen to be general manager.

'We've only been living here a few months,' Nell said. 'I'm still getting used to the size of the house. We lived in a two-up two-down across the road before. Now I have a maid and I think we will need a cook.' She looked embarrassed, and a little sad, at the thought.

Lizzie remembered how her sister had loved to cook, and her ability to get dinner quickly to the table. The standard of daily fare at number seven Lower Street had changed considerably after Nell had left home, Mrs Carey being a reluctant cook and Lizzie an unskilled one.

'Have Ma and Pa been to see the new house?' Lizzie asked. What would they have made of such riches in comparison to their own cramped cottage?

Nell shook her head. 'You know what Ma is like. She can hold a grudge for longer than anyone would think possible.'

Lizzie's heart sank at the words, even though she knew them to be true. And when, all too soon, she had to leave to be back in Middle Street, she wasn't surprised when, as she made her farewell to Nell at the door, her sister said, 'I've told Ma I've seen you but she's not in a mood to forgive you for vanishing without a word, Lizzie. She refuses to meet you, or even speak about what you've been doing.'

Nell paused. 'I did tell her where you're living now. I thought it was as well she knew, in case word somehow got back to her. I'm afraid it just made matters worse.'

Lizzie had expected as much but was cast down all the same and struggled to hold her emotions in check. Despite her best efforts, her lip trembled as she said, 'And my sisters? Can I see them? And my little brother?' Her heart turned over at the thought.

Nell bit her lip. 'It will be hard. If Ma found out . . . ' Then, seeing Lizzie's expression, she added, 'Give it time. I'm sure we can find a way.'

Lizzie walked home, barely noticing the growing chill of the late afternoon. Her soul was warmed by the hours spent with her sister's family and she carried her happiness with her all the way back to Middle Street. It sustained her through the following week, but by Sunday she was impatient to see Nell again. As she had mulled over the visit, questions occurred to her that she wished she had asked. She could only store them up in her mind and hope that another opportunity to meet would present itself before too long.

CHAPTER EIGHT

Lizzie was confused by her newly awakened wish to see her family; during her time in Canterbury, and at Betsanger Court, she had barely thought of them. Now that she was back in Castle Bay, her heart ached for her sisters, and Nell was her only link to meeting them again. How quickly she had moved from wishing to avoid all her family to longing for them. Perhaps it was Nell's acceptance of her work in Middle Street that had transformed her thinking. Their mother, though, would be far from easy to convince to see her errant daughter.

As autumn turned and winter moved in, Lizzie managed infrequent meetings with Nell. Mrs Franklin was less than keen to offer her another Sunday afternoon off, but with the girls' help, Lizzie managed to escape Bay House for an hour or two here and there, to walk with Nell and catch up with any news. Nell had begun to probe more deeply into Lizzie's previous year or so away. Lizzie had found herself able to talk about her time in New Street, and even about Adam Russell's proposal, but had not ventured beyond that.

Nell had been indignant about the awkward position Lizzie had found herself in. To her surprise, Lizzie had felt the need to defend Adam. 'I understood it,' she said. 'He needed a mother for his children, who knew me well, and I knew the running of the house. In his eyes, it made perfect sense.'

They walked on, the east wind scouring their cheeks and bringing tears to their eyes.

323

'To be honest, I realise now that if I had married him, my life would have been easier,' Lizzie confessed. 'Do you suppose Ma would have been prepared to forgive me for running off if I'd returned a respectable married woman, with a ready-made family?'

'But you didn't love him, Lizzie,' Nell said simply. 'You could never have been happy.'

Lizzie was silenced by her sister's conviction. And, in truth, she didn't really believe her own words. Adam Russell was not the man for her and her decision to leave had been the right one.

Nell invited Lizzie to spend Christmas Day with the family. 'The girls are longing to see you again,' she said.

Lizzie was torn. Christmas at Nell and Thomas's home was a delightful prospect: she could imagine the dining room decorated with fir boughs, candles burning, a delicious roast goose on the table, ready for Thomas to carve. But the girls would also expect a special dinner in Middle Street, where it would no doubt be a raucous, gin-fuelled occasion. And who would cook for them if Lizzie didn't? She doubted Lydia Hayward would be prepared to step in on such a day. So, regretfully, she had to decline Nell's invitation.

'But I will ask Mrs Franklin for a Sunday afternoon off in the new year,' she promised. 'In fact, I'll tell her I'm taking one.' Lizzie laughed at her own boldness, but she was as good as her word.

'I'll be off next Sunday afternoon,' she told Mrs Franklin, in the first week of January. 'And one every two months after that.'

Mrs Franklin declared this an outrageous proposition, but Lizzie stood firm. 'I work very hard for you. Despite your insistence to the contrary, we both know that it's not a position you'd find easy to fill. So either the girls can sort themselves out when I'm away or you could ask your sister whether she would be prepared to step in again.'

In the end, a compromise was reached. Lizzie roasted a fowl on the Saturday, to be served cold on the Sunday. She prepared the vegetables before she left and Annie agreed to roast the potatoes and boil the carrots and swedes. Lizzie left a cake to serve as dessert, but despite her efforts the girls complained.

'It's not the same as when you cook for us. The gravy was too thin and we want a hot pudding, with white sauce.'

Lizzie was unmoved. 'It won't hurt you to have something dif ferent once every eight weeks. Maybe you could stir yourselves to make some of the things you say you miss.'

It turned out that one of the girls, Kitty, was a fair cook and quite capable of managing the dinner occasionally. Once it was agreed that she would do so, in return for the others funding her week's supply of rum, harmony was restored. Lizzie had some time with Nell and her family, and the girls at Bay House enjoyed the dinner they felt they deserved.

'Do you think you could swap a Sunday for a Saturday in July?' Nell asked, on their Sunday together in May. 'There's an open day at the brewery and I've asked Ma whether she can spare Ruth and Jane to help me serve teas. It would give you a chance to meet them. Ma won't come – she'll say it's too far – and the others are too young and would just be a hindrance.'

'I'll start thinking how to manage it now,' Lizzie promised. It would be difficult, she knew. Saturday was a busy working day at Bay House. She was in constant demand from late afternoon to the early hours, to fetch, carry and shop. But Nell had said the brewery open day would start at ten o'clock in the morning and finish at four in the afternoon. She could surely escape for an hour or two within that time if she planned carefully.

On the designated July Saturday, Lizzie was in the kitchen bright and early, ready to serve breakfast. She'd warned the girls of her plan, asking them to cooperate, and they had agreed. But it seemed cooperation didn't extend to rising any earlier than usual to eat. Lizzie banged around in the kitchen, hoping to stir them into action, then gave up. She would plan to be away by midday and back again by two. That would give her nearly an hour at the open day, which should be plenty, given her interest was in seeing Ruth and Jane rather than touring the brewery.

Just before midday, Lizzie was tying on her bonnet in front of the glass in the narrow hallway, the kitchen set to rights after breakfast, although several of the girls still sat at the table.

'I'll be back in a couple of hours,' she promised, then hurried from the house before any of them could find an excuse to delay her. It was a hot, sunny day, not ideal for making a fast-paced walk to Hawksdown, and by the time Lizzie arrived at the imposing gates to the brewery her dress was sticking to her back and her forehead beaded with sweat. She'd forgotten to ask Nell where she was setting up her tea table but it would surely be easy enough to find. She hoped it would be inside one of the buildings, or at least in the shade. Intent on finding it, she set off across the main courtyard, walking past one of the brewery drays, a large carthorse harnessed in the traces. She paid it, and the two men conversing beside it, no heed until a voice called, 'Lizzie!'

Recognising Thomas's tones, she swung round. He would know where she could find Nell. Then his companion spoke. 'Lizzie? Lizzie Carey?'

She shaded her eyes against the sun, then half stifled a gasp. The man with Thomas, wearing a white shirt and leather waistcoat, was someone she had never expected to see again. She thought she had successfully defended her heart against all memories of the bitter disappointment he had caused her, but with Joe standing before her, it all came flooding back and she knew she had failed.

CHAPTER NINE

'I'm in search of Nell,' Lizzie said, addressing Thomas and ignoring Joe completely.

'You'll find her through there.' Puzzled by her abrupt manner, Thomas pointed through an archway into another courtyard. 'She's set up her table in the corner.'

Lizzie hurried away before anything further could be said. She was sure she could feel Joe's eyes boring into her back, but she didn't turn. Somewhat agitated, she cast around the crowd in the courtyard in search of Nell's tea table. All the men were drinking ale but she spotted a cluster of ladies in the far corner, where tall buildings cast welcome shade. They were holding glasses and teacups and Lizzie hastened over.

There, behind the table, Nell was dispensing tea, aided by her maid and two girls who could only be Ruth and Jane. They had changed in the time Lizzie had been away: they were already taller than Nell and their dark hair gave them a strong resemblance to their father.

'Hello, Nell,' Lizzie said. 'Is there anything I can do to help?'

'You managed to get away,' Nell exclaimed. 'Ruth, Jane – look who's here.'

The sisters stopped what they were doing – plating slices of fruit loaf – and stared at Lizzie. With a sinking heart, she took in their stony faces.

Ruth was the first to speak. 'Ma said you were back.' She turned an accusing look on Nell. 'You didn't say she would be here today.'

'It's open to everyone, not just brewery workers.' Nell was defensive. 'Lizzie, let me get you a cup of tea. Or a glass of lemonade – you look hot.'

Flustered by the reaction of her sisters, and aware of curious looks from the ladies standing nearby, Lizzie gratefully accepted the lemonade and stood for a moment, at a loss. Then, resolute, she moved towards Ruth and Jane.

'I'm sorry I went off without a word,' she said, in a low voice. 'I hope one day you can forgive me. I resented all the work Ma expected me to do, but it was wrong to leave as I did.'

Ruth wasn't mollified. 'And who do you think had to do all the work after you left?' she demanded.

Lizzie, ashamed, looked at her feet. Ruth could only have been thirteen at the time, Jane two years younger. Girls had to grow up quickly in the Carey family.

'We were supposed to go to the charity school,' Ruth continued. 'But we had to look after Mary, Alice and Susan instead.'

'And Peter.' Jane finally spoke.

'Peter.' Lizzie couldn't prevent a smile. 'Was Pa happy to have a boy in the family at last?'

'He dotes on him,' Jane said. 'But we all do.'

'I don't,' Ruth said.

'I hope I can meet him one day.' Lizzie had finished her lemonade and stood holding the empty glass.

'I doubt Ma will let you through the door. She says you're a disgrace to the family.'

Ruth looked pleased, Lizzie thought. 'I may be working in Middle Street, but not in the way Ma thinks,' she retorted.

Ruth gave her an odd look. 'Ma heard all about what you were doing in Canterbury. Working for that woman who pretended to be better than she was, bringing shame on the family.'

Lizzie frowned. Ruth must have got the story confused. Hannah Russell's character certainly didn't fit those words. Perhaps she was referring to Mrs Bullivant, but that didn't make sense, either.

Neither Ruth nor Jane seemed to have anything further to say to her, busying themselves with handing out the cake, so she moved away and returned the glass to Nell. 'I'll go now,' she said.

Nell gave her a look of sympathy. 'So soon? Not quite the welcome you hoped for?' she asked.

Lizzie grimaced. 'Indeed. But I shouldn't have expected anything different. I don't suppose Ma has wasted any good words on me now she knows I'm back.'

'I'll talk to them,' Nell promised. 'I'm sure next time you see them, it'll be a little easier.'

Lizzie gave her a wry smile and turned to leave. Then she remembered the shock she had experienced on arrival. 'I saw Thomas as I came in,' she said. 'He was standing by a brewery dray, talking to a man who was holding the horse's bridle. Do you know him?'

'I expect it was Joseph Powell, the stable manager,' Lizzie said. 'Thomas wanted a horse and dray out on display for the visitors to see. Why do you ask?'

'I thought he looked familiar,' Lizzie said. 'But he's not who I thought he was.'

It was partly true, she supposed. She smiled and nodded farewell to Nell, busy with a queue that had formed for lemonade, and cast a surreptitious glance towards Ruth and Jane. They had returned to slicing cake and ignored her. Trying not to sigh, she made her way back through the crowd towards the archway. Anxiety at the thought of passing Joe as she left the brewery made her legs weak. Why had he addressed her today after ignoring her in her last few days at Betsanger Court? She wouldn't respond if he spoke, she decided, looking anxiously towards the dray to see whether Thomas still stood there.

There was no sign of her brother-in-law, and a crowd of recent arrivals was clustered around the dray. Joe was busy answering questions so Lizzie hurried past and out onto the road.

She turned her face north and set off towards Bay House. She would be back in good time, but she didn't relish the girls' questions.

They would ask whether she had had a good time, and what could she say? That she had bumped into the man who had spurned her, and her younger sisters had wanted nothing to do with her? She almost laughed. It was not the outcome she had hoped for, after looking forward to the day from the moment Nell had mentioned it.

Lizzie was busy as soon as she stepped back through the door, and she was glad of it. It prevented any further rumination. One of the girls had lost the dress she wished to wear later that day, and had accused Nancy of taking it. 'You always liked it,' she screeched. 'You said the colour didn't suit me and it would look better on you. I'm going to search your room – I know it's there.'

'Oh no you don't.' Nancy had her by her hair, forcing Lizzie to step in and separate them.

'Stop it, the pair of you. You brought the dress to me to change the colour of the trim,' she said to the accuser. 'Don't you remember?' It was clear she didn't – she had drunk a quantity of rum that day. 'I'll have it finished for you before this evening. But only if you apologise to Nancy and then go up to your room.'

A grudging apology having been issued and accepted, the house settled down. Lizzie knew that the warm weather meant the girls would go out that evening to parade along Beach Street or visit the taverns in search of custom. She would have an hour or two to herself before they began to return, sailors on their arms. Until then, she wouldn't dwell on how she felt after seeing her sisters – and Joe.

CHAPTER TEN

Nell sent a note to Lizzie on the Monday after the brewery open day, asking whether she could arrange an hour or two when they might meet. Lizzie ignored the note. She felt mean doing so, but she didn't want to be reminded of anything to do with that Saturday. A few days later, Nell sent another note – again, Lizzie didn't respond. A week passed but Lizzie's resolve didn't weaken. She had no intention of going anywhere near Nell's house, for fear of bumping into Joe, and she had no wish to be reminded of Ruth and Jane's reaction to her. If that was how the Carey family wanted to behave, so be it.

Nell would not be thwarted, though. Another note arrived.

Lizzie,
   I know you are avoiding me, but we must talk. I have something important to tell you, something I feel sure you will want to hear. I will wait for you on the seafront, next to Throckings Hotel, at two o'clock on Friday.
Your loving sister, Nell

Nell meant to intrigue her, Lizzie knew, and she was indeed curious. But what could she possibly have to say that would change anything with regard to Ruth and Jane? Would she have arranged for them to be there, too? She resolved not to go – she couldn't face the disappointment of another meeting. Yet, as the days passed, she changed her mind time and again. In the end it seemed mean to leave

Nell standing alone, waiting, so she told the girls she had errands to run, took up her basket and left Bay House just before two o'clock.

The sun was hot but a breeze made the temperature feel pleasant and Lizzie's spirits lifted. She remembered how important it had once been to her to be outside in the fresh air, how she had longed for Betsanger Court when she, Agnes and Christopher had had an enforced stay in Canterbury. Now she spent too much time in the dark basement kitchen. She resolved there and then to make more of an effort to be outside every day. The work at Bay House constantly expanded – perhaps if she was less visible the girls wouldn't keep filling her hours with trivial errands, gossip and mending.

'Lizzie, I'm so glad you came.' Nell seized her and gave her a hug, knocking her sister's bonnet askew with her parasol.

Lizzie was somewhat taken aback by the effusiveness of her welcome. She supposed it was to make up for Ruth and Jane's coolness towards her.

'Shall we walk?' Without waiting for an answer, Nell set off towards the southern end of Castle Bay and Hawksdown. Lizzie quickened her pace to keep at her side.

'You said you had something important to tell me?' Lizzie prompted.

Nell stopped so abruptly that Lizzie had walked on a few paces before she realised. Puzzled, she turned back.

'I barely know where to begin.' Nell, always so calm, seemed flustered. 'You remember you wanted to know about our stable manager, Joseph? Well, at the open day he asked Thomas how he knew you, and Thomas told him that he was your brother-in-law. Joseph is quite new to the job and I'd hardly seen him, except at a distance, but Thomas had told me about him and was full of praise for his work. He's already following some of the ideas Joseph suggested to improve the delivery rounds.'

Nell paused and looked at Lizzie, as if to gauge her reaction. Lizzie kept her face impassive, a skill she had perfected at Betsanger Court, but her heart was beating wildly.

Nell commenced walking again. 'Joseph told Thomas you had worked at the same place as he did, Betsanger Court.' She gave Lizzie a sideways glance. 'You told me you didn't know him.'

'I said he wasn't who I thought he was,' Lizzie corrected her. 'Which is true.'

Nell gave her a sharp look. 'Well, at the end of the open day, I went to find Thomas and he was out at the front of the brewery, talking to Joseph, who was getting ready to take the horse to the stable. When Joseph saw me, he looked shocked and said, "You're so like Lizzie!" I was taken aback. Then Thomas introduced me as his wife and your sister. I asked Joseph how he knew you, and he explained about Betsanger Court. He said there had been a falling out between you, for which he was sorry. He mentioned receiving a letter from you after you had left, and that he would welcome the chance to talk it over with you.'

Lizzie snorted in derision. 'Well, it's a bit late. He had the chance to talk to me when I was there. He didn't want to know.'

Nell stopped again, and faced Lizzie. 'I was really surprised that he poured all this out to me, and in front of Thomas, too. He was obviously upset after seeing you, and then when he saw me, with us looking so alike, I suppose he couldn't stop himself. Lizzie, I don't know what happened between you, but I think you ought to hear him out.'

Lizzie realised her right hand was at her throat, unconsciously smoothing over the outline of the ring suspended beneath the neckline of her blouse. She quickly returned her hand to her side. 'I've no wish to talk to him,' she said. 'He made his decision to cut me out of his life. I respected it, accepted it and I've moved on.' To her annoyance, her voice shook as she spoke.

'Well, that's a shame,' Nell said, 'because he's waiting here to talk to you.'

Horrified, Lizzie saw Joe a few yards away, sitting beside the path, the dray close by and the horse placidly cropping grass.

'How could you, Nell?' she demanded. She looked about her,

thinking to turn and walk back the way they had come, but Nell had her by the arm.

'It won't hurt to listen,' she pleaded. 'Just give him five minutes.'

Lizzie tried to shake her off but the next moment they were standing in front of Joe, who scrambled to his feet.

'I'll walk on a bit,' Nell said, nodding to Joe. She left Lizzie standing awkwardly in front of him.

Joe didn't look comfortable, either. He shifted from foot to foot and opened his mouth several times as if to speak, then shut it again.

'Well?' Lizzie demanded, losing patience. 'Nell said there was something you wished to say. I don't have much time – I need to get back to work.'

Joe swallowed hard. 'Lizzie, I got your letter after you'd gone. I didn't know you'd leave so soon. Susan told me you'd already left when she gave it to me. I wasn't going to read it, I was so angry at the time. But I kept it and read it a few days later. You said how you felt about me, and that you would wear my ring. I wished then that I had been able to talk to you about what Mrs Bailey told me, and to hear your side of it.'

'Mrs Bailey!' Lizzie stared at him. So whatever it was that had tarnished her reputation at Betsanger Court had come from the housekeeper. 'But what on earth did she say about me?'

When Joe didn't immediately reply, she plunged on: 'I told you about the problem with Mrs Simmonds, that I'd never worked for her. Surely she wasn't peddling rumours about that.'

'No, it was about your baby. You never told me you had a baby.' Joe gave her an accusing look. 'Although she did say you'd had the baby after you'd worked for Mrs Simmonds, and I began to wonder whether any of what you'd told me had been the truth.'

Lizzie had no idea what he was talking about. 'A baby? I've never had a baby. Where did she get such an idea?'

'You keep a lock of her hair in your prayer book,' Joe said. 'She found it there, tied with a ribbon, "Grace" written on it in your hand.'

It was Lizzie's turn to open her mouth to speak and fail to find the words. Finally she managed: 'Susan warned me on my first day that Mrs Bailey was a snooper. I didn't care, because I had nothing to hide. Grace was the baby I looked after in Canterbury after her mother, Hannah, died. She wasn't mine but I loved her. I felt like her mother, because I cared for her from birth, and it broke my heart to leave her behind. I cut the curl so I would always remember her just as she was, a perfect, beautiful little baby. But she was never my child. Shame on you, Joe, for believing malicious gossip.'

Lizzie was so indignant, she practically spat out the last few words. She took a deep breath, to control the anger in her voice. 'I thought better of you, Joe,' she said. 'Why didn't you ask me, instead of believing Mrs Bailey? I can't think what I could have done to her to make her behave like that. She's an evil witch.'

Lizzie turned on her heel and stormed back towards Castle Bay, leaving Joe, crestfallen, at the side of the path.

CHAPTER ELEVEN

Once more, Nell sent Lizzie a note, asking whether they could meet. At least she had the good grace to apologise, Lizzie thought, skimming the page before she threw the paper into the fire of the range, watching the edges singe before the flames took hold.

She was furious with her sister's meddling. First Ruth and Jane, now Joe. Her face grew hot at the memory of their conversation. But one thought nagged at her: what had she done to make Mrs Bailey behave as she did? She had an inkling as to why the housekeeper disliked her. She hadn't enjoyed being overruled by Mrs Bullivant, who told her to place Lizzie in charge of the children in the nursery, rather than Hester, her own choice. Susan had warned her that Hester was Mrs Bailey's favourite. But blackening her character with everyone in the household, including Mrs Bullivant, seemed like an extreme form of revenge for something outside Lizzie's control. And how had she uncovered Lizzie's link to Mrs Simmonds, after she had done everything possible to keep it secret?

She continued to brood on the matter over the next few days, causing the girls to say, at not infrequent intervals, 'Cheer up, Lizzie.' She would plaster a smile on her face and try to shake off the bitter feelings left by the encounter with Joe, but she was never successful for long.

Another note came from Nell a week later and Lizzie burned it, as before. Then, a few days later, a third note arrived, this time in an unfamiliar hand. Lizzie turned it over, looking for clues. Could it be from Joe? Heart pounding, she unfolded it and began to read. She was confused at first, for the content was not as she expected. A glance at the signature made her rethink, and she began to read it again.

Dear Lizzie,

You will no doubt be surprised to receive word from me, but my intention is two-fold.

First, your sister, my dear wife, is distraught that she has caused you pain and upset in her efforts to help, and I find it hard to stand by and see her suffer.

Second, I have discovered that I am to blame in no small way for the injustice you experienced at Betsanger Court. I would welcome the chance to set things straight and hope that you will agree to meet me. I always walk with the children after church on Sunday. If you are able to join me at half past eleven, you will find us on Hawkshill Down. I look forward to seeing you there,
Respectfully yours,
Thomas

Lizzie was puzzled. What part could Thomas possibly have played in her dismissal from Betsanger Court? It was clear there was only one way to find out. She would have just enough time to get from her church service to the suggested meeting place, but Kitty would need persuading to take charge of the Sunday dinner until she returned. This was easily done, since Kitty had spent more than she had earned that week and needed money to sustain her rum habit.

It was a glorious August Sunday when Lizzie made her way to Hawkshill Down, which was carpeted with wild flowers in white and shades of pink: ox-eye daisies, milk vetch and sainfoin. Agnes would have enjoyed collecting a posy here, she thought, as she spotted Thomas walking with his daughters on the far side. She hurried to join them, conscious that Nell would be expecting him back. Did she know he had arranged to meet Lizzie? The children would certainly tell her, if not.

Thomas greeted her, and the girls, delighted by her presence, each seized a hand and skipped along beside her, Lizzie listening to their excited chatter. She cast an occasional curious glance at Thomas. He wore a grave expression and, after ten minutes or so, he said to his daughters, 'There's something I need to talk about with Lizzie. Why don't you go and gather some flowers to take back to your mother? Stay where I can see you.'

They found a particularly abundant patch and sank to their knees among them. Thomas turned to Lizzie. 'We don't have long, so I will be brief. Nell told me what had happened – how she had tried to help sort out what she saw as a misunderstanding between you and Joe, but ended up making matters worse. I could see how upset she was but, at first, I assumed you'd had a sisterly disagreement, which would be mended easily enough. When you didn't reply to her notes, I found her weeping on several occasions.'

Lizzie looked down at her feet, embarrassed at hearing her behaviour described in this way.

Thomas made no further comment, but proceeded: 'Imagine my astonishment, then, when Joseph came to me and said he wished to leave his position. I was taken aback – he's an excellent worker, had settled well and seemed happy. I pressed him for his reasons, and he became agitated, saying he couldn't stay knowing you were nearby and that he had caused you harm he felt unable to address. He felt his presence would spoil the relationship you had with Nell and he didn't want to be the cause of further damage. I confess to being irritated – it's hard to find good, reliable people and it looked as though I would have to let him go over a misunderstanding that could surely be put to rights. So, I made one last attempt to change his mind. "Tell me how you caused this harm to Lizzie," I said.

'Then the whole story spilled out. I suppose Nell had told me some of it but perhaps I wasn't paying close enough attention. Anyway, when he said it was now clear that the housekeeper, Catherine Bailey, had been intent on causing mischief between the pair of you, I realised I had played a part in this whole sorry tale.'

Thomas stopped and glanced over to where the girls were

amassing quite an armful of flowers. 'That's enough,' he called. 'Leave some for others to find.'

'But how can Mrs Bailey have anything to do with you?' Lizzie was confused by his words.

'I was supposed to marry her,' Thomas said simply. 'She was called Catherine Morgan then, and worked in the kitchens of Mr Cooper, the owner of the brewery. But I realised I'd made the wrong choice, and I married Nell instead.' His face softened. 'And I've never regretted my decision for a single moment.' He sighed. 'Catherine was furious and, in a way, I can't blame her. I was clumsy in my dealings with her. I hardly saw her after I broke off our engagement. She left work immediately, and a little later I heard she had married the son of Mr Bailey, the boat-builder. I suppose I was relieved to hear it. I've barely given her a second thought since.'

'She was widowed, apparently, and has been working at Betsanger Court since it was built, two or three years ago.' Lizzie's mind was racing. 'But why do you think she behaved as she did, Thomas?'

'She must have worked out that you were Nell's sister – there's only one Carey family in Castle Bay – and that you were my sister-in-law. I suppose she couldn't forgive my happiness, but she hadn't found a way to hurt me. I can only guess she saw a way to do it indirectly, to cause harm to the family, through you.'

Lizzie thought back to how she had regretted giving her real name on her first day at Betsanger Court, and how she had given a false address in Canterbury. Yet Mrs Bailey had referred to her returning home to Castle Bay. With a sinking heart, she remembered her parting shot: *Give my regards to your sister's husband.*

'She sent her regards to you on the day I left,' Lizzie said. 'I never understood how she knew we were related or what she meant. Now I see. I called her an evil witch the other day. A vindictive, evil witch is more accurate.'

Thomas and Lizzie contemplated the revelations of the past quarter of an hour in silence. Then Thomas called to his daughters, 'Time to go home. Will you join us?' he asked, turning to Lizzie.

She shook her head. 'I must get back. But thank you, Thomas. You've given me a lot to think about.'

She said goodbye to the girls, who threatened tears of disappointment that she was leaving them, until she promised to join them on another Sunday very soon. Then she walked slowly back to Bay House, shaken by what she'd heard. By the time she'd reached the front door, she'd made a decision. Having vowed she never wanted to see Joe again, she knew she needed to talk to him about what she'd just heard. Then a thought struck her – Thomas had said Joe wanted to leave, but he hadn't said whether or not he had persuaded him to stay. Could he already have left? Had she missed her chance to undo some of the damage caused by Catherine Bailey's malicious actions?

CHAPTER TWELVE

Down in the kitchen, Kitty had the Sunday dinner well under way and there was the usual light-hearted atmosphere around the table as the girls talked over their week, their discussion punctuated by raucous laughter. Lizzie had intended to step in and take over the cooking, but Kitty took one look at her and exclaimed, 'Why, Lizzie, whatever has happened? You look as though you've seen a ghost.'

The girls stopped chattering and stared at her. Nancy pulled out a chair. 'Sit down,' she commanded, 'before you collapse. You're as white as a sheet.'

Lizzie sat down and burst into tears. The girls were full of concern, clustering round her, offering handkerchiefs and soothing words. Annie thrust a glass of brandy under Lizzie's nose. 'Drink this,' she said. 'It's good for shock.'

Lizzie's sobs finally subsided, to be replaced by hiccups. Her face was burning, her cheeks damp and her eyelids swollen. The girls sat down again and resumed their conversations, in muted tones. She was glad to be given a few minutes to collect herself. 'Small sips,' Annie urged, pushing the brandy glass between her fingers. 'It will help.'

Reluctantly, Lizzie complied. The shock of the alcohol hitting the back of her throat and spreading its warmth through her eased her spasms and the hiccups stopped. She blew her nose and made to stand up.

'No you don't,' Nancy said. 'It's our turn to look after you for a change.'

Lizzie didn't argue. She sat back, and listened to the increasing volume of chatter, managing a smile or two when she heard a risqué fragment of gossip. Kitty set the dinner on the table and Lizzie, with much encouragement, managed to eat a small amount although her appetite had all but fled. After Kitty had served a cherry tart for pudding, Lizzie began to long for the clearing up to be done and the girls to leave the kitchen so she could have the place to herself for a while. But they had other ideas.

'Now then,' Nancy said. 'Let's be hearing who's upset you so and we'll see what we can do to help.'

Reluctant to expose her private life to them, Lizzie resisted. But they wore her down, wheedling the story out of her bit by bit until they had it all. To Lizzie's surprise, she didn't feel shame as much as relief. Their indignation over Catherine Bailey's behaviour raised her spirits a little, but they were far more inclined to leniency towards Joe than Lizzie was.

'But why did he believe her poisonous words?' Lizzie protested. 'Why didn't he ask me about it?'

'He'll have had his reasons,' Kitty said. 'The only way to find out is to ask him.'

'I think he might have left town already.' Lizzie felt tears start to her eyes again. 'I fear it's too late.'

'Well, we'll have to find out, won't we?' Annie got to her feet and began the table clearing, her words causing Lizzie some anxiety. What on earth would Joe make of it if the girls set out to track him down? After the upset over whether or not Lizzie had worked for Mrs Simmonds, she wasn't sure it would be a good idea for him to discover she was working at Bay House in Castle Bay's notorious Middle Street.

On Saturday evening, almost a week later, Lizzie was settling in the kitchen, looking forward to a quiet hour or so while the girls were out in the warmth of a summer's evening, showing off their new dresses and hoping to entice customers. She heard the front door open and Annie's voice called down the stairs: 'Lizzie, a visitor for you.'

She leaped to her feet, alarmed. Was it Nell? Or, more worryingly, Thomas? What would he make of her living arrangements? The footsteps on the stairs told her it was a man and the next moment Joe was framed in the doorway, ducking slightly to avoid banging his head on the lintel. 'Hello, Lizzie,' he said.

'But . . . How . . . ?' Questions coursed through Lizzie's mind.

He shrugged. 'It doesn't matter. Can we talk, Lizzie? I owe you an apology. I know that now, thanks to Thomas. And I'm so sorry I behaved as I did. I was misled, but you were right in what you said that day when Nell brought you to me on the green. I should have asked you about Catherine Bailey's words, not believed them without question.'

Then Joe explained how, during the fortnight in October when the rain had kept Lizzie and the children confined to the nursery, Mrs Bailey had drip-fed him a succession of lies. She'd seen Lizzie and Joe on more than one occasion during their secret evenings together, and started by warning him off.

'She's not who you think she is, Joe. Be careful. I'm only telling you this for your own good,' she'd started. And day by day she'd embroidered her tale, persuading him that Lizzie had a secret child, born by mischance when working for Mrs Simmonds. She'd had to leave her establishment, and seek work elsewhere, ending up at Betsanger Court. The baby had been left behind and her wages went to pay for its care.

'I thought of our afternoons in the stable yard with Agnes and Christopher, and how they were the best part of each day for me.' Joe's voice shook. 'And of our evenings together, how lovely they had been and how you had sought to convince me you'd never worked for Mrs Simmonds. You seemed so fresh, so honest – I trusted you completely. Then I heard what Catherine Bailey had to say and I was persuaded to look at things in a different way. I was devastated. She took pains to warn the staff against you, too. She said she had no wish to speak out of turn, but she thought it was something they ought to know, that you were not the person you pretended to be. I have no doubt the story was embellished every time it was repeated.'

It's little wonder they began to behave towards me as they did, Lizzie thought bitterly. I was trapped in the nursery, not knowing any of this, unable to defend my good name. By the time we were free again, Mrs Bailey had poisoned everyone against me. She remembered Cook's snub when she had taken the children into the kitchen, the small portions that began to appear on her plate at mealtimes.

'I'm not proud of myself,' Joe said abruptly. 'Looking back, knowing what I now know, I can't understand why I didn't speak to you about her accusations. But she phrased it as though she was only saying these things to protect me, to prevent me making a terrible mistake.' He stared at his feet. 'When you left so abruptly I confess I was pleased. It was awkward, having to work in the same place as you, seeing you every day. Then I got around to opening your letter. Suddenly I could hear your voice, just as in our conversations together before . . .' He paused. 'Just as in our conversations by the owl field. And then I began to have doubts. I was no longer sure who to believe. Mrs Bailey seemed to feel that after her revelations we had some sort of special relationship. Her familiarity made me uneasy. I stuck it out for another year, then told the Bullivants I had to leave for family reasons. They gave me a good character and I got the position at the brewery here – Isaac Turner, the head coachman, had heard about it. He knew I wanted something that offered a bit more independence and he thought it might suit.

'I know I've hurt you very badly. I hope you can see how I was misled. It doesn't excuse what I did, but if we could try . . . if we could be friends?' Joe threw her a look of appeal.

He was still standing awkwardly in the doorway, shifting from foot to foot.

Lizzie, seated at the table, tried to marshal her emotions. What did she want to do? She couldn't say for sure – she needed to think it all through. 'I can't give you an answer now,' she said finally. 'You'll have to give me time.'

Disappointment clearly written on his face, Joe turned to go.

'But thank you,' Lizzie said, softening. 'Thank you for trying to explain.'

He nodded, and she listened to his footsteps returning up the stairs, the front door opening then closing behind him. Not ten minutes later, the first of the girls returned and Lizzie's whirlwind of a Saturday evening was under way. She would have no further chance to think about Joe's words until her walk to church on Sunday morning.

CHAPTER THIRTEEN

Lizzie had fallen into bed in the early hours of Sunday morning, exhausted as usual. When she woke with a start at just after eight o'clock, she couldn't work out why she felt excited. She had to set aside the sensation; it was a scramble to get ready in time for church, and to leave the table set so the girls could help themselves to breakfast.

It wasn't until she was hurrying towards the church, the sun already warm on her cheeks and a haze forming over the still sea, that she recognised the reason behind her unusual feeling. It was because of Joe's visit. Her anger with him had evaporated and given way to relief. There was an explanation for what had happened at Betsanger Court. It still hurt to contemplate how easily he had been swayed by Mrs Bailey's words, but Lizzie also had to acknowledge that the woman was a formidable opponent. Her authority, as housekeeper, made it hard to question anything she said. Lizzie experienced a surge of un-Christian rage. She would like to see her face-to-face and tell her exactly what she thought of her.

She stopped for a moment at the churchyard gate and breathed deeply. Then she walked up the path and into the cool interior, nodding at Sunday acquaintances as she passed along the flagstone aisle and took a seat in her usual pew. To discourage conversation with her neighbours, she knelt and bowed her head as if in prayer. In fact, she was thinking of Joe. He still had feelings for her, despite Catherine Bailey's attempts to turn him against her. He wanted them to establish a friendship. And she knew that was what she wanted, too. She was half inclined to keep him waiting for an answer, to make him suffer as she had. Then she scolded herself – what was the point of denying her own feelings? She had believed she had successfully shut the door in her mind on all the bewildering upset of her final days at Betsanger Court. Now Joe had forced that door open and she wasn't inclined to close it again.

The music told her the service was about to start, so she sat back in the pew, raising her eyes to where the wooden arches of the nave soared to the rafters. She allowed herself a small, secret smile. She would confront all the hurt and anger and set it free.

On a cold day in December that year, Lizzie walked up the pathway to another church, St Mary's in Hawksdown, the church near the brewery, where her sister had married Thomas five years earlier. She hadn't been able to attend that wedding – Mrs Carey, angered by Nell leaving the family, had decreed it too far to go and too difficult to manage with so many small children in tow.

Lizzie breathed deeply to steady herself, exhaling a white cloud that hung briefly on the frosty air. She was glad of the green velvet cloak that enveloped her, a loan from Nell for the day. The flat white heads of Christmas roses, mingled with rosemary in her simple posy, shook a little in her grasp. She turned to the man at her side and nodded.

'Ready?' The look her father gave her was full of pride. He had been the first member of the Castle Bay Careys to visit Lizzie, following a meeting with Nell at Lower Street in November to see if she could effect a family reconciliation. No stranger to Middle Street and its taverns, he had had no qualms about calling at Bay House. He had embraced his daughter, while Nancy, Annie, Kitty and several of the other girls watched.

'I've missed you, Lizzie,' he'd whispered in her ear. There had been tears after that, including in her father's eyes, and bottles had come out so they could drink a toast to new beginnings.

Mrs Carey and the older girls had proved harder to placate. In the end, at the start of December, Nell had sent a note to Lizzie. She was to call at the house in Lower Street at midday on Sunday, after attending church. It had been a rush – Lizzie was by then going to services at St Mary's in Hawksdown – but she had got there on the stroke of noon. Mrs Carey had been as frosty as the weather Castle Bay was now experiencing, and Ruth and Jane had pointedly taken themselves off to the tiny kitchen, banging the pots and pans as they started dinner preparations.

Mary, Alice and Susan had been far more interested in their visitor. They had been too young when Lizzie left to remember a great deal about her so had no prejudice against her.

Lizzie settled herself on the floor, where they were sitting by the fire. 'And who is this?' she asked, knowing full well. Their little brother was propped up against a chair, a now even more battered Arabella in his lap.

'Peter,' Susan replied helpfully.

'And he loves Arabella, too?' Lizzie attempted to pick up the doll, causing Peter to wail and clutch it to his chest.

Lizzie had come prepared, with a pocketful of sugar mice. Once harmony was restored, Peter decided he would be friends with her. By the time she left, even Ruth and Jane, drawn in by the chatter and laughter at the fireside, had reluctantly abandoned their kitchen sulk and joined their siblings in getting to know their sister once more.

Mrs Carey had few words to offer her daughter, and those she uttered had come as a shock.

'You've disgraced this family, Lizzie Carey. You might have convinced Nell you were working as a nursemaid, but I know better. I had a lady come and visit me – she said I ought to know that my daughter had been working for a notorious bawd in Canterbury. What do you have to say about that?'

Rendered speechless, Lizzie could only stare at her. Finally, she found her voice. 'What woman? What was her name? What did she look like?'

Mrs Carey didn't know her name, but the description she offered was one of Catherine Bailey. The complex reasons behind her behaviour had not only led her to ruin Lizzie's relationship with Joe, but with her mother, too. Lizzie had mended one, but was there any hope for the other?

The Careys would be inside the church now, Lizzie reflected, seated among the congregation, waiting for her. The organ music rang out through the open doors as she and her father progressed up the path into the simple, white-painted interior. Lizzie scanned the pews – there was her mother, staring fixedly forward, but all the children had turned to look. They were smiling and pointing – Lizzie heard Susan say, 'She's here! She's here! She looks like a princess!' Lizzie's much-loved Grandpa Walter sat nearest the aisle, Eliza Marsh – Thomas's mother – at his side, Peter squirming on his lap. She gave her grandpa a special smile – it was the first time she'd seen him since her return. On she walked, past Thomas and Nell, and their children. Nell was already dabbing her eyes with a handkerchief.

Familiar faces filled the pews on the other side, too. The girls from Bay House sat there, dressed in their finest clothes. Lizzie beamed, delighted to see them. Annie looked particularly pleased with herself. It was she who had persuaded Joe to come to Bay House and talk to Lizzie. When Lizzie asked her about it later, she'd said, 'Not all my customers are sailors, you know. Some are local. I know some of the brewery workers – it was easy to get word to Joe.' Annie felt she deserved all the credit for Joe and Lizzie's reconciliation and Lizzie wasn't about to disabuse her of the notion.

Mrs Franklin had declined her invitation, saying someone must stay in Middle Street to keep an eye on things. In reality, she was annoyed that Lizzie would be leaving Bay House after her wedding. Her sister, Mrs Hayward, had no qualms about accepting. Wearing her best outfit, she was seated – smiling broadly – in one of the pews taken up by the exuberant Bay House girls.

At last, Lizzie turned her attention to the altar. Her hands shook even more and she was relieved when Nell's eldest daughter, Clara, ran forward to take the posy from her.

Joe stood there, his back towards her. His broad shoulders filled his jacket and she saw him surreptitiously run a finger around inside his shirt collar. He'd never been comfortable in formal dress, she reflected, remembering him in his coachman's outfit. He turned, then, to look at her, his expression serious. She was close enough now to look into his hazel eyes, and all other thoughts drained away. It was as though just the two of them stood in front of the minister, the small congregation no longer present. Lizzie could scarcely breathe, until the minister's words broke the spell and she and Joe turned to face him, uttering words that afterwards she had no memory of saying.

His grass ring had taken its rightful place on her left hand, but she feared it too brittle to last. A simple fine gold band now anchored it, but after the wedding she would keep Joe's handmade ring safe in a small wooden box he had made especially for the purpose.

The brief ceremony over, Lizzie and Joe turned to face their guests before walking back down the aisle, hands clasped. Joe had no family there – the distance being too great for them to travel just for the day – but Lizzie hoped the warmth of the welcome from her own family (or most of them), and the excitement of the Bay House girls, would more than make up for any disappointment. Nell had insisted on hosting the wedding breakfast at their house, close by and, after Lizzie and Joe had endured the traditional shower of rice, all the guests hurried there to escape the cold.

Lizzie and Joe's attempts to establish a friendship had lasted all of two weeks. It became apparent very quickly that they longed for something more: a return to the way things had been a year previously. The best revenge on Mrs Bailey, Lizzie had reflected, would be to let her malicious words make no difference to them whatsoever. They picked up their courtship where they had left off, but they treated it with great care, only too aware of its delicate nature. The Bay House girls and Nell were having none of it, though.

'What are you waiting for?' Nancy asked Lizzie, one day at the end of October. 'We all know how you feel. When are you and Joe going to get wed? We need a party!'

At the same time, Nell was paying a visit to the brewery stables to have a word with Joe. 'I'm so pleased you and Lizzie have patched things up,' she said. 'But you wouldn't want to let her slip through your fingers again, would you?'

Joe, alarmed, was about to ask her what she meant, when she continued in a rush: 'I was thinking that a winter wedding would be lovely. Just before Christmas, perhaps. Then we can all spend it together. And maybe it would help the family to forgive Lizzie. What do you think?'

And so, as autumn progressed to winter, and Joe and Lizzie's bond deepened, it seemed only natural that a wedding was agreed, without the words 'Will you marry me?' needing to be uttered. Lizzie looked around Thomas and Nell's dining room, decorated with fir boughs and ivy in honour of the occasion and of Christmas, just a few days away. Their guests mingled, glasses in hand, the volume of their conversation rising as time passed. Mrs Carey kept herself aloof at first, conversing only with her younger daughters, but to Lizzie's surprise and delight, she came over to her and, a little grudgingly, wished her joy. Lizzie, on impulse, kissed her cheek, which sent her hurrying back to the safety of her family. It was a step in the right direction, Lizzie thought, and saw Nell smiling encouragingly.

'Well, Mrs Powell.' It was Joe's voice behind her.

She turned to find him brandishing a sprig of mistletoe. 'Well, Mr Powell,' she replied, 'I wonder what you have in mind?'

Joe didn't reply, but drew her into his arms and pressed his lips to hers. Lizzie, her head a little hazy from the glass of wine she had drunk, relaxed into his embrace, dimly aware of clapping from their guests and whoops from Nancy and Annie. As she and Joe reluctantly pulled apart, Lizzie felt as though her heart must burst with happiness. After all her missteps and enforced new starts, her life was finally taking the right direction, with Joe at her side in Castle Bay, surrounded by her family and friends.

EPILOGUE
JANUARY — JUNE 1832

In the New Year, Lizzie and Joe moved into one of the brewery cottages in the row where Thomas and Nell had once lived. Lizzie thought Thomas had pulled strings to make this happen, but he shook his head. 'Joe has an important job. The drays start to leave the building at dawn and some don't return until long after the workers have left. There's a stable lad to help, but I can't risk any delay to the ale getting out to our customers. And the horses need to be rubbed down and rested on their return. You'll soon see that your husband needs to be on hand at all hours.'

His words were true, Lizzie discovered. Often times, she turned over in bed, putting an arm out to wrap around Joe's warm body, only to find a cold space, where he had slipped away after midnight or before dawn to take care of the horses. No stranger to hard work herself, she didn't mind. Although she felt a little bereft, having left her days at Bay House behind. Joe hadn't asked her to give up her job, but Lizzie knew that the hours couldn't be made to work and the daily walk to and from Hawksdown would be too much. She didn't miss her lumpy pallet in the damp room off the kitchen, but she did miss the girls. She called in to see them whenever she was in Castle Bay, to have a cup of tea and catch up on the gossip. They complained frequently about the skills, or lack of them, of the women Mrs Franklin found to replace her. None of them lasted long.

'Can no one turn a seam, or stitch an invisible repair?' Kitty complained, showing Lizzie a dress with a rip that now looked as though it had been darned. So Lizzie agreed to take on the sewing tasks, since it appeared the girls were constantly dissatisfied. It gave her a small income, which she supplemented by taking on similar work in the Hawksdown area, found by placing a card in the window of the local greengrocer.

She helped Nell with her daughters, her sister having shared the news at Christmas that another baby was on the way. Nell declared it must be a boy, for this time around she was suffering a great deal from sickness and weariness. Lizzie was glad to be of service – it helped to fill the long hours while Joe was at work. And being with the girls reminded her of the happiest times in her past, the hours spent in the company of Gabriel, Frances and baby Grace, Agnes and Christopher.

The manner in which she had left the house in Canterbury, slipping away without a word to the children to explain her departure, was increasingly on her mind. She began to formulate a plan as her longing to see them grew. First, though, she needed to find a way to finish the piece of Hannah's whitework she had taken with her when she left the Russell household. At the time, she had imagined she would teach herself the technique and complete it, returning it to accolades from Adam, who appreciated the work it involved. She had had no time to touch it, though, and she was ashamed still to have it in her possession. A chance discussion with Annie, after the return of a dress Lizzie had repaired, led to a happy outcome.

'It's hard to believe I have no sewing ability, when my grandmother is such a skilled seamstress,' Annie said ruefully. 'And not only a seamstress, but she does beautiful whitework. I have a collar she made, but I never wear it for fear of damaging it. Let me show it to you.' Annie hurried from the room, returning with a collar so finely stitched it looked like a piece of lace.

Lizzie stared at it, turning it over in her hands. 'It's beautiful,' she said at last. 'I have a piece of whitework, too. But it is unfinished.

I made myself a promise that I would complete it to return to the family it belongs to.'

'Then why don't you?' Annie was puzzled.

'Because, unlike your grandmother, although I can stitch a seam I have no skill with embroidery.' An idea struck Lizzie. 'Does your grandmother still do whitework? Would she take on a commission?'

Annie shrugged. 'Her eyesight isn't what it once was, but I can ask her.'

After some discussion, Lizzie reached agreement on a way forward for Hannah's unfinished piece. When it came back to her, tears filled her eyes. She wanted to return it to the family at once, but couldn't think how.

Her opportunity came when Joe asked her if she'd like to accompany him on a trip to Canterbury the following week. 'I have to take Mr Cooper's private carriage to the coachworks there so a repair can be made to the chassis. We will have three or four hours to spend in the city. What would you like to do?'

When Lizzie told him, he seemed startled, but as she explained her reasoning he nodded. 'It's not what I expected, I have to confess, but I'm more than happy to support you,' he said. 'That is, if you want me with you?' he added hastily.

'I do,' Lizzie said.

The day of the trip to Canterbury was filled with pleasant summer sunshine, even at the early hour when Joe and Lizzie left Hawksdown. Lizzie was wearing her best Sunday dress and bonnet, and nervously clutching a basket on her lap. She sat up at the front, beside Joe – it didn't seem right to sit inside. The journey took just over three hours and she was glad to climb down at the coach-maker's and shake the dust from her clothes. Then she took Joe's arm and they made their way through Canterbury to New Street. Here Lizzie knocked at the door of the Russells' house, taking courage from Joe's presence. She had a moment's doubt when the knock wasn't immediately answered. But then the heavy door swung open and Judith stood there, smoothing her apron.

She stared at Lizzie for a moment, as if trying to place her, then her face broke into a smile. 'Lizzie Carey! How lovely to see you. I've often wondered what became of you. And here you are, looking so well.' She stepped back. 'Won't you both come in?' She looked from Lizzie to Joe, and back again.

'This is my husband, Joe. I'm Lizzie Powell now.' She always felt proud when she said those words. 'We won't stay long – I don't want to disturb you. Is Frances here? And Grace?'

Judith led the way to the kitchen and gestured to them both to take a seat. 'They are out, I'm afraid, with their mother. Their new mother.' She cast a glance at Lizzie to gauge her reaction. 'Adam married again shortly after you left. Someone he knew from the cathedral congregation.'

So Lizzie had guessed correctly. 'Are they happy?' she asked.

'The children? Yes, I believe so. They will be back soon. You can see for yourself.' Judith offered them lemonade, which Lizzie gratefully accepted.

'And Gabriel?'

'He does well at school,' Judith said.

Barely five minutes later, Lizzie heard the front door open. She glanced at Joe and he smiled reassuringly. Frances rushed into the kitchen, followed at a slower pace by a young woman holding the hand of a small girl, who could only be Grace, although she was unrecognisable as the baby Lizzie remembered.

Lizzie and Joe got to their feet, while Judith introduced them to Olivia, the new Mrs Russell.

'Ah, so you are the Lizzie Frances still talks about so fondly,' Olivia said. As expected, she was the blonde young woman, glimpsed at the cathedral with the Russell family when Lizzie had attended a Sunday service with Mrs Bullivant. Lizzie remembered seeing her among the Sunday congregation when Hannah was still alive, but had no memory of her being close to the family.

'Are you still painting?' Lizzie asked Frances, desperate to see whether she bore her any ill-will for the way she had vanished from their lives.

Frances had grown – she was taller and thinner in the face – but to Lizzie's relief, she seemed eager to engage with her. She had a sketchbook now, she said, and hurried to fetch it so she could show it to Lizzie. Grace was staring curiously at the visitors so Lizzie scooped her onto her lap, burying her face in her hair for just a moment to try to recapture her baby scent.

'This is Grace,' she said to Joe, giving him a meaningful look. She wasn't about to confess to having cut a curl from her head in front of Olivia and Judith, or to explain the trouble it had caused her.

After ten minutes spent examining Frances's sketchbook, Lizzie said they must take their leave. 'I have another visit to make,' she said. 'But, first, I wanted to return something. Frances, this belonged to your mother, Hannah.'

She took the piece of whitework from her basket and spread it on the table. 'It was unfinished,' she said, 'so I took it away with me, intending to complete the work your mother had started. She wanted the family to have it, to remind you all of her, but she was too ill to work on it. And I didn't have the skill. But I found someone who does.'

Everyone gazed at the piece: Hannah's arching foliage now enclosed a representation of the house in New Street, drawn by Lizzie for Annie's grandmother to copy. Three small figures filled the space beside it. After much deliberation, Lizzie had chosen to show the children at the ages she remembered: the ages they were shortly after their mother died. Baby Grace was depicted lying on her back gazing up at the foliage, Gabriel sitting beside her, and Frances next to him with a bunch of flowers clutched in her hand.

'It's beautiful,' Frances gasped. Lizzie looked at Judith and saw tears in her eyes. She couldn't speak, only shake her head.

Olivia, astonished, reached out to trace the stitching with her finger. 'Such skill,' she murmured. 'Adam will be so pleased. He'll be here at any moment.'

357

Lizzie experienced a sense of rising panic. She'd felt sure he would be at work that afternoon, for she was wary of seeing him after the way she had left the house all those months earlier.

'We're all to go to a special service at the cathedral this evening, in honour of the Dean,' Olivia went on. 'I believe he has served the cathedral for twenty-five years. Adam is coming to collect us.'

Lizzie got to her feet. 'Then we mustn't detain you.' She looked at Joe. 'Come. We must be on our way.'

'Please stay,' Olivia begged. 'He'll be so disappointed if he misses you.'

Lizzie looked at Joe. He stayed seated and nodded imperceptibly, so she sat down again, heart pounding. It was just moments later she heard the front door open.

When Adam entered the kitchen, Gabriel trailing behind him, he seemed taken aback at the scene before him. His gaze swept over Lizzie and Joe, without seeming to register their presence, before settling on Olivia.

'We have visitors,' Olivia said, flustered. 'Mr and Mrs Powell, from Castle Bay.'

'It's Lizzie,' Judith said impatiently.

Adam swung around and peered intently at their faces. 'Lizzie,' he said. 'Why, I never thought to see you again. Where have you been? What have you been doing? And you're married now.'

'I'm so very sorry, leaving you as I did. It was wrong of me.' Scarlet in the face and intent on apologising, Lizzie ignored his questions. Memories of her agonies over the decision came flooding back.

Adam waved his hand, as if to brush away her words. 'It's of no matter now.' He looked at Olivia. 'As you can see, I am a fortunate and happy man.'

'I'm glad you were settled so quickly,' Lizzie said. She didn't mean to imply anything by her words but a faint blush rose to Adam's cheeks. Perhaps he was conscious of how soon after her departure he had set his sights elsewhere.

'Look what Mrs Powell has brought for us,' Olivia said, somewhat bemused by the turn of the conversation and seeking to distract. She pointed to the piece of whitework, still laid on the table.

Adam stepped forward to take a closer look. Head bent, he gazed at it for several minutes in silence. When he looked up, Lizzie saw his eyes brimmed with tears.

'Why, it's quite beautiful,' he said. 'Did you stitch this?' He addressed Lizzie directly.

'No, such work is quite beyond me,' she said, rueful. 'Hannah started it. She intended to finish it, for the family to keep as an example of her whitework. She wanted it to be a surprise. I took it when I left, hoping to be able to finish it myself. I failed, but I was able to find someone who could complete it.'

Adam reached out and traced the outline of the house, and the three figures in the foreground. 'Thank you,' he said simply.

Lizzie got to her feet. 'We really must go. You have an engagement this evening and we shouldn't keep you any longer.'

They left in a flurry of goodbyes. Lizzie looked back to see the family on the doorstep, Adam with his arm around Olivia's shoulders, Grace in her arms, Frances and Gabriel standing in front of them. It was the picture of a happy family and she felt immense relief.

Joe took her arm again as they walked along. 'That was a lovely thing to do,' he said quietly.

Lizzie gave him a tremulous smile. 'I'm glad. But now for something I've been dreading.'

She led him to a less familiar part of town, where the grand houses had pillared front entrances and space between each one and its neighbour. Lizzie marched up the steps to the dark-painted door of one, and pressed the polished bell. After a few moments, the door swung open.

'Is Mrs Simmonds at home? I have something she has been expecting.'

The maid who had answered looked startled and hesitated, then stepped back to let them in. They waited in the entrance hall while she went in search of her mistress. A few minutes later, the tap of heels announced the arrival of Mrs Simmonds.

'Well,' she said, surveying Lizzie, then Joe, 'this is unexpected. To what do I owe the pleasure?'

Lizzie stepped forward, took a few coins from her pocket and spread them on the marble surface of the hall table. 'There,' she said. 'The money I owe you for the coach fare from Castle Bay to Canterbury. And not a penny more in interest.'

Then, with a defiant look at her adversary, she took Joe's arm and swept towards the door, the maid running to open it for them. Lizzie heard Mrs Simmonds laugh, but she didn't try to detain them. On shaky legs, Lizzie descended the steps to the street.

'And now we can celebrate,' she said, as relief coursed through her. She led Joe to the banks of the River Stour, where a few benches had been placed in a small riverside garden. A couple vacated one just as they arrived and Lizzie quickly slipped into their place, setting her basket beside her. She removed a package wrapped in a linen cloth and opened it to reveal a pork pie, sliced into quarters, bread rolls, a slab of crumbly white cheese and two apples. Then she handed Joe a bottle of beer from the bottom of the basket, and took one for herself.

They were both hungry after their early start, and the birds that gathered, hoping for titbits, were sorely disappointed. Lizzie shook the few crumbs out of the cloth and folded it back into the basket. Then she removed her bonnet and settled her head on Joe's shoulder with a contented sigh. Her work was done. She and Joe had considered paying a visit to Betsanger Court on the way home, then discounted it. Although Lizzie longed to see the children, she reasoned that Christopher would be at school, Agnes would likely be upset and, although it would be pleasing to show Mrs Bailey that her unjust words had failed, and that she and Joe were married, she wasn't sure she was ready to face her yet. Her anger against her was still too strong.

Nell had made enquiries and discovered that Mrs Bailey had an aunt on her father's side, living in Canterbury: a Mrs Simmonds. The last piece of the puzzle had fallen into place. Lizzie could only assume that the housekeeper, recognising the name Carey on first meeting her, had made the connection with Thomas, who had so disappointed her. Did a wish for revenge take root then, and grow when Mrs Bullivant interfered with her household decisions, over-ruling her and making Lizzie nursemaid in Hester's place? Had she discussed it with her aunt on one of her visits to Canterbury, gaining the information about Lizzie that she then embroidered and used to such destructive effect? Even her claim to widowhood was false, it seemed, although that hadn't stopped her making a play for Joe once Lizzie was out of the way: Mr Bailey was still alive in Castle Bay. She had simply left him.

Nell's discovery had helped Lizzie to cope with her anger and distress. She no longer racked her brains to discover what she had done to deserve such treatment. Mrs Bailey, she decided, was un-hinged. So, for now, she was content. Warmed by gentle sunshine, in the company of the only man she had ever loved, who that day had supported her in laying to rest an important part of her past, she thought herself blessed with more happiness than she could ever have deserved.

ACKNOWLEDGEMENTS

Grateful thanks to my agent, Kiran Kataria, for her eagle-eyed appraisal of the novel's first draft, as well as her patient explanations of practical matters (royalty statements ...). Eleanor Russell, my editor at Piatkus, has been unwaveringly supportive and encouraging during a difficult time, while Tanisha Ali, Elena Torres and the rest of the team have guided the book on its way with great efficiency. Hazel Orme's meticulous attention to detail has thankfully ironed out my grammatical errors and sometimes erratic punctuation, curbed my tendency to overwrite and caught more than one bizarre slip-ups.

Uncertain health has dogged me throughout the writing of this book too, including a long spell in two hospitals. I can never thank my family enough for all the care they have shown – and continue to show – throughout this time. I have been greatly moved by all the visitors who came to see me, in Kent and in London, bearing gifts, taking laundry away, shopping for me and generally doing everything possible to lift my spirits. They continue to do so, leaving me humbled by the thoughtfulness, generosity and kindness of so very many people.

Do you love historical fiction?

Want the chance to hear news about your favourite authors (and the chance to win free books)?

Suzanne Allain
Mary Balogh
Lenora Bell
Charlotte Betts
Manda Collins
Joanna Courtney
Grace Burrowes
Evie Dunmore
Lynne Francis
Pamela Hart
Elizabeth Hoyt
Eloisa James
Lisa Kleypas
Jayne Ann Krentz
Sarah MacLean
Terri Nixon
Julia Quinn

Then visit the Piatkus website
www.yourswithlove.co.uk

And follow us on Facebook and Instagram
www.facebook.com/yourswithlovex | @yourswithlovex

PIATKUS